HER

MEMOIRS #1

ONE

BREATH

TO

THE

NEXT

Danube Adele

DANUBE ADELE

COPYRIGHT

One Breath to the Next © 2021 by

Danube Adele

Print Edition

ISBN: 978-1-7-331916-2-3

DEDICATION

To the heroic men and women of the military

who answer the call—

thank you.

ACKNOWLEDGEMENTS

I want to thank my good friends and

loving family for always being willing to listen

to my spontaneous plot bunnies.

I blame the alcohol.

Table of Contents

CHAPTER 1

MASON

"Two more. Give me two more, Garcia. Do it now. Go." I used my no-bullshit voice despite the fact that my own teeth clenched in reaction to the pain etched on his face.

"I can't do it, Mason," Jay Garcia snarled through gritted teeth, even as he pulled the weights attached to what was left of his calves from his wheelchair. A guttural cry tore from his lips. His entire body shook with the effort and the agony. Sweat poured off him as the weights rose hesitantly to the top of the pulley and fell back, completing a rep.

"The fuck you can't. Two more," I replied inches from his face, ignoring the swell of empathy that erupted from deep in my soul seeing the pool of moisture in his eyes. Jay had mountains to climb to meet his recovery potential.

"One more!" He growled, his eyes angry and slitted. If Jay could talk while he was pumping weights, he wasn't working hard enough.

"Three more!" I taunted him. "You can take a fucking bomb to the legs, but you can't do three more reps?"

"Fuck you!" Jay roared. His dark eyes turned pink and glassy with shimmering moisture. It threatened to spill over. His legs jerked on the pulley again, his arms braced against his wheelchair. The shining stack of heavy steel rose halfway up the pulley, paused for a fraction of a second, then got yanked all the way up.

"Life isn't going to hand you a fucking trophy for effort, Garcia. Push yourself. Don't give up. Again. Go. Now."

"I'll fucking kill you," he groaned.

"When you can fucking walk again, I invite you to try, asshole. Now quit your whining and lift the fucking weights."

"Fuck you! Fuck you, motherfucker!" His face was red, and the veins in his neck and temple started to bulge. But lift the weights he did. Two more times in quick succession—like I knew he could—before he set the weights back with a heartfelt cry of release that came from somewhere deep in his barrel chest.

Shouts and applause erupted from the small crowd that had gathered to watch our training session, a few calls of congratulations sprinkled here and there before people went about their own workouts again. The tears that had been threatening streamed down Jay's cheeks as an emotional, hoarse sob ripped from the depths of his chest, making his large upper body shake with the force.

"Yes. You. Can." I clasped his forearm in a secure grip, locked eye contact, and crouched close by his wheelchair. "I got you, brother. I got you."

"I know it." He nodded, using his left hand to swipe at the moisture on his face. "I don't deserve it, but I know it."

"Bullshit. We all deserve it."

Jay shook his head as more tears dripped down his scruffy face. He had stopped shaving in the last week or so, refusing to accept care, and I knew why. In combat, when bad shit went down around you, it ended up becoming your living nightmare. It sank sharp, poisonous claws deep into your soul. Turned you into a beast, and when you looked into the mirror, you couldn't see yourself anymore.

Jay's demons were riding him hard. From the moment he'd come in this morning, I could see he'd had a bad night. Maybe he'd had several in a row, judging from the bags under his eyes. There was a new sense of fatigue clouding him, and that was dangerous. He wasn't giving his workout the same heart he'd started with a few months back.

"What's going on?" I asked. He knew what I was asking. He didn't even try to deflect.

"Tammy left." Jay swiped at his eyes. "She said I wasn't even trying anymore. Packed her shit and took off a couple of days ago."

Fuck. The worst time for it to happen. He'd been making progress. "Why would she say that?"

"We've been fighting for the last couple of months. She said it was like she was living with a stranger. It's been almost six months since I got back and nothing's changed. I don't talk to her anymore. I don't see her. Shit like that." He paused. His lips thinned into a tight line, like he was trying to control a well of emotion, and he sniffed sharply. Still, a few renegade tears fell down his cheeks. "I don't blame her. She deserves better."

I bit my tongue, refusing to say something

negative about a woman who should have had the patience to let Jay readjust to not only civilian life after living in a fucking war zone, but also to now living life as an amputee, his legs missing from the knees down. He hadn't shared the details of how the bomb hit, but I was sure it was as fucked-up as the rest of the stories I'd heard from guys coming back, my own included.

I shook my head, my words quiet. "I'm sorry to hear that."

He sniffed, gave a final swipe to his eyes and hung his head. "Stopped taking the meds."

"Why?"

"They aren't doing any good. Can't fucking sleep anymore. Don't want to sleep."

"Nightmares?"

He nodded.

"You talking about your shit with someone?" I asked quietly. "There's all different kinds of therapies they could offer you. Other kinds of medicines that'll maybe work better."

The answer was already in his eyes when he looked back up at me, dark and grim. His jaw was set square, tensing when he gave a sharp jerk of his head.

"What the fuck, dude?" I shot out in a low voice, wanting to make sure the conversation stayed between us. "You need help. You can't deal with this on your own."

He could only shake his head. The fact he was starting to head down this path meant he was heading toward a fucking unacceptable conclusion. Too many soldiers had already taken their lives. There was no way I was giving up on Jay Garcia. I didn't know what visions haunted him at night, but I knew how they could fuck with a person. It had taken me years, but I'd finally made some inroads.

He wouldn't look me in the eye, and I knew what it was. Worse than the injury that had permanently changed the landscape of his body was the feeling of worthlessness and being unable to forgive himself. He'd done something he felt he couldn't live with. Just like me. That shit lived on a reel in your psyche just waiting for unguarded moments to hit play.

Like now.

Talking with Jay sparked the sharp memory of relentless heat under a desert sun. The heavy weight of my pack. Rivulets of sweat.

My breath caught in the back of my throat as I fought to smother the memory, tried to ignore it, swallow it down, and press on. I needed to make sure Jay was all right.

"Talk to me, Jay."

He shook his head a final time, took the brake off his wheelchair and pushed away. "I gotta go. I've got an appointment to get fitted for new prosthetics. Some high tech shit. I'm about to become the bionic man." He forced a carefree smirk.

I was relieved he was still going to the appointment. If he ever stopped coming to the gym or started skipping doctor visits, it would be time for an intervention on his ass. Until then, it was natural for him to go through the rollercoaster effect of ups and down. Recovery, both physical and emotional, took time. And it sucked that his girlfriend of the last two years had decided to jump ship.

I gave a quick nod, lightly clapped his shoulder, and stood. "That happening today?"

"Yeah." He paused as if a thought had just occurred to him.

"What?"

He looked like he wanted to say something, but

then he shook his head. "Nothing."

"I hope you know if you need something, I'm here for you." There was so much he needed. I knew this, but his life was out of my control. There was nothing I could do but encourage, prod, badger... He wheeled himself out of the automatic glass door that led to the rest of the gym, and I prayed I wasn't watching a dead man taking his last breaths. I never wanted to see that again.

A sudden image lanced my heart. It was crystal clear. In vibrant color. Details sharply outlined in my mind.

Gasping breath. Gurgling blood. The sky reflected in wide blue eyes that slowly turned lifeless.

That's when it hit. I'd let myself go there. Let my mind pull up the bits of memory. Enough to get triggered. Always. My throat squeezed down, my chest banded tightly, and my heart beat like a wild thing trapped in a too-small cage trying to get free. Fuck me. Not now. My office was so far away. Across the entire fucking gym. I couldn't reach it.

I tried to relax, struggled to take a breath. Fought the tunnel vision starting to take over. It wasn't working. Instantly, I looked for my saving grace.

Where was she?

My gaze turned wild while I tried to maintain my cool. I looked through the glass walls out into the main gym area, searching for the girl who had the ability to calm me with a single glance. She was here. I'd already seen her. She was here every day. I moved through the sliding door and felt the wheezing start, the fight for a single breath. If I couldn't calm down soon, I was going to pass out.

She wasn't on a cardio machine. She wasn't using weight machines. She was by the free weights, standing perfectly still in front of the mirror, her tranquil indigo eyes already watching me. Captivating me. Our eyes locked. I fell into the endless pool of calm peacefulness reflecting back at me. She was a little thing. Fragile. Precious. Probably only came up to my shoulder, but she housed special powers that were far greater than her size.

Don't look away, I thought desperately, already feeling my chest ease.

I won't, she seemed to say, holding me up with a look.

Was it seconds or minutes later that I could take a deep breath again? Feeling foolish and vulnerable, I broke the connection. Moved with purposeful strides across the gym until I reached my office and closed the door, still breathing heavily. Dots of sweat coated my upper lip. My whiskers rasped as I wiped the back of my long-sleeve T-shirt along the moist skin, but I still didn't let her out of my sight. I brought up the security monitors on my computer screen, found her in the same spot. She was looking toward my office door, blotting sweat from her slender neck with one of the white towels we provided.

There was something about her that spoke to me, something gentle and pure. Innocent. Uncorrupted. Lacking in artifice. There was a warm, comforting energy about her that I was addicted to. As if she were on a frequency that connected to my soul and eased the chaos that bombarded me, yet we'd never had a single conversation. She was an angel. My own personal angel.

Her   name   was   Layla.

CHAPTER 2

LAYLA

I almost chickened out.

The deep, bone-jarring bass from the house music at Zeke's on the Boardwalk, a dull thud reverberating through the bathroom door, underscored my self-doubt. With the metal latch blocking the outside world from entering this single-stall restroom, I confronted my own fears in the rectangular mirror.

The moment lasted the length of time it took me to inhale and exhale deeply, fighting a flash of anxiety that churned my stomach and made me want to run home, a place where I now felt safe, and lock all the doors.

Frigid. I can't even keep my dick hard for you. Coldhearted bitch. If I'd known what you were going to be like…

My eyes burned. I cringed at my reflection, hearing the echoes of *him,* of my past.

For the first time in almost two years, I was ready to make my move, finally take a fresh step forward, put myself out there. Then *his* voice— mean, ugly, menacing—snuck out from a hidden place in the deepest, darkest nightmare part of my mind.

Shame bloomed in my cheeks at the harsh words. They hit like an evil feeding tube to my soul. Sexually inadequate. Broken. Classless. Worthless. For a moment, I was buying into it again, feeling small, insignificant, wanting to slink away and forget all about this foolish plan that brought me here. Good thing I'd built up immunities over the last two years. Two years of fighting past what I'd been trained to believe about myself. Two years of reminding myself that wanting to be happy, confident, and content with my life was not a personal flaw. It was a right.

I'd worked hard to turn *his* toxic words into my own personal battle cry.

It was always a choice. A decision made from the inside, like turning the page to a fresh new chapter. From one breath to the next, a new world could open up if I let it, if I made it happen. I could make anything happen.

Lifting my chin against the invisible monster that still tried to throw its weight around, I shut the door on the echoes of the past. There was no way I was going to let him keep controlling me. *I* left *him*. My decision. My life. Mine.

I pushed myself away from the porcelain sink, shoved out through the women's bathroom door and re-entered the bar, a fire lit from within me. The dulcet tones of Bob Marley singing "Let's get together and feel all right…" now spilled gently from house speakers, overlaying the din of conversation. People were having a good time, some bobbing to the reggae beat, others singing the words drunkenly while they danced, the atmosphere spiked with short bursts of laughter here and there.

I stood back, surveyed the crowd, and zeroed in on the first step of my plan. It would only happen if I was brave enough.

Despite the beachy, casual décor, I still couldn't relax. What I was about to do, what I was setting myself up for, had my heart jackhammering a hole in my chest. Tonight, I was finally taking charge.

Tonight, was a step forward as the new me. The stronger me. The me that took what she wanted rather than the sad, naïve me that sat back and simply accepted whatever she was handed.

Tonight, I was going to fuck Mason Garrett.

The word fuck, a new vocabulary word that my old self would have shied away from, slid seductively through my mind. The old me shied away from everything, afraid of what people would think, afraid I wasn't smart enough or good enough, afraid of being criticized for mistakes. I was always afraid of looking like I'd come from the poor side of town, where the only living things thriving were the weeds that broke free from the pavement cracks.

The new me liked the feel of that word on my tongue, savored the hard consonant sounds of it rolling from my lips, enjoyed the tingle of it down between my legs. Fuck. The new me said it a lot. Said fuck it. Said life was too short. Said invite him for a good, hard fuck.

I wasn't looking for hearts and flowers. Not anymore. I was looking for something raw and animalistic. Hot. Hard. Fast. Temporary. Who could turn that down?

I caught sight of him at the bar.

He was half seated on a corner stool with one foot casually resting on a wooden rung, talking with the staff behind the bar. He loomed larger than life. His navy thermal stretched across his impossibly broad shoulders and tapered down toward the waistband of his denim. Large, worn combat boots finished his look.

As always, being near him was enough to make my abdomen clench, make liquid heat gather at the apex of my thighs. I let my eyes close for a moment, enjoying the pleasure of it. It was a beautiful part of being human that I'd missed for so long I thought there was something wrong with me. Heat. Desire.

The first time that had happened, I'd been nearly paralyzed with my embarrassment.

I'd been on my way out of the gym almost a year ago, and I'd seen Mason yank the bottom half of his shirt up to wipe sweat off his face. At the same time, he'd exposed not only the ripple of muscles crisscrossing his abdomen but also a thin line of golden hair that trailed enticingly down the middle of his stomach. My gaze had followed the trail south to where it disappeared beneath his athletic shorts.

My breathing had stuttered to a halt for the first time over the sight of a man. I'd stood there confused, almost not recognizing the symptoms for what they revealed. My heart pounded like crazy;

my breathing turned shallow. My panties grew wet with my secret girl parts pulsing hotly, clearly knowing what they wanted. Then a terrifying thought occurred. Would he know what I was thinking if he looked at me?

The fear that it was somehow reflected in my eyes had squelched the discovery of new pleasure, made me anxious to avoid dreaded ridicule. I'd scurried off to work, mortified by my own body. Fresh heat tinged my cheeks anytime I happened to remember that particular moment. And yet, I also chose to remember it often. It wasn't the last time I left the gym with wet panties.

Initially, I'd been afraid that Mason would be contemptuous, or worse, pitying, if he knew how my body reacted to his. That was the kind of treatment I'd been trained to expect from a man. Hurtful. Thoughtless. Disdainful.

Until I caught him watching me right back.

"Layla! Glad you could make it."

I blinked back to the present. Rowdy grinned boyishly from behind the bar, his usual dark shaggy hair pumped up rock star-like with gel.

"Damn, but you look good, girl."

"Hi, Rowdy. Thanks." I gave a small smile.

"We're playing our first set in about an hour. Until then, let me know if you need anything," Rowdy added with a playful wink before moving down the line of customers to get more drinks made.

I gave a short nod, but then my eyes immediately went back to Mason, noting the way his sun-kissed brown hair curled ever so slightly at the base of his nape, noting the play of muscle beneath his shirt when he straightened up from leaning on his elbows.

Over the last several months, I'd made a study of how Mason's thick muscles moved when he was dripping sweat during a workout, bunching and flexing with each exercise, each repetition. The sounds he made, grunting and panting as he strained under heavy weights, were sounds I listened for. I looked to meet his eyes across a busy room or see them reflected back at me in one of the many mirrored walls. He was silent but powerful, and my body was hyper aware of him at all times.

It took a moment for him to face me, almost as though he paused to think about it first, but when he did, the effect was no less than it was at the gym. The familiar sight of his rugged, masculine features, square jaw and sensually shaped lips caused warmth to radiate through my veins. Striking silvery eyes locked on mine. There was no looking away. His gaze had its usual impact: my heart tripped up, and my abdomen simmered with heat.

His intense eyes were mesmerizing. So much was said without making a sound. Unspoken needs and demands went unanswered because they were always frustratingly remote.

"Layla." He rasped my name in his deep, bass tone, a bit growly, a bit rough, scraping against my senses so that I could feel him clear down to my toes. It was the first time I'd ever heard him say my name aloud.

"Mason…" His name caressed my lips on a whisper.

With the crowd of people at the bar, there was just enough room to slide in beside him, let my hand rest easy on the polished wood grain, my nails manicured to look feminine for this occasion when they would normally be nude. Even with my heels on and him half seated on a barstool, I had to look up into his eyes. His gaze was piercing and direct, and as usual, conveyed the same reserve that taunted me every day at the gym. I wanted to get past his wall. I wanted to get past the polite manners and respectful distance.

I took the plunge.

"Can I buy you a drink?" A nervous flutter had my pulse catching here and there. Would he refuse? Up close, he was even bigger than I'd realized. I waited to see if that familiar twinge of panic would tweak my stomach. Big men usually made my nerves multiply exponentially, but nothing happened.

Relief fed my confidence.

I knew Mason was different. I'd first seen him rehabbing disabled vets at the gym. He never gave up on them. He took care of the guys that came back from war damaged. Maybe that was the reason I trusted him. Maybe I was a little bit damaged. Deep down, I knew he wouldn't hurt me.

"I didn't know you were coming." Devastating my sense of control, the deep timber of his voice rolled over me when he leaned forward, his quieter tone giving a sense of intimacy. In this crowded room, it was just the two of us.

I took a half-step closer, feeling the pull of his gravity, wanting more of his personal sphere. His knee, still propped on one of the stool's rungs, grazed my hip. The move didn't go unnoticed. His eyes searched my face, analyzed, did a slow scan of my top, which was wide-necked and falling off one shoulder, revealing my cami's lace. The top curve of my breast was visible above the neckline, and I couldn't stop the warm flush that rose up my chest and spread to my neck.

A moment of feeling shy had me looking down at my crimson fingernails before glancing back up to his face. I knew I was probably being ridiculously obvious. Added to that, he was making no move to relax, smile, or touch me, even casually. If anything, the look in his eyes had become more closed off. Unreadable.

Breathe.

I wasn't ready to give up yet. I'd already come this far, fighting successfully against the ghost of my relationship past to get here. Tilting my head back, I looked up at him. There was comfort in his beautiful eyes that were partially veiled by dark lashes. I felt like I knew him, though I'd never talked to him before now.

"Rowdy told me the guys were playing tonight. I thought it might be fun to watch."

"Do you know his music?"

"Never heard it before. To be honest, I didn't realize he worked here nights. I thought he just worked for you at the gym. Now I find out he's got a band as well. When does he sleep?" My smile was brief while my fingers nervously tucked strands of my long, dark hair behind my ear, unused to having it in my periphery. I usually kept it up in a ponytail, but tonight, I'd let it hang loose in its natural waves around my shoulders.

His attention followed the movement of my hand, and I wondered if he could see the vein pulsing madly in my neck.

Then his eyes were back on mine. His words were brief. "He works hard. They're good if you like funky jazz."

"I like all kinds of music."

"Then you're in for a good show. Good riffs."

I didn't want a good show. I didn't want to talk about music. I wished I were more confident in knowing what turned a guy on. Not just any guy. This guy. Searching out Rowdy, who was helping someone a few customers down from me, I reached for the bill in my bra that I'd stashed before entering the bar. Liquid courage? Maybe. I turned back to Mason. "I'd like a Corona. Can I buy you one, too?"

His fingers, hot against my sensitized skin, kept me from pulling the money all the way out. He carefully slid the bill back under the neckline of my cami, lingering for a moment longer than needed on the top swell of my breast. Moving a few inches north, he found a lock of my dark hair curling over my collarbone and wound his finger through it, testing its texture between his thumb and index finger before letting go. Then he was looking at me again, his eyes a shade darker.

Without breaking eye contact, he called out to Rowdy, "Two Coronas. Put it on my tab."

My breathing went shallow and trembled between us on the exhale, my voice sounding a little bit higher than normal when I said, "Thank you."

Just one light touch of his fingers and already my nipples were budding and swelling. I'd stopped feeling embarrassed by it all some time ago. He had the ability to get my blood pumping with a look, much less a touch. It was amazing, like finding out I had secret powers that I was desperate to explore. It was time for the next step. I wanted to feel what came next. I wanted to read to the end. I was tired of always hitting the cliffhanger and being left to wish and wonder. What would it actually feel like to have amazing sex with someone I was attracted to who wanted me back?

Deliberately, I let my hand fall to rest on his leg near his knee, although the bold move made my face flame. His thigh was hard, wider than the span of my spread fingers. His flesh was hot, even through the denim.

He looked to where I touched him, was quiet a moment. I worried that he was about to push my hand away, but if anything, he leaned closer, capturing me with a look once again, his voice growing a shade quieter. "I've watched you."

His scent was intoxicating. He was close enough that it enveloped me, a combination of whatever soap he used and his own unique essence. I took it into my lungs and stifled the sigh that wanted to escape. "I know."

"Six a.m. sharp. Spandex pants. Sports bra. Tank."

I couldn't look away from his pale eyes, silently willing him to say he wanted what I wanted to make this easier on me. "Almost every morning for more than a year."

"More than a year." His nod was barely discernable, more of a slight dip. "Why now?"

I knew he was asking why I'd decided to approach him after all this time of keeping to myself, maintaining my distance. Cat and mouse. Catch and release. Like playing tag adult style with the promise of something dark and sexy to come day after day. "Maybe I needed time to see who you were."

He pulled back a bit, lips tightened as though an unpleasant thought came to him. His tone went flat. "Who am I? What did you see?"

He was disengaging, pulling away; I didn't know why. All this time, I'd watched him interact with his employees, his customers, the men he rehabbed. My being here wasn't a spontaneous decision made in a drunken moment at a bar. I saw exactly who he was.

My chin jutted. "I saw your strength of character."

He searched my face. With sharp attention, he leaned in toward me. "What does that mean?"

"Strength of purpose. Respect. Loyalty. Friendship. Reliability. Trustworthiness."

His jaw clenched for an instant, then relaxed. He smirked, grabbed up the Coronas Rowdy had placed on the bar. He handed me my own in the process, and clinking his bottleneck to mine, muttered, "Don't put a spin on it. I'm just a guy. Don't go painting me with bright colors." He took a drink, but despite his casual words, he watched me over the rim of his bottle.

"There's no spin here." I used his own words back at him. "You weren't the only one watching.

T-shirt. Bike shorts under loose athletic shorts. A bandana tied back over your hair. I have to say I'm surprised that your whiskers are a golden brown when your hair is so dark."

I gave in to my desire and tentatively reached a hand toward his face, not caring that my fingers shook ever so slightly. Pausing a moment, I waited for him to flinch away. When he didn't, I caressed the bristles along his square jaw, my thumb pausing at his lower lip before drawing a line along the fullness of its bottom edge, lingering. He held his breath while I explored. Then we both exhaled.

I set my hand on his leg again. "Your staff respects you; you're fair and treat them well. You're passionate about helping the vets find their way back to as normal a life as they can manage. Your gym facility is top-notch because you know you have a responsibility to your customers. It all tells me you're someone I can trust. Otherwise, I wouldn't be here now."

While he shook his head, negating my words, his knees closed in, bracketing my hips, keeping me close. He didn't want me to step away. I didn't think he was even aware of his contradictory words and actions, but my heart punched out a little faster with the pressure. I barely heard him remark, "You don't know me."

"What about you?" I could feel that he wanted me, but he was holding back. Would he blow me off for being fanciful or somehow filled with romantic ideas of the future? I wasn't. And I wanted to lay all my cards on the table. "Why haven't you come to me in the last year?"

"I didn't want you to get the wrong idea." He took another sip of his drink, but his eyes dipped south to the welcoming slopes of my cleavage and lingered, like he couldn't help himself, like he could feel the ache in my breasts and wanted to answer the call. I was doing it. Breaking through the barriers. Still, he growled. "I don't do relationships."

"What if I don't have the wrong idea at all?" I urged my fingers up his thigh, stopping halfway up to watch for reaction. His jaw flexed. His breathing got heavier. Success gave me a buzz of pleasure, and for once in my adult life, I felt sexy. Being the aggressor was a rush. "I don't do relationships either. But what if I got tired of just looking and wanted … more?"

"More how?"

"Isn't it obvious?" Heat thrummed in my veins and emboldened me. I wanted him to burn from the inside the way I was. "Or do I have this all wrong?" I let my nails dig into his thigh.

His nostrils flared on an intake of oxygen. "Did you come alone?"

I took a small step closer, fitting more snugly into the V created by his spread knees. The power of my arousal was demanding action. I was close enough to feel the heat coming from his chest when I leaned closer, a few inches separating our lips, to murmur, "The only reason I came tonight is because you were going to be here."

He was silent but continued to hold my gaze. His eyes narrowed. He was quiet long enough that a hint of insecurity snuck in and disappointment threatened me. I'd gotten into the situation without thinking about how to leave if it didn't go as planned. I started to pull away, but he trapped my hand under his own on his knee and kept me in place. Even as my breath caught, loving the feel of his warm skin completely covering mine, he said, "I don't think you know what you're doing here."

He didn't trust the invitation. "Maybe not. It's my first time doing this."

His cloudy eyes, dark with conflicting needs, dropped heatedly over the top curve of my pale breast yet again, his jaw tight, hyper-focused on the one spot. He looked back at me, and that was the first hint of predator that shifted his gaze. "First times can be dangerous."

"Not if you're careful. Not if you know the score."

His hand wrapped around my wrist, but he didn't pull it off his leg. Instead, he ran his hand up my arm and pulled me closer into the V of his thighs before settling it on my hip to keep me there, forcing me to arch back to keep looking into his face. My flesh felt like it was sizzling beneath his hot grasp. I couldn't look away. His eyes demanded my attention.

"What's the score?" he asked so low it would have been hard for anyone outside our intimate circle to make out his words.

"Need. Don't you feel the need?" I was starting to breathe faster. This was going to happen.

He leaned down so the warm breath from his lips touched my ear, enveloping me completely within the circle of his personal space. "What is it you want, Layla?"

The way he said it was dangerously soft. Silky. My breath hitched on a hard beat. A ripple effect sent hot tingles with lightning speed to my girl bits. My womb contracted so pleasurably I barely held back a moan. I didn't move back. I loved being in his personal space.

With trembling breath, I leaned even closer, finally letting my nipples have their greatest desire, which was to brush their aching points along the firm muscle of his chest. I left no space between us at all, and with my lips touching the vulnerable skin of his neck, just behind his lobe, I whispered, "I think you know."

"If you can't even say it—" His lips were on my ear.

"I want to see if you can make me come as hard as I've fantasized about for almost a year." That's when I pulled back to catch his reaction.

The hunger in his eyes became all-consuming. He searched my face for signs of authenticity. It didn't take long for him to make his decision. One inhale, one exhale, and he stood, linking his fingers through my own and pulling me down a hallway that was beside the kitchen.

There was a door marked Office, and he'd barely pulled me through and shut it before my back hit the closed door.

There was a fraction of a second where I saw the dark intent in his eyes before Mason's lips, hot and demanding, captured mine on a wave of raw hunger. Engulfed in the feel, the taste, and the scent of him, blood swooshed deafeningly, my body a live wire of vibrant, hot tingles. My hoarse cry of pleasure punctuated the silence. It had never been like this before. Never. Ever.

His large hands, even tangled in my hair, were gentle, holding my head at the perfect angle to deepen the connection before his tongue slid along the seam of my lips and then plunged inside, hot and velvet as it rubbed mine. Sharing the sweet, bitter tase of the beer he'd been drinking was the sexiest thing that had ever happened to me. Corona was my new favorite flavor. I sucked on his tongue, eliciting a growly moan and the surge of his body crushing up against my own. The rigid length of him pressed against my abdomen, and the wild thing inside me woke up, demanding I let her out.

So I did.

"This has been driving me crazy, sweet girl. I couldn't stop looking at it, wanting to see what was under there," Mason growled. One of his hands slid down my neck, and his fingers traced the delicate, silky lace neckline over my breast, his eyes hooking mine with a silent question. Never had I been asked before. The answer was yes.

"Do it," I breathed. My words weren't completely said before he tugged the blouse and strapless bra down until my breasts were propped above the wire lining for his view, the dark pink nipples exposed.

A moment of doubt, a twinge of unease, fluttered through my mind, and my breath caught at the back of my throat until I saw the look on his face.

"Layla." Almost reverently, he murmured my name while his stormy eyes worshipped the sight of me. "You're so beautiful."

His thumb rubbed back and forth over the pouty tip just before his lips latched onto it, and like a direct conduit to my sex, the heat and suction from his mouth gave me a jolt of electricity that had me arching into him and crying out with the sudden, sharp pleasure of it. Panting through the waves of heat, I floated in a fog of arousal that was more potent than I'd ever known was possible. He helped me uncover the secrets of my own body.

"I had no idea," I moaned, my fingers cupping the back of his head, curling into his thick dark hair. "No idea. Ohmygod. Mason. Don't stop."

And he didn't.

His lips and tongue sucked at it. His teeth took nibbling bites, his tongue rubbed at it, and my secret parts pulsed furiously, making my panties wetter than they'd ever been before in my life. Strange mewling sounds came from my parted lips, and my hips rocked toward him involuntarily, inviting him to take, wanting to feel him right at the center of where everything was heating and swelling and needing.

"You like that?" He pulled back from my nipple, leaving it dark red, puffed to a hardened, achy point, and shiny from his mouth.

"So much," I whimpered without shame. "So much."

"I want my mouth all over you." He leaned in to nip at my neck and ear. "Want my tongue to fucking taste every part of you."

"Yes," I cried. That was what I wanted. All of it. For the first time.

Against my lips again, he murmured, "Thought about doing this so fucking many times. Wanted to just…"

And his hand was back on my breast, kneading it and pinching my swollen nipple. He caught my panting moan with another hot, open-mouthed kiss that gave me a taste of him. Mason. Clinging to his biceps to stay upright. He was addicting. I was drowning in sensations, exhilarated by the need that danced through my veins. We were feasting on each other like there was no guarantee of tomorrow.

Heavy breathing and sounds of pleasure feathered between us when a harsh rap on the door startled us. Mason's lips ripped away from mine. Both of our chests were heaving.

Rowdy's voice sounded like it was right next to my ear when he called, "Bethany's here, bro. She's looking for you." The knob turned as though the door was about to be opened.

Fast acting, Mason leaned a quick hand against it right beside my face, keeping it closed. It jerked me out of the sensual haze I'd been floating in, my eyes wide on his. Oh my God. Did anyone hear me moaning in here? The door was so thin. Who was Bethany?

"Mason? What the hell are you doing? Let me in," an impatient female voice drifted easily through the door between us.

"Hang on!" Aggressive impatience edged Mason's tone, but when he looked back at me, his eyes were still hungry, his lips swollen from our almost violent kisses. He braced his other hand on the other side of my head, caging me in, his eyes riveted on mine. "I can't do this right now. I have to—"

"Dammit, Mason. Don't keep me waiting," the woman snapped, another sharp rap on the door.

"We have a date. Remember?"

"Fucking hold on a minute, Bet," he growled back. "I'll be right with you."

Bet? Reality filtered through instantly, and with it, immediate shame. The same moment I'd been reveling in as a personal victory suddenly became shadowed. How did I keep ending up on the wrong side?

"She's waiting," I whisper-hissed, a hot flush riding clear up to my hairline.

He had a date. A date! My insides withered. My heart pounded. How could this have happened? How could he do this to me? Except, I'd done it to myself. I'd thrown myself at him. And I had said it was casual. But now I was going to have to walk by her looking like I'd been making out with her guy, because I had.

I hadn't known about her, or I never would have done any of this. He even had a pet name for her. Bet.

"I have to go." My words were barely audible and rushed.

A feeling of urgency pressed me. I couldn't look at him as I yanked my clothing back into place like I was hiding the evidence. But I hadn't known. I would never want to hurt another woman. I wasn't my mother who could smile with evil glee while flirting shamelessly with a man in front of his wife. I cared about how my actions affected others.

"Layla—" He was frowning down at me, seeming at a loss, watching me scramble. He had something to say, but I didn't want to talk to him. I didn't want to look at him. I didn't know what to say. I'd never done this walk of shame where everyone knew what I'd been up to.

"No, really. Let me get out of your way," I squeezed words out from a throat tight with tension, eyes burning with self-contempt.

Let them be the workhorse, baby girl. Get what you can from them while you're still young and pretty. Take from them before they take from you. My mother's slurred speech and mocking laughter, common after nursing vodka and juice most of the day, interjected my thoughts. I could see her glassy-eyed, mile-long stare in my mind's eye, could hear her "motherly advice" that she often repeated while absently petting my hair, and my throat swelled.

The moment my clothes were back in place, I needed to escape. Now. Just get out. God, I felt so stupid. There was no way I was ever going to be like my mother. I'd worked so hard to do things right.

"Layla, it's not what—"

"Let's not keep them waiting."

Wanting the conversation to end, I spun around in place, opened the door, and found an exquisite blond with an impatient look on her face not a foot away from me. It took less than a second to size her up. Absolutely gorgeous. Casually elegant. Higher in the pecking order socially than I was.

Her long hair was tied back in a sophisticated ponytail, and she wore a slinky slip of a dress with spaghetti straps that showed off cleavage created by very well-rounded breasts. No bra. She was several inches taller than me and had that effortless sort of body that was fine boned and naturally slender.

She looked me over in the same instant, then dismissed me. Her next sentence made my face instantly overheated like I was on fire.

"What the hell, Mason? What's with the groupie? We have plans."

Groupie?

All this time, all the fantasizing late at night under my covers, and he was never mine to touch or kiss. He belonged to another woman. But Rowdy had said…Didn't matter. Mortification bombarded me.

Mason had a girlfriend.

CHAPTER 3

MASON

"Oh God," she whispered.

Layla's expressive blue eyes were bleeding hurt, her gaze darting between me and a smug-looking Bethany. She couldn't hide what she was thinking and feeling. I knew what was going through her mind, and it was bullshit.

"Layla—" I snagged her forearm to stop her from leaving, but she yanked back like I'd burned her.

"I'm so, so sorry. I didn't—I wouldn't—I've got to—" She flushed a painful hue that only got worse with each half-stuttered group of unfinished words. The entire situation had spiraled south from one moment to the next.

"Yes, you should go. Three's a crowd," Bethany stated with some aggression, her arms folding impatiently across her chest, deliberately giving the impression of owning some piece of me here.

"Excuse me," Layla whispered.

"Layla, wait!" I growled, helpless to make her listen when she looked like a cornered rabbit bent on escaping. "Give me a second here. It's not—"

Before I could get the situation under control, she snaked through the door and darted past Bethany. I surged forward to follow, but Bethany hooked a surprisingly strong hand around my bicep, stopping me with a firm grasp.

"I don't have all night." A hardened expression replaced the smug look. "You agreed to meet with me, and I have things to do after this."

"I said I'd be right with you. If you don't like it, you know where the door is." Scowling, I pulled my arm free from her talons, stepped out into the hallway, and searched the growing crowd. Not a sign. The need to follow rode me hard. Pumped full of equal parts lust and frustration, I was ready to blaze a trail through the crowd, find her in the parking lot, and explain the situation, but with my first step, a voice of reason stopped me in my tracks.

She deserves better. You'll fucking corrupt that sweetness, and she'll end up hating you. You can't have her. You'll only hurt her.

"No," I muttered under my breath.

Yes.

"No," I whispered again as my heart clenched with an unfamiliar longing. She'd felt so right. It was like I'd known her forever. Everything fit. There was no way I would let myself hurt her. That is, I wouldn't knowingly try to hurt her. I'd kill myself if I hurt her. "Fuck."

Resentful, I hammer fisted the side of the doorframe, my anger rushing hot and bitter through my veins.

I hated living like this. And Layla was likely driving away thinking I was a dick who played her, that I was some asshole who didn't fucking care, that I was a douche who didn't have respect for women, which was all utter bullshit. All of it.

What the fuck just happened?

We'd been balancing the edge of the fulcrum perfectly for more than a year. I'd walked the line. I'd done the right fucking thing even through the pull between us, through countless times I'd wanted to simply ask her to coffee. Hear her voice. Know the secrets she kept behind her big blue eyes. Instead, I'd left her alone.

How long was I supposed to live like this? How long was long enough?

But even as the thought came, guilt hit me like a big crashing weight slammed into my gut. Pinpricks of heat broke out across my skin making my airways grow tighter, and I knew I was riding the fine edge of yet another panic attack. Two in a day. What the fuck? I'd barely made it to the office before the compulsions had hit earlier. Fucking compulsions.

The patrons dancing to music just down the hall barely registered as the symptoms slid into play.

Thoughts flew faster than I could keep up with. The situation was beyond my control. I couldn't handle being out of control. I couldn't handle chaos. Chaos was death. I needed to be in control. Nothing was in my control in this moment.

The whispers of the past broke through a crack in *the* mental door. The one that led to sounds of shouting. Sporadic gunfire. Shit that usually stayed locked up out of sight. Twice in a single day, after I'd been able to go weeks and even months between episodes. This was why I had rules I followed. Personal rules. It was the reason I'd never approached Layla over the last year, even though I couldn't stop watching for her, memorizing each piece of her.

Now she thought I was a player.

My chest grew tighter, the chaos in my mind becoming overwhelming. I was trying to stuff the memory of lifeless blue eyes back away where it belonged, or I wouldn't be able to function.

I needed to get this fucking meeting over with, so I could calm the fuck down again.

Fucking Bethany.

Why the fuck had I agreed to meet with her? She was nothing but trouble. Perpetual problems that had nothing to do with me. Always wanting someone else to solve her life for her. Meanwhile, Layla was running off, maybe crying.

I stepped back through the office door. Closed it behind me with a sharp crack, feeling like my jaw was going to snap I was clenching it so tight. It was getting harder to pull in a lungful of air. I was fighting for it. Trying to keep it under control.

And fucking Bethany was standing there watching me with a smirk, limiting what I could do in the moment unless I wanted her to know what was happening, which I refused to do. I had to listen to some kind of bullshit from her, and the compulsions, the damned compulsions, shoved me to the very edge, stabbing at my mind. It was either give in or pass out.

My heart tripped over itself, hammering into my chest. Memories of explosions, wailing cries, and panicked shouting layered my brain with toxic smoke and white noise that limited what I could take in right now.

"Say what you've got to say," I snarled, needing her to get the fuck out. Fast.

"You don't have to be a dick."

I barely heard her. The longer I ignored the compulsions, the more my chest felt constricted, as though squeezed in a vice, until I was nearly wheezing again. *Tunnel vision. Can't breathe. I have to give in before I start panting like a fucking dog.*

Hoping to make it look casual, I sucked in a shallow breath and stacked the file folders on the desk, setting them flush with the edge of the desk closest to the wall, ostensibly to get them out of the way, all while fighting the tremors attacking my insides, making my hands shake ever so slightly. I lined up the laptop parallel to the front edge of the desk. I put the extra pencils into the square pencil holder, which I moved so it was perpendicular to the top left corner of the computer near the back side of the desk.

Already my mind was quieting.

Finally, I set the two office chairs in front of the desk parallel to each other and took extra time to make sure they were perfectly perpendicular to the desk, before gesturing for Bethany to take a seat. The tunnel vision receded, but my heart was still clenching hard and fast. Luckily, I'd taken the edge off the panic attack. I wasn't good, but neither was I going to black out.

I sat on the edge of the desk, barely holding it together. Sharing an office with old Zeke was my own special kind of hell because he was the least organized individual I'd ever met. If I sat in the chair and paid any attention to the rest of the office, I'd be compelled to organize every single item, put things in perfect geometric alignments to have a sense of rightness in the world. I needed parallel structures, perpendicular angles, straight lines, and symmetry.

I breathed through the lingering anxiety and deliberately brought up an image of Layla from earlier in the day, the soft, serene beauty of her face when our eyes met, the steady calm that was always part of her essence. *Don't look away. Please. Stay with me.* She kept her sights on me, taking up the space of the horrific memories, spreading warmth, a small smile curling her lips. Then she was saying, *It's okay. You're okay.*

That was new. She hadn't spoken to me before in my imagination. It was enough of an anomaly that it stopped the runaway train in its tracks and had me sitting back bemused.

I focused my thoughts back to the present. My muscles began to loosen.

I didn't want Bethany to see my weakness. She'd always found humor in it.

She noticed anyway. It was hard to miss, especially with a stray rivulet of sweat making its way from my temples, the sheen of it patching my T-shirt at my pits. Her eyes reflected a sharp ugliness masked within a humorless smile as she sat back and stared at me. That was the risk of knowing someone for so long. She could read me better than anyone.

As usual, she was amused when she said, "Still doing the arranging thing? God that used to drive me insane. Sometimes when I was pissed at you, I'd deliberately go through every room in the apartment and move things around."

45

It didn't surprise me. She'd always had trouble living in her own skin much less dealing with the kind of problems I had. Still, her presence brought back old memories of the pain we put each other through, and I was ready to get her the fuck out. God forbid she show a little care, maybe some empathy. Any occasion with her was jarring to my psyche. And while I didn't blame her for needing to move on from our relationship so many years ago—it was the best thing for both of us—neither did I want to be reminded of that time.

"Get to it. Why are you here?"

"Why the fuck are you rushing me?"

"Either talk or leave." More deep breaths. I wasn't going to die. At least, not now. That was always the root struggle when I was triggered. Fight or die.

"Such a tough guy, right? It always has to be your way—"

"If I had my way, you wouldn't be here," I ground out, on the edge of telling her to take a hike.

"Trying to get back to your little girlfriend? You can't. I wouldn't have thought she was your type anyway." Bethany's tone was clipped, the familiar tightening of her lips telling me she was pissed off.

She was looking for a fight. I knew the signs.

"My type isn't your concern."

"I thought you liked the skanks with fake tits and no names. This one actually looked like a decent human being. Does she know what an asshole you are?"

"Not talking about Layla with you." The office was hardly bigger than a walk-in closet, which meant her cloying perfume began permeating the small space. After the delicate floral scent of Layla's skin, Bethany's musk was heavy and invasive. I wondered if I'd ever liked it.

"Fine." Her movements were sharp as she dropped her bag unceremoniously on the floor in front of the desk, finally taking the seat I'd offered. "Someone should warn her not to expect anything from you."

I bit off the sarcastic words that came naturally. I realized how automatically Bet and I could resume our verbal sparring exactly the way we'd left off when we'd broken up three years ago. I had an epiphany: She was still trying to do our dance, but I didn't have to dance with her anymore. It was a small moment of victory for me, a moment when I could let the irritation deflate and step back from the situation. See the forest. There was no point anymore, and it only wasted energy.

"Mention Layla again, and we're done." For a moment, she glared at me, her jaw clenched with residual aggression. She actively swallowed whatever her next words were going to be.

"Fuck whoever you want. It's not my concern." She dug a file out of her bag and slapped it on the desk next to me. "I have a business proposition for you."

"What is this?" It really wasn't unusual that she'd spill venom and still expect to be listened to. She hadn't changed, but that didn't surprise me after knowing her so long. We'd grown up together since we were five. We'd been through a lot of shit together. There was no way to completely walk away, particularly when she had a tendency to be self-destructive.

"I'm working for a new company that sells supplements. Protein supplements. Vitamins. Weight loss. There's a whole range of products that have successfully given people the results they're looking for."

I flipped open the file and saw glossy pictures of the entire product line, men and women looking toned and scrubbed up so they were shiny and clean on the label in their athletic gear. "What do you want me to do with this?"

She leaned back in the chair with an unapologetic look of expectation. "I want you to sell them at the gym."

I flipped through some of the testimonials promising that the products were "phenomenal" and that they "worked magic." One of the testimonials was from Bethany herself. Interestingly, she made a claim to have been significantly overweight for much of her life—which I knew for a fact was bullshit—before trying the product and getting amazing results. Impatience mixed with exasperation when I closed the file and folded my hands over it. "What the hell is going on? Why are you doing this? I thought you were working for some law firm. Weren't you a paralegal or something? Going to school? Living with someone?"

The fire in her eyes faded a bit. The casual give-a-shit shrug seemed forced. "I quit. It wasn't working out."

I thought that she'd been living with one of the partners but couldn't be sure. "Why not?"

Her face suddenly looked tired. She rubbed a hand over her forehead. "It's not something I want to talk about right now. What I need is for you to

49

take a look at the products and purchase a regular supply. I think you'll find the wholesale prices to be quite reasonable. Once you've selected which of the products you want to buy, we can draw up a contract."

"Sorry, Bethany. I don't sell supplements. I don't believe in supplements." I was protective of my gym. It was the lifeblood that kept me sane, a labor of late nights working through a business degree, novice mistakes that took me to the edge of bankruptcy a time or two, and times when I had to go without before I wasn't operating in the red.

"Such a boy scout." Her eyes went frosty. "I happen to know you're doing well. Well enough that you could buy into this bar. Well enough that you just bought a freaking condo a few blocks off the beach. And you fucking owe me, you bastard."

"How do you figure?"

"I needed stitches that night. Fucking stitches because of you."

Her little outburst had some of the effect she was looking for. Shame and regret swamped me, but that was it. I wasn't surprised she'd done the research on my finances. Bethany was always looking for the angle. She was always looking to work a situation until she got what she wanted. Shaming, guilt, tears, poor me… It worked on me when we were living together, but not so much anymore. I wasn't responsible for her.

"I don't owe you shit, Bet. I work my ass off. You should try it some time." I wasn't going to feel bad because I'd finally found some success.

"I'm trying here. Christ, Mason. Would it hurt you to at least look at the information? See what it's about? This is my job. I fucking need the money." She leaned over and let her finger run over my knuckle in a casually idle touch. "And who knows, maybe we could have some fun again. I remember how good it was between us. A bottle of wine. Chocolate-dipped strawberries. You remember that time? It could be that again. Don't you think?"

I pulled my hand away. "No, I don't."

"Why not?"

"I'm still the same guy."

Her eyes turned cold, angry, and her lips tightened again, but now her face was flushed with emotion. I knew this didn't have anything to do with me. I hadn't talked with her in more than a year—the last time being a quick greeting when we ran into each other in town—much less spent significant time with her. Something else was going on in her life, something she wasn't going to share, and I was glad for that because I didn't want to know. I was no longer on that merry-go-round.

"Bet, you don't really want me. We both know this. Weren't you living with someone? I thought it was serious." When she refused to look at me and instead glared at some imaginary point on the wall above my head, I knew I was right. "I'd recommend thinking real hard about what you're doing before you do something you can't take back." She had it in her to do a revenge hookup. It was something she'd pulled with me, and I knew from experience that she'd feel like shit afterwards.

"God, you're an asshole," she muttered, stuffing herself back into the chair with her arms crossed. "Whatever."

"You need to talk about the problems with him, Bet, whoever he is." Maybe her tears did still work on me. I could see them making her eyes shiny, but this time, they looked genuine. The bluster was missing from her demeanor. "Look, I'll read this stuff. That's it. That's all I'm promising."

"Yeah, all right." She nodded. "I'll get back to you in a few days. See what you think."

"How's your mom?"

She took a deep breath and stood, like the information was part of the weight she carried. "Hanging in there. Cancer's gone. Had to sell the house, though."

"I'm glad she's better. My mom always asks about her."

She gave a short smile that fell as quickly as she formed it. "She'll be glad to know."

Against my better judgement, I asked, "Are you going to be all right? Do you need some money?"

"I need … I don't know. Peace."

Didn't we all?

She stood up abruptly, slinging her bag back over her shoulder. Her face went back to its taut lines, which was how she squared off with the world before confronting it. I hoped she would find what she was looking for. When she opened the door, the house music was still on and "Uptown Funk" drifted in on a wave of talk and laughter from the crowd. It was muffled again when she closed it, and I found myself staring at the door for the second time.

My brain backtracked, and I was again worried about whether Layla got home okay and considered strong-arming Rowdy for a possible phone number in order to check on her. If he even had it. If she even wanted to hear from me again. The thought that she possibility wouldn't sent a short pang through my chest.

I could still feel the warmth of her body pressed to mine, smell her delicate perfume. Her lips were so soft. She tasted amazing. And she thought I was a bastard.

What the hell had I been thinking bringing her back here?

I'd promised myself I would only look, but the moment she came on to me at the bar, all bets were off. Even as I told myself not to sink into her eyes, they got a stranglehold on me. There was a vulnerable quality to them, a fragility. And yet, she knew how to turn on her beast mode at the gym.

She attacked her workouts with a sort of a take-no-prisoners mentality. She worked with a singularity and dedication that often had her gritting her teeth. All or nothing. Balls to the wall. There for the workout and not the social opportunities. She was no gym bunny. She'd kept to herself and bled pain with satisfaction. It was almost like she was not only facing but also defeating an unseen enemy.

For my own part, I feasted on the sight of her every morning. She had a habit of listening to music from her earbuds while on the cardio machine for one segment of her workout, and whatever she listened to made her hips swing in rhythm. I was an expert on the shape of her ass. Fuck. It was a thing of beauty.

I'd be lying if I said I didn't want to continue what we'd started in here, which was why it was a good idea to let her go. She didn't know me, and I didn't want her to. Seeing Bethany's face when she walked away three years ago was hard enough. The shitstorm nightmare of that breakup had almost been more than I could handle. There was no way I could go through it all again when things went south, which they inevitably would.

The darkness in me hid a monster in the deepest shadows, waiting to strike out.

She would have hated me more if I'd actually fucked her.

At this point, I had to give in to my compulsions, which were triggered by my new business partner's philosophy of abstract disorganization. Fucking Zeke and his flower child, the-universe-will-provide take on life had me attacking the desk. Sticky notes were stuck haphazardly in random spots on the computer and desk calendar to remind of supply orders that needed to be placed. Then there were stacks of papers that included bills from suppliers, reports on our current supplies, and payroll shit partly stacked on top of a file cabinet, partly on another section of desk, and the rest casually resting on the floor, with no apparent rhyme or reason to its organization.

How this place was still open I had no idea, and the compulsions could not be ignored any longer, especially since Zeke wasn't likely going to show up again any time soon, as sick as he was. Giving in was like rebooting my system. Setting me right. The sooner I jumped in, the sooner I'd feel like myself again.

It took me an hour to go through everything, set up computer spreadsheets, create paper files for the hard copies we had, and develop a filing system. I was sweating by the time I finished, but only because low-level anxiety had my heart pounding a shade harder until everything was in its rightful place. My world was nearly on its axis but for one thing. I had to know about Layla.

My heart settled back to its normal pattern only after I promised myself I'd ask about her, talk to her. I didn't actually want her thinking I would ever knowingly hurt her.

With that settled, I finally left the office to do a walk-through of the club, see how business was going. If I was going to keep this place alive for

Zeke, I needed to know the lay of the land.

Rowdy was working his ass off behind the bar. He was smooth. Knew how to juggle the alcohol and still make customers feel welcome. It was a good skill, and he'd trained the bar staff well. They were efficient and professional. Bartending was probably something I needed to brush up on. You never knew when it might be necessary to fill in. Part of the success of a place was knowing it from the ground up, the inside out, the cost of the ounce sold versus the ounce bought from a wholesaler.

"Water?" Rowdy asked tossing a look my way, his eyes missing nothing. I probably looked like shit. He was handing someone change, but when the guy refused it, offering it as a tip, he gave a quick, "Thanks, man," before depositing it in the tip jar behind the bar.

"Water sounds good." I scrubbed a tired hand over my face and wished not for the first time my life were different. When you fucked up bad enough, there were no take backs. You couldn't get a do-over like you could in elementary school kickball games. You had to live with the consequences.

"Or something stronger?" Rowdy arched a brow in question, still searching my face.

"Water's good. Look, did you see Layla take off?"

"She went out the back door," he responded with a blank expression while filling the glass and setting it in front of me.

"Did she look upset?"

He was quiet a moment, wiping down his workstation. "Hard to tell. Her head was down, and I only caught a glimpse."

I rolled the glass between my hands, appreciating the condensation. It cooled my palms and gave me a moment to think. "What do you know about her?" I wasn't sure why I was asking except to further torture myself with glimpses of what I couldn't have.

He studied my face for a moment, always a straight shooter, even with his hair gelled up special for the show he was going to put on soon. He seemed reticent, and I wondered if it was because he was interested in her himself. It was noteworthy that just the thought of him asking her out sent a blast of anger to my gut. He finally said, "She's a good girl. She's been through some things."

"How do you know her?"

"Met her at the gym when she first started.

Worked with her on some exercises. She had some kind of hang up about her ass." He smirked, which had me frowning for a brief moment. "Girl doesn't appreciate her assets. Anyway, she does web design. Fucking genius shit. Really creative. Was talking with her earlier today about setting up a site for my band helping us figure out how to direct traffic our way. Told her she should hear our stuff tonight to get a feel for us."

"Computer stuff." It was more of a quiet statement as I tried to piece together the puzzle.

Rowdy absently tidied the condiment holders that he used when making some of the cocktails. He was about to turn things over to another bartender so he could join his band on stage. "She's been really cool about offering us a discount on shit. She knows the band is struggling financially, and she's still willing to help us out. I wouldn't want to see her get hurt."

It sounded like a warning. Normally, I would have been pissed to have some punk kid try to school me on my personal business. Would have probably gotten up in his face. But I couldn't legitimately work up the emotions under the circumstances. Rowdy had integrity. I respected him. And there was something about Layla that gave off a sense of fine china. She seemed to bring out the protectiveness in the guys that knew her. She didn't want to own the room when she entered it and acted more like she was weathering a storm when she received unwanted attention, rather than basking in it.

"I understand, man. I do. Thanks for the info."

He gave a brief nod. "I'll see you on Monday."

"Monday."

The revelry continued around me, surging as the band took the stage and revved up the crowd before starting their first song. Layla should have been here to listen. What I'd done with her, to her, replayed in my mind. She smelled so good. Felt so good. Hearing her soft, husky moans had had me wanting to wrap myself around her and find a happy ending for both of us. My cock jerked in my pants with a vicious influx of heat, but I needed to let go of that image. First off, it wasn't going to happen, and second, I had a job to do. The ache in my cock had to be ignored, something I'd been able to do successfully for the last year.

Rowdy's band, Finding Waldo, wasn't half bad, and they brought with them a small following who added color to the bar. That color was green and had dollar signs. Drinks were bought, food got shuttled out of the kitchen, and there was dancing, talking, and laughter. A haze of smoke touched my nose, and within moments, I had a customer escorted outside so he could legally finish his cigarette on the sidewalk.

All very professional. Again, there were good people getting trained well. The bones of the place were solid. Part of what I was doing while moving around the establishment was analyzing the experience from a customer's point of view, and what I could see was that things were a little sloppy. Dust on ceiling fans, on the liquor cases. Rust in the sinks, the drains. Bathrooms not checked regularly. Some spilled drinks not cleaned adequately, leaving sticky residue on the table and floors. A few times I could feel the bottom of my shoe peeling off the floor. Systems and procedures needed to be reestablished. That was all.

Since Zeke had taken more of a backseat in his business, things had begun to slide, details missed. After he'd told me he was sick with the big "C" disease and was going to have to let the business tank, I'd offered to buy in. He'd been a mentor to me long ago. Supported me when I was desperate and falling apart. There was no way I was going to let his business die after he'd worked his entire life to build it. There was no question that I was going to help him out. With medical bills racking up, we needed to keep the money coming in.

It was a packed house, a good sign for a Saturday night. Friday had had fewer people, and the weeknights even less than that. There needed to be some kind of draw to get more business during the week. It was something I was going to have to research. Weeknight promotion possibilities.

I just needed to stay focused and remember that rules and systems kept things running smoothly.

I'd almost broken my rules with Layla. I wasn't going to get emotionally and physically involved with anyone. It wasn't safe. Bethany was case in point. Hurting someone I cared about yet again would destroy me.

CHAPTER 4

LAYLA

"Did you see his cock?"

My brows arched.

"Was he hung? I'm not looking for a police sketch-artist description here, more of a how-did-it-feel kind of description, you know? Were-you-able-to-comfortably-walk-the-next-day level of detail. See where I'm going with this?"

In a tribute to Princess Leia, my impossibly cute, petite friend, Blessing, had wound her thick, shoulder-length blond hair into two buns on either side of her head, wore Divergent-esk combat boots, skinny-style utility pants that looked painted on, and a Rosie the Riveter shirt with the caption *She Persisted*, an interesting juxtaposition to her deliberate choice of black-rimmed bifocals sitting on her nose.

Yes, bifocals, since she couldn't see much past the bridge of her nose. She refused to wear contacts. She had some kind of eyeball phobia. Her big, round, baby blues blinked at me from behind thick lenses with pure delight, eager for some juicy description of my night.

"Comfortably walk? Are you really going there? Oh my god," I moaned, feeling the heat crawling up my neck, but the words brought naughty imagery to mind, and my secret girl parts involuntarily tingled just thinking about it all. I frowned. My parts were so easily excitable when it came to Mason. That was my problem in a nutshell.

"Did you doubt I would? C'mon. You know me better than that. Look, I gave you time and space to get ready for this conversation because I could see your adorable attempts to hide from me in your computer space, using your squinty-eyed look to appear all engrossed in your computer screen."

"I do not have a squinty-eyed look."

"You totally do, like that would stop me from sniffing out good dish." She gave an exaggerated smirk and shook her head like that was pure crazy talk. "I've been more than patient, so spill. It's time to share the feast."

Big sigh. I didn't know how to feel about what happened. I'd stepped into the gray area, unsure of what was right and wrong. This was new territory for me.

My emotional seesaw had swung between anger and embarrassment over the last two days. Between "What was I thinking?" and "Way to go, girl!" Yes, with the exclamation point. Because I had relived it over and over, play-by-play like Skinemax porn in my mind, sometimes with acute mortification, but most of the time with intricate sensory detail of his hands on me.

I remembered the way my body went haywire with a crazy mix of heat and desperate need just from kissing. Kissing! It was insanely amazing to truly share myself with someone for the first time, which was different from any kind of sex I'd had with Brady.

Luckily, I'd had a couple of days to process the whole event, effectively draining much of the emotion from it. I was frankly surprised the conversation hadn't taken place when I first walked through the door, since she'd known what I was going to do, had even helped me plan it from the get-go.

Granted, she'd been on a conference call to the Netherlands most of the morning. Aside from her business where I worked as a web designers, she had a sideline passion, a gig that kept her up late into the night. She had designed a steampunk-fantasy video game, one that had been years in the making, her techy love child, something with warriors and dragons and magic and such, and damn if it hadn't finally been recognized for the stroke of brilliance that it was by those who produced such things. That was the only reason she hadn't been up in my face any sooner than lunchtime, when we went up on the roof of the loft we worked out of, wondering if "our plan" had worked.

Blessing's smile faded the longer I was silent.

"Uh-oh. Was it cringy? From the expression on your face, I'm going to guess that the sex was not good." She scrunched her nose.

"No, it's not that." Though I normally told Blessing everything—the good, the bad, the terrifying—because she'd been my biggest hero during one of my darkest moments, I couldn't stop the spread of self-conscious heat that pricked my cheeks because his touch had been so very good. "We didn't actually have sex."

Blessing scowled instantly. Not surprisingly, she'd been rooting for me to get laid. "You chickened out." It was more of an accusation.

Defensive, I was already shaking my head in denial. "No, I didn't. I swear."

"What did you try? Did you wear the mini? I bet you threw on those stupid jeans even though I told you they can act like a damn cockblock. It's about easy access." She punctuated her last few words with her chopsticks, stabbing them toward me before scooping up another piece of her salmon roll from the local sushi takeout place and dunking it in wasabi-enriched soy sauce. It looked tasty, but I was on a tighter budget than she was. Especially now.

I sighed, setting my peanut butter and honey sandwich down. "They aren't stupid. They're cool and comfortable. Trying without trying."

"They also make it harder for him to reach your pussy."

"Oh my God. You did not just say that word." My cheeks heated instantly.

"What word?" She looked genuinely confused.

"The...p-word."

Blessing froze mid chew, surprise popping up on her face. She swallowed. "You're kidding me. You object to the word pussy?"

"It's not that I object to it." Change took time. Some words vibrated with power, and I wasn't sure I was ready to wield that kind of power just yet. At least I was using the word fuck in my mind pretty regularly. I was proud of that.

"You deliberately make a plan to fuck a guy you've been fantasizing about for more than a year, but the word pussy embarrasses you?"

"It just sounds dirty." It had the power to get me hot and bothered, embarrassingly so, in an instant. It also reminded me of the porn I'd begun watching. I always imagined it was Mason and me doing the scenes whenever I watched. My imagination was fertile. So fertile, it felt like everyone could see it on my face.

"Fuck yeah! It should sound dirty. Good and dirty in the very best way." Blessing dropped her chopsticks to face me. The look of determination she leveled my way made me suddenly fearful. "You need to take back the word pussy. Fucking own the shit out of it. Make that word yours. Say it."

"What?"

"Say it. Pussy."

"This is ridiculous." I took a nibbling bite of my

sandwich, shaking my head with a nervous twitch of laughter.

She palmed her own sex the way a guy would palm his junk, and my eyes rounded seeing her hand there before skidding back up to her face again. She nodded and said, "Repeat after me. This is my pussy. I own this shit. I am responsible for its health and well-being. Do it."

"You're crazy. I'm not grabbing myself."

"Your pussy. And yes, you are. I swear, I will keep this up and hound you until you do this. I will follow you down the street, into the grocery stores, the library, the gym—"

"Blessing—"

"Grab your damn pussy!"

"All right, all right. So freaking bossy." In my mind, I'd said *fucking bossy*. I gave her a good glare and set my sandwich down to lay a hand over the denim at the apex of my thighs.

"This is my pussy. I own this shit…" she paused, waited for me.

Though my face was vibrating with heat, I knew she'd make good on her promise to harass me, so I dutifully repeated, "This is my…pussy. I own this shit."

"I am responsible…"

"I am responsible for its health and well-being."
We finished the last part together, and I was glad no
one else was on the roof to hear this completely
embarrassing conversation.

"Pussy."

"Pussy."

"Pussy." Her lips quivered, and now I knew she
was playing with me.

"Pussy. I got it."

She laughed. "Your homework is to say it out
loud ten times a day until you don't blush or
hesitate when you say it. I also wanted to see how
many times I could get you to say it."

"Whatever." But I laughed.

She went to pick up her spring roll from the
foam container and continued the conversation we'd
been having. "Access. That's all I'm saying."

"You're going to eat with that hand?" I asked
with a smirk.

"You betcha. I'm a special kind of fabulous."

She popped it in her mouth and closed her eyes for a moment of pure flavor appreciation. "So, no more dodging. What happened? You wore…"

I was not generally a skirt-wearing kind of girl. I basically had two dresses in my closet that were used for weddings and funerals which was why, for this occasion, we went shopping. Blessing insisted that I "show off my legs, my ass, and my tits because they totally rock." Put like that, how could I say no?

"I did not wear my jeans. I wore the mini."

"Good girl," she mumbled around another mouthful before swallowing. She smiled and sighed. "Fantastic. Go on. You went to the club, and he was there."

"He was. And I almost chickened out, but I didn't. I walked right up to him and asked him if I could buy him a drink."

"*You* asked *him*. How very feminist of you. Why be subtle when you know what you want, right? Here, here." She lifted her plastic cup of iced tea in a singular toast before taking a hefty slurp from it. "Then what? C'mon. Don't make me drag each and every word out of you. Did anything happen?"

There was no way I could repeat to her what I'd

whispered in Mason's ear about how he'd starred in my sexual fantasies. It was so personal; it would feel like I was making trivial something that had taken all my courage to say. Communicating needs or pleasure had never been part of any sexual experience I'd ever had in my life. Pretty quickly after moving in with my ex, all flirtatious play dried up. Anxiety ruled the household. There was nothing sexy about that. Pinpricks of dread started gathering in my chest just from the remembering, but I fought them off.

I used my personal affirmation exercise, which was a deep breath in and a reminder of my own personal strength on the exhale: *I* left *him*.

I sped through the rest. "We kissed and touched in his back office…"

"And it was good?"

Understatement. "Really good. Amazing, actually. Anyway, then this girl walked in. Turns out, he has a girlfriend. And she's like…beautifully perfect. Totally hot. Like, Beverly Hills Barbie hot or Malibu Barbie hot." I shrugged as though playing it off lightly, even though my stomach clenched in protest because Rowdy had said Mason did not have a girlfriend when I'd tried to cleverly find out, and I'd never seen her at the gym before. Ever. I mean, how was I supposed to know? The darkness bled through even though I was trying for playful when I stated, "Who knew?"

Just when I was getting on the sexual freedom bandwagon with someone who made my body sing, I discovered he wasn't available to play with. That thought revved up old feelings of injustice, that somehow the universe was determined to put its boot on my neck, a position I was used to being in. Make me eat dirt perpetually. It didn't matter that I lived on the up and up, worked hard, tried to do right by others. I kept finding myself on the short end of the stick in life.

It was particularly painful when, for once, everything had felt so right.

My helpful brain kept serving up the memory on a silver platter, the experience itself life-altering. I'd felt so needy, so horny, in a way I'd never felt before. My…pussy had wanted to feel him. The suctioning force he'd used on my nipple had made me cream my panties instantly, and he'd pressed that hard erection into my belly. Arousing rather than frightening.

Of course, once I'd gotten home, my self-criticism began.

Should I have rubbed his cock? Was that what he'd been waiting for? I should have told him I didn't really know what I was doing, because I'd never done any of this right, according to Brady, and he'd been the only man I'd ever been with. But forget all that because Mason had a girlfriend. He didn't actually want to have sex with me, and I kind of forced it. Had he felt coerced into the situation?

It was a mortifying thought. I painfully understood coercion.

Blessing was studying my face, looking somber, her chopsticks resting on her plate, her hands clasped in front of her chest. "You're letting the past affect the future, sweetheart. Sex is the best kind of fun. It shouldn't be stressful. It should be play in its purest form, not something to constantly second-guess. And you didn't know he had a girlfriend, and if he'd wanted to play it straight, he could have told you right up front. It's not complicated and not worth the dialogue you probably have going in your mind right now."

She'd hit the nail on the head. My chuckle was brief and lacking humor. "Yeah, well this is me you're talking to. I don't always get things right."

"I hate that bastard." The words blew right out of her mouth as she slapped the lid down on her food container. I knew she was referring to my ex. "I hate him with all my heart. He trained you to constantly doubt yourself, to think there was something wrong with you."

"I don't want to talk about him." Firm. There was no nonsense to my tone. Almost two years had gone by since I'd lived with him, and I was working hard not to give him any more airtime than I already had.

"All right. I'm just…Sorry." She shook her head and huffed out the negative feelings on a growly breath. Adjusted her glasses on her nose with a quick, irritated touch. "All in all, this was a success. This was a fantastic success. You do not have any kind of sexual dysfunction. You can absolutely get hot and heavy with someone and take it to the finish line just fine. Next time, you'll have a great big orgasm that rocks your goddamned world. I swear it. And I'll tell you what. Mason, he's the dick for doing anything with you when he knew he had a girlfriend."

I winced inwardly, not wanting to think of him that way, not wanting to think of Malibu Barbie with her hands on him, and yet the obvious… "I know that. Logically." How often did emotion work in a logical, linear, cause-and-effect pattern?

"Then why feel bad?"

"It's going to sound stupid." I picked at my sandwich, tearing a bit of crust off, and popping it in my mouth while I contemplated whether to share yet another ridiculous story from the melancholy tales of my life. "Here's the thing. He wasn't mine to touch. He was hers. I was taking something that didn't belong to me, and it made me feel awful. Wrong. Ashamed. It was like being in elementary school again and having the lunch lady slap my hand because I was reaching for a tray of food I couldn't pay for."

Because in any given situation, I always seemed to be on the outside looking in, wishing I could participate but not having enough capital, either financial or social, to do so.

"She slapped your hand?"

I nodded. "It was traumatizing. All these kids saw and laughed. I think I was eight or nine. I can even remember the food on the tray. It was a chicken burger with tater tots and those green apple slices that have caramel dipping sauce in the packet. I was so hungry because we didn't have food in the fridge that morning, so you know, no breakfast. I'd been dreaming of lunch all day, wanting it so bad.

"I never forgot the shame of it. My mom had forgotten to fill out the cafeteria application for free lunch, which I qualified for, unfortunately. Anyway, this little perfect blond girl, a little Beverly Hills Barbie in training, was right behind me with one of those smiles that actually had an evil twist to it. At least it did in my memory. She took the very tray I'd had to put back with one of those in-your-face kind of superior looks, saying how good everything smelled in this really exaggerated voice that only little kids can achieve to increase the torment in any given moment. She had money. She could afford the tray. She took it and paid for it. She was in my class, and by the end of the day, she had everyone calling me 'Punky Brewster.'"

Blessing's eyes blazed with anger on my behalf. "I hope you beat her ass."

"Nope. I hid out in the library."

"The beginning of a beautiful relationship?"

"Call me a bibliophile."

"Please, please, please. At least tell me she ended up a drunk prostitute doing guys to support a meth habit by the time she left high school."

"More than likely ended up going to Stanford or something like that. Rich girl. Dressed well. Good grades. Family that took care of her. Truthfully, we'd moved to a new school by the time fifth grade rolled around, but she existed at every school, you know? She was everything I wasn't, had all the basic things I should have had, and she never had to work for them or question that they would be there." I took a deep breath thinking back to *the girlfriend*. "It was just so unfair. *Bethany*, or Bet, as he called her, was perfect. Not a hair out of place, expensive-looking clothes, and he belonged to her. She had a claim on him. Perfect body. Perfect teeth. I bet she has a car, too. Something elegant to match her style. I'm so tired of blond bimbo Barbies taking over the world."

Blessing gave me an arch look gesturing toward her own hair, noting the color. "We're not all bad."

"You're hardly a bimbo." I knew I was being small and petty hating this girl so much. She wasn't even the problem, but she reminded me of all the baggage I carried. It sucked.

Blessing laughed. "More like a total nerd. And, I told you I'd teach you how to drive."
"I know, I know, but it's not like I can get a car right now anyway. There would be payments, gas, insurance. I just can't swing it yet." There were side effects to growing up in poverty. Not knowing how to drive was one of them for me. "And I know I'm being bitchy and all that, and it's wrong to criticize her. It's not like I know anything about her or that she did anything to me personally. She was fine. She could be on the verge of curing cancer; I don't know. The thing is, I was the one with my hand

caught in the cookie jar, taking the tray that wasn't mine. I mean, there was no way she didn't know what was happening in there." I hadn't exactly been mute.

"Did she seem mad?"

I thought about it a moment, not having reviewed those details. There hadn't actually been any kind of dramatic reaction from her. "Not really."

"Maybe, just maybe, and this is a super crazy idea to consider, I know"—which was the clue that Blessing was about to bomb me with her sarcasm, so I waited for it, let her own it, run with it— "but maybe she wasn't his girlfriend, and you are totally jumping to the wrong conclusion."

Hmmm. Something to consider, but nothing to get my hopes up about. "Maybe so. Anyway, I'm over it. Something else happened that's more pressing and potentially problematic."

"What's wrong?"

"Nadine showed up."

Her lips thinned. There had been more than a few drunken episodes when Blessing and I were both still living in San Diego. "When?"

"She was waiting outside the apartment complex with some guy Saturday night."

They'd been leaning against his car smoking cigarettes, laughing at nothing substantial, listening to music playing too loudly from his car radio in what was usually a pretty quiet, working-class neighborhood, which was bad enough, but the air seemed tinged with the sweet herbal scent of weed. Of course, they both denied having or smoking or ever seeing when I made a casual comment about it.

Whatever. I'd wondered if the cops would show up or a neighbor would come and complain. At least it hadn't been alcohol, which was her first love. She'd have been laid out on the sidewalk, otherwise. It was what she kept choosing, again and again, instead of a close relationship with me.

"Sober?"

My sigh journeyed from the very depths of my soul. I glanced out over the tops of the other buildings to see the Pacific Ocean beyond the Manhattan Beach pier in the distance, then tilted my head back to appreciate the crystal blue, cloudless sky, wishing life could be simpler, less exhausting.

"She's claiming forty days of sobriety. I was glad to see her alive and looking fairly healthy." While I knew, logically, that it was unlikely, my heart wanted to believe.

"It's been a while." Blessing scowled.

"A year, maybe, when I first took her to rehab. I was so full of optimism, willing to give it all to help her. Literally." My sister had always been so pretty when we were younger, her curling strawberry blond hair a testament to having different fathers since mine was dark. It was always in a flyaway page boy style, framing eyes that were the exact same color as mine, ocean blue, which we got from our mother. Last night she'd looked hard. Like she'd tumbled through a rough patch in her absence.

"What does she want?"

"Place to crash while she gets back on her feet." It was with mixed feelings that I let her into my personal space, a place that was sacred to me. It wasn't the greatest place, but it was mine. I'd worked hard for it. Independence. I didn't owe anyone anything. Of course, the first thing she'd done? She'd smirked unpleasantly, giving it a brief glance, then huffed a snide comment. *You should have stayed with Brady.* The air had deflated from my lungs instantly. She had that power.

Blessing whistled a breath, taking on a cautious tone. "How do you feel about that?"

"I…" Joy and pain. I loved seeing her, my older sister Naddy-pie, who'd always taken care of me as a kid, protected me with the fierce kind of loyalty of a mama bear. And, I hated being confronted with who she'd become, an emotional terrorist who held me hostage for her life. I loved the potential for finding the close relationship we used to have. I hated the everlasting hope I kept getting suckered into feeling and the inevitable disappointment I'd been trained to expect when she fell apart and left again.

She broke my heart every single time. I never learned.

"Not sure?"

"I don't know. I mean, I want so much for her to be…whole."

"Happy."

"No, more than that. Happiness is an emotion that comes and goes. A scoop of ice cream makes me happy until I have to work it off with an extra thirty-minute run. Then, I'm not so happy. I want something more lasting for her. Contentedness. Room to breathe and let whatever demons are riding her just go."

"You aren't giving her money, are you?"

"No." I shook my head. At least I could say I'd learned that lesson. "Said she had some. She had a part-time job that she was hoping would become full time soon. A manager was going to transfer somewhere leaving an opening here, yada, yada, yada. I didn't listen to the details. She was gone all day again Sunday and came back late at night. Was sleeping when I left. I told her where my hideaway key was located. Probably a stupid move. Anyway, we haven't had time to catch up. I have no idea where she's been or what she's been up to." We'd played this drama out a few times in the last several years. It was hard to believe anything she said. The awful truth was if her lips were moving, she was lying.

"You don't need me to tell you to be careful here, but I'm going to say it anyway. Be careful. I understand your need to help, but don't let her take you down."

"I won't." I couldn't be mad at the advice. It was gentle compared to the thoughts I'd had. A part of me wondered if my TV would still be there when I got back home today.

Blessing grabbed her lunch remains, stood up, and sent a surprisingly accurate shot over my emotional fortress of a wall, hitting me right on the bull's-eye. "And you are hiding from Mason."

Wary, I eyed her, seeing the smirky twist of her lips. "How do you know?"

"Your hair was dry when you got to work." She did her impression of a chicken as she walked backward clucking "bawwck, bawck-bawck, bawwck."

Busted. I always caught a shower in the women's locker room after my workout.

I flashed her my pretend fangs, not sure she even saw them before she whirled around to head back down to our office. For all my talk of being this tougher, take-no-prisoners, new-and-improved me, I *had* chickened out this morning. Instead of hitting the gym first thing, per my usual routine, I'd decided to make it there after work, figuring Mason would likely be gone by the time I got there. He was always there in the morning to work out with guys in his Rebuilding Lives program for injured vets, but I had to imagine that he didn't spend the entire day at the gym.

But what if he was there?

I took the last few quick bites of my sandwich and made my way back to my desk with my lunch bag in tow, still chewing while my mind considered different possible scenarios where he confronted me, or we ran into each other. It was going to happen. Absolutely. Was he going to look at me through different eyes? I mean, of course he would. That was a stupid question. But what would that look like? Would he be all superior and smirky, or would he pretend like nothing happened?

Tension simmered in my body the rest of the day, the kind that had me feeling jumpy and unfocused. My mind searched for and rejected different words and phrases I could use in a variety of scenarios, all while trying to review accounts, update sites, and return calls. The realization finally arrived, that there was nothing I could say that would make things right again.

We'd opened a box marked "do not touch," and there was no going back.

CHAPTER 5

MASON

"She's here."

"How long?" Frustration tag-teamed my anxiety. Avoidance tactics. She was hiding from me, giving me too much time to think. Worry. I needed to look into her eyes and know she was all right. I needed to explain I wasn't a dick, even though nothing could happen between us, but she never showed up. I'd watched the door all morning.

Added to that, Jay Garcia had been a no-show, which added to the shit show in my brain. Had he gotten his prosthetics? Was he stewing about his now ex-girlfriend? He hadn't missed his training since his darkest moments earlier on.

But this was exactly my problem. This was it. I needed to be able to predict my world, and when shit got beyond my control, I started having symptoms again. Even had a fucking nightmare the previous night. Woke up drenched in sweat, shouting, ready to take cover, with gunfire echoing in my mind.

It was five in the morning when I got to work, fighting tremors the entire way. Compulsions that I figured I had under control, had been able to manage successfully, were now driving the bus, grabbing me by the throat, squeezing, shoving me back until I complied. When everything was in order and accounted for, it was safe.

I refolded the towels with military precision, reorganized the complimentary bottles of shampoo and soap that were shelved in the supply closet to make sure they were in appropriate groupings. That's when I noticed that the various bottles of cleansers we used on the floors and weight machines weren't lined up right with the labels properly displayed. So, I took care of that.

And she hadn't shown up. I watched for her long after she would normally have come. All it'd taken was one night to put everything in jeopardy. I was in danger of sending a splintering spiderweb crack through my precisely, carefully ordered world. I'd made too much progress to let myself regress, and if this told me anything, it told me I clearly wasn't ready to let anyone into my sphere.

And still, I could fix this. Set it right again. I needed to. I needed her to be my angel.

Staff came, noted the crazy in me, the frenetic pace, the dark cloud hovering, and gave me space. I'd been driving myself nuts until Rowdy, who must have picked the short straw, tentatively approached while the rest of my employees watched us covertly from behind the desk. He convinced me to "go chill," with the promise that he would let me know if Layla showed up.

For the first time in memory, my own staff kicked me out of the gym for a "surf break" because I was driving them nuts.

That's when I took a breath and realized I was doing more harm than good. I respected my core group—Rowdy, Shay, and Amanda—too much not to see they were trying to be my friends and look out for the business. They knew enough of my story to understand, but I didn't want to impose on that goodwill. I'd simply nodded, knowing I was worthless, and driven off to seek a place that would allow my mind some peace and quiet, free from worry and anxiety. The beach.

"She just arrived," Rowdy answered.

"Thanks, man." I disconnected the call and took another hit of the ocean breeze, drawing it deep into my lungs, letting it infiltrate all my cells.

The ocean had a calming effect on me when I let it do its magic. The sun was setting over the water, and like others around me, I took another minute to soak it in, watch it dip, acknowledge powers greater than myself, acknowledge that I didn't have control over most things and that it was still going to be all right. Riding the waves gave me space to breathe, and it pounded the shit out of me with unrelenting force more than a few times. It was humbling. Surfing required me to refocus my energy, channel it elsewhere.

It also made it clear why I couldn't get involved. It took so little to overstress my psyche and make me worthless for a whole day. While that was better than what used to happen—weeks and months shot to hell—I was still fucking broken. Broken. And no one deserved the kind of shit I brought to the table.

Still, I needed to make things right with Layla before I could let this thing go. Not seeing her had totally fucked with my world, and I needed to get us back to how things were.

Within twenty minutes, I'd managed to rinse off, change, and haul ass to the gym. I slipped inside just in time to find an unobtrusive perch on the front desk from where I could watch Layla attack the bench press. Her dark hair was sleeked back into a ponytail, and she had her spandex shorts and tank on.

As always, my mind hooked into her frequency, that level of quiet calm that I usually found every morning just seeing her. She was the start of my day, and today, she'd ditched me.

The after-work gym-goers populated the main room, creating a buzz of activity; music played through the speakers, and members socialized between exercise sets. It was the busiest time of day, the gym floor more crowded with bodies than at any other time.

Rowdy, who was my number one go-to guy in both of my business ventures, threw me a quick nod and returned to checking in members on the computer while I leaned against the desk to wait her out. She'd thrown more weight on the bar than I'd seen her use before, and she was hitting it hard for the first two sets, working in total beast mode. On the third set, she slowed, her muscles tiring.

She had fans. A couple of guys were lingering by the free weights a short distance away. Their eyes followed her every move reflected in one of the mirrors mounted on the walls, like they were on the hunt, as if they wanted full access to what they could see. I didn't like it. She either hadn't noticed them or was ignoring them in the middle of all the activity taking place around her. One leaned in to say something to the other, neither one ever taking their eyes off her. They both grinned at the comment and continued watching.

I could easily imagine what was said, and it made my jaw clench.

While I couldn't blame them for looking—she was sexy as fuck in her sweaty spandex that outlined her curvy little body—a slow burn started in my gut anyway. I wanted to smash their faces against the mirror. They were fucking vultures, circling her, and she was unprotected. I knew what they were thinking as they watched her, and she had no clue. She looked so small and defenseless. She barely cleared my chest when she was standing in front of me. Guys were fucking dirtbags, and that included me.

Before one of them made a move on her, I casually strode over to "spot" her, making sure to make eye contact with the two douchebags standing by the free weights. When they caught my glare, they suddenly found shit to do, and I got behind her, letting my fingers hover under the metal bar she was pressing up.

She gasped her surprise, her dark blue eyes

focusing on me, searching my face, the bar paused in an extended position, suspended over her head. For a moment, her eyes seemed starved, taking me in, lingering on my lips. A flush spread up her chest and neck, and I wondered if she was reliving Saturday night in vivid detail like I was. Then she was panting under the weight, the bar wobbling dangerously.

"Pay attention," I growled, feeling the heat of that look she'd given me clear down in my dick. It twitched with the sudden pooling of blood in the region. I had to breathe through the unexpected surge of need in such a public place. It left me feeling too vulnerable. I scowled down at her, snapped, "You're going to hurt yourself. Finish your reps."

Her eyes whipped back to the bar. She bobbed it twice more, but on that second time, it paused mid lift, her arms shaking to get it the rest of the way up. Her teeth were clenched. She grunted with the effort, and still, it remained fixed at the halfway point.

In an aggressive take-no-prisoners command, I gritted, "Dig deeper, Layla. Push it up. Push. Push. Push."

A sudden light in her eyes told me she was grabbing hold of my energy, working with me.

Emitting a final snarling growl, she found her inner reserve and shoved the damn bar up like she owned the fucking thing. I helped her guide it to its resting spot, highly respecting that she was indeed a badass. She wasn't here to look pretty. She was here to kick her own ass. I admired the shit out of that.

It was also the sexiest thing I'd ever seen.

"Good work," I murmured, coming to the front side of the bench while she recovered.

"Thanks." Her words were husky, tremulous, coming out on tired, shaky breaths between sexy full lips that I remembered tasting over and over again. I remembered how they felt beneath mine.

The memory was a bitch, hitting me square on when I was trying to do the right thing, and it was there between us when our eyes met and held. Then hers headed south, taking inventory of my chest, my fucking cock that wanted to salute a greeting. I did the same, noting the outline of her nipples, her narrow ribcage that rose and fell with each deep breath, and the hollow of her stomach with delicate hip bones sticking up. I'd had my hands on her. Felt that soft skin. I fucking wanted to again.

Silence stretched.

She gave a quick look around as though realizing

what she was doing. An adorable flush crept over her skin, and she sat up on the bench. Averting her eyes, she grabbed at her towel, busying herself with blotting at the moisture on her face before draping it over her shoulders. Then she stood, facing me.

"How did you know I was here?" she asked.

Remembering the shit day I'd had, my frown was instant. I took a few steps closer to her, wanting to keep our words between us. She was forced to look up at me, her blue eyes rounded with sudden nerves. Though quiet, my words shot out on a trail of frustration, rapid and gruff. "I told Rowdy to call me if he saw you. Why did you run off? Why are you avoiding me? What the hell, Layla? You fucking started this."

"I… I…" She shook her head back and forth, showing a helpless, fruitless search in her mind for words that weren't forthcoming. Then resignation filtered down over her features, along with the truth. I saw it in her eyes first—the softening that contained a silent apology—before I heard it in her voice. Her tone was gentle when she finally admitted, "I didn't know what to say to you. I felt…feel stupid and ridiculous."

"There's nothing about you that's either stupid or ridiculous," I stated gruffly. Unable to help myself, my eyes tracked rivulets of sweat doing a freefall into her shirt between the mounds of her breasts. Her nipples were still hard, outlined clearly by the second-skin tank she had on. I wondered what they would taste like right the fuck now. Salty-sweet?

She caught sight of where I was looking and crossed her arms over her chest, which only plumped her breasts higher. Fuck. I could see burying my face there. With her breathing going sharp and shallow, her eyes took on that hungry look again that told me she was fighting the same heat that was burning through me. She wanted me. And we were surrounded by people. Before I ended up with a raging hard-on, I stepped back from her.

"We need to talk." I tilted my head directionally toward the exit. "There's a coffee shop next door. It's pretty quiet at this time."

"I still need to do my cardio." It was a weak attempt to put off the inevitable.

I fixed her with narrow eyes. "We'll call it a hydration break. Just ten minutes. Then you can come back and finish. You can't avoid this, Layla. There are things that need saying."

She took a few quiet breaths, her mind working as she stared up at me, and I fell into the soft blue pools of her eyes that could see into me more than I was comfortable with. They pulled me in until I felt lost in them. And still, my mind remained settled. Calm. That's what she did for me.

"I just need to grab a sweatshirt."

"I'll meet you out front."

She finally nodded. The rest of me sighed in relief at that nod, because since the first moment I'd laid eyes on her, she'd become part of what kept me whole. There was no way I could afford to fuck this up. From the first moment Layla entered my life, she'd become necessary.

CHAPTER 6

LAYLA

The Bohemian Café had a quirky personality, and I liked it.

Deliberately mismatched chairs in rich wooden tones, their cushioned seats covered in different embroidery fabrics, were paired with all differently sized and shaped wooden tables arranged in configurations that were nonuniform. Everything was clearly secondhand and looked a bit worn, including the Spanish tile flooring.

Local artists had hung a variety of canvases anywhere there was wall space available, making for a vibrant scene with a relaxed vibe. It was welcoming and homey but did nothing to calm the storm brewing inside me.

My body buzzed with overstimulation, emotion,

hormones, all mixing together in a big cauldron of I-have-no-idea-what-will-happen-next. I crossed my arms over my chest, my fists grabbing onto my sweatshirt's bulky fabric for added reassurance. Mason pulled his wallet out, giving the cashier a casual greeting before looking back at me over his shoulder, a questioning arch to his dark eyebrow, clearly asking what I wanted to purchase.

The realization that I'd left my purse in the locker room made my stomach bottom out. I gave a sudden alarming glance down at my empty side, followed by a fearful rush to jump on my own error before he could, automatically expecting some form of ridicule, so I ridiculed myself before he could do it.

"Nothing. I forgot my...It's...okay. I'm just so stupid. I don't ever think..." How freaking ridiculous. How had I expected to pay for myself? Freaking dummy. It wasn't like money grew on trees, but here I was going into a place of business without even thinking about it.

My eyes suddenly burned after hearing my own thoughts. *Money doesn't grow on trees, Layla. Some people, not you of course, but some people in this world need to work for it.* It was Brady's voice. Brady who'd often put me in my place when we were out in public with a statement like that. He'd done it knowing he controlled the money. It was one more way of controlling me. Owning me.

Mason scowled. In his cut-this-shit-out voice, he said, "Layla, you need fluids."

"I've got water back in my locker." I didn't want anyone doing anything for me. I didn't want to owe anyone anything. I couldn't trust anyone. I had a moment of horror, feeling moisture blur my vision, but I blinked it away rapidly.

His eyes narrowed with some unformed question that I didn't have an answer to. He didn't ask it and only motioned toward the display case, which I was thankful for. With his deep voice gentling, he said, "Layla, I'm going to get you something, so you better choose."

Equally hateful to me was strangers looking at me, possibly judging me, and it felt like we were drawing attention to ourselves, particularly the cashier who was watching us with a vague, practiced smile that probably covered for the exasperation she was feeling. "Vitamin water," I answered, just to end the moment.

"Make that two," he added.

I took a breath in, and on the exhale, reminded myself again: *I* left *him*. *He* was no longer in my life. No one owned me. I made my own money and took care of myself. I wasn't helpless.

Mason grabbed up our drinks and tossed a bill on the counter, waving off the change. He handed a bottle to me and led the way to an empty table. Being that it was a weeknight, the place was virtually empty. Private. He pulled a chair out for me, the thoughtful gesture registering in my heart, making me pause for the briefest moment before I sat. No one had done that for me in the past.

He sank into a seat across from me, and I couldn't help but drink in his familiar face. I loved the way I could get locked into his compelling eyes with their striking pale silver color, brooding storm clouds that I now knew could go dark with need when they looked down at me hungrily. There was a rightness to this moment—the piece of my day that I hadn't realized was missing fit the space I'd left gaping open when I'd ditched my normal workout time. I hadn't gotten my fill of him during the morning hours. A year was a long time to get used to having someone fill a part of your day, and I'd denied myself.

He shifted forward. His dark blue T-shirt with a surf logo on the front stretched across his broad chest, and his elbows rested on the table, pushing into some of my personal space by accident rather than design. His large form took up more than half the space we inhabited, with his legs bracketing mine that were primly crossed under the table. Intimate. Personal. His scent came across the small space, sunscreen mixed with a tinge of his own musk, and I found myself relaxing enough to lean in ever so slightly, just an inch closer, to get more of it.

Nerves got the better of me as the silence grew.

"I'll pay you back for the water," I offered quietly, and immediately wanted to face palm. Buying someone a bottle of water shouldn't be that big a deal, so I needed to just forget about it, but I couldn't. I was riding the edge of my anxiety with the situation I'd created between us. This was a new game to me. I didn't know the rules. I didn't know what he wanted to talk about.

Mason glowered his opinion down at me, his dark brows furrowing over the bridge of his nose, and shook his head, which left me feeling petty and small. Defensive. I folded my arms across my chest and leaned back again. Before he could say anything, I took the offensive. I looked him straight in the eye in a silent challenge.

"I'm not sorry about what we did Saturday night. Even if she is your girlfriend. I figure it wasn't on me to put the brakes on the situation."

His somber expression relaxed. A hint of a smile curled his lips. Masculine satisfaction looked good on him. "I'm not sorry, either, and she isn't my girlfriend. It was a business meeting."

Relief gave me a boost of pleasure at the same time it loosened the tension in my shoulders. "I'm glad. I didn't want to think you were the kind of guy who'd be with other women when you had a girlfriend."

"I'm not. But you rabbited out before we could talk. I didn't want you thinking I would screw around with a woman's emotions, and particularly not yours." He reached over to uncap my drink for me, his large hands surprisingly agile and graceful, then set it back down in front of me. "Have some. You need it."

"Thanks." I picked up the bottle and stared down at it a moment, thinking of what happened after Malibu Barbie had almost walked in on us. In the spirit of being honest, I came clean. "I panicked. Saturday night. I know a lot of girls do one-night stands and can breeze their way through a situation like Saturday, but I've never done something like that before. You know, tried to hook up with someone at a bar. You're only the second guy I've ever…been close to." I looked back up at him, hoping he understood what I was saying without me having to spell it out. I didn't have it in me to get too personal in this moment of confession.

"I figured it was something like that." He wasn't surprised. It was like he'd read me from the beginning. "Why?"

"I told you Saturday—"

"I don't mean why did you choose me, but why did you choose to do this at all? Why not meet a nice guy and go the traditional route?"

The brief, non-humorous chuckle spilled from between my lips before I could stop it. Self-conscious, I dropped my eyes and ran a hand over my hair, smoothing sweat-dampened strands back toward the rubber band that tied it off. That reaction was only the tip of the iceberg. The possibility of having my will drowned out completely by some careless man the next time around was not something I was remotely interested in experimenting with. I couldn't lose myself again.

"I tried that." I looked back at him, hooking into his beautiful, silvery eyes. "It's not something I want to do again. Ever."

The thought alone of being in another live-in, monogamous relationship was enough to tighten my stomach. A sense of claustrophobia edged my nervous system with pinpricks of panic. Emotional prison. Who needed that? Not me. And yet, neither did I want to stop living, breathing, experiencing all that I could. I gulped some of my specialized water and recapped it.

"After one relationship?" He shook his head as though what I'd said didn't make sense. "Not even interested in one of the ex-military guys in my program? I hear chicks dig uniforms."

"Never that. Not in a million years." My response was sharp, my tone hard, and it had come out of me so immediately, it startled even me, but the associations were there. The military precision of Brady's closet, the hospital corners on the bed, the criticism of my housekeeping and how it was never good enough, shaming me into doing tasks over and over again to get them "right." My heart thudded with the memories.

A flare of suspicion, brows bridged over angry eyes, had him asking in a dangerously quiet voice, "What happened, Layla? Did he fucking hurt you?"

I took a few moments, then answered in a calm voice so as not to betray the depth of the emotional baggage that came with having this conversation. If Mason knew the battles I still fought internally, he'd probably think I was a basket case, and I didn't want my past ugly anywhere near my present or future beauty.

"I don't want to explain an ex-relationship right now. That's not what I'm here for."

He watched me in that intense, quiet way of his, that concealed what he was going to say or what he could be thinking. I thought he was going to force more questions, but then he let it go. Nodded his agreement.

"We don't have to talk about it now, but we do have to talk about Saturday."

"What about Saturday?"

"I've thought about your proposition, and while I'd love to take you up on it, I don't think it's a good idea. Casual sex with no expectations."

"I get it. It's fine." My answer was quick, an instant rebound off a basketball hoop. I worked to sound cool, but his response was crushing. My eyes burned. I fought off the image of Brady's smirk in my mind, fought off the fear that the things he'd said about me were being confirmed by a third party. Embarrassment made my next move one of flight. It was awful sitting here with a mental file folder overloaded with sexual fantasies I'd had about Mason when he didn't feel the same way.

"What do you get?" He studied me, analyzing

my expression like he could see into my mind. "Because I haven't actually explained myself."

"You don't need to explain anything. I get it. You don't want to do this with…with me." I went through the motions of lifting my lips into a small smile, afraid some part of it was trembling with the effort. There was no way I wanted to hear why he didn't want to have sex with me. It wasn't the first time I'd heard the list of what was wrong with me. I wasn't that brave. Not with Mason. "We don't need to do this anymore."

"What are we doing?"

"You are about to tell me that you aren't into me that way, maybe something equally horrible like 'it's not you, it's me.' I mean, that's fine, but I don't see a reason to keep this conversation going. We are in agreement."

"That's not what I'm saying at all." He looked genuinely surprised. "I just don't want this to go badly, and it has the potential for that. I don't want to hurt you, Layla. You aren't a casual fuck. You might think so, but you're not."

"You don't get to tell me what I am or what I'm not. I don't need another man telling me what I'm like."

"That's not what I'm saying."

"And I don't need you to pretty this up for me. I'm a big girl."

"You think I'm not into you?" His voice grew a little louder with a look of incredulity on his face. Now curious eyes burned a hole through my fragile composure. The eyes of the few others in the shop bore into me, and I couldn't take it. I'd had enough of people feeling sorry for me in public to last a lifetime.

"I can't do this," I whispered, and was out of my seat and exiting the coffee shop, shoving through doors, and making a beeline for the gym.

"Layla, wait up."

I only got past the short alley where the big dumpsters were located between the businesses before I stopped, unable to ignore him completely. I wasn't that girl who could storm off with a dramatic gesture, particularly not if it was away from Mason. So, I paused, feeling helpless to my own emotions, and leaned against the wall between the buildings. I took a breath and braced my hands on my hips, looking down at my scuffed old tennis shoes that I used for my workouts. Mason had only been a few steps behind me. He moved in close, hulked over me, cornered me up against the wall so I could feel the heat of his body.

My first glance was at his lips, my first deep breath his scent.

Why did I have to be so attracted to him? Why did he have to smell so good? Why did I have to like having his hands on me?

"You keep running from me." His voice was deep and gravelly with his frustration.

"We don't need to make a big production here. Let's just forget I ever brought all this up. I get it, okay?"

"Layla," he growled, dipping his head to my eye level, so I was forced to look at him. Even under a darkened sky with only the dimmest lights illuminating us, I could see the hard determination on his face. He was going to finish this conversation and make sure I understood every excruciating detail of his rejection of me.

"What," I snapped.

His voice went husky, and the back of his fingers lifted to brush aside a few stray strands of hair from my forehead. "You don't get shit. How could you even think I wasn't into you after Saturday night?"

Not knowing how to answer, I shook my head

and gave a one-shouldered shrug.

He leaned in to touch his lips to my ear, the words vibrating against my sensitive skin as he spoke. "I almost forgot where we were and fucked you against the door. You are all I've thought about. Your sexy lips and how they moved against mine, how your nipples tasted like fucking sugar and spice, and when I wasn't thinking of that, I was wondering how fucking soft you'd feel if my fingers were deep inside you."

"Mason…" I exhaled against his cheek. Shivers attacked. I don't know if my gasp was completely internal. His words had spun a web of desire that caught me as efficiently as a spider would catch its prey. My breathing fluctuated, and realizing that my lips had parted, I closed them and tried to breathe deeply again, regain control.

"For two days, I was going nuts. All I could think about was seeing you on Monday, and then you weren't even fucking here."

"I couldn't…"

He leaned in further so that his lips rested on the actual skin of my ear, the rough whiskers creating a perpetual electrical charge that set off nerve endings all over my body. The need that had been tamped down most of the day was burning hotter than ever.

"You proposed a game, and I wish so fucking much that I could play, but I can't. You have no idea how badly I want to feel my cock inside you."

"Then why?" I was so confused and turned on.

"I don't want you to get hurt. You aren't a casual girl. You aren't a one-nighter."

He'd said "cock" and "inside you." My imagination had me there instantly, eagerly, on the same page. My...pussy was suddenly feeling too hot. The heat surged, but so did my frustration at his rejection. "Don't tell me what I can and can't do. You don't know me."

"Think about it." He stepped back, looked down into my eyes again, trying to make me see his truth. "It took you a year to approach me. You wanted to get a sense of who I was first, remember? That's what you said at the bar."

"So?"

"So, that's not how casual happens. That's how relationships happen. You wanted to trust me and like who I was before you opened up to me. Think this through. What happens after we fuck a few times?"

"Nothing. Life goes on."

"That's why I can't do this with you. Your expectations are completely unrealistic. We're going to keep seeing each other at the gym unless you plan on going to another gym."

"What? No." I shook my head.

"I can't be that guy that fucks you without ties when I see you every day. That's not how you do a casual hookup." He looked frustrated. "I need you here. At the gym. I need to be able to see you and talk with you. Sex fucks that up. I need your friendship, Layla. I'm desperate for it. I mean it."

"Friendship. Got it." The word had me shuddering internally, even while I was trying to stay cool and calm on the outside. What a horrible word. It slammed the brakes on all of this. "I have to go."

"Layla—"

"Look. I'm not going to argue with you about this. You're out. Fine. You had your talk with me. Can I go about my business now?"

"But are you still looking for a casual hookup?" he asked.

I looked away from him, unsure of what I was going to do now that he didn't want this. His eyes were boring holes into my face, willing me to assure him that I would never do that. One thing was certain: I'd eventually figure something out. There had to be someone out there I might want to share time with. Maybe he was right about the whole casual thing. It made sense that you weren't supposed to see a one-night stand every day. Another stupid move on my part. I never should have come on to Mason. Pure ignorance on my part.

"Dammit!" Mason snarled his aggravation when I didn't answer. "Layla, you don't understand what you're inviting. Fucking a random guy is dangerous. You're going to get hurt. Why do you need to do this? Why are you looking for some random guy to fuck you?"

"It's none of your business anymore." It sounded so crude the way he said it. I felt the color rise in my face, a sense of shame that made me angry. Why did every other person get to enjoy sex but me? Why did every other person, but me, get to experience what it was like to want someone, to feel the tingles, the blood rush, the excitement, the intimacy?

"I can't stand the thought of some trashy guy who doesn't deserve you fucking you over!"

"I want to be fucked!" The word came out of my mouth loud, and the power behind it filled me up. I grabbed hold of it. Shoved it in his face. "I want to be fucked over and over until I can't take it anymore. I want to know what it feels like to be fucked in the heat of passion when I'm so wound up all I can do is come mindlessly. I want to know what that's like."

"Layla…" My name was a gruff sound exhaled between us, like defeat. His breathing was heavier, his hulking form suddenly moving closer again, like he couldn't stop himself until his thick arms caged me up against the wall. "You can't fucking say that shit to me."

"Yes, I can." I glared up at him, now only inches away. "I know what I want, and I'm going to make it happen. There's nothing wrong with wanting to chase orgasms with someone else. I'm tired of using porn to chase them on my own."

"Fuck. Layla." He ducked his face into the curve of my neck and inhaled my scent like he was trying to regain his control. Then he was rasping in my ear. "Fuck. You touch yourself while watching porn. I can see it in my mind. So, fucking sexy. There's no way to come back from that."

"There's nothing wrong with…"

"Not a thing…"

Mason's lips moved up my neck, his whiskers a

burning pleasure that prickled the sensitive skin until he captured my own lips in a deep, scorching kiss. Instantly, my toes curled, and I moaned with the feel of my blood turning thick, and of hot, teasing tingles radiating throughout my body. He ground his hard cock into my abdomen, and I loved the feel of it because it belonged to me. It was mine. I'd created it. Me.

The sense of heat and urgency had us grasping at each other, molding our bodies by feel to that perfect fit that seemed unique to us.

"Just like Saturday," he muttered against my lips. "I can't get enough."

"My body is on fire for you." My words were breathless and shaky. "It's so powerful."

"I can't stay away," he growled, and his tongue coaxed my lips to part enough that he slipped it inside, caressing my own with a velvety heat that had me rising on my toes to get closer, taste more, build on top of the brewing storm that was only the beginning of what I needed from him. But just when I was starting to cling like a vine, my fingers stabbing into his hair, he pulled away, breathing raggedly. Scowled down at me.

"What?" I gasped, the cold night air touching overly warm skin.

He shook his head, still breathing heavily, twined his fingers through mine, and pulled me back along to the gym. My brain was so fuzzy, I wasn't sure what was happening until he shoved open the door, so a rush of air conditioning whooshed around us.

"Finish your workout." It was the last thing he said before he stalked off toward his office.

Bemused and confused, I saw the new employee smirking at me from behind the front desk, like he'd been in on our little secret. He was dirty blond, lanky, somewhere in his mid-twenties, and with a smartass twist to his lips. Had he watched us through the glass doors? A quick glance over my shoulder showed me that he had a perfect line of sight. I caught my reflection in the glass door since the light was behind me. I looked like a hot mess.

My lips were swollen, my hair was a little messy, and my eyes were super round and dilated. Just as quickly, my head whipped back around to him, reading into his smirk, disgust curling my stomach. He'd watched us. What exactly had he seen? Heard? How loudly had I yelled that I wanted to be fucked?

"We close in an hour."

"I know." My face felt like it was the color of the

sun.

Just then, Rowdy came up and addressed the new employee with barely restrained irritation. "You have work to do. Get it done and report back to me."

The smirk never faded. It was accompanied by a shrug before the new guy moved off toward the men's locker room, a hint of cigarette smoke following him.

"Everything okay?" Rowdy asked in all seriousness, his eyes assessing my face.

"It's all good." I forced a smile. I felt so obvious.

"All right. Let me know if you need anything, okay?"

"Sure thing."

And where had Mason gone off to? Was he going to come back out? What had happened? Did it mean he'd changed his mind about what I'd offered? I was so confused. He was blowing hot and cold.

I headed for the elliptical machine and got started on the last leg of my workout. With too much time to think and nothing but drama to sort through, I found myself drifting back to the first time I'd walked in the gym.

Big men made me nervous. It hadn't been that long since I'd left Brady, and I was still jumping at my own shadow. I'd snuck off one day leaving no more than a note and was still looking over my shoulder, my breath catching any time I saw someone tall, fit and blond in my periphery. Then add in that Mason was using his big, scary man voice, shouting at this poor disabled guy. In that exact moment, I was instantly shoved back in time to the nightmarishly beautiful, perpetually spotless, townhome I once shared with Brady in San Diego.

The memory flashed me back to the kitchen, white knuckling the barstool the only outward sign of my anxiety. Dread burned through my stomach, not knowing if I should sit down or keep standing behind it. It was like I was a kid facing my punishment, hoping that daddy wouldn't get mad.

Tension had all my muscles feeling tight, stiff. My jaw ached from forcing a casual smile, hoping if I gave the impression of being relaxed and happy, it might change his mood, change the trajectory of his next set of behaviors. It never worked. But maybe if I jumped the gun...

You seem upset. What's wrong? I asked. My smile remained firmly in place though my pulse pounded out a warning.

Brady's lips stretched into his own version of a smile, but it was one that had no goodwill attached to it. There was a silky, sinister polish to it, and it never reached his eyes. He made a point of getting out the bread, meat, and cheese from the fridge, grabbing the mayo and mustard. A knife. His silence was more frightening than anything. Finally, he said, *I got a bill from the school.*

I'd wondered when it would arrive, and even though it was addressed to me, he'd opened it. Read it. I had no right to privacy here. *Right. That's my bill. I'm taking some computer classes at the community college. Nothing major. We talked about this.*

You *don't have any money. And* we *said that you had enough to do around here that you weren't getting done.* He made a point of holding his sandwich up as evidence. It was a reminder that I hadn't cooked anything today, another point of contention. Early on, he'd badgered me about learning to cook. Yet another symptom of growing up in poverty with a mother whose various addictions were more important than her kids: most of our food had come out of boxes, was severely processed, and only needed water and heat. Nutrition, cooking, healthy meals were foreign concepts I'd had to learn after leaving home.

No, we *didn't say that. That's what* you *said.*

As expected, everything headed south from there. It had been a long night. Tears. Anger. Shouting.

Then there was Mason and his big-man voice, and I hadn't even been a gym member for one day.

I'd stood frozen that first day, seeing Mason and his client working the weights. Mason was in this guy's face, taunting him, and this guy was shaking, straining, and turning an alarming shade of crimson. His teeth were clenched with an inner rage. Familiar panic and anxiety had my heart pounding with fear.

But then this magical thing happened. In the midst of rude sounding, growling epithets being exchanged, mixed with cries of what sounded like pain and agony, a goal was somehow reached. The snarls became shouts of jubilation, and Mason hugged the man who had pushed himself to the very limits of his arm strength on the weights because both of his legs were missing. They gave each other powerful claps on the back in one of those solid man hugs. They'd both been in complete control of themselves the entire time.

"Good work, brother," Mason had said in what was soon to become the voice I most associated with him. Calm. Supportive. Warmth reflected in his gruff delivery. It baffled me. I'd expected a fight. Shouting. Name-calling. Belittling. Maybe some punches thrown. The tension between the two men dissipated instantly, leaving me disoriented.

That wasn't the moment I became attracted—still convinced I was not a sexual person and was somehow lacking, still feeling like a victim rather than a survivor—but it was the moment I began studying him. Every morning, he took on the role of PT for a group of guys that were desperate to keep hanging on to some semblance of a normal life, some flavor of control. Most days weren't goal makers, and many days over the year had been breaking points. It was emotional, somehow a form of psychological therapy.

Sometimes guys came in with a steady bead on what they wanted to accomplish and what they had to do to get there. Then there were days where someone came in with a wrathful anger that required self-punishment using the weights, or maybe they came in unable to muster one iota of strength to even try. Mason took on many roles. Sometimes he was the taskmaster, and sometimes he was just the listener, but always, the sessions ended in positive, life-affirming kinds of ways. The guys loved him.

I kept to myself, tried not to let my observations

become at all obvious, but I couldn't stop myself from trying to understand what kind of man he was. Never in my life had I been near a man who behaved in a way that was anything other than selfish and careless. It took time, persistent evidence, to start believing that he was different.

It was a few months later when the fateful "abs" incident happened and my mind latched onto the image of me pressing open-mouthed kisses on all his beautiful man muscles that lined his stomach, but the fantasy hadn't been going long before it'd been replaced with another fixation. His butt. Seeing how taut it looked, how his clothing, whether it was athletic shorts or jeans, outlined those muscles perfectly and had me thinking about cupping them, testing them out.

Again, no sooner had I envisioned that little fantasy than a new one had come that involved my teeth and his neck, and on it went. It was a fateful day that I realized I wanted him. He had this strong beautiful body, and I simply wanted to be naked with him, something I'd never felt with Brady. It was like my body was waking up after being in sleep mode for most of my whole life.

Then there was the day I had the courage to let him catch me watching him, the excitement palpable, and instead found myself caught by his magnetism, his own eyes electric. It was like he'd reached out and told me he wanted me with just a look. It was also the first time I discovered porn on the internet.

"Layla." Rowdy approached again when I was nearly finished with my cardio. "I meant to tell you we have another gig in a few weeks."

Remembering that he saw me run out before his band played, had me biting my lip in guilt and lowering the intensity on my machine so I could keep moving and talk at the same time. "I'm so sorry I didn't get a chance to hear the band the other night. Something came up."

"It's fine. Life happens." He had his usual friendly smile in place, his longish dark hair pulled back in a cute, micro man bun to keep his look professional while at the gym. "Everything went well. I just wanted to tell you we've got some other gigs coming up soon. I was thinking I could email you some details if you're still interested in seeing us live."

"Sure thing. I'd love to see you guys, but we should also meet in my office. Email me some of the cool websites of bands you like. That will let me get a sense of their online presence so I can best help you. There are so many options, and with new technology continually being created, we can have some fun with this."

"That's a good idea."

"Great. Let me know."

He gave me a wicked smile. "Mason's been looking for new ways to advertise. He's always wanting to stay current. I think he should know more about what you do. I'm going to mention that to him."

My groan of dismay was all inward. I didn't need anyone to intervene in what was already an awkward, embarrassing situation. "No. Really. I don't need—"

"And listen…" This was the part where his cautious tone forewarned me that he was going to bring up what had happened at the club in some way. "I'm not trying to get into your business in any way, I promise. I just want to say that he's a good guy. Complicated for sure, but seriously one in a million when you get to know him. He was worried about you the other night."

"He was?" The question came out in spite of my attempts to play it cool.

"He wanted to follow you out, make sure you were all right. It was making him nuts that he couldn't go with you. I'm pretty sure he considered getting your number from your account here, but I don't think he wanted to seem like a stalker. And just so you know, Bethany went on her way not long after you left."

There was satisfaction in knowing the beautiful creature didn't have a hold on him and pleasure in knowing that he'd worried. I hadn't misjudged him, something I'd done painfully badly with Brady. "Thanks, Rowdy."

"I need to walk my client out the front. I'll email you soon," Rowdy promised and reached around to hit the button on my machine himself. He upped the intensity with three pushes and walked off, calling out to someone he'd been working with.

I upped the intensity of my machine by one more push of the button and was running again.

Mason was still holed up in his office when I decided to leave, and I refused to be a clingy girl who kept chasing him down. Despite what Rowdy told me, Mason had said he wasn't on board. I refused to force myself on him, and I headed out front to where I'd locked up my bike.

I would have noticed the guy sooner if my mind hadn't been preoccupied, but his voice in the darkness nearly made me jump out of my skin. He was in the shadows by the corner of the alley, watching me leave.

"Gotta smoke?" he asked.

It was that new guy. I cringed inwardly and felt a mild sense of outrage, seeing the look on his face. He was obviously leering at my breasts and barely skimmed his eyes back up to mine when I zipped my hoodie closed.

"I don't smoke," I muttered, turning to my bike. He gave me a weird, creepy feeling that prickled my skin.

"You're the one that rides that thing?" He took a few steps toward me. He was almost as tall as Brady was, just not as muscular. Thinner. But that didn't matter. I didn't like the look in his eyes. There was a coldness there that I understood at a bone-deep level. I was intimately acquainted with that look.

I ignored him, a low-level panic building because he was distracting me enough that I fumbled the combination three times before I got my lock undone and shoved into my gym backpack.

He half smiled and half sneered. He knew he was making me uncomfortable and was doing it deliberately. I got hit with a small dose of adrenaline, sensing some kind of undefined threat.

"Ride safe. You never know who's out there. Watching." Then he pulled the hood up on his sweatshirt, concealing his face, and walked away.

I didn't waste time getting the hell out of there.

CHAPTER 7

LAYLA

The creepy feeling resided in my mind and body like an unwanted passenger.

It was only now, after riding my bike for nearly two years around town, that I became aware that I was a lone female riding the streets at night. I started seeing shadows where there weren't any, wondering if that was a car slowing to pace me or just a guy looking for an address. In other words, imagining things.

While I was certain that I was being silly, getting home was a relief...until I saw my unlocked, not-even-fully-closed apartment door and froze.

My heart kickstarted.

Alarm bells blared through my nervous system,

knowing I'd left it closed when I went to work in the morning. Someone had gone in. Were they still in my apartment? Should I call the police? Was my sister all right? She was the only other person who would have been in there.

Could Brady have found me? He'd once said he could find me anywhere.

"He's in San Diego, dummy," I told myself and forced a deep, fortifying breath into my lungs, but even as I dismissed the thought, my heart raced. "Not going to start jumping at shadows. This is my life."

I took a tentative step closer and held my breath to listen. There was no noise from inside. My heart pounded as I tentatively reached out a shaky hand, pushed the door all the way open, and then waited a beat. When nothing happened, I walked in and froze for the second time.

The living room was an explosion of clothing and shoes. There was no burglar; it was just my sister. Not only did it appear that she'd dumped every item of clothing she owned into various piles on the stale brown living room carpet, but there were also half a dozen or more boxes of personal items half spilled out with odds and ends. Where they'd come from, I had no idea. The room looked like it belonged on the show about hoarders. There was hardly one square foot of clear carpet to step on.

"Are you kidding me?" The whisper ejected sharply from under my breath, anger replacing the fear.

Again and again, we reenacted the same scenes. It was the only thing I could count on with her. Anger and despair. Over and over again, she sucked the contentment out of a space and left it tainted with oppressive tension and self-centered destruction. The feelings struck hard and fast. Why did I believe anything might change? Because I wanted it to? A sliver of hope? Searching for the ray of sunshine through the dark clouds that followed her perpetually?

A calming breath slowed the destructive words in my mind.

"I'm glad she's here. I'm glad she's not dead somewhere on the streets. I'm glad she's decided to stay with me while she figures things out," I whispered, trying not to clench my teeth. I had to keep repeating this, because the offense she dealt didn't end with simply leaving my apartment the victim of an unnatural hurricane that was her personal crisis.

Oh no. It was never that simple. She could

always find a new way to scrape her nails along the proverbial chalkboard. In this moment, the added offense was the fast-food container perched haphazardly.

My sister was asleep curled up on the couch, the TV's blue light flickering over her body. A white foam box was open right next to her feet on the cream-colored material I'd been so proud of purchasing. The container was partially filled with something that looked like Pad Thai with orange grease pooling in one of the corners, and it was on the verge of being upended. All it would take was for her to straighten her bent legs, which she could do at any moment, and all that orange grease would be splattered on the material, never to be gotten out.

Dammit!

It showed her typical disregard for anything beyond herself, and it made me angrier still that I couldn't risk letting her see the depth of my anger, which went well beyond this one moment in time. It was an accumulation of painful moments, of disrespect and negligence, that had cut deeply in the last several years, but I couldn't level her with my feelings. I didn't want my anger to be the reason she went back to using, if she was actually clean. I didn't want to add stress to an already full plate of sobriety and the challenges that likely entailed. She was fragile. She needed understanding and stability, not a confrontation that would lead to no good outcome.

Still, irritation burned. Resentment simmered. There was a damn table not five feet away.

I fought back the snarl and quickly grabbed up the fast-food container, reminding myself she didn't understand. I needed to explain it to her. She didn't know that I'd worked my ass off to not only afford this apartment but everything that was in it too. It was a cheap apartment in a less-than-attractive neighborhood, and everything was secondhand, but it was all mine. I was proud of it.

Angry breaths seesawed from my lungs. I was near to hyperventilating, hating the feeling of helplessness. It seemed to be a theme in my life.

But only if I let it be. Action followed thought. Logical thought could only follow the release of emotion. I just needed to breathe it out. Then we could have a real conversation. Deep breaths. In and out. I could choose a different course of action if I just let go of the feelings and let myself think clearly. Nothing good came out of only reacting.

Naddy and I needed to sit and have a talk. Set up some ground rules we could both live with, which did not include greasy food on my beautiful sofa.

I was going to have to be careful. If there was anything I'd learned in my dealings with her, it was that if there were any hint of accusation, she'd either storm out, start a depressive crying jag, shut down into a comatose state of mind, or threaten to use again.

It hurt so much to see her like this. Where had courageous Naddy-pie gone, the girl who stood up for me and not against me? She needed that courage back in order to make herself better.

Her beautiful, familiar features were relaxed in sleep, and I could almost see the ten-year-old she'd been. For most of our elementary years, we'd been inseparable, playing together, doing our homework together, trying to figure out life without the consistent help of any emotionally invested adult. We'd had each other.

Do your homework, Layla-bear. C'mon. We'll do our homework together. She'd say it with this mini-adult, authoritative inflection to her voice.

But I don't want to. I can't do the times tables. I'm just dumb. I'd gone through a whiny-voice period, but Nadine had always been patient and kind with me. She was the one who taught me what unconditional love really meant. It was why I kept letting her back in.

No, you're not. You just have to memorize them. Let's make up a game. We laughed ourselves silly making up rhymes for the times tables. *Four and eight jumped out of the closet and yelled "boo!" because they turned thirty-two. Eight and eight fell on the floor, but when they got up to shake themselves off, they were sixty-four.* The rhymes hadn't made sense, but I still remembered them to this day.

Other times, she was making up fairy stories about dispossessed fairy princesses who were best friends and sisters living in the trees of a beautiful forest. Of course, we were the princesses, and we'd make believe we had wings so we could fly. On windy days, we'd be so certain we could fly that we'd run down the sidewalk of one of the trailer parks we'd lived at and flap our arms wildly. I could still hear the sound of our giggles. Regardless of our mother and whatever boyfriend she had in any given period of time, we'd always had each other. Naddy'd been my mother, more than my mother ever had been.

I was smiling as I came back from the past. Big sigh. She'd always been there for me until one day she wasn't.

Eat first. Then share with her, calmly and kindly, that I do not allow food to be eaten on my couch.

Period. Simple enough. Oh, and don't leave the door open or unlocked. It didn't have to be made into a big deal.

Thoughts of food had my stomach growling, aching for the leftover pasta from the previous night. Something I'd learned while living alone was that if I made extra when I cooked, it meant cheaper eating over the long haul and less work on another night. With pasta, that could mean leftovers for up to two additional nights. Just thinking about it had my mouth watering and improved my disposition.

I went to toss Nadine's fast-food container into the trash under the sink, got a load of the kitchen, and felt sucker punched yet again. Dishes were piled up in the sink. An empty box of crackers, a carton of milk that was only about a tenth full, which was not even enough for a bowl of cereal in the morning, and my newly bought orange juice bottle void of any actual juice, were all sitting on the counter alongside the empty bowl of pasta. Empty. Gone.

There was no freaking way she'd eaten it all by herself and had fast food on top of that.

I glared over at Nadine's sleeping form.

I opened the fridge door, sort of double-checking that my eyes hadn't deceived me, and noted that not only wasn't I wrong, but even more was absent from the shelves, too. Things like deli meat, cheese, and nearly half a loaf of bread, things I'd been counting on for my lunches this week, were almost completely gone. What the fuck?

"Nadine." Her name came out like a whip cracking on the air. She jerked awake instantly, startled, blinking owl-eyed, looking around to reorient herself. It was a good thing I'd moved the food container. Her legs would definitely have knocked it over.

"What? Where? Are you okay?" She looked around groggily, trying to process what was happening. She seemed out of it, and immediately, I was looking for redness of her eyes and lucidity in her gaze. It was automatic, not even something I thought too much about. Did she seem abnormally impaired or was this normal sleep fuzz of the waking brain.

I tried to keep an even tone and still my words were clipped. "My fridge is empty. Why is all the food gone?"

"Fridge?" Cognition returned, and she gave a rueful smile, looking painfully like our mother. They had the same heart-shaped face, the same guiltless, blue eyes that could beguile all with their charm, and the same inability to identify any sense of personal responsibility over their own thoughtless actions. "Rocky, Billy, and Weasel were hungry. They have big appetites."

The humor on her face, the complete lack of any and all remorse, apology, or recognition that she was doing anything wrong, made my frustration roar back to life. "Rocky and who? Weasel? You let strangers in my house and let them raid my fridge? What were you thinking?"

"They aren't strangers. I've known them for years. We were roomies for a while down in Mission Beach. You'd get it if you saw them. They're hot," she grinned and winked. "We hooked up again a week ago. They were doing a job down in PB and convinced me to come back up with them."

"What does that have to do with my food being totally gone?"

"They even gave me a ride around town so I could get all my stuff before bringing me back up here, and I wanted to repay them. They said they were hungry, so I invited them to eat whatever."

It wasn't yours to give. I hated feeling so petty about food, but the fear of ever having to be reliant on anyone else ever again was making my throat constrict. Getting to this place in my life had taken years of planning, thought, and careful spending. She was threatening this with her wrecking-ball attitude. Wrecking balls didn't care if they tore down your entire life. They just swung away and smashed whatever was in front of them.

Memories of being in that San Diego townhouse popped up. The ghost of an argument from times past taunted me. I was so helpless.

I want to have my own money. I was shouting. Crying. *I need to apply for a job. There are things I want to do.*

What more do you want? I work my ass off. I fucking give you everything, but it's never enough, is it? Never. You always want more, more, more. I could give you the fucking world, and it wouldn't be enough because you're fucking selfish and self-centered. You don't think about anyone but you, even though all you have to do every fucking day is wake the fuck up and take care of the fucking house and cook some damn food when I'm tired from working a long fucking day.

I'd spiraled with the shame and tried to make it up to him by submitting to the sex he wanted. It always left me feeling demeaned and dirty. I was an object in his world. That was all. The discussion about me getting a job had been closed. He always knew best. Being that he was almost ten years older than me, it seemed like he did have everything under control, which I'd convinced myself was a good thing after years of living with my out-of-control my mother.

Life with Brady was predictable. There was no more revolving door of my mother's men to contend with, no longer did I have to worry about moving every year or so to escape her debtors, and never again would I have a fridge that was empty or utilities that had been shut off from lack of payment. By that definition, it was easy to convince myself that Brady did take care of me.

Coming back to the moment, I took a deep breath, but I was still royally pissed. "I don't like having people here who I don't know."

Nadine was starting to get ruffled. Her smile faded and indignation had her brows meeting over the bridge of her nose. "I'm an adult, Layla. I'm not a child, and if I want to have friends over, that shouldn't be a problem. I'm not using, and they aren't drug dealers."

"I didn't say they were."

"But that's what's going on in your mind, right? I am never going to get cut a break here, am I? Even when I fucking try to do better, you get in my face."

It was so unfair. The dam broke. "I am the only one who has ever offered you a safe place to stay and regroup, and if I'm gun-shy, it's because you've lied to me multiple times over years. What reason do I have for trusting you?"

"I'm not like that anymore."

"I want to believe you, but I was also the only one who managed to scrape some money together to pay for rehab where you decided to walk out after two weeks and get high, so if I'm less than trusting of what you do and who you hang out with, I have good reason."

She threw her arms up impatiently and stood in a huff. "I wasn't ready for rehab at that point. I told you at the time."

"But you accepted the placement anyway."

"I didn't want to disappoint you yet again!" She bit her lower lip when it trembled. "But I couldn't stay."

"You didn't think about that before I sold anything and everything I had that was even remotely valuable and lived on three-packages-for-99 cents noodles and peanut butter sandwiches for most of a year. That would have required you to be considerate and think about someone besides yourself. Look at this place! It's a freaking mess and you've only been here for a few days." I'd nearly been bled dry from that rehab stint.

Her chest heaved, trying to contain the emotion that was making her hyperventilate. "Why the hell did I even come here?" She grabbed a pile of her clothes from the ground and dropped them into one of the boxes before she marched over to another pile, and scooped everything into her arms, and dumped it in as well. Alarm that she was leaving cut clean through my anger.

I was being such a shit. She wasn't high or drunk. She was trying to do better. "I'm sorry, Naddy. Please stay."

She ignored me. Her eyes turned pink and she sniffed, but she kept stomping around the room, gathering her things. I didn't want her to leave again. I didn't want to be in the dark about whether she was safe.

I got in front of her, blocked her from another stack of her things, forced a hug on her, and pressed my cheek to hers. She didn't respond at first. Kept her body stiff, but that was okay.

"I don't have to be here. I have other places I can go. I've got people from San Diego to Venice Beach willing to put me up. I'm not a total loser. I have friends, you know."

"You came to me because you knew that I would take you in. You know that I love you and want you to be healthy and happy in this life, because that's what you deserve. You know that we take care of each other."

"Layla..." The fight drained, leaving a tired, disconnected voice behind. She gave a half-hearted pat to my back and let her arm drop again. It was an empty, pacifying gesture meant to put an end to the moment, lacking in any real feeling of love or tenderness. It hurt.

"Naddy, I'm sorry."

"I don't think this is going to work out." She pulled away, taking a few steps back, crossed her arms protectively over her chest.

Guilt clawed at my insides. I could afford to buy more food for this week. I wasn't that strapped for money. And I had plenty of peanut butter and honey. Living on peanut butter wasn't such a bad thing, really, but the thought of her leaving terrified me. If she didn't get better, one day, I'd get a phone call, and that would be that.

She'd taken care of me for so many years when our mother wouldn't. She'd been my rock for so long. I bit back the sob that welled in my throat, feeling how alone I was without my sister before the drugs and alcohol grabbed hold. I missed her so much. She was in there. I knew she was. Now it was my turn to take care of her.

My second biggest fear was being poverty-stricken. My first was losing my sister. There was no question.

"Please stay. I want you to stay."

"You're not acting like it." Her voice was smaller. More fragile sounding. "And I get it. I've done some shitty things, but I don't want to live here feeling like an imposition."

"You're not an imposition." Being around Nadine meant living in chaos, and it'd be hard to go backward when I'd made such great strides moving forward. But she was my sister. We were at a point in life where she needed me.

"I want to be able to invite my friends over if I'm going to stay here."

My instinct was to say "hell no," but if I was letting Nadine live here, I needed to be reasonable. "Okay. You're right. When do you get paid?"

There was a moment when her facial muscles relaxed into a blank expression. It was an infinitesimal movement of smaller facial muscles, as though she didn't know what I was saying. She asked, "Paid?"

"Your job?" Had that been a lie? Was this where she was playing me? Had I already fallen for her line of bull? "You started working, right? You told me you had a job."

"I do!" She spouted the words quickly. Too quickly? I no longer had the capacity to be objective about anything she said, seeing guilt on her face the same way I'd been jumping at shadows on the way home. I was newly aggravated when she smiled and insisted, "Of course I do."

And just like that, the tension returned. "Why don't you sound sure?"

Her smile died, and she made a sound of exasperation. "Here you go again! Making accusations. What are you trying to say?" She let her lower lip pout outward a bit. Quiver. This time, it felt like I was being worked, but was I really? She challenged me. "You think I'm lying? I was asleep, Layla. You woke me up. Sorry if I was a little groggy. It happens to us little people. We can't all be perfect when we wake up."

Again, because this well was deep, there were so many things I wanted to say, but nothing that would help the moment, and nothing that could be taken back once said. I bit my tongue and let the anger wash away. I'd been played so many times, but what if she was being truthful this time?

She relented with, "I understand where you're coming from. It's not like I've been a saint. I'm sorry for those other times."

"I know. It's just that if you are going to be living here, you need to contribute."

"I know."

"And I'm not comfortable with your friends lounging around my place all day, because I can't afford to feed everyone." What I didn't say was that I didn't trust the kind of friends she had a tendency to make because she wasn't exactly making a lot of good choices. In any case, the tension broke yet again. I released a big breath of air.

Nadine ran a hand through her hair and pushed a sigh from her lips. It was a good sign that she wasn't fighting me about any of this. The sound was more of resignation. "No, of course not. I should have thought of that."

More gently, I added, "And you can't make some huge mess and not clean up after yourself. Your stuff is all over the place. I came in here to eat, and it's absolutely disgusting. There's trash and dirty dishes everywhere."

"I'm sorry about that. I should have cleaned up, but I fell asleep."

As long as we were doing this, I went for it. "Most important, more than anything, please eat at the table." I walked around the couch and sank down on one edge of it. My fingers ran over the fabric I'd fallen in love with at first sight at the yardage store. "I bought this couch when it was ripped up and falling apart. I figured out how to repair it, how to reinforce cushions, and how to make a cover for it. It was hours and hours' worth of work, and that material is more expensive than the couch itself. Please do not eat on it."

She looked at the couch dutifully with a nod of agreement. "Okay. I gotcha."

"I'm glad you're here, but we need to work together." There was an echo through my mind of similar words said long ago. I smirked, realizing who'd first said those exact words to me. "Roles are reversed, it seems."

She cocked her head questioningly. "What do you mean?"

"You used to tell me we needed to work

together. Remember? And you'd get so mad at me for not cleaning up the kitchen whenever I made a mess. Whew! I remember that."

Nadine got a faraway look in her eyes before they turned hard. "Yeah. I remember." Her words were cold, deceptively soft, and caught me off guard for a moment. Then she looked down at her bare feet and back at me with a faint smile.

"My favorite times were when we'd take a picnic outside and eat on the grassy field at the old, overgrown Little League park," I continued, wanting to sink into the memory of that Naddy who was troublefree and satisfied with the world at large. "I know we were eating crap food, but eating it with you outside made it seem like an adventure. I didn't have to see that mom was passed out drunk yet again or that the place was barely habitable. You made sure there was some kind of food. Remember fairy princesses? I was just thinking of that."

There was a sad twist to her small smile, and she sat back down next to me. "I remember. I remember doing your hair every morning. You always had so many knots."

"You'd brush it. Braid it. We'd take turns singing with the brush in front of the mirror."

"God, we were entertaining." She shook her

head, but then her smile fell. "I also remember hiding with you when mom came home drunk with someone."

"Yeah, but you were always there to keep me from feeling afraid."

"Sometimes I felt like you were my baby. I'd play dress-up with you, like a living doll."

"You took the best care of me. I loved those times together. I miss you." My own eyes stung. "I want you to be healthy."

Her lips flattened into a hard line. "Yeah, well, shit happens."

We were having a good moment, the first one in years. Then, just like that, as things always were with Nadine, it shattered. *Come back to me.* "There were so many times I really needed you, and I felt so alone living with Brady. I wanted so much to be able to call you and ask questions. Things were going so badly."

"How were things going badly?" She tilted her head, her brows creasing.

"So many ways. He kept me alone. No work. No school. Made me feel like I was worthless so that I would be grateful that he kept me around." Some things were hard to say out loud because, if I were being honest, part of me still worried that somehow, they were true or I'd gotten things wrong, misinterpreted them, and shame sat with a strong presence on my shoulder. Had he had the right to call me names in his frustration? "He used to call me a coldhearted bitch."

She frowned. "That's harsh."

I flushed tomato red, the heat making my cheeks feel warm. My next words came out on a whisper. "Sex was always about him. For me, it was painful, and horrible, and he made sure to tell me it was my fault, that I was frigid or something."

For a moment, dismay hovered over her face, but then the smirk was forced back. "Like I said. Shit happens. Everyone gets theirs."

The remark chilled me. It was something Mom would have said, only now Nadine was saying it. Did she mean I deserved bad things to happen to me? Why? Did she resent me? Here I was hoping—I always hoped—we could talk and share. Find some part, even just a remnant, of that relationship we used to have as kids. Before I could stop myself, I was reaching out again. "What memories do you hold on to from childhood?"

She shrugged and leaned back, almost as though she were taking a step away from me physically. "I remember being stuck having to take care of you. I remember a mother who didn't give a shit, and I remember wishing I could fucking be anyone else living far away somewhere on the other side of the earth or some shit."

My shock must have shown on my face because Nadine only laughed and shook her head derisively. I would have been more hurt by her words, but they seemed to be turned inwardly. This emotion was about her.

"Still so innocent. You're lucky."

It sounded cryptic. What she meant by that was lost on me. I was hardly innocent.

"I'll get my stuff picked up." She was emotionally shut off. I could feel the void. She went around picking her stuff up to shove haphazardly into wherever there was space in her boxes and bags, but she was finished with this conversation. Later, when I was warming up a can of condensed soup, it wasn't a surprise when someone knocked, and she called out a careless "bye" and left without another word.

I wanted to cry.

CHAPTER 8

MASON

"You have to come, sweetheart. We haven't seen you in months, it's your dad's birthday, your brother's in town, and everyone's coming over."

I was only half listening to my mom, not because I didn't like hearing from her, but because Layla had walked into the gym and was about to start her workout. She'd changed her time to the evenings for some absurd reason, and I wanted to be out there in case anyone tried to hit on her. I was not okay with that.

"When is this thing happening?" I asked absently, watching the security monitors on my computer. One of the cameras had a good view of the weightlifting area. Layla was using the free weights, doing work on her biceps and triceps, wearing the usual spandex that outlined the curves I'd had my hands on twenty-four hours ago. My hands were itching to cup and trace and knead all those curves yet again.

I watched Rowdy approach, talk to her through her first set, likely something instructional, because she nodded her head and adjusted her form as she continued lifting.

"Saturday in two weeks," my mother chirped, sounding upbeat. "We'll grill up some steaks, and I'll make some French fries and some kind of vegetable. I think your sister is going to make a fruit salad, and your brother is going to buy some kind of dessert. It's all covered."

"I'll be there. I'd never miss dad's birthday." I watched Rowdy walk away. Layla put the weights back, shaking out her arms a few times to relieve the muscle burn, and chose heavier weights from the rack. She began another set.

"I'm so glad. It wouldn't be the same without you."

"I'll put it on my calendar."

She paused a moment before adding, "You know, you're welcome to bring anyone you want."

That focused me in on the conversation again.

"Yeah, I know. You remind me at every event."

"I'm just saying. No pressure, but we're always happy to set another place at the table."

"It's just going to be me, Mom. No one else." A brief, renegade image of Layla, the silky brown texture of her hair curling around my fingers, her blue eyes fierce when she was arguing with me, popped up in my mind. Mom would love her. She had that air of sweetness about her. Wait. What the hell was I thinking?

"I want to see you happy, Mason."

"I am happy." It wasn't a lie. After swimming against the current for so long, learning how to be a business owner and trying hard to learn where the pitfalls were located before I fell into them, it was amazing to finally see success. I'd been pumping money back into the business, living small, saving and skimping long enough that finding myself flush through hard work was energizing. Satisfying in a quiet, comforting way.

"You're working all the time."

"Mom, we've been over this. I'm a business owner. Two now. It comes with the territory."

"But you aren't leaving any room for the good stuff in life. The things that make it all worthwhile.

152

People. You know"—she hesitated uncomfortably, and I knew what she was going to say just before she said— "it wasn't your fault. None of it was."

"I'm not going to talk about this, mom. Not now."

"You never want to talk about it. You need to talk about it. You need to keep going to that therapist." She kept pushing, not realizing she was forcing that door wide open, the one in my mind that I kept on lockdown. It widened to emit sounds from the past.

Sirens. Handcuffs. The memories alone were a noxious force running through my body. "I tried that. It didn't work." So many more fucking nightmares. Was I awake or asleep? The perpetual chaos going on in my brain. In fact, therapy had made things detrimentally worse. Exponentially more painful.

"You only went for a month, Mason. You need to go longer than that. Months. Sometimes years. And maybe you need someone different, but in the end, it'd be for the good. You haven't let yourself heal."

"No."

"Medication, sweetheart."

"Never."

"But Mason…"

And George was dead anyway. G-man who liked to play a little ukulele and spontaneously sing made-up songs with the most pathetic, groan-worthy rhymes. My hand started shaking, my eyes burning. What the hell was going to a counselor going to do for me now? I had to live with this. There was no way to heal. Ever. It was better to numb out with work.

"I've got to go."

"Don't be mad at me. I love you."

"I know." My words were short. I knew it bothered my mother to hear that tone, but I needed this talking point to end. The memories needed to stay buried. I didn't have the luxury of living in that fucked-up state of mind. Already, my pulse rate spiked. My heart was a mallet pounding against my chest, filling my ears with the mad rush of blood pumping.

"I'm your mother, and I'm worried about you."

Her words hardly registered as echoes of the shouts and screams of pain pinged randomly through my mind. I couldn't hear myself think.

"Mason? Are you all right?" My mother's voice sounded distant. I'd put the phone away from me as my lungs fought for air. Fought the constriction. Fought for oxygen. I was hyperventilating.

Then I looked at the monitor. Layla was there, working her set. Calm. Serene. Beautiful. I could imagine that she was systematically breathing with each lift of the weights, her teeth clenched, her eyes fiercely focused. Her lips were soft and generous, and her body fit the contours of my own so perfectly. An errant thought fucked with my head, took me in another direction. *Had she watched porn last night? Chased down an orgasm on her own?* An image of her on my bed, her own hands squeezing her breasts, needed to be shut down immediately, especially with my own mother on the phone.

My heart calmed, and I chuckled.

"Mason? Are you still there?"

"Sorry. I'm here. I'll see you then. Let me know if I can bring anything." I continued watching Layla until one of the guys from yesterday edged back into the monitor frame. He was some kind of a pretty boy, Zach Efron look-alike, and he was deliberately grabbing weights that were huge, sending her a grin in the mirror, some form of greeting that got her attention.

"I will."

On the monitor, Layla's smile was brief and shy when she replied something that had the guy chuckling at the same time that she retreated a step and looked to her weights again. The asshat didn't realize he was making her uncomfortable. He took up a stance with his own weights closer to her, a smirk on his face, like he was warning other guys off with his presence. Pretty Boy was looking to score. There was no way in hell I was letting that happen.

"I love you, Mom. Gotta go. I'll see you soon."

I was already walking out of my office when I disconnected and pocketed my phone. I had a bead on Layla and barely noticed Shay was behind the desk until she got my attention.

"Mason," she called out, "I've got a problem to discuss with you."

"What problem?" I almost put her off but realized that was unreasonable. Shay was normally friendly and upbeat, so I was surprised to see a "life sucks" look on her face, brows drawn, lips tight. She was folding towels fresh from the dryer behind the front desk, barely contained frustration edging her lips. "Why are you doing Greg's work?"

"Because I want to leave before midnight, and I can't find Greg. He's probably outside on a smoke break or something." Her movements were sharp, jerky, and aggressive. She snapped out another towel, smiled a cheerful 'bye, see ya' tomorrow!' to an exciting customer before the smile fell instantly and she continued folding.

"What's going on?" The pull to be by Layla's side as a deterrent to any Romeo that was looking to hit on her was strong, but I forced myself to find out what the problem was.

"I'm hearing complaints about how messy the men's locker room is getting." Movements emphasized her words as she worked with determined efficiency. "He's not keeping up with supplying the towels. The toilet paper isn't being replaced. The sinks are getting gunked up. I've shown him how to fold and stack the towels a couple of times in the last week, but I still find them in the cupboard looking like a five-year-old did the job. Just sloppy."

Irritation bit my insides. The idea that any of my members had felt unhappy with the service they were receiving chafed. I'd spent years being a fucking workhorse, and to hear that this new kid was trying to coast on my dollar left me feeling burned. "When is he on the schedule again?"

"Tomorrow." Her nose wrinkled. "I don't like him. You know, I'm not trying to get the guy fired, but he's cringy."

"How so?"

"Hard to describe. Makes my skin crawl. The way he looks at me? But it's not like he's looking at my parts or anything. I don't know. Maybe this is my mad talking right now. Don't listen to me."

"I trust your instincts, Shay. Tell me if he treats you inappropriately. Immediately."

"I will." She stacked the neat pile of perfectly folded towels into a plastic bin and produced a tired half smile. "Maybe I'm just done in? Michael and I've been doing some hardcore triathlon trainings, you know? Bumping it up? Trying to jump to the next level? I'm pretty worn out."

"You guys need to make sure you take a day. Eat some carbs. You can't train that hard every day."

"That's what Saturday is going to be. We're going to relax, get some massages, and go see a movie or something."

"Good. I'll talk with Greg. If he can't do the work, he can't be here. He gets one more chance, and he's only getting that because of his brother, who I have only the utmost respect for."

"Cory. Glad he went off to college, but I miss that kid." A smile leaked out the corner of her mouth as she hefted the basket on her hip. "Cory was a great guy."

"A real superstar," I agreed.

"Too bad his brother is such a shit." She laughed and headed for the supply closet.

Pretty Boy was moving on Layla by the time I approached the weight stand. He was saying, "There's a great little Italian place near the pier. Have you been?"

"No," she gave the same small smile she'd given before, which pissed me off because from the guy's posturing, it encouraged him, made him feel confident. She should have told him to fuck off, but instead, she carried her weights back to the rack and shook her arms out again. Was she seriously letting this guy take my place? There was no fucking way.

"I've heard it's good. A buddy of mine went last week and recommended it. I was hoping to get over there myself, but I could use a companion."

There was no way she was going out with this joker. She was not going to chase an orgasm with him. Layla didn't have a chance to respond, because I came up behind her and whispered in her ear. "I need to see you in my office."

"Now?" she asked, her blue eyes rounded, looking back and forth between me and the other guy. Irritated that I was interrupting, Pretty Boy compressed his lips in a tight line. I'm sure he was biting back some rude comment. He was smart to do that.

"Right now. It's important."

"Oh. Okay." She grabbed up her towel, quickly waved over her shoulder at Pretty Boy, and followed me back across the gym. Shay had moved on, and Amanda was now behind the desk answering phones. She gave a quick smile to Layla who followed me behind the desk and into my office, where I shut the door, blocking us from view.

"What's so imp—"

My fingers cupped her face, and I bent to catch her lips, hot and hard. A squeak of surprise was followed by a breathless moan as the powerful spark ignited between us. Relentless need fed desperation. I licked the seam of her lips, demanding entry before sliding my tongue in to rub against the velvety feel of her own. I got a taste of her again, sweet and supple, giving and taking, and even better than memory. Then her hands came up my back, her nails digging in, and she did some of her own damage, pressing me close as her tongue caressed my own. My heart thundered against my chest, the blood rushing south, my cock harder than I could ever remember it being. Our lips played with fire, and she rubbed her soft abdomen against my raging hard-on until it felt like I was going to explode.

"Fuck," I muttered, needing to pull my hips back. "Every fucking time you make me crazy."

"Mason," she whispered, taking nibbling, sucking bites of my lower lip, sending arcs of electric heat straight to my dick, her hands pulling me closer to rub her stomach on my cock again. "I want more. Please."

Her words worked a growl from my chest as I could only think of getting my dick inside of her and fucking her on my desk until she was coming all over me. "Fuck."

I grabbed her arms from around me and held them at the base of her spine in one of mine. Her breasts pushed out to me, tantalizing and irresistible. With my free hand, I pulled down on her sports bra until the stretchy material propped her bare breast up to me again, pretty as a picture with a pink nipple that was stiff and hard. I'd been dying to know what she fucking tasted like during a workout, and with that in mind, I plumped her breast up to my mouth and sucked hard, letting my tongue rub all around the stiff peak. Sweet with a hint of saltiness from her workout. Fucking delicious.

A hoarse cry came from her lips followed by panting breaths. "You're going to make me come. That feels so good. Mason!"

"Are you wet?" I eased off to give a final lick.

"Yes. Ohmygod."

"I think you should wait," I responded, lightly rolling the tip between my fingers for good measure before replacing the fabric.

"No."

She gave a protesting little hiss when I pulled back, until my other hand palmed her ass, kneading the firmly rounded flesh there. Groaning, she pushed into my cock. She was this sexy fucking goddess, every move sensual and driving me nuts. There was no way to resist, especially when she looked dazed with lust and hungry for more. I knew I was crazy to have her in here now, but then I feasted on her lips again, plump and pink from getting worked over by me. I liked this look on her. I'd put it there.

"Why aren't you coming in the morning anymore?" I asked against her lips.

"Been needing more sleep." She nipped at my lip again, which earned her a good mouth fucking with my tongue that had her panting again by the time I ended it with soft, sipping kisses.

"Too many fucking guys come at this time. I'm going to have to fight them off you."

"Why?" She pushed up on her toes and took her own kiss, slid her own tongue into my mouth, twisting it against mine, giving me a good mouth fucking, and I almost forgot where we were right there and then. This time, I was the one panting sharp breaths.

"Because you aren't going to fucking chase down orgasms with anyone else." My hand slid down her spandex-clad thigh, hooked it, and brought it to my hip, letting my dick access the sweet spot right between her legs by bending my knees some. I couldn't remember why this was a bad idea anymore, but I sure as fuck wasn't going to let anyone else have access to her sweet little body. I was the one making her wet. I was the one that was going to take care of it. Fantasies. That was all we were doing. Indulging in fantasies. What was the harm?

"Oh my God." Her eyes went unfocused, and she ground her sweet little pussy helplessly against me, her leg curling around my hip. Little breathless cries came out on soft puffs of air from between her kiss-ravaged lips, and my cock throbbed painfully. If we didn't stop now, I was going to rip that damned spandex off her.

"Fuck." Reluctantly, I eased away, not wanting my first time inside her to be quick against a door.

"Mason? What…Why are you stopping?" A desperate tone infused her voice when she said my name. I liked how it sounded, husky and sex-filled. Needing.

"Not here."

"But—"

I touched my forehead to hers. Fantasies. Harmless. "Here's what I need you to do. Finish your workout, and when you're done, meet me out front. Don't wear any fucking panties."

"No panties?"

Her eyes looked a deep indigo with arousal, cheeks flushed, lips swollen, and I almost went with plan B, which would have been to bend her over my desk and fuck her until she was screaming my name. She wanted me as much as I wanted her, but there was no way I was going to do that to her here.

"Go." I pulled the door open but stayed inside because my cock was fucking hard as a rock. "I need a couple of minutes."

Absently, she nodded and took a deep breath, running a hand over her hair and workout shirt before stepping out again.

It took thirty minutes of focusing on desk work before I had things under control again, and by under control, my dick wasn't making a tent anymore. Went over the books for the gym. Went over the books for the club, which got my attention. Numbers weren't adding up. I was going to have to investigate what the problem was. Zeke's should have been making more, but somewhere, there was a money leak. I was going to have to spend the next few days at the bar figuring it out. I needed to look at the expenses, what was bought, how often, what was charged.

It was the perfect activity to get my mind on other things. By the time I felt like I had my shit under control again, I knew Layla would be close to done, and I went out on the gym floor. My eyes immediately found her on the elliptical machine, and all that control went back to shit.

It was like the floodgates had opened from that

first moment that I touched her at the bar, when she whispered in my ear, floated the words come and fantasy, showed me how much we'd been on the same page for a whole fucking year. Before, I'd been satisfied with letting my imagination run things, choreograph hot sex scenes where she was vocal and limber. Now, I wanted reality. The need to take her was riding me hard, and I hoped to Christ she was close to being done on the machine.

With earbuds in, she was rocking out to something that had her legs pumping on the machine, her gorgeous ass moving back and forth to the rhythm. I wasn't the only guy noticing, which had me unreasonably tense. I needed to mark her. Needed to keep other guys from thinking they could do any fucking thing with her.

Coming up behind her, I saw there wasn't much time left on the computer readout. She had about ten minutes. Stepping into her line of sight produced a startled jump and a quick, self-deprecating smile that pursed her lips. She had one of those mouths where the top lip was fuller than the bottom. Fuck. What I wanted to do with those lips.

"Out front in ten?" I asked, noting the bounce to her tits as she moved. The front view was as hot as the rear. She was covered in sweat. It was dripping down her neck, and I fought the impulse to catch it with my tongue.

"Twenty," she countered, a shy smile curving her lips.

"Fifteen."

"I need a quick shower," she protested.

"Fifteen." I didn't want to wait the extra five. It was hard enough keeping my hands to myself while talking to her.

Twenty minutes later, she was wearing a simple long-sleeved, fitted T-shirt that had a low V-neck. It showcased the soft pale skin of the tops of her breasts. She was also wearing the same short skirt she'd worn that first night at the club. Her legs looked smooth and toned. Sexy. I wanted to run my fingers up that skin to see if she'd followed my directive.

Our eyes met. She fed me a secretive smile that teased an enchanting dimple from her cheek. It was quiet. Intimate. Warmth coated my insides.

"My Jeep is over there." With my hand riding low on her back, I guided her to my car and unlocked the passenger side. She turned to face me, biting her lip nervously. I could see the vein in her neck pumping like mad.

"What's the plan?" she asked.

"I thought we'd go for a drive." Reaching behind her, I opened the passenger door, then crowded her with my body into the V of the open door. Out of sight from the general public, my hand grasped her hip and slid around to cup her ass. I was getting a hit off the sound of her breath catching. Her nipples called to me. Stiff, outlined by the thin layer of T-shirt in the balmy air.

"A drive?" She was all breathless. I wondered if she was already wet for me.

"A special drive. Jump in."

"All right." She tossed her bag onto the floorboards before she carefully climbed up on the seat. I gave my assistance, kept my hand on her waist, made sure the shoulder belt was flat across her chest, let my fingers slip under her shirt to give a teasing stroke of her hard nipple. I was sure I heard a soft mewling cry before I stepped back and shut the door.

"Do you care where I drive?" I asked, once I was behind the wheel.

"Anywhere is good."

City lights reflected off the windshield in the darkness of the night. My Jeep had particularly fat tires, so we were riding higher than most. The soft top was stored in the back, so the air ran freely over our skin once we pulled out onto the main boulevard. It didn't take long for Layla to fish a hairband from her bag and throw her hair into a ponytail.

"Good workout?" I asked, pulling out onto the main drag, wanting her to feel comfortable. Her voice was soft and husky. I could listen all day.

"I couldn't concentrate." She gave a quiet laugh and shook her head.

"Why is that?"

Her eyes found mine. "I wanted to see what you were going to do to me."

We pulled up to a light before I asked her my next question, wanting to see how she was going to react. "What would you want me to do?"

Even in the semi-dark of the interior, she flushed a violent shade of red, but she held my gaze. "I want to feel you inside me. I've never come with anyone before."

"Fuck." I realized I was saying that a lot these days. A horn honked, reminding me I was on the road and the light had turned green. I accelerated, letting the silence speak, letting the undercurrents of electricity build before asking, "Do you know what I want?"

"What?"

"I want you to come all over my fingers harder than you've ever come in your life." I turned to get on the freeway. "I've thought about having you here many times. It's one of my own fantasies about you."

"Oh…" Squirmed in her seat.

That's when I reached over to put my hand on her thigh, felt the smooth, supple skin, the momentary tensing of her muscle. Peripherally, I noted her head swiveled back toward me, dark wisps of hair blowing with the wind as she tried to read my intent, but I kept a careful eye on my driving. I moved my hand north, my fingers getting closer to her sex.

Her breathing became more labored, but she didn't stop my hand. No, she wanted this. She moved her legs farther apart in invitation. Angled her body toward mine.

"I've been thinking about this for the last hour. I could hardly get through my exercise," she admitted.

"I was ready to carry you off that fucking

machine." Passing lights from the freeway illuminated the smooth skin of her face that was tilted back.

The slightest shift of my hand brought my fingers flush against her silky, bare, soft folds that were already wet with need, and no panties in the way. "Good girl," I breathed.

Her lips parted on a soft moan that burned a path straight to my crotch, instantly making me so fucking hard.

"Did you watch porn last night?" I asked. That image alone fucked with my head all night and all day. I could imagine her in bed, maybe with her tablet or phone propped up next to her.

"What?"

"Porn. Did you watch it?" Probably had her fingers in her panties, or did she have a vibrator?

"Mason!"

"I'll stop if you don't answer." I swirled my fingers around her clit, spreading her slick juices until she was gasping for breath before pulling away the slightest bit.

"Don't stop," she cried out instantly. Her body was quivering with need.

"Tell me the truth." I moved my fingers back into the hot, honey warmth of her pussy, letting my fingers trace around and rub her clit slowly. "Porn. Did you watch it last night?"

"Yes." Her hips curled into my fingers seeking more friction. Pressure. I held off, giving her only enough to frustrate. "Mason, please," she moaned, breathing my name through her lips.

"What was the scene?"

She panted, "Lonely hitchhiker."

I rewarded her with more pressure, dipping my fingers toward her center where more of her wetness coated her lips. "Did he pick her up?"

"Yes."

"What happened next?"

"She sucked him off."

"His cock?"

"Yes."

"I want to hear you say it." I eased off again, and her lips exhaled soft puffs of air.

Her eyes met mine, hungrily, when her lush lips formed the words, "She sucked his cock."

I exhaled my own groan, my cock swelling impossibly thick and hard with every word, every expression coming from her. "Did you like watching that?"

"Yes," she moaned, my fingers working around her sensitive flesh again. "Then she got on him and rode him."

"Good girl," I whispered. I fucking needed to have my dick right where my fingers were playing. "Did you stick your fingers in your pussy while you watched? Did you pretend it was you?"

"I pretended it was us."

"That's right." I wanted to see her come. "It will be."

"I want it to be," she gasped, her hips moving with my fingers.

My fingers worked her over, moving around and around her throbbing clit, stopping to trap and pinch her swollen flesh between my middle and index finger before plunging back into the center, finding her wet opening, and sliding my middle finger in.

Another gasp escaped from her lips, her face flushed with need, her eyes unseeing out the front windshield. She was beautiful and wild. Open. Her pleasure became my own. Her cries fed my arousal until the animal was beating at the cage, demanding to be let out.

"Pull up your skirt."

CHAPTER 9

LAYLA

My hands shook as I pulled my skirt up to my waist.

Mason gave a glancing stare down at where his thick middle finger disappeared inside my pussy, a look of hunger in his eyes before they went back to watching the road.

"So soft. So wet. Work your hips on my hand," he whispered in his deep smoky voice.

I hesitated a moment, knowing we were out in public, knowing that this was all so surreal. I was pulsing around his finger. Pure heat pumped through my veins while my mind struggled with the knowledge that if someone really paid close attention, they'd see the look of desperate need on my face. I'd be exposed. Vulnerable.

There were only a few cars on the road, and none of them were paying us any attention. Then the idea of coming with people around us, not even aware of what I was doing, took hold. His fingers were inside me while a tired-looking, overworked woman drove like an automaton just a few lanes over, her face looking like a permanent grimace was etched across her brows in the half-shadows of the night. I recognized the expression. She was disillusioned by life, accepting that this was all she had in store for the future. I was not going to become her.

Pushing back against the seat with my legs splayed and his fingers gently rubbing the glistening core, I took the reins. Cupped his large hand with one of my own and guided his finger in and out, in and out. The burning need grew at my core. Spread. Tightened its hold while I moved my hips with subtle jerks. Moved his fingers with secrecy, my breathing hoarse and choppy. I had to work for it. Earn it. Fight for it.

This was what I wanted. Needed. Ached for.

"That's it. This feel good?" Mason growled, his finger curling, quickening the rhythm just a bit, pressing against nerve endings that shot sensation through my body until I clenched my teeth to dam the cry of pleasure that fought to erupt.

"Yes. Oh, God, yes," I breathed. My eyes were closed, head tilted against the headrest, the play from passing lights dancing across my closed lids.

"Like this?"

"Just like that. Just like that," I panted. The tide built. The wave crested. Held. Kept me on the very edge. My body tightened, the muscles in my core squeezing against his fingers in warning.

"Are you going to come? Touch your clit. Come for me, sweet girl." Voice hoarse and breathing heavier, Mason was there with me.

"Yes—" The word was a breathless whimper. My free hand moved down to touch my clit as ripples of pleasure told me the wave was about to break.

"I want to hear you."

"Yes, yes, yes," I quietly chanted. The rush was building. My voice was barely audible. "Don't stop. Don't stop."

"I won't, baby. I won't."

My toes curled, my hips jerked, my back arched, and I gasped out a silent cry as the wave crashed over me, splintered me into pieces. It left me shuddering and panting, my pussy clenching around his fingers, and the forever freedom that assured me once again that I was a woman with a wonderful mind and body that I wanted to share and that there was nothing wrong with that or me. As the shudders subsided and I pulled his finger out of my core, he lifted it to his own lips and sucked my own arousal from them.

"Sublime," he growled.

A faint smile touched my lips, self-consciousness peeking out from around a mental rock. "Really?"

"And you look beautiful when you come. I could watch that all day."

It took a moment for me to get my next words out. I watched him drive for a few beats and said, "I want to know what you look like when you come." This was a moment that showed me I was new and bright and shiny, because with nothing more than the desire to give him back pleasure that he'd given me, I sat sideways facing him. I reached over to place my own hand on his thigh, inches from where I could see the evidence of his erection.

He didn't stop me.

Slowly, savoring the feel of his muscles flexing under my touch, I let my hand slide up along the material of his athletic pants.

He still didn't stop me. It was almost as if he was holding his breath.

My heart pumping just a bit harder, I cupped my hand around the hard length of his cock and was rewarded with the sound of him sucking breath inward.

"Shit." He reached for my hand, but instead of taking it off, he held it on. Worked to help me stroke him just right from the outside. He growled a groan, deep and guttural, that made my pussy pulse with renewed desire. I wanted him to fill me. Pound into me.

I moved to hook my fingers around his waistband, but he stilled the movement.

"We can't." He laughed with a bit of an edge. He didn't push my hand away but held it there without stroking for an extra few seconds. "I'm going to crash into something. You're making me crazy."

"Then let's go back to the gym. Shouldn't everyone be gone by now?"

He gave a short nod, and within a few minutes, we were heading back, but I reserved the right to continue my own form of torment, letting my hand stroke the length of his thigh before coming back up to stroke and squeeze his shaft ever so casually. It was a promise of things to come, so to speak. He drove with his head resting back against his seat, his teeth gritted.

"This was your fantasy?" I asked, easing my hand back to his thigh again.

His nostrils flared when he took a deep breath and looked over at me. "One of them. I've been obsessed with the idea of having access to your pussy with no panties to get in the way. I just wish it wasn't so dark. I wanted to see you."

"Tell me another." I felt drunk with the feel-good chemicals coursing through me. This was heady stuff, and that Mason had thought about me had me grasping for more.

He gave me a side glance, then said, "You tell me one of yours first."

"Mine?" I could feel the heat climbing into my cheeks, my bottom lip sucked nervously between my teeth. My heart pounded with intimate knowledge of secret things I wanted him to do but had never ever said aloud before. Somehow, the darkness gave me courage. "Well, I have this one… I'm in the shower at the gym, and you…" I trailed off, my heart pounding harder.

"What do I do?" he prompted. His pale eyes blazed with the heat still radiating from his body.

"You…" My cheeks were probably glowing from my confession at this point. In a whisper, I finished the sentence. "You lick me."

"Where?" Mason's deep voice slid to an even lower register, became seductive.

"You know where."

"Only if you tell me," he insisted, the words rough in his deep rumbly voice. "Where do you want me to lick you, Layla?"

"My pussy." I can barely hear my words with my heart pounding so hard.

"Do I make you come with my mouth?"

"Yes."

"Because I would love to make that happen. I would love to suck and lick your pussy until you can't think anymore."

His words and images were so deliciously dirty, my own voice got shaky. "I've never done that before."

"Your ex is a fucking moron," he stated, a dark shadow crossing his features. "Tomorrow night.

Plan your workout to end when we close, and then take your shower. I'll fucking make you come with my tongue on your clit and my fingers deep inside of you. Watching you come is now my new favorite hobby."

"Oh my…" I needed to take a deep breath as the blood pooled between my legs with just his words. "So, are we doing this? Sex without expectations? No relationship?"

"I don't know what this is." The question seemed to draw out his frown further, like he was still conflicted. "I know we both said we aren't doing a relationship thing."

"Maybe we should have some rules, you know? Keep things simple."

"Like what?"

"Like, no dates. No sleepovers."

His brows furrowed as he considered what I was saying. "Just sex."

"Fantasies. I tell you mine. You tell me yours."

"We burn off some steam together?"

"Yes."

He nodded, a more thoughtful expression on his

face. "I guess we could give this a try."

We turned into the outdoor mall where the gym was located, its elegant, understated façade sitting dark except for the overhead signage. There were a few inside lights left on for safety and security. It sat in the far corner of the row of businesses taking up the largest corner lot. I was ready to take up where we left off, even reached over to slide my hand up his thigh when Mason exhaled an exasperated breath.

"What the hell is Greg doing hanging out still?" The other businesses were already closed for the night, making the lot fairly empty and ominous to me. He was propped up against the building watching us drive up, his lips twisted in a little half-smirk, while listening to his earbuds. "The gym closed half an hour ago."

I snatched my hand away, made sure to have my skirt firmly in place, though without my panties, I was feeling exposed. At this point, having a witness to what we were planning to do was uncomfortable and strange. I preferred to keep our business private, and if he saw me enter with Mason now, he'd know for sure what we were doing. At least, that's what it felt like. The sexy mood was dying. "Mason, I don't think…"

He was already shaking his head, pulling into a

space near the door. Pitching his voice low, he said, "Yeah, we can't do this now. Tomorrow."

The engine was still idling, covering our conversation. "Yes. Tomorrow."

His sudden grin was mind-scrambling. He leaned closer. "That's one you owe me."

It took a moment to realize he was talking about orgasms. I was suddenly mirroring his expression, feeling more lighthearted than I could ever remember feeling with a man. "We keeping score?"

"Of course."

"Gotta know who's winning."

"As far as I'm concerned, we're both winning. I can't wait to finally know what you taste like."

Jesus. I took a deep breath and squirmed to relieve the simmering ache that was starting up again right between my thighs.

Mason had a knowing glint in his eyes. "I know this is getting you hot, sweet girl, but do not get yourself off tonight. Save it for me. I want to give you your orgasms. Wait for me. It'll be worth it."

"Mason, you're killing me," I groaned as another wave of tingles flooded my abdomen. I took a breath and blindly reached for my shoulder bag, not losing eye contact. "I really want to kiss you, but we're being watched right now."

"Give me your phone. I'm going to give you my number." He waited for me to dig around my bag and activate the home screen before giving it to him. He then punched in numbers and hit send. His own phone rang from the cup holder he'd placed it in. He shut it off and shoved it back into his pocket.

"Tomorrow," I said, putting my phone back in my purse.

"Tomorrow." He looked around the lot. "Where's your car?"

I shook my head. "Don't have one. I ride my bike everywhere."

The grin flattened and concern wrinkled the skin between his dark brows. "Why don't you have a car?"

Knowing I wasn't ready to go into any kind of true explanation, I pulled the strap of my bag over my shoulder and opened the car door. "I don't know how to drive. I'll see you tomorrow." Then I was out the door and, after closing it, strode to the bike rack without looking back. My bike lock was already in my hand, my fingers quickly spinning each tiny number wheel to its appropriate symbol, when I heard Mason's door open and close.

"Greg, what are you still doing here?" Mason called out.

"Just waiting for a ride," Greg replied casually. I could feel his eyes on me, and I deliberately ignored him.

Then I was on my bike, which was strange and uncomfortable in a skirt without panties, but getting home was the goal. Just then, an old, beat-up sedan—in bad need of a paint job and new belts, the bass pumping—pulled up and came to a stop. Greg pushed away from the building, gave a short nod to Mason, and got in the car. A brief blast of music hung on the air before the door was closed, and then the car was once again in motion, driving away quickly.

"Hey, are you going to be okay? How far away are you?" Mason looked around the darkened streets, sounding reluctant to part ways with me. "It's dark. It's late. Why don't we throw your bike in the back of the Jeep, and I'll drive you home."

His concern warmed me, but I didn't want to make this a regular thing. There was no end date to my riding a bike, and I refused to begin depending on anyone else for anything.

"Thanks, Mason, but I'll be all right. I do this every day. I'll see you tomorrow." Before he could protest any further, I pushed off and made my way along the sidewalk, the cooler air touching my face that now wore a big wide grin.

Mason was going to eat my pussy.

CHAPTER 10

LAYLA

"He gave you a big O while he was driving?"

Today was Cowgirl Day, which meant Blessing was wearing jeans, her cowboy boots, a fitted paisley shirt that was tied at her midriff, and her hair in two thick braids on either side of her head. She loved playing with her image. You could tell when Blessing was feeling off, because she would be dressed like a "normal" person rather than a trope.

"Yup. Going down the highway. Cars passing us." I took a deep breath when my heart reacted to the memory by pounding more swiftly.

"I knew it! You've been wearing a shit-eating grin all morning." Blessing hooted and clapped.

I was leaning against the counter in the little kitchenette where all the coffee goodness was housed, sipping from a mugful I'd just built with some cream and a decadent dash of chocolate syrup that I would normally skip because of my strict nutritional rules. Today I was saying "fuck it." We were taking a quick midmorning break, and as expected, Blessing was calling me out on the smile that'd kept appearing at random times on my face since I'd arrived.

Memories of Mason's words that were so dark and dirty, and the way his big hand looked between my pale thighs after I'd pulled my skirt up for him, kept replaying in my mind. It wasn't hard for someone savvy to guess what I'd been up to, and Blessing was definitely savvy.

"He must have mad skills." Her eyes sparkled with glee. "He got you off without killing you."

"That's putting it mildly. He made me see stars." I was blushing, as usual, but I was also excited to spill some of the details. "He made…the experience…all about me. It was like his goal was to rock my world without even thinking about his own pleasure." Never had Brady given a shit about how I was feeling, whether something felt good to me. It was always about him getting what he wanted. All the time.

A sudden flashback had me squeezing my eyes shut. *Brady's face over me in our bed, holding me down while he pounds into me. I can't move, but it hurts. I can't breathe. I can't say anything, or he'll tell me why I'm broken. He'll tell me what a coldhearted bitch I am, and how if I just relaxed, maybe I'd start to like it. I've learned this lesson. If I pretend to enjoy myself, it'll end sooner, but I feel nothing. Tomorrow, I will be empty, used, worthless, and sore.*

Brady was always rough, and if I winced, he liked it more.

I opened my eyes, determined to replace that memory with the one from last night. Just the one time of playing intimate games with Mason had enlightenment me. I felt cared for. Connected. The proverbial lightbulb went on, and I suddenly realized a "no shit, Sherlock" fact: Brady had simply been cruel. He was a cruel person. It was one thing to know something logically, and another to actually believe it. I finally believed it. After last night, the doubts had disappeared over the horizon.

"Mason is a good man." Blessing pushed the button on the coffee maker and leaned back again to eye me with delight. "I like him already. So it was a come-to-Jesus moment?"

"More than ever." Just thinking about him was

getting me horny. I was going to need fresh panties before the end of the day at this rate.

"Finally. You deserve someone who's going to get things right for once. When is this going to happen again? Soon, I hope? You know what they say. Practice, practice, practice."

"Tonight." I laughed, then waited a second before admitting, "We're going to do the sex thing. No strings. We talked about it last night."

"He changed his mind?"

"Yes."

"Shit! The possibilities are endless. Hours of fun if you play this right."

"What do you mean?"

"Do some role play. Doctor and nurse. Prisoner and prison guard. Professor and student."

"What?"

"Maybe a Japanese cosplay character? You could be the helpless female warrior, and he could be the terrifying alien with a big cock whose only purpose in capturing you is to have hot sex with you from multiple orifices at the same time."

That should have sounded frightening, but it

gave me pause trying to picture the logistics before my mind did a mental shake of itself. "You need to get laid."

"You are right." Blessing fanned herself and sighed. "Been too long. Too long. But the game is close to launch. I have some friends testing it. There's a tech team I'm sort of partnered with."

"Testing it?"

"Looking for major flaws. It's a shit ton of work, but I'm personally coding it to make it a more unique experience. I don't want thousands of hours to go down the drain because solutions don't work or somehow the user experience gets tainted. In this industry, if it gets around that something is unplayable, you're dead in the water. I want to make sure it's solid. Rock solid."

"That makes sense." She'd poured her soul into this game, and from the little I'd seen of it, there was no way it wouldn't be the coolest, most sought-after game available before too long. Emotional. Dramatic. Good plot structure to the game. Complex. I'd seen some of the art she'd produced for it, and it was nothing short of hauntingly beautiful. She wanted to do a full-on launch by Christmas of the following year.

"So, a couple of things on the news front. First of

all, my nephews are going to be here in December for about a week." She poured her own coffee and started to fix it up.

"This Christmas? As in next month? That sucks for the kids, right?"

"No, the week before actual Christmas. My brother and his wife need some adult time, which they decided to take in Hawaii."

"Oh." I whistled my appreciation. "Nice. One day I'll travel there. Who am I kidding? One day, I'll travel anywhere."

"One day." She held her mug up in a silent cheers. "If I make some major bucks from this deal, we'll celebrate by going. We need some mai tais on the beach with some cabana boys. Or is that in Mexico?"

"Either place sounds like a plan."

"And the other bit of news, we're going to have another tenant in this joint. Someone bought the suite of rooms next to ours, and from what I understand, he's going to do some reno starting soon. Our roof patio is actually a shared space, so we might see the guy up there at some point." Blessing fanned her face dramatically stating, "And this is how the realtor described him when I saw her locking up, also stating that he was a hottie."

"So, your nephews are here, and we'll have eye candy in the near future?"

Blessing owned the north side of the top two out of three floors of the building, with an additional, attached loft space that I'd never actually stepped into it was so private. The third floor was a studio that she'd converted into her living space, while we worked on the second floor. Yes, she came from money and could afford things, but she'd always been generous to a fault. She hadn't allowed herself to become entitled by it.

"And you're going on an orgasm bender. Good plan. Sounds like things are about to get busy around here. Well, I'm going to be out for most of the rest of the day getting some shit done, so this is all you." We high-fived each other, and on that note, Blessing went up to her loft to do some kind of work for her game. More and more, she was leaving the website business in my hands with cryptic mutterings about just giving me the damn thing.

I didn't want a handout, but could I buy into it? I had a little money saved. How much would that cost? The idea of having something of my own, some piece of ownership in something I'd earned that would prove I'd really risen above my upbringing, made me giddy. Excitement flashed through me considering the possibilities. This was success.

It was after lunch when I was sitting at my desk, ready to finish some updates I'd scheduled for clients this week, when my phone rang. It was Mason. Just seeing his name flash across my screen gave me mad butterflies that bashed themselves against the sides of my stomach like they were on a suicide mission. My pulse went haywire, but my grin was instant. I had to take a deep breath before answering.

"Hello?"

"Did you make yourself come last night, sweet girl?" His gruff voice penetrated through my layers of clothing, rolling through all the highly sensitive parts of me that remembered what he was capable of. With one sentence, he awakened my body, got it humming like it was embedded with a live wire.

"No, I didn't," I answered in a soft, low voice, looking around, making sure Blessing hadn't somehow magically reappeared, unable to help sounding breathless. It was one thing to talk about how he made me feel; it was another to actually demonstrate it. "I thought about it, but then I went to bed."

"Did you watch porn?"

It took me a few seconds to override the mix of excitement and fear that had my mouth going dry. I'd never talked so much sex before with anyone else. It took a few breaths to remember that this was the new me, the me that wasn't embarrassed and didn't apologize for the things I wanted. "Yes, I did."

"What did you watch?"

My voice pitched even lower, became a whisper, when I admitted, "There was a girl in a bikini on the beach. She was laid out on a blanket, somewhat hidden by sand dunes. Only a few people around."

"What happened next?" The bass tones in his voice curled through my senses with wicked encouragement.

"A guy came over and sat with her. Talked with her. She asked him to spread oil on her skin. He rubbed it all over her back and her butt, kneading it. Then she turned over." My breathing felt a little shaky.

"Did he fuck her? Right there?"

"He rubbed more oil into her stomach and shoulders first. Then he let his fingers slide under her top and played with her breasts. Then he got more oil and slid his fingers over her stomach and into her bikini bottom."

"I'd pull it off you," he said huskily. "I'd want to see that beautiful fucking pussy you have. I didn't get enough of you last night."

"He did that," I breathed, feeling the image he described. "He took them off, and his fingers were inside of her."

"Did he make her come that way?"

"Yes. She was helpless to it. He made her come more than once." And she'd spread her legs open, trusting, and unable to stop from feeling all the wonderful feelings that lit her body up. I'd watched, alone, wanting to be that woman and wanting Mason to be that man.

"Have you ever come more than once?"

"No." When I was with Brady, I'd never come at all. At. All.

"You will," he promised. "It's my new goal to give you as many orgasms as I can at any given time we're together."

I exhaled a whimpering sigh, a hint of a breathless sound, into the phone just thinking about having his fingers inside me again. "I want that."

"Fuck," he groaned. "I can't wait to see you at the gym tonight. I have plans."

"It feels like such a long time from now. Hours. I don't know how I'm going to get through it."

"I knew I shouldn't have called you."

"Are you…hard?"

"Shit, yes. Like a rock. Are you wet?"

"Soaked. I'm going to need to keep extra panties with me from now on."

"Fuck." He chuckled in a self-deprecating manner. "Just hearing you say the word panties gets me going. I still have hours of work to do and no ability to concentrate, and I fucking need to concentrate on this."

I thought I heard frustration. "What are you working on?"

"The books at Zeke's."

"Is everything going all right? You sound stressed."

He was quiet a moment before admitting, "I think one of the bartenders is stealing alcohol. The numbers aren't adding up. Sales are down but costs are up. In the last few months, we've had to purchase more. We're bleeding money somewhere, but I don't know where. I'm going to have to cross-reference and compare sales over the last year to see when this started. See if I can find a pattern."

"Sounds like a lot of work."

"It is." He sighed, and I heard the creak of a chair like he was sitting back. "I was starting to go cross-eyed with this shit and wanted to take a break to hear your voice."

"I'm glad you did."

"What are you working on?"

"Usual stuff. Updating websites to include whatever a client needs and/or requested, phone calls, keeping up with the invoices."

"You like what you do?"

"I do." I leaned back in my own chair, eyeing the website that was currently up on my screen. It was for a local landscaping business that was expanding and needed more options for customer information and interaction opportunities. "It's exactly perfect for me. I love art and design, but I can't draw worth a damn, so this is one way of being creative. It also helps people who are trying to achieve their dreams, and that feels good, too." It had taken me a long time to even realize I needed a dream. Only because of a chance encounter with Blessing had I finally realized I was wearing blinders.

"Rowdy thinks we should have a website for both the gym and the bar."

"It's a great strategy to drive business your way. Pictures of what you offer, specials, upcoming events, you know. It helps get the word out. Good way of marketing. Each of your businesses should have a presence on all major social media platforms, where you advertise and update info. Honestly, it's a good thing, even if it is a lot more work."

He groaned. "I know you're right. I'm just not a social media kind of guy. I think I made a personal account a few years back on Facebook, but then I totally forgot about it. Maybe you could make room in your schedule to talk with me more about that."

The thought of having him in my office space had me feeling giddy. "Absolutely. Let me know."

"It'll have to be after I get these books cleaned up. With Zeke being sick, he's let things go. It looks like we're losing about a thousand in alcohol sales per week. I need to figure out what the hell is happening. I think it's going to take a few days."

The disappointment was sharp. "Will I still see

you at the gym tonight?"

"Bet your ass." His voice was low and husky again. "And don't worry about your panties, sweet girl. When you're with me, you aren't going to need them. We close tonight at ten. Plan accordingly."

"That's exactly when I plan to be all sweaty, needing a shower."

"Fuck." He took a deep breath. "I need to go. I'll see you tonight."

"Bye, Mason." It was several minutes of staring off into space after disconnecting the call before I realized my office line was ringing and that I needed to get some work finished. I thought back to what Blessing had said.

Was I about to embark on an orgasm bender? I sincerely hoped so. The shiver that trickled down my spine told me I liked the sound of that.

CHAPTER 11

MASON

Sitting in the office at Zeke's, there were two things I knew for certain: first, Layla was going to arrive at the gym soon, which was frustrating because I wasn't already there, and second, I had no patience for Bethany, who showed up at the bar just when I'd been ready to leave for the gym.

"Bet. What's up? I'm running out now." She was standing in the doorway to the club's office when I opened the door to leave. She looked chipper until she noted my scowl and pushed past me with a snort, ignoring my attempt to bar her from the room. Short of running her down, I had to let her in, but I sure as hell didn't need her bullshit. With a frown, I muttered, "You need to make this quick."

"Hey, Grouchy," she tried a teasing tone in an overly friendly voice, plopping herself in one of the office chairs like she had all the time in the world. It only served to piss me off that, once again, she was inserting herself into my life uninvited. Crossing one leg over the other, she raised questioning brows and stated, "I'm following up to see what you think of the products. I'm ready to sign you up to be one of my regulars."

Biting back the harsh words on the tip of my tongue, I followed her in. To muffle the sound from the house speakers, I shut the door, but I didn't sit down. I didn't want her to get comfortable. "I left you a message about this already. There's no information in the file that shows what ingredients are in the products or how they were tested for safety. I want to see the trial runs. I want to read about potential hazards and side effects."

"I gave all of that to you, silly," she laughed playfully, though knowing her so well, I could see that her eyes were watching me with sharp intent. She wasn't going to make this easy.

Fuck. I wanted to get going. There was no way I was going to miss time with Layla. Besides, she was going to be wearing her usual spandex, and I didn't want some horny bastard to get the wrong idea.

"You gave me testimonials, Bet. That's not the science behind it."

"They're users of the products. Their input is very valuable."

"Bethany, those can be faked. You know that." I waited for the storm that was potentially going to come. She wasn't known for handling disappointment well. When she was involved, it always turned into a shit show. "In fact, you gave a testimonial. Which product did you use?"

"This is ridiculous." Funny that her smile faded instantly, her lips forming a tight line of irritation.

I couldn't help the resentment in my tone. She was wasting my time. "Which product did you use?"

"Which…" her eyes narrowed. She was trying to think of an answer. I didn't give her time to think. She was so full of shit.

"Product," I spit out. Crossing my arms across my chest, I confronted her. "You gave a testimonial. Tell me about it."

"It was g-great. I loved it." She tried to blink innocently, sort of shrug her shoulders, like that said it all.

"Which one was it? You have about a dozen you're pushing here. Which one, and why did you stop?"

"I-I like the vitamins."

"Get your story straight, Bet. In your testimonial, you claimed the diet shakes were amazing." I pinched the bridge of my nose, thinking of all the work I needed to catch up on at the gym since I'd spent most of the day at the bar. I didn't have time to wade through this bullshit drama first. Only Bethany had the ability to give me a headache in less than five minutes. "From my point of view, what you've given me is a load of crap, and I don't take chances on something that looks like a scam."

"Look, I didn't expect to be quizzed here. I've tried several of the products, and all of them were great." She was getting defensive, getting her back up. I knew her well. She'd double down on her lies before ever admitting to them. And I didn't want to argue anymore.

"Safety is crucial, Bethany. There's no FDA approval on these supplements—"

"Supplements don't need to be FDA approved." She thought she had me with this statement, her lips curling into a smirk.

"I'm aware of that. It's the reason why I want to see the science." I leveled her with a stare, made eye contact so she could see I was entirely serious about this. "Show me the science if you want me to take you seriously; otherwise, I don't want to hear any more about it. I won't endorse products that I don't feel completely confident about. My gym members are too important to me."

She rolled her eyes, the exasperation coming out in painfully familiar ways when she sneered, "These products have been sold worldwide."

"Tell me who bought in the U.S. I want to see how the supplements are being received by the clients."

She paused a moment, having her bluff called. She took a breath. "I can't do that."

"Sure you can. Just a few companies. Some names, numbers? Surely you remember. Anyone who's enjoying good results is going to be happy to share them."

"Look, I don't have that information."

Finally getting to the truth. "You didn't actually sell anything to anyone."

"Yet. I haven't sold anything yet. But I'm sure they did." She raised her voice and stood in frustration. "I'm new to the company. I'm still trying to prove myself, but they aren't going to lie to me about this." I couldn't have been happier knowing she was no longer living with me. Now if she would only get her shit together...

"You think they wouldn't lie? I couldn't even find their company online. You didn't have to pay for any training, did you?"

She looked affronted, snapping, "No, of course not!"

What was it going to take to get her out of my office? I wanted to get the fuck out of here, be done with this whole situation. There was a reason Bethany and I weren't together, and the longer she stood here, the more she reminded me of all the ways she'd undermined our relationship. She'd always been selfish, looking out for herself first, second, and third. I fought the compulsion to search for straight lines, geometric shapes. My chest tightened, and I closed my eyes, let Layla's voice play through my mind. Sweetly melodic. Playful. Thoughtful. Sinful.

I took a deep breath, and my chest loosened up again. "Look, I said it before, and I'll say it again. Get me the science first. Then we'll talk."

She glared at me for several seconds, fighting the

urge to vent while recognizing that I hadn't completely denied her yet. With her face set like an angry bull getting ready to charge, she snarled, "I'll see what I can do."

I knew she wasn't going to be able to get anything substantive from this company, and in reality, I was only putting off the inevitable showdown when I told her no. Something was going on with her, but she was no longer any of my business. My business was finding Layla, which got put off again when I tried to leave.

It was a Wednesday night, normally a quiet night at the club, so it was no big surprise that there were only a few patrons sitting at the bar watching MMA on the big screen. It wasn't a live fight, which gave me an idea to start televising the pay-per-view events on our screens. Layla's ideas to develop a web presence was excellent. Then we could advertise on a website. And, there had to be ways to drive business, even on hump day. Getting input from employees and customers, to see what they wanted, could be an interesting experiment.

Heading behind the bar, I approached Magnus, one of the assistant managers who was also lead guitar in Rowdy's band, and said, "I'm heading out."

Magnus had been with Zeke for years. Knew the

place inside and out. At first glance, he looked questionable with sleeves of tats and a few facial piercings, but once you got him talking, you'd know he had a degree in music and loved to teach what he knew at one of the middle schools part time. He was also near to my size and walked drunken, belligerent customers out to the sidewalk whenever necessary. There were always women trying to flirt with him on any given night.

"You mind if I ask who the chick in your office was?" he asked, his eyes trained on the exit, like he'd watched someone leave. "She didn't pay for her drink. Asked for a bottled water."

"She wouldn't." I exhaled, reached into my pocket to pull out a bill, but he waved me off.

"I already covered it."

That had my brow rising. "You didn't have to, but thanks. You might see her around. Her name's Bethany."

"An ex?" He assessed my expression, for what I wasn't sure.

"From years ago."

"She was here looking for you yesterday. Saw her by the women's restroom." His gaze remained steady on me. "You guys getting back together?"

"Why? You interested?" Part of me wanted to warn him off for his own sake, but that would have been a dick move on my part. She wasn't evil, and he was a good guy. Who was I to tell anyone anything?

"Just want to know the lay of the land."

I could respect that. "We're not getting back together. Not sure what her deal is yet, you know, why she's here, but I guess I'll find out soon enough."

He nodded in reaction, but there was still more behind his eyes. "You seen Zeke lately?"

Giving my phone a quick glance to see if there were any missed texts or calls, I shoved it into my back pocket and answered, "Not for a month or so. Just talked to him by phone when I needed some question answered about the books."

Magnus smirked and asked, "He kept books?"

"Not regularly." Remembering the original question, I asked, "Have you seen him?"

He finished wiping down the counter with a shake of his head, but he didn't look at me. I had the impression that his head shake was more of an emotional response of frustration than actually answering my question. He finally looked up at me and said, "You should go see him."

"Something going on?" I asked, trying to read between the lines.

"He's not doing well."

"I talked with him last week. He sounded all right. Didn't tell me anything new."

"He stopped going to treatment."

Gravity weighted that statement.

"You're shittin' me." What the hell was he thinking?

"I wish."

I took a deep breath, knowing what had to happen. Instead of going to the gym, I was going to have do a one-man intervention. "All right. Appreciate the heads up."

Zeke's place was a quick ten-minute drive from the bar. He lived in a small one-bedroom apartment farther inland, a nondescript gray and white structure with three floors of residences. Eyeing the corner unit on the third floor, I noted the blue light of a TV flickering against the otherwise darkened windows. He was either watching television in the dark, or he'd fallen asleep watching.

Ringing the doorbell got no response. Neither did knocking. A sense of urgency that he might be hurt had me reaching for the knob, and as always, it was locked. I searched under the mat, the potted plant, above the doorway, and I scored the location of the extra key. Without hesitation, I let myself in and was immediately hit with a cloud of stench.

"Zeke," I called out, wanting to pull the neckline of my T-shirt over my nose. "Hey, man, it stinks in here."

I flipped the light on in the entryway and saw the kitchen immediately to my left in the small apartment. There was crap all over the counters, in the sink, and the fridge wasn't completely closed. Stepping past the kitchen into the living room, I saw it was in much the same condition as the kitchen, and Zeke was sprawled out on the couch in the middle of it all. From the sound of his snores, he was out, the light from the television flickering over him.

"Zeke," I lowered my voice, now that I could see he wasn't in danger. I turned on a lamp next to the end table and got my first glimpse of him. Shirt stained with food, boxers instead of pants, greasy-looking, patchy gray hair that looked like parts were becoming matted, and body odor that was strong enough to make my eyes water.

Then I saw the empty bottle of Jack Daniels on the floor. Maybe this was where some of the extra liquor was going every week. Here and to whomever was bringing it to him from the club. That was going to stop.

"You're drunk," I muttered under my breath, concern wrapped around my guts. Something bad must have happened. This was not the strong-willed, opinionated Zeke I'd come to know and respect. This Zeke was passed out, not just sleeping. From the number of empty bottles littering the room, the news had to have been significant. Shit. Did they tell him he was dying? My heart tightened at the thought. After all the shit he'd been through, didn't Zeke deserve a break?

Stopped treatment and was drunk.

A big sigh rushed from my lungs. He was a mess. And so frail. With no one to take care of him.

How could he do this to himself? How could he let himself fall so low when he was the reason I'd raised myself up? Anger bit at my insides. He should have fucking told me what was going on. Always helping others and never asking for help himself. It was time for an intervention, but it wasn't going to happen now. Tomorrow. When he was sober.

But neither was I going to leave him twisting in the wind in his filthy apartment.

Grabbing a plastic garbage bag from under the sink, I went around collecting all the trash and setting the full bag by the door before grabbing up all the dishes and soaking them in the sink. It took nearly an hour, and the whole time, I had my eye on the clock, feeling stuck between a rock and a hard place.

I was sure Layla was at the gym by the time I was near to done and knowing there was a narrow window of time for me to find her there had me doing a rush job. There was no way I was going to fuck tonight up by missing her. I took care of the big chunks. Got the dishwasher going and the food cleaned up.

I left Zeke a note on the coffee table, right where he couldn't miss it, that said he needed to take a fucking shower, we needed to talk, and I would come by with groceries in the morning to cook some breakfast. Then I grabbed the trash on my way out to my car and dumped it.

It wasn't until I was parked in the gym lot that I recognized my chest was tight. There'd been a part of me that figured she'd be gone. Seeing Layla's bike still locked up eased it a bit, but not enough to be comfortable. I needed to see her eyes. Only when

I looked into her eyes would I be able to completely relax.

Jumping out, I went inside and saw that it was ten minutes until closing and Layla was getting off the elliptical. The machine had stopped, and she grabbed her towel from the bar and stepped down onto the black mat. As she turned from the machine, her lips were tight, like she was disappointed, which was wrong. Never should that expression be on her face.

I beelined for her.

I may as well have had tunnel vision for all that I noticed of what was happening around us.

It took a dozen strides to get in front of her, but the moment I did, she stopped short. Her eyes widened when she looked up into mine. I could finally take a deep breath. Relief nudged her lips into a small, welcoming smile, like she was genuinely happy to see me, and my heart suddenly expanded with a stab of warmth that left me speechless.

She was so pretty.

And she was mine.

The thought barely solidified before I was propelled to action.

I didn't give her time to say anything. I took her small, soft hand tucked inside of my own and pulled her back toward my office with the thought that I needed to show her she was mine. I pulled her inside, out of public view, shut the door, and sank into her, backing her into the hard, wooden surface so our bodies touched.

My hands cupped her face as our lips met. Instant heat crackled between us. She was sweet. Soft. Feminine. Perfect. I ravaged her with a hot, open-mouthed kiss that instantly had her moaning, plush lips moving against mine, responding in equal measure, kissing me back with the same intensity. My cock went hard, it's new, usual state when she was around or when she wasn't around but was thinking about her.

"I'm sweaty," she protested against my lips. That just told me I wasn't doing my job right, so I plunged my tongue into her mouth, owning it. I rubbed my tongue against her smaller, silky one. Her whimpers of pleasure made me crazy to hear what she sounded like when she was coming. Only for the lack of oxygen did I back off, both of us sucking in air, eyes drawn back to each other. Unable to help myself, I brushed my lips to hers back and forth a few more times. They were swollen from my kisses, and her eyes were dazed with arousal. That satisfied something primal inside of me. I needed to keep that look on her face.

"What—" she began, but I gave her another gentle kiss that had her nails digging into my back, which made me growl with the pleasure of it. Had a woman ever made heat shiver down my spine?

"Sorry I'm late. Something came up," I finally murmured against her lips.

"I didn't think you were going to come," she whispered against my own. Then she kissed my lower lip and sucked it between her teeth to give me a sharp little bite. My cock ached with the pressure, and I had to grind it between her hips, groaning with the need to bury it inside of her.

"Why didn't you call me or text?"

"I thought you'd changed your mind," she breathed against my lips. "I didn't want to bother you."

Her words had me frowning—how could she ever think she was bothering me? —but I put her hand on the front of my jeans and squeezed it over my length. "Does it feel like I changed my mind?"

On a soft exhale, with her hand running the length of my cock and a shy smile curling her lips, she breathed a simple, "No."

"Go get your shower, and I'll kick everyone out."

CHAPTER 12

LAYLA

My body was throbbing in all the right places.

"Layla, we're on for tomorrow?" Rowdy asked from the front desk where he was shutting off the computers. It was clean-up time. Looking around, I could see there were no other patrons on the floor. My face flushed like it was obvious I'd been sucking face with Mason in his office. Added to that, not only were my legs shaky, but I was definitely very wetly aroused, and my thoughts were all over the place.

"Tomorrow?" It took a moment to think. Thursday. Tomorrow. Rowdy had emailed earlier to come meet with me and discuss what he wanted for his website. With an overly bright smile, I nodded eagerly. "Yes. Tomorrow. I sent you the address, and I'll see you…tomorrow." So dumb.

"Awesome." He grinned and headed for the door, his athletic bag slung over his shoulder.

"We're closing." Shay came up behind me and circled the desk. There was an apology in the tone of her voice like she was trying to politely suggest I get out, and I felt my face flaming with further embarrassment. I felt so conspicuous. He'd pulled me into his office in front of everyone, and now, no one was here, but I was just standing around like a…what did Malibu Barbie call me? A groupie? I didn't know what to say. Luckily, Mason stepped out of the office and saved me.

"I asked her to wait for me. You go on home, Shay. I'll close tonight."

"Really?" she asked with a megawatt-bright smile, but just as quickly, she spun and disappeared into the room where the employee lockers were located. I heard her saying, "Don't need to tell me twice."

The look he gave me was scorching and had the effect of making my heart pound harder. His gaze lingered on my breasts that were still beaded to nippled points, still reacting to him, craving his attention. When his gaze moved lazily back up to mine and locked on tight, it told me to carry on, with a heated promise in their depths that he was going to join me soon, which made my pussy clench in reaction.

Holy cow.

When had that ever happened to me off a single look? Inhaling sharply and needing to break the spell, I turned away, headed toward the women's locker room. I heard him telling others the same thing he told Shay, adding that he had work to finish up since he'd been gone all day. It helped me to feel less obvious.

The women's locker room was empty when I entered, thank God. Getting soap and shampoo out of my locker, I left my sweaty workout clothes in a plastic bag and walked to the shower with a towel wrapped around me sarong style. The material stimulated as it rubbed. My skin was more sensitized knowing he was here, and that he was about to come find me. I was having trouble catching my breath. Excitement and nerves mixed together was a heady cocktail.

The moment was significant. Magical. An event that would mark an important shift in my life.

Going after what I wanted.

Actually wanting someone.

Wanting. Period.

My body hummed with energy. Tiles felt extra cold against my bare feet. The slide of the curtain on the metal railing echoed in the silent room. With a turn of the knob, needles of sharp, stinging, hot water pelted my fingers as I checked for temperature. I was about to take a step over the threshold into the new world I'd picked for myself. Of course there were some doubts. I ignored them and stepped under the torrential spray, hyperaware, listening for the telltale sound of footsteps or the feel of a cooler breeze created by a door opening or closing.

Anticipation kept my heart racing like I was doing a fast mile, leaving me breathless.

Any moment, he was going to show up, no one else was going to be in the building, and I was going to be completely naked in front of him for the first time.

It was exhilarating and frightening at the same time. I was almost in over my head, but I wouldn't have it any other way.

Lathering up, I slipped soap over my nipples that were already stiff and achy. Swollen, like they were making their own demands for attention. Just grazing them with slippery fingers was lighting a fire, the suds swirling over my body and down between my legs.

What part of my shower was he going to walk in on? More goosebumps rippled down my shoulders just thinking about it. Adrenaline tripped through my body like it was on an IV line being fed into my veins. This build-up was almost more than I could handle.

The scent of jasmine filled the air as I shampooed my hair, then closed my eyes and tilted my head back, rinsing the suds away. When I lifted my head again, opened my eyes, he was there, and my breath hitched.

Mason's pale eyes with their dark slate rim watched through the gap in the curtain, shadowed with hunger, eyeing my body like he owned it, like there was something primitive taking over inside his mind. His look dialed straight into my nervous system and made everything accelerate. Blood whooshed in my ears. Respiration turned shallow.

A hot pulse pounded between my legs.

This was like starring in our own private porn scene. It felt a little bit like we were doing something forbidden, him being in the women's locker room, watching me shower while he was still fully dressed. Imagining what we looked like from the third person perspective made the need to crawl up his big, strong body and rub all over him, like a feline in heat, even stronger. I'd never needed anyone before, but I needed him.

His eyes trailed down over my bare skin. In the past I would have covered up, but this time, in a heart-pounding bold move, I let my fingers skim the path his eyes took, letting the water dance over me. He looked ready to eat me alive, and a rush of power flooded me. Something I'd never felt in my life when it came to men.

"Turn it off." His rough voice was barely recognizable. His own eyes were dilated, his breathing heavy. Looking down his masculine frame, I could see his cock already straining against the front of his cargo shorts and felt an answering surge of heat.

Reaching out a hand, I shut off the stream of water.

Backed a step until the tile wall was flush with my spine.

Invited him to look his fill. Peripherally, I could see my chest rise and fall more quickly, my breasts beaded and begging for attention.

"Sexy as fuck," he murmured quietly. His words

sent a secret thrill deep down inside me.

Mason pushed the curtain aside and stepped into the stall, his size eating up the space the moment he passed the threshold. My breath got caught up again, then whooshed out in a rush, my chest nearly brushing his the closer he came.

He lifted his hand between us, and we both watched as his thick fingers reached out to me. A shiver worked itself down my neck as the heat from his fingers burned into my skin before tracing water droplets along my collarbone. When the droplets fell in rivulets, he followed their pathway in a soft caress, slowly, gently, to the peak of my breast before his thumb rubbed agonizingly over my stiff nipple.

I gasped a needy whimpering sound. The heat spiraled in waves down my abdomen to that one sweet spot between my legs. My voice was a tremulous whisper when I said his name like a sensual ache. "Mason."

"So beautiful. So sensitive," he rumbled, bending so that his lips were almost touching my ear. His thumb continued its reverent caress, plucking at my nipple, causing me to pant my pleasure when he said, "Did you know they were so sensitive?"

"Ohmygod," I whispered harshly, trying to keep his question in mind. My back arched toward him, hands flattened on the wall behind me for stability. His fingers moved to my other breast, giving it the same hot treatment, and another mewling sound I hardly recognized trembled from between my lips before I could say, "I didn't know."

And I hadn't known. No one had ever taken the time to touch me. Pleasure me.

"Is this what you wanted?" he asked and nipped my earlobe before letting his lips soothe the sting. His fingers switched breasts again, continuing the torture with his one hand while the other braced a forearm above my head, effectively trapping me with this one touch. He could make me come like this.

"Yes."

"You wanted me to find you like this?" He continued to rub and pluck, almost casually, at the dark pink, puckered tip, and the heat was building exponentially.

"Yes," I answered breathlessly.

"And play with you?" He leaned down to suck the tip into his mouth, surround it with wet heat and his tongue curling around it before his fingers were there again. His husky voice was back at my ear when he added, "Make you come a few times?"

"Yes. Please."

"Then show me."

"Sh-show you?" I turned my face as the scruff of his cheek rubbed along my neck. A shiver touched my skin with the contact.

"Show me you want me," he whispered, biting at my neck again.

"I do. Mason…" My hands slid up his chest, noted the feel of his hard muscles. I cupped his face and pulled his lips to mine, where I captured them in a kiss that showed him the scorching need I had raging through my body, years' worth being unleashed in a single moment. It was the first time I'd ever initiated a kiss, and I went all in, tilting my head to have a deeper connection, my hands sliding up into his thick hair to grab the back of his head. Hold him right where I wanted him.

His groan vibrated from a deep place in his gut, and he lost some of his control.

He scooped me into him, crushing my breasts to his hard chest. Wrapping his fist in my long, wet hair, he tugged my head back and invaded my mouth with the wet heat of his tongue, owning me, rubbing against me, toying with me until I was wild and whimpering, our tongues tangling, mouths angling for deeper penetration.

I was helpless and safe and turned on at the same time, rising on my toes to wrap my arms around his neck and plaster myself against him, and that's when his other hand slid down to cup my ass before letting his fingers slide even further between my cheeks until they caressed the swollen lips of my pussy, just rubbing around the cleft. His finger slid through my wetness, grazing my clit, and I cried out against his lips.

"So wet," he murmured into our kiss. "So soft."

"More. Mason, please." I was getting him all wet, and he didn't seem to care.

It was just where I needed his touch. I opened my legs wider, giving him easier access, but his finger did the same dance, sweeping between my swollen lips, just barely touching my swollen nub. I wanted more. I writhed against him spontaneously, grinding against the steel heat of his erection, wanting to incite him to more action. He was so big and hard against my belly. For the first time, I wanted to see, touch, experience a man. This man. But he held himself in check,

In a single move, he grabbed my forearms,

pulled them down from his neck and pinned them to the tile on either side of my head.

"I need to lick your pussy," he growled. "I've dreamed of going down on you and eating you out all fucking day. Yes or no."

"Yes." There was no hesitation. I was beyond feeling shy. The need to come was too great.

Then his lips were at my neck, taking nipping bites on their way to my breast. He raked his teeth over the aching tip but didn't stop his descent down my abdomen. When his breath fell on my pussy, he looked up at me. Pale gray eyes were stormy with need, forcing me to stay connected when he scooped one of my legs over his shoulder, opening me wide. It was the hottest sight I'd ever seen. Then his lips were brushing gentle kisses on either side of my thighs, the scruff of his whiskers brewing a storm of tingles that arrowed to one overheated, pulsing place right at the top of my thighs. I was leaning against the wall, grabbing at his shoulders for support.

Then his lips hovered over the trim dark curls that were moist from both my shower and my arousal. He looked back to me. Deliberately pulled my lips wider and placed a suctioning kiss right on my clit.

"Ohmygod!" I cried, my hands going back to his hair reflexively.

His tongue rubbed the swollen flesh, nipped and sucked at it until only my keening cry echoed from the shower stall. He licked a line along my slit, up and down, stabbed at my center, until I was riding the tight, sharp edge of tension. He lapped at my juices as they gathered with each attack of heat, and then came his fingers. First one, then two, slid through my opening, curling in just the right spot, sliding in and out while his tongue and lips found my clit again, hyper-accelerating the electrical heat of pleasure racing through my body.

I was practically riding his face, my hips pumping into his fingers greedily.

"Oh Mason!" I panted harshly, my fingers digging into his scalp to hold him right where I needed him, gasping each breath in quick succession. "I'm going to come. Don't stop. So close."

He growled his pleasure. Increased pressure. Nipped and sucked even harder on my clit while adding a third finger to tunnel inside me. The scorching fire built between my legs until they shook. Until my toes curled reflexively. Until my orgasm hit with the full electrical charge that had my body jerking, my breathless cries in sync with each convulsion against his face. Inner muscles squeezing against his fingers.

"Too much," I whispered, now pushing his head away instead of pulling, and he chuckled. Kissed my inner thighs.

"Beautiful. I could watch you come all night," he gently withdrew his fingers from inside me and stood.

His lips sought mine, and I could taste myself there. It was tangy and sexy and the poignant evidence of my own sexual needs that had long been ignored. It tasted like freedom, and it was addicting.

I wanted more. I wanted him inside me.

To that end, I licked along the seam of his lips, and when he opened, I used his own moves on him. Slid my tongue in, reveling in our combined tastes. Where before, I'd let my tummy rub his erection, now I had my hand there. I fisted his thick length, squeezing and stroking through the cargo material, just the way he'd shown me in his jeep.

The strangled groan encouraged me to undo his belt and the top buttons of his shorts before working my way under the waistband of his boxer briefs. He was so hot and hard. When my fingers closed over the velvety length of his erection, he pulled away from our kiss with a hiss, resting his forehead on mine.

"Fuck, Layla," he whispered against my mouth, sounding tortured, but doing nothing to stop me. He rubbed his lips against mine and rocked his hips into my hand. "That feels fucking amazing."

"I want to make you feel good."

"You do."

"What if I put my mouth on you?"

"Only if you want to."

The sound of metal clanging, like a metal locker door banging against metal, startled us both. We quieted. Listening.

"There's someone else in here," I whispered.

"There shouldn't be. Stay here. I'll check it out." His scowl was dark when he stepped back and re-buttoned his shorts. He tossed me my towel and closed the shower curtain, securing my privacy. I heard his receding steps and felt the rush of cold air against my skin with his absence before wrapping up.

Had someone heard us? Did he miss shooing

someone out before joining me? Maybe someone had been relaxing in the sauna and gotten stuck? I mean, was there any easy way to sneak out of a room where people were going at it?

When Mason didn't come right back, I went to get dressed and pack up my bag. Strangely, I couldn't find my panties. Mystery overlaying mystery. Had Mason taken them? Kept them as a souvenir or something? He was proving himself to be a kinky one. I pulled on my jeans and sweater from earlier and exited the locker room. He was at the front desk reviewing footage, a frown in place. He shook his head and came back around the front desk to place a light kiss on my lips, leaving his hands resting on my waist.

"We don't have cameras in the locker rooms, but I'm not seeing anyone moving around the floor, either."

"It was probably nothing."

"Probably." But he didn't seem convinced. "I swear there was no one in here. I locked up the front. It's still locked."

"Then everything's okay, except for you." Feeling bold, I let my fingers slide down his hard abs to the front of his jeans, feeling where there was clearly a tent going on, but he caught my hands fast, a rush of air hissing between his teeth.

"I don't think now's a good time." There was still heat in his gaze, but his attention was torn. The moment had passed, and I was feeling a little vulnerable.

"I don't want to leave you like this again."

He surveyed my expression and gave me a crooked smile, let his hand slide over my backside with both hands, kneading firmly. "Let's just say now you'll owe me two." My sex convulsed with a belated spasm. It was already anticipating a next time when he added, "I plan on collecting."

"I can't wait."

In a move that still seemed unreal, in this new world where we were now becoming lovers, Mason planted another scorching kiss on my lips that had me clinging, my body getting ready for round two. Against my lips he whispered, "I'll see you tomorrow."

The pull to stay was strong. I didn't want to break the connection yet, so I found myself leaning closer to ask, "But what is your next fantasy?"

A sparkle touched his eyes; his lips quirked. After studying my face a few moments, his lids slid half-mast. "You surprising me."

My grin was automatic, as was the color splashing my cheeks, which was weird because I'd just had him between my legs wringing cries of pleasure from me. "I can do that."

"Counting on it."

With no other reason that I could think of for staying, I walked away feeling punch-drunk. With a sigh on my lips, and my mind working out possible surprise scenarios for Mason, I didn't notice the new young guy smirking at me until I was within a few feet of him, unlocking my bike. It was the familiar knowing glint he'd displayed previously that had me cringing and worrying. It was the same creepy smile he'd flashed the day before.

Was he the noise we'd heard?

Goosebumps hit me, which had me shoving my lock into my bag quickly.

Even under darkness of the night sky with only the inconsistent lighting from the closing businesses, when I couldn't see the exact color of his eyes, I could still see that he was x-raying my body through my clothes with a look that made me feel exposed, and mildly alarmed.

"Have a good night," he saluted.

I hopped on and pedaled away as fast as I could

go.

CHAPTER 13

MASON

"I figured it was you."

Zeke, Ezekial Jackson, scowled, looking like ten miles of bad road. His thinning gray hair stuck up at odd angles, deep grooves lined his mocha face, and his words scraped over rusty vocal chords when I entered. I'd used the hideaway key but figured my offerings, a food bag consisting of breakfast burritos, would chill him out since he likely hadn't consumed anything solid in over twelve hours.

It was almost 11:00 a.m. I'd come earlier and finished cleaning the place up while he'd sawed logs on the sofa, not having moved a muscle since the night before. The place wasn't perfect, but it no longer smelled rank.

And Jay had been a no-show again today.

Fucking Jay Garcia. What the hell was he thinking?

"Get a shower, and we can eat." I set the bag down on his small dinette table. "I'll get some coffee going."

He glared at me a few moments, looking fragile when I'd only ever seen him tough and scrappy, but then he nodded, and with great effort, levered his body off the sofa, still wearing his stained undershirt and boxers.

This was an all-time low. I'd never seen him looking so wrecked, which was why I recognized it wasn't anger but shame that soaked his eyes when they slid away from me. "Give me ten."

It was closer to twenty, but he emerged from his bedroom looking more like his old self, if a little subdued. I had food laid out and had just poured coffee for two, first handing him some aspirin and a glass of water for the hangover he was likely suffering with in silence.

Silent suffering. It was what we'd been trained to do in the military. But what had happened to cause him to shut down so completely? What was he suffering from? He nodded his thanks and popped the pain meds before drowning them with a healthy gulp of water.

"Eggs, potatoes, cheese, bacon. Mild hot sauce."

He grunted an acknowledgement, then asked, "From Maria's on the corner?"

"Yeah."

He hitched his jeans, looser now since he'd been sick, and sat in one of the chairs, old with cracked plastic upholstery. He'd put on a sweatshirt with the logo of the club, but he was now swimming in it, his frame was so thin. Hunching over his plate, he took an appreciative sniff of the food stating, "Woman makes a mean burrito."

"That she does."

We ate in silence for a few minutes. Comfortable. I'd opened a window to let in a breeze, hoping to air the stale food smell out of the space while he was showering earlier. It wasn't until after he'd pushed his plate away to make room for his elbows that he looked me in the eyes again. "I ain't gonna lie. I'm in a bad place."

"I can see that." There was a void, a dullness to his dark brown eyes that let me know he'd crashed headfirst into a ditch.

"My daughter won't see me."

He saw the surprise on my face, his gaze steady,

analyzing my reaction.

"You didn't know I had a girl." He nodded to himself, picked up his mug, and took a sip before adding, "No one does."

"How old is she? What's her name?"

"Her name is Clara. Don't know her married name. Forties? Forty-six, forty-seven maybe?" A faint lift of his shoulders only emphasized how thin he was. He'd once been robust with good health, and now he looked frail, barely able to eat a quarter of the food I'd brought him. After a deep breath, he added, "Not even sure. She doesn't want me to know details. She's married. Has kids. That's it."

He was a grandpa. I set my food down and wiped my hands on the small paper napkin I'd nabbed from the fast-food bag. "She won't see you?"

"I was all fucked up after Vietnam, you know?" He cleared more of the gravel from his throat before talking again, his eyes going vague, no longer focused on me, as they looked inward toward his memories. "I mean, I had no emotions. I couldn't feel anything for a long time. What I'd seen. What I'd done. I had to shut all that shit down in my head."

I nodded, understanding where he was coming from. It had been a bullshit war that had left a lot of guys dead if not dying from the inside out.

"But I shut out Violet, my wife. You know, they didn't have a lot to give us when we came back." He waved a hand in the air encompassing the world generally. "Now it's all over the news. Everybody knows that guys come back with all kinds of mental problems, but back then, no one talked about it. No one. And the world fucking hated us. Baby killers and shit. We came back after getting fucked by the government only to keep getting fucked over at home. There was no help for a long time for me."

"PTSD."

"Yeah. Exactly. Anyway, Violet tried to hang in there for a couple of years. She did. She tried. I give her credit for that, but I just didn't have anything to give her. It was like I could see her drifting away from me as time went on. One of the things about her that I used to love was her smile. She was always smiling, always happy, but by the end, she'd stopped smiling. Absolutely miserable. I did that to her. After a while, I broke down her spirit, and she stopped trying so hard. She gave up on us a little at a time, and I couldn't blame her for it. When she finally packed up, I still couldn't feel a thing. Not for a long time. Not until years after she left, and by then, I was drinking."

"And Clara?" I asked.

"Clara. Cutest little thing. Perfect. I didn't want to get her dirty. She deserved so much better. I stayed away." His voice cracked, eyes got shiny. He paused a moment to breathe, gain control again. Pressed his thin lips together before admitting, "I kept pictures. Violet was good about sending them to me every year so I could see her grow up. Violet knew I was all fucked up. She was a wonderful woman. A saint. Eventually remarried. Nice guy. Had more kids. Started smiling again. It was all I wanted for her."

"So where does Clara come into this?"

"I wasn't right in the head again for a long time. You know, I was living my life in a bottle, barely keeping my ass from living on the streets. Wasn't calling regularly. Didn't keep promises. I was a fucking shitty father. I know that. Always letting her down. Hurting her. But the worst thing I did was show up to her high school graduation drunk off my ass. It didn't go well." He bent his head to his hands, hiding his eyes for a moment, scrubbing at his face before lifting his head.

I winced, thinking about it. "What happened?"

"Let's just say, she told me never to contact her again. I tried to apologize a few times after, but she"—he waved a hand dismissively with a sweeping gesture while trying to find the right words— "refused to even entertain a single moment more of my bullshit. And everything about me was bullshit at that time. I couldn't fault her for that."

"You've tried since then?"

"About a month ago." He leaned on his elbows again. "I've had nothing but time, you know? Since I've been sick? Time to think. Time to remember. Looked at all the old pictures and realized every damn thing I missed out on. Everything came crashing down on me. It was like, every time I hit the crossroads, I sided with the devil. Made all kinds of wrong choices."

"That's not who you are anymore, Z." He was looking like a shell of himself. The more he shared, the more he seemed to dig down into the ditch. It was like he was looking to die.

He just shook his head and continued. "Well, I got to thinking that maybe Clara had a right to know that I wasn't doing well, just in case she had any feelings left for me. I didn't want to do any more damage by up and dying without at least giving her a chance to chew me out for being a rat bastard all her life. Something. At least, that's what I told myself. But really, I was aching to see her again. Somehow get back something from what I'd lost. Look into her eyes again and tell her how sorry I am that she didn't get a better deal in life. I'm just so fucking sorry."

"And?"

"My letter was returned unopened. Violet told me she wouldn't even touch it." Now his lip quivered, his eyes welled up. He struggled to take a breath, fighting the emotion that was making his throat work convulsively. Ultimately, he lost the battle and the tears dropped.
An ocean of grief radiated from him, and my words couldn't ever be enough, and still, with my own voice turning scratchy, I said, "I'm so sorry, Zeke. So sorry."

"It's all gone, Mason. I don't get that time back," he growled and slammed a fist on the table making the plates and mugs rattle. "I had it all, and I couldn't see it. I couldn't appreciate it until it was too late. I fucking lit my world on fire and burned it to ashes, and there's nothing I can do about that. I just don't give a fuck anymore. I don't. I can't."

"Is that why you stopped treatment?"

"You're damn right it's why I stopped. I'm tired of this, Mason, I'm just so fucking tired. Tired of the fucking pain and disappointment. Every single day. What the fuck have I done with my life? Nothing memorable. Nothing significant. Nothing I can take credit for. Nothing I can hold up and show her. No wonder she doesn't want to see me." Each word dug him into a deeper and deeper chasm where he was rejecting everything, even me, and fury rose up from my gut.

"That's bullshit, Z."

Tears were freefalling down his cheeks. "It's not. I did nothing. I am nothing."

"I get that you're feeling low, but you've been the light for a lot of guys. You cannot stop treatment now. You can beat this shit. Your doctor said."

"You aren't hearing me! I'm a bum, Mason. A bum. And I'm tired of being this person, this loser!"

"You fucking saved my life, old man." The sudden shot of anger had my lip curling, my fists clenching where they rested on the table in front of me. "You made me believe I could live again. You. It may not mean anything to you, but it means a fucking lot to me."

He waved a hand, and it almost felt like he was dismissing me. "You only think that, but you'd have

245

been fine either way."

"You're fucking doing it again. Don't light your goddamned life on fire yet again. You want to feel good about your life? Learn from your fucking mistakes and recognize when people care because they're counting on you. The guys at the VA count on you. I count on you. Are you saying they don't matter? I don't fucking matter?"

"I'm just saying you have a father, and he's a good one."

"He had no fucking clue how to help me, and it's no shot on him. I was ready to eat a handful of pills, and there was nothing anyone in my family could have said to me to make me stop. I needed you to pull me out of the black hole I was stuck in, and you did. It was fucking dark and deep for a long time, but you found me in there. That was the power of you. You saved me. Are you telling me it was all bullshit? Don't fucking disregard me, Z. You've been like a second father to me."

"I'm not disregarding you," he snapped, affronted, and maybe with a hint of surprise on his face that came through when he paused. Maybe he hadn't realized his impact on me. Maybe I hadn't told him.

"You fucking are. And you know what? You're

disregarding your daughter yet again."

"The fuck I am!"

"The fuck you are. You have good odds of living through this disease with treatment but zero odds without it. If you're dead, will she ever have the opportunity to change her mind? Figure out she's ready to take a chance on you again now that she's older and wiser? You're playing with your life, and when you do that, you're playing with hers. Even if my feelings mean nothing to you, hers should. Maybe she won't ever come around, and maybe she will. But she won't have a choice if you hit the fucking crossroads again and side with your demons."

"It's not like that!"

"Whatever. Do what you're going to do."

I shoved away from the table, adrenaline pounding through my heart with a relentless ache. He caught up with me at the door. Grabbed at my arm. For being a scrawny, sickly guy, he had a strong grip.

"I did things, Mason. Things I can never forget." The anger drained from his face, leaving behind defeat. "I killed people. Innocent people who hadn't done anything to me. I was an artist and a hippy before I got drafted. Fucking had dreadlocks and smoked weed. I wasn't meant to kill. You don't want to be like me."

"If you don't deserve a better life, I sure as hell don't have any hope." He was ready to be done with his life over something that he'd had no control over. The sounds grew louder in my ears. The explosion. The shouts. The smoke. The desperation. Lifeless eyes turned skyward. My own cries. Hoarse and helpless.

He tried to argue it, but the well of pain was already seeping through my own mind. I hardly registered his benign assurances. "Mason, you're not like me. You got your whole life ahead of you."

Gently and carefully, I pulled free of his grasp. Backed up a step toward the door, seeing another set of eyes in my mind with the crushing knowledge that he was no longer on this earth.

"Z, you can always know that you were following orders given to you by our government, but I will always know I killed my best friend."

CHAPTER 14

LAYLA

His silvery eyes found mine in one of the many mirrors, pausing long enough to show me raw pain reflected there, like something or someone had sucker punched him. My heart contracted sharply.

At the time, I was putting one foot in front of the other on the elliptical machine, letting my body warm up before I punished it with more speed and endurance for forty-five minutes. So concentrated on Mason's state of being was I, that I almost tripped on the machine. I had to grab at the handlebars and get my feet under me.

His pain was mine in this moment. There was an instant desire to comfort him.

What happened? Did someone die?

I cocked my head ever so slightly in question, feeling the concern spread from my heart to my expression.

Immediately, he broke the connection. Let his eyes drift over the room. Something had to be seriously wrong. I'd studied him long enough to know that. Then he moved on without looking back. Head down, he went to his office behind the counter and shut the door.

At first, I wondered if I should leave him alone. Sometimes people needed to handle their problems on their own, and who was I to interfere with his process, but the other voice in my head argued back. No one should feel like they're alone. He was always there for everyone else, but who was there for him?

It was imagining him sitting at his desk needing support and having no soft spot to land on, that had me turning off my machine and heading straight for his office. I knew this wasn't what we agreed to be for each other, but I couldn't let someone I cared about feel alone when they were upset.

"Hey, Layla!" Amanda looked up from the computer system where she'd just checked in a member. A friendly smile automatically kicked up the corners of her mouth and eyes, her own dirty blond curls thrown into a careless bun on top of her head. "What can I do for you?"

"Well," I stopped at the counter, unsure of how to get past the gate. "I just saw Mason come in and need to talk with him. Would it be possible for me to slide on through for a few minutes?"

"For you, absolutely. Come on around." As easy as that, she did a Vanna White sweep of her arm toward his closed door that was slightly off and around the corner from where her workstation faced the entrance.

Forcing a confident smile, I pushed through the waist-high swinging gate, scooted around the counter, and paused just outside the door. I lifted my knuckles and knocked lightly. Hearing no sound, I tentatively let myself in, closing the door behind me.

Mason was leaning his elbows on a filing cabinet, staring down at his hands. He didn't move. Gave no indication that he even heard me come in other than the slightest tilt of his head my direction. I moved closer a step.

"I wanted to see if you're all right." My voice matched the quiet of the room.

He still didn't turn around.

"I hope you don't mind. I was worried."

When he still didn't respond, a shadow of doubt crept over me. I stepped back toward the door, rethinking whether I really knew him at all. Who was I? Just a girl he'd gotten off a couple times. That was it. And now look at what I was doing. Always being stupid. My stomach knotted.

A fool. Always reaching for air.

"I can...leave you alone."

He cleared his throat, and it was gruff when he said, "I knew it was you. Your scent."

I hesitated. Go or stay. Balancing on the threshold in my mind, feeling strangely fragile, I asked, "Is that good or bad?"

After a pause, he admitted, "It's...comforting. I know it's you."

A breath that I hadn't even realized I was holding escaped my parted lips, but a surge of warm relief followed.

On silent feet, I moved the few steps to get behind him, reached a hand to touch his back, simply rested it there against the hard muscles by his shoulder blades. He was tense. Muscles bunched. "You seemed upset when you came in."

"I'm fine." He ducked his head, scrubbed a hand over his face, and let out a sigh that seemed to have a tremor to it.

"What happened?"

"Nothing, really. I mean, not nothing, but…" He shook his head like he was having trouble getting the words out. "A good friend of mine has cancer. He's giving up. Doesn't think he's deserving or some shit." He cleared his throat, likely fighting a well of emotion, and hung his head.

My heart clenched even tighter. I'd struggled with this one. Maybe still did at times. Was I deserving, coming from a background of filth and a mother that couldn't have cared less about my well-being? Had Brady seen the same things in me that my mother had? An unworthiness? What about my sister? She was the one person who'd sacrificed herself to take care of me, yet she was dying in slow motion right in front of my eyes. She didn't think she was worth anything either. But that wasn't right. None of it was.

"We all deserved to live our best lives, whatever that means," I murmured, partly to remind myself.

Reaching as high as I could, I massaged his shoulders with gentle pressure. He dipped his head, resting it on folded arms, letting me touch him, seeming to appreciate the human contact since he wasn't pushing me away. I worked my hands down either side of his spine, squeezing, rubbing, and caressing his flesh, not with any sexual intent, but with genuine care. When I got to his waist, I slid them down his hips and around to the front of his thighs, spooning my own body to his back, like I could take some of his pain.

"It hurts to see people you care about being self-destructive. My sister's like that." I set my cheek against the center of his back, drawing my own comfort. "She's an addict. Drugs and alcohol both. Almost two years ago, I found her in her apartment. I couldn't find a pulse. Couldn't see her breathing." I sucked in a shaky breath, finding myself there once again—the blue pallor of her complexion, the desperate urgency.

"I'm sorry, Layla." His gruff tone was still gentle, the warmth of it finding its way into what had always been a cold, lonely place in my heart. Reaching down, he grabbed one of my arms and wrapped it around his waist, holding it there. Comforting. Supporting.

"I was doing CPR and screaming for help. I

don't actually remember screaming. Truthfully, I barely remember anything. Everything about that day, from the moment I realized she was dying right there, feels like a blur of undiluted fear and adrenaline, but by the time the ambulance arrived, I hardly had a voice, so I figure I must have been. Even the next day, I had a sore throat."

"Did she make it?"

"Barely. I was freaked out because my showing up to the apartment where she'd decided to crash for a few months was pure serendipity. She just happened to be house sitting at our cousin's house nearby instead of one of her usual spots in San Diego. I just happened to be on my way to work and planned to pop by to grab the sweater I'd left, a sweater I didn't even really need. It was summer. It was warm. But what would have happened if I hadn't shown up, or she'd been somewhere down south?"

"She would have died."

"No doubt. So, I got her into rehab. Sold everything. Maxed out my credit and got her to go. Before two weeks were up, she left. Was high or drunk or something within an hour of leaving the place."

"There's nothing you could have done."

"I know that, but part of me wishes she could see how much she matters to me, how much it would hurt to see her completely gone from this earth. It's not her time yet. She's too young to wither away."

"My friend's name is Zeke."

"The club on the boardwalk?"

"Yeah," he nodded. "He's amazing. One of the strongest people I've ever known. Had to fight his way through mental illness after coming home from Vietnam, and he's done the most selfless work with other guys coming back from war, telling them they'll get to the other side of this. He's saved lives but now doesn't want to fight for his own, even though he has a good chance of beating this thing."

"He's fighting his demons, just like my sister Nadine. I just wish I knew what they were." I rubbed my face against his back again. "Maybe you need to remind him of his own words. There is an after if he wants it, and he still has time to make it right when he gets there, whatever his demons are."

He took a deep breath. "I'm not giving up on him. I'll ride his ass until he starts his treatment again."

"I'm not giving up on her. She's at my apartment right now."

Mason stood up to his full height and turned around, his hands coming to rest on my hip bones, his thumbs absently moving in soft circles. "Thanks."

"For what?" I looked up and was caught in his eyes. They were red-rimmed and moist, shadowed with emotion. There was pain there, and it was deep. Haunting.

"Checking on me. Caring about me." His big hands squeezed reflexively on my hips.

"I didn't want to see you hurting alone." I let my own hands travel along his body up his strong chest. One of my hands continued up to his jaw before cupping his cheek, my thumb rubbing away some of the wetness from beneath his lashes.

"Shit," he ducked his head and swiped impatiently at his own face, like he hadn't known there were tears there. It was like he was ashamed of showing his emotions. "Sorry."

"It's okay." Before I could help myself, I reached up to cup his cheeks, wanting him to look at me again. I missed his eyes when he wasn't looking at me. "It's okay."

When he finally looked back up at me, leveled me with his eyes, I couldn't help but stand on tiptoe, bringing my lips to his, caressing them with a gentle soothing touch, brushing back and forth over his soft flesh. I wanted to take away his pain.

When I would have slid back down to my heels, he held me in place, taking over. His lips lingered, sipped, slanted over mine to deepen the kiss. It went to the next level almost instantly. Hotter. Harder. I whimpered, fresh sensations skittering over my flesh.

It caught up to me in an instant. The tingles. The heat spreading deep in my abdomen where it balled up, anticipating, simmering.

In the next moment, I was airborne. Hands under my butt, he lifted me to his frame. Automatically, my legs curled around his waist, and my arms circled his neck, but it was only to transport us to his big office chair, where he sat us down with me straddling him, feeling his thick, hard shaft searing me between my legs.

The kiss turned desperate and all-consuming.

The fire was starting to burn out of control. His hands slid up my ribcage to rub against my nipples, causing me to arch, automatically pleading for more contact, more friction. They hardened instantly, and I moaned into his kiss. The fabric of my tank and sports bra were so thin, it was almost like I didn't have anything on.

Without even thinking about it, I was rocking my pussy against his hard shaft. He was already pulling my tank south, sucking an achy tip into his mouth.

But I didn't want to make this about me. I wanted this time to be about him, where he lost control, where I could make this powerful man unravel under my touch. Where I could make him feel better.

"There's something I've been wanting to do," I whispered against his lips.

Not wanting him to stop me, I pushed off his lap. Even as his fingers flexed against my flesh in protest, I backed up to the door. The quiet click of the lock echoed loudly in the room, desire warring with hints of fear as I stared him down, looking for any microscopic, negative reaction to cross his features.

Giving him time to protest, I moved slowly, deliberately, a step and then another until I was standing over him. It was only when I pushed his legs farther apart and knelt between them that the knowledge of what I was going to do to him was reflected in his stormy gray eyes. They grew darker, the intensity sharpening when my face was level with his straining denim. I wanted to do this, have him trembling under my fingertips, be in control when I'd never been before.

Our eyes met and held with my fingers undoing the buttons of his fly. Nerves had them shaking, but his reaction soothed them. He watched hungrily. The intimacy was gripping. Addicting. I couldn't look away from their dark, steely depths. I could hardly breathe.

This was a first for me.

Initiating.

Fresh butterflies swarmed my abdomen.

Heat pooled between my own legs.

Finally breaking eye contact, I peeled back the edges of his jeans, revealing black boxer briefs that barely contained his erection. I ran my hand over the cotton material that hugged his thick, hard cock. Grasping the waistband, I freed his length. Velvet skin over steel length, my fingers wrapped around his thick girth and squeezed. I loved the hissing sound he made, the shudder that went through him at my touch, the way his cock jerked in my hands. It pulsed and grew even thicker from my touch. I had this much power at my fingertips, and it was even better than I could have imagined. Resting on my knees between his spread legs, looking up at him with aching need radiating from my entire body, I was filled with triumph.

"You sure you want to do this?" he asked.

I glanced up at him from under my lashes. "I watched a video last night to learn how to make it good."

His eyes flared. "Show me."

In answer, I bent to nuzzle my face along his rock-hard length, loving his clean, musky scent.

His breathing grew heavy.

Still holding his gaze, I licked his shaft from root to tip, just the way I'd watched the girl do it on the porn video, before kissing the tip and licking tangy pre-cum off the top. Then I slid my entire mouth over the top of him, sucking and licking his cock, flattening my tongue, and bobbing my head, his cock impossibly thick and scorching hot in my mouth.

"Oh fuck," he gritted out in a low, guttural tone. "Fuck, Layla. Just like that, baby. Just like that. Feels so fucking good."

So sexy. The look on his face was a man on the edge. I moaned my reaction against his thick flesh, loving every part of this.

He sucked in air with the vibration. Another small amount of pre-cum dotted his tip, and I swirled my tongue over it, savoring the essence that was him.

"Your lips on my cock is sexy as fuck." His voice was hoarse in his attempt to keep it low. "You're going to make me come so hard. So fucking hard."

I doubled my efforts, moving my hand down to cup and caress his balls. His growl was primal. He panted out each breath, his muscles tensed like he was trying to control his own reaction. I wanted him to feel as helplessly addicted to this demanding need burning between us as I was. His hand gripped my ponytail and guided my head, forcing it down over his cock. Instead of resisting, a new rush of sizzling arousal washed over me. Saliva dripped over his length, his mushroom tip tapping the back of my throat, making tears slip down my cheeks and my clit throb with swollen sensitivity, wanting this so much.

"I'm going to come," he warned, pulling on my ponytail to get my mouth off of him.

My hands curled around his thighs, and I kept his cock in my mouth, keeping the rhythm of sucking and bobbing.

"Layla, fuck. Oh, fuck," he snarled just before his body jerked and warm cum slid over my tongue and down my throat, a little tangy, a little salty, and all him. His head fell back on his chair when the last jerk of his body signaled the end of his orgasm. I gave his still-semihard cock a gentle, sucking kiss on the tip, pulled his boxer briefs back up, and used my hand to wipe at the moisture on my face.

My body was still humming with need, and I wasn't sure what to do next, but he had his own idea.

"C'mere." He was watching me from beneath slitted lids, still breathing heavily. I took the hand he offered and let him pull me to his lap. He turned me to face away from him, so I was leaning back into his chest. A shiver skittered down my back when he nuzzled my neck and bit down on my earlobe. In a thick voice, he whispered, "That felt so fucking good."

"I'm glad." My words came out in a breathy tone. "I love making you feel good."

"But we're not done here."

"We're not? Oh!" I gasped at the feel of his hands sliding up to cup my breasts. He rubbed and plucked at them while I sucked in each breath, fighting the moan that managed to escape.

"Shhhh," he murmured in my ear, still playing my nipples with delicious precision, each stroke pushing me toward the cliff. "We don't want anyone to hear, do we?"

"No," I whispered, but my hips were squirming with restless movement in his lap, my pussy needing attention.

Mason hooked my legs over his knees and spread my thighs wide. It was such a vulnerable position. I was so open. And I loved it.

Then his fingers were sliding beneath my spandex and underwear, through the short, groomed hair of my pussy, and unerringly to my hot, wet center. A strangled cry was muffled behind my closed lips as the wave of pleasure swept over me.

"Here?" The deep, rough timber of his voice vibrated against my ear. He pushed through the moisture, his thick finger sinking deep inside me, swirling around. "Is this where you need me?"

"Yes," I hissed, sliding my own hands over the top of his, shamelessly helping him, only to find him stopping his movement. A protesting cry squeaked from me.

"Grab the arms of the chair, Layla. Hold on tight."

Only after I did as he told me to did he move his finger again, curling against that special place that had my back arching, my mouth open with a silent cry. The heat sizzled through my nerve endings.

"Shhhh," he whispered right by my ear, moving his finger in and out of me. "So fucking wet. Sucking me in. I can imagine what you would do with my cock inside of you."

"Mason…ohgod," I choked out, imagining it. "So good."

Then he added a second finger, pumped them in deeper, rougher, letting his palm rub my clit with every thrust of his fingers. Harder. Faster. My hips curled to meet the penetration, the need to come taking over every thought, the singe of pleasure scorching me from the inside out.

"Yes, yes, yes, ohgod, ohgod, ohgod, Mason!" His free hand covered my mouth the moment I exploded. The electrical charge that surged through my body curled my toes first before shooting up my entire body until I was crying out into his cupped hand. My pussy spasmed around his fingers that were wringing every pleasurable convulsion from me until I collapsed back onto him feeling comfortable. Satiated.

And free.

"Sweet girl," he whispered against my ear, letting his hand drop from my mouth. My breath was still coming out in trembling puffs. "I love making you feel good, too."

There was no hint of panic or fear tainting this experience, making me feel queasy with a fight-or-flight response. Maybe Brady's hold on me, on the inside, where he'd still been able to reach me, was finally gone.

A surge of elation warmed my heart.

We remained there in Mason's chair. I was curled up in his lap with my face resting in the hollow of his neck, my finger drawing random shapes on his firm chest. He was absently toying with the end of my ponytail. It was a silence that was both comfortable and filled with a sense of tenderness. Somehow, this didn't feel like the casual hookup that we'd agreed to. It had felt like… more.

That realization came with a hint of fear.

What was this? What were we doing? Was I setting myself up for another downfall? I knew I trusted him, but did I want anything more? A few weeks ago, I would have been adamantly against the idea. Now, I wasn't sure.

The only thing I knew for certain was that I wanted to keep seeing him, being with him, talking with him, sharing these kind of intimate moments with him. This felt like a connection. This was the answer to the question that I'd asked myself after leaving Brady: Why would anyone subject themselves to the imposition of another's will? And now I had a fledgling of an understanding. There didn't have to be an imposition of will. There could be a partnership, an agreement that everyone had to be okay with what was happening. One person did not have to control the entire relationship.

Was it all right to admit that I liked this?

CHAPTER 15

MASON

There was all kinds of wrong in having Layla curled up like a contented kitten, but I ignored the feeling because I'd be damned if I was going to end this…whatever this was, something I refused to analyze or label in this moment for fear of ruining it.

But the pull…the draw felt magnetic. She fit me, like a second puzzle piece that I didn't know was missing. I didn't want to be parted from her.

There was a single sharp rap on the door.

When Layla would have scrambled from my lap, I pulled her closer, letting my hands speak for me. I ran soothing, kneading fingers over the shape of her thigh, outlining her delicate hip bone with my thumb, tracing the firm muscles of her abdomen, and back down. Her sigh was a soft, contented sound in my ear. My dick twitched with interest. She was practically purring under my touch while I responded absently with, "Yes?"

"We're officially closed, the checklist is done, and I can lock up on my way out," Amanda called through the door.

If the gym was now closing, that meant we'd been in here for over an hour. I hadn't even realized the time passing so swiftly, but I wasn't surprised. Keeping Layla close satisfied a weird, protective need I had for her. From the first moment of seeing her, it had grown stronger. That, and she fit up against me perfectly. Soft. Gentle. Necessary.

"Great. Thanks," I answered Amanda.

"And, Zeke just showed up. Said he wants to talk to you."

That got my attention.

Layla's head swiveled back to see me; her brow arched as she recognized what this moment might mean to me. Maybe it was foolish, but it was like I could already feel her energy reaching out to me, stroking me, encouraging me. I could drown in the sweet blue depths of her gaze.

"Zeke? He's here?" I called out as though to

clarify, but in reality, needing time to process.

"Yeah. You want me to tell him you're busy?"

Layla shook her head earnestly and whispered, "You need to talk to him. I'll go get cleaned up and give you guys some space."

After a moment, I nodded back and called out, "Tell him I'll be right out."

The moment she scooted off my lap, it felt cold and empty. I frowned, realizing how much farther this had gone than I'd been ready for. There was no way this could end well, but a sense of bewildering helplessness gripped my chest. Stuck betwixt and between. I didn't want to go back, but I had no idea how to go forward.

"See you here tomorrow?" She smiled up at me, readjusting her clothes. For the most part, she was put back together, but there were still tells. Her lips were slightly puffy, and her ponytail was a bit off-center with more strands dancing along her jawline, having been pulled out of the holder.

My dick jerked again remembering my fist around that hair, directing it around my cock. Deep breath. I needed to calm my shit if I was going to have a serious conversation with Zeke, but I couldn't seem to completely separate from her.

Even if it was only for a few more minutes, I wanted to keep her by my side before I forced myself to confront the reality of our situation.

There was no way I could ever risk hurting her. She was too important.

Noting that I'd been staring at her for the last several seconds, she cocked her head in question. Fucking adorable.

"I want you to meet Zeke," I stated, coming to a decision.

In the way that was becoming so familiar, she searched my face, looking for some kind of meaning or reason for my request, interpreting something unknown to me that must have been written in my expression before saying, "Okay. I'd like that. Do I look okay?"

"You look beautiful."

She flushed a faint pink with the compliment, ducked her head for a second, like she wasn't used to hearing nice things said to her. "Mason..." But she didn't know what else to say and simply shook her head with a faint smile tickling her lips.

"You ready?"

She ran a quick hand over her hair and clothing.

"Ready."

Zeke was leaning on the counter, his hands braced there as though holding himself up tiredly. If I wasn't absolutely sure the office might smell of sex, I would have taken him there. His eyes were moist, his face tense when I came around the corner. "Mason."

"Zeke, you need a chair?"

"I'm not a fucking baby," he groused, even though I rolled a chair from behind the desk. That's when he caught sight of Layla. "Oh…I'm sorry."

"For what?" she asked, a grin stretching her cheeks and making her eyes sparkle.

Damn she was pretty. It was hard to concentrate.

Then she added with a wink, "You're not a baby."

He grunted and sat, but there was a flash of humor in his eyes when he sat back and looked up at us, leaning an elbow on the counter.

"Zeke, this is Layla. She's my…" I wasn't sure what to call her. For a split second, there was a pause, but quickly, I recovered and said, "She's a member here. Layla—"

"Zeke," she was already approaching, bending just a little bit to reach out a hand. He took it in both of his. "I've heard so much about you."

He grimaced, grunted. "Well, I'm a bastard, sure, but I can do better. I promise." He was really talking to me when he said that, and I nodded.

Layla scoffed, "I heard you do wonderful things to help others during their hardest times. I'm glad. Sometimes, people need help and don't think anyone cares."

He muttered his response, something that sounded like the tone of a "thanks" without actually saying the word.

"He does." I nodded. "And there's still more to be done. Jay, one of my morning guys, hasn't shown up all week. I think he's going through some shit right now, and it doesn't look good. Can I get you to go with me to his place tomorrow?"

Zeke nodded. "I can do that. After."

"After?"

"After my treatment."

My throat tightened for a second. Then I nodded. "Sounds good. You need help with that?"

"Naw. I'm good."

"All right, then."

Layla beamed a brilliant smile my way, her eyes looking shiny with emotion. "I'll leave you guys to the details. I'll get cleaned up and grab my stuff. It was nice meeting you, Zeke, and I'll see you tomorrow?" She looked up at me.

Without letting myself think on it, I slid a hand around her neck and pressed a gentle kiss to her lips, more because I needed to feel her one more time, answer the pull that was perpetually there. When I pulled back, her eyes were wide. Searching mine again.

"Be safe," I murmured.

She nodded. "I will."

CHAPTER 16

LAYLA

By the time I finished a quick shower and got all my stuff together, Mason and Zeke were no longer at the front counter.

If I was being honest with myself, I'd half hoped he might join me in the shower again. His large, rough hands being so gentle with me was good therapy for both mind and body. The more he was with me, large and imposing with his height and muscles, and yet thoughtful and kind, was retraining my brain to accept that not all big men equaled damage.

At the same time, I knew it was likely better to get some space. I had things to think about after being with him today.

The lobby was empty when I came out of the

locker room. It looked like Zeke had left, and Mason was probably back in his office closing up. I wasn't ready to confront my feelings again just yet, so I decided to leave. Pushing through the glass door that had been left unlocked for me, I dug through my bag, double-checking that I had my phone and key ring somewhere within the bottomless recesses. I was thinking, not for the first time, that I needed a better system or a different bag.

It took a moment of standing there dumbfounded, staring at the empty bike rack, swiveling a quick look all around as though maybe I'd gone to the wrong bike rack, before the reality set in.

It was gone.

My heart squeezed with disappointment and anger. I hung my head, needing a moment to gather my thoughts. Who in the heck would have wanted my bike? It was a piece of junk I'd bought from a secondhand store. Why would they bother?

"Missing something?"

My head snapped up at the disembodied voice in the darkness. I saw the new employee, Greg, standing off in the shadows, leaning up against the building, watching me. The hair on the back of my neck stood up. It struck me suddenly how dark it was, how little light fell on this side of the building, how few people were around the strip mall after everything was closed down.

I was essentially alone.

Greg usually had a smirk on his face. It was his default expression, like he found the world to be something laughable and beneath him, but he looked different tonight. He was breathing heavier, his eyes completely focused on me, and mean, like he was looking for a confrontation. A silent cry scratched at the inside of my throat. My skin prickled with the beginning of panic.

I knew that look on his face too well. It was an evil look. I'd managed to escape it by leaving my ex, but I'd never forget it.

Old survival strategies were never far away. I tried to keep my voice steady, not give away the fact that my stomach was clenching, my muscles were tensing, and I was white knuckling the set of keys in my hand. "Yeah. It looks like my bike is gone."

He started walking toward me with very deliberate, casual steps, a smile twisting one side of his mouth. "Maybe I could help you find it."

"No, it's all right. I can call an Uber." As much as I wanted to run, I felt like I was facing a feral animal. He would chase something that ran. No, the best bet was to work my way back into the building. Yell for Mason.

"It seems like I saw it around here." He chuckled, coming a few steps closer before pausing, still a half a dozen feet away. I fought the urge to back away. I didn't want to show that I was scared. It would be like waving blood in front of a shark.

That's what he reminded me of. There was something in his eyes. It was a flash of knowledge, a glint of cruelty, a holding of his breath in anticipation, like he was excited to play this cat and mouse game with me, that warned me he had something to do with my bike's disappearance. I was sure of it. I'd become an expert of physical tells when someone was about to hurt me in some way. That was what I'd taken away from my relationship with Brady.

The trick was to keep things calm. Cool.

Fear squeezed my heart, but I took a breath. Forced a faint, regretful smile.

"It's all right. These things happen. Thanks, but I can get Mason..." I slid my hand in my bag, cursing the state of mass disorganization that kept me from being able to find my phone with quiet stealth.

"Mason, Mason. You sound pretty cozy with him."

"We're friends."

"I can be your friend. I could give you a ride. My friend will be here any moment." He suddenly moved toward me again, and though I didn't want to look weak by stepping back, I didn't see any alternative.

A wash of helplessness poured over me. My phone was somewhere at the bottom of this stupid bag. I couldn't find it. Would Mason hear me if I screamed? The walls were thick. Were they soundproof?

"No!" I said forcefully, backpedaling a step, my hand up as though to stop him. It was trembling.

"What's wrong?" He paused, a grin spreading his lips wide, like he was feeding off my fear. His tongue slid out to swipe over his bottom lip, and the way his eyes took a walk over my body felt obscene. His next words confirmed it. "I thought you liked dick, sweetheart."
"What?" My heart was hammering up high in my throat. I stumbled back a few more steps toward the doors, not wanting to turn my back on him.

"Dick," he said with deliberate emphasis on the consonants. He advanced a few more steps, closing the gap between us. My thoughts raced, unable to settle on what to do. He added, "You like the boss's, don't you?"

"I don't know what you're talking about." Why was he doing this? He was trying to intimidate me, which meant he was either a bully or actually going to hurt me.

Where was Mason? There were a dozen steps between me and the front door. Could I make a run for it?

"I heard you in the locker room a few days ago. He was giving it to you hard, wasn't he?" Then he pulled a pair of panties from his pocket. The familiar pair that had gone missing from my gym bag. I'd left all my sweaty clothes in a plastic bag right on top of the bench.

He stuck his nose in them and took an exaggerated sniff, sighing with pleasure before shoving them back into his pocket again.

Horror held me frozen in place. "Oh my God. That was you? You grabbed my…"

"The back door was still unlocked. I heard you loud and clear." He mocked a high-pitched cry, but

I was too afraid to be embarrassed. "Singing so pretty. Will you do that for me?"

Backing up a few more steps, I yelled, "You're sick. Stay away from me."

"I can give it to you good. I know my friend wants to give it to you. There he is now."

A pair of bright lights suddenly swung wide coming so fast from the street entrance that it rocked with the force of the turn. Its motor revved loudly before coming to a screeching halt at the curb in front of the gym doors.

Taking him by surprise, I spun to rush the door, but I didn't get more than a few steps before he caught my arm in a hard grip and swung me around.

"Don't be in such a hurry," he snarled, crushing me to his chest, trying to get hold of my hands.

"Get off me!" I shouted, shoving at his chest, struggling to keep my hands free, but he was too big. My bag fell to the floor. I screamed, "Mason!" Greg pressed his body to mine, lifted me off my feet to shove me toward the black car. His lips were near my ear when he snarled, "Your fucking boyfriend fired me this morning."

"Mason!" I screamed again, kicking at his shins, and trying to shove myself away from him. "Leave me alone!"

"Shut the fuck up!"

But his hands were busy trying to secure me, so I screamed over and over again, desperation making my voice loud and shrill, fighting to twist away from him until suddenly, he was gone.

The black car shot away in a massive engine roar.

"Hey!" Greg shouted, scrambling up from the ground. "I was only fucking around."

But he didn't get to say more when Mason's fist smashed into his face, the horrible sound of flesh pounding flesh loud in the stillness of the night. Greg fell to the ground when his gut caved in with the force of Mason's kick.

Mason's voice sounded like death when he ground out through clenched teeth, "Stupid prick. Try finding a job from prison!"

The scream of sirens slit through the chaos.

"She likes dick. What can I say?" Greg taunted, spitting blood on the ground, and giving an evil grin. "She was all over me, begging for it."

CHAPTER 17

MASON

A primitive need to destroy churned in my guts like an angry, seething monster.

"She was all up on my dick, begging me for it, making moves on me. I didn't do a fucking thing wrong. The girl fucking loves dick. How come she comes on to me, and I go to jail? That's the most fucked up shit I've ever heard," Greg snarled, running his mouth. "Why else do you think I have her panties? She gave them to me."

Layla gasped, hearing his words, her body going stiff against mine. She was shaking her head almost violently whispering, "No."

"Don't listen to him, baby," I said against her temple, fighting to keep the rage out of my voice while holding her to my chest like she was about to get yanked away from me. She had a death grip on two fistfuls of my sweatshirt like she was never letting go, which was a big part of what kept me from charging with the ferocity of a bull seeing red.

She needed me.

Realizing he had our attention, Greg's snarl turned into a sneer. Even as the cops cuffed him and shoved him up against the cop car to pat down his pockets, he taunted, "She moans so pretty when you're fucking her, doesn't she? And when she comes, she screams like a wild animal."

"Quiet down!" one of the officers commanded.

With the hot surge of fury pounding viciously through my veins, I was ready to go Hulk stomp the motherfucker until he was comatose despite the cops being present. I stuffed the reaction, but I still couldn't contain the growl that seemed to come from deep inside.

"Oh my God," Layla whispered in a voice aching with embarrassment, letting go of me so she could bury her crimson face in her hands until the officers came to her for questioning, which did nothing to quell the restless anger that sent a charge through my veins, keeping me tense.

Then she'd stepped away from me, out of my

reach, when there was a threat sitting just feet away. It left me with disturbing panic and unreasonable anger. I kept pacing, keeping an eye on her and an eye on him, developing that tunnel vision thing again. I wasn't going to let anything more happen to her. I couldn't fail someone I cared for again. I couldn't, or I was going lose my shit.

As it was, I took deep, even breaths, counted backward from twenty, and reminded myself that she was fine. I'd gotten to her before they could take her.

This time, the words whispered through my mind, spiking another slash of fear through my gut. Even knowing that she was fine, my heart suddenly pounded like I'd just done a quarter-mile sprint. I was getting light-headed.

But she was all right. She hadn't blown up. She wasn't in pieces. Pieces.

The flash of memory came without warning.

The men were roasting each other, innocent, unknowing, believing that I'd done my job. They had no clue I'd missed something.

Words shouted in another language, the urgency catching us a millisecond before the ear-shattering explosion went off.

My breath was now shallow. I was panting, ready to hyperventilate.

Where was she? I needed her.

She was still with the cop.

I needed to see her face. Dive into the calm blue waters of her eyes. Sink into their depths and trust her to hold me there until my mind could be whole again, until the voices of the dead drifted back into the abyss of my dark memories that roiled from all I'd seen and experienced, that I still couldn't let myself think about much less talk about.

The tunnel vision was shrinking down, darkening the world outside my scope. When it came on this suddenly, it was sometimes the symptom right before I lost consciousness. Sweat sheened my face, cooling with the night breeze.

"Layla," I rasped almost silently, barely recognizing my own voice. Just in time, the cop finished with her. Layla made her way back to my side, her arms hugging her middle, her eyes trained on her shoes.

The panic attack eased off a bit simply because she was next to me, except she was now maintaining emotional distance, looking away, off toward the mountains. Her eyes were hidden from me. She was giving me her shoulder, her wavy hair now mostly dry after her shower, falling in soft waves down her back.

She'd put up a wall that clearly said "don't touch."

What was going on?

What was she thinking?

Why wasn't she looking at me?

My airways relaxed enough to let me breathe, but my heart still pounded with a fierce determination. This was my fault. I'd let her down.

I needed to talk with her, but I couldn't. The fucking cops were exacting in their investigation, which was good, but it was keeping me on the fulcrum of a scale, seesawing back and forth with threatening anxiety.

We spent another half hour answering questions and going over the security tape when I almost lost my shit all over again. It was like there was a perpetual growling animal trying to work its way from deep inside, and it wanted to smash something. Clearly, the douche had been waiting for her to come out before preying on her. He'd damaged the bike to get it off the lock, then hid it around the corner of the building before relaxing with his cigarette against the wall.

The black car showed up, but it was at the wrong angle to see the fucking license plate, and fuckwit Greg denied knowing anything about a black car at all, laughing about it to our faces.

"When he gets charged with kidnapping, he'll change his tune," one of the officers told Layla, his face grim. She'd simply nodded, giving the officer the same tight smile she'd begun giving me. I sensed her fear, felt her nervous glances.

"If you think of anything else, give me a call," was the final instruction given by the last of the cops that lingered. His was now the final of three cop cars still parked in the lot throwing red and blue light against our faces.

When Layla remained silent, hidden a few steps behind me, I nodded. "We will."

"My card." The officer cast a worried glance over my shoulder toward Layla. "Make sure she's all right. If she needs to talk to anyone, we can offer some numbers to call."

"Thanks." I took it and waved him off as he got in his car, shut off the flashing lights, and eased down the road.

I couldn't take the distance anymore. I spun

around and confronted her, staring down at her until she finally met my gaze. Wary blue eyes were so big and round, they dominated her face.

"I'm taking you to my place," I stated, my voice gruff and uncompromising like it was a command. I realized I was coming across kind of caveman-like but wasn't able to help it. "You can't be on your own tonight. Let me take care of you. I have a spare room."

Her eyes glittered with unshed tears, but she still held herself back. I thought I could detect a tremor, like she was still shaking with either the shock or the chill, but she obviously didn't want to be touched, and it was ripping me up inside. "I should go home. I have work tomorrow."

"This was fucking traumatic, Layla. You should call in sick and take a rest day." I wanted her to talk to me. Tell me what was going on in her mind. Share this with me. Let me in. But she stayed remote, and I didn't know how to reach out.

"I don't know."

I'd agreed to her non-engagement rules, non-emotion rules that in reality couldn't be followed. Fuck the rules. Tonight changed everything. I knew I was coming on strong, but it was for me as much as it was for her.

"Do you really want to be alone?" I scrubbed my hands through my hair in frustration. "I can't fucking believe this happened. And who the hell was the guy in the car?"

She was so vulnerable. No defense skills. What would have happened if I hadn't been on my way out, which was the real terror that kept my body unsettled, wasn't it? Revved. On alert. Looking for more danger.

I needed to teach her some shit. Simple defense moves. Make her safer in the world. How the hell was I going to keep her safe from the fucking world? So many fucking ways to die. She was so soft and vulnerable. Her big blue eyes were too trusting and invited the bad guys in.

"Please," I managed, barely able to soften my tone.

"Um…" She looked down at her feet, then away toward the boulevard. She let her eyes trail the cars as they drove by, people seated behind the wheel ignorant of the fact that something dark and threatening had nearly become a tragedy right here in front of my business.

I locked on to her expressive eyes, could almost hear the back-and-forth argument going on in her mind. She ran a distracted hand over the top of her hair, smoothing away loose tendrils from in front of her face.

I didn't realize I was holding my breath until she nodded, looking down at her shoes, and said, "Um…Okay."

CHAPTER 18

LAYLA

"Are you all right?"

"I'm fine." I said it automatically, keeping my voice soft and steady, not wanting to cause further issue. I'd already watched Mason prowl the exterior of the crime scene like a feral animal, fists ready to pound flesh, one second away from attacking. He was so big, so strong, and the way he'd clenched his jaw nearly the entire time, a muscle ticking rhythmically right at his jawline, had kept me silent.

I was an expert at reading body language. It was a survival tool. You had to notice the details to know what was about to come and how best to handle it.

For now, if I was quiet, I wouldn't draw attention to myself.

Mason was simmering with irritation or maybe even anger that he'd had to jump into the fray and save me. I knew he was going to turn passive aggressive and start cross-examining me when we got to his place.

His place.

What was I thinking? I was smarter than this. The rules were there for a reason. We'd agreed. Nothing personal. But here I was going to his place.

My heart started beating erratically. Cold sweat gave me an overly warm, clammy feel, even with the November chill in the air. My thoughts began spinning too fast to grab a single one.

The world was back to feeling off-kilter in a way I hadn't felt for a long time. Memories, past and present, mixed together to create a confusing, whirlwind of feelings. The healthy strategies I'd worked so hard to learn, so I could hold off those images of past horrors, had deserted me, left me exposed and vulnerable.

Helpless.

Painfully vivid flashbacks of another time when I was completely helpless, of Brady stalking me in our old house, menacing, using his size to frighten and his intellect to manipulate, played behind my eyes. Tears of worthlessness over his cruel words and heartless behavior were a permanent scar on my soul. The terror of believing I was still stuck in that nightmare continued to have the power to wake me gasping for air, leave me trembling for the rest of a night. There had been too many nights of crying over heartfelt wishes that withered away and died on the vine because Brady never found joy in me, in who I was.

But who had I been? My eyes burned as the answer readily popped up.

He was always there in my mind, his frightening voice, more than ready to tell me about who I was. Too often, his words were mean, vicious, soul-killing and implanted right where they could stab at me over and over again.

No money. No job. No education. No skills. No real family to speak of. That's who you are, Layla. You're lucky I'm still with you. You'd be out on your ass if not for me. You better be good for something around here. Now wait for me upstairs.

Trapped. Weak. Pathetic.

What was I doing here with Mason? In his car? He looked so mad. Why did I get in his car?

Memories spilled out unfiltered, and now my

body was on red alert. Ready to jump and run. Hit the gas pedal with both feet and never look back. Flight. Illogical fears had me jumping at the shadows in my mind, seeing danger everywhere I looked. Knowing that the chaos in my mind was unreasonable didn't stop the spiral. I had to fight the tears that clogged my throat as we drove under city lights, hating with a vengeance that dark voice in my head that was always ready to provide the abuse I'd grown accustomed to.

When would it stop? When would it lose its power over me? I thought I was healed. I thought that episode in my life was finally over, in my rearview mirror forever, but here I was reliving the horror of it all again, flashes of moments, his voice, his face, overwhelming feelings of despair.

Because I was weak. I was too afraid to ask the real question I needed answered. *Was Mason blaming me for this?* So I answered for him. Of course he was. I was blaming myself, so why wouldn't he?

I curled up against the door of the Jeep and rode the frightening mental roller-coaster in silence. It left me careening dangerously around the sharp corners with unanswered questions.

The what.

The why.

Some guy tried to kidnap me. Take me away to, what? Rape me? Kill me? So crazy, but things happened for a reason, right? Nothing happened out of the blue. There was usually a causal chain to follow. I sat with that hollow feeling in the pit of my stomach wondering how this found me. What did I do wrong this time?

How did I cause this?

But I didn't really think I had, did I? I'd learned better than this, right? But would Mason agree?

It was Brady who always twisted things, so they were my fault in the end. The good times were fleeting but were enough to keep me hooked, hoping for more, yearning for the happy times when Brady was kinder, when he smiled, when he approved of what I was doing, none of which was all that frequent. What was the lesson here? Don't become emotionally invested. The good times never lasted long.

And I had no reason to believe otherwise with Mason.

"Are you sure you're okay?" His words were slightly louder, more curt. Gruff. He sounded like gravel skidding under tires, and my fears were confirmed. He was angry. I should have walked home or gotten a ride from the officers. I needed to get out of his way.

To answer his question, I nodded and gave a brief affirmative sound that wasn't actually born into a word, a tilt of my head in his direction, a small, forced smile that felt stiff, but never made eye contact with him. "You know, I'm fine. I can go home."

I felt more than saw the frown he sliced in the dark space between us before he challenged, "Maybe I'm not."

I wasn't sure what that meant, but it did little to calm the whirling dervish building speed and momentum in my stomach. This was my warning system telling me to brace myself for things to come. The push and pull between fear and longing twisted in my gut.

While one voice in my head reminded me that Mason isn't Brady, another pointed out that I'd also thought Brady was a good man at one time.

I cared about Mason too much at this point.

Would he end up being my downfall?

How was I going to get out of this?

There wasn't enough time to calm the footrace of clumsy chaos in my mind before we pulled into his short driveway, and then it was like the gates were closing in behind me with a clang, cutting off escape. The tremors started, first in my hands. I balled them into fists, crossed my arms, and hid them in my pits, trying to make it look like I was cold.

If he noticed, he would say something scornful about how weak or stupid I was, wouldn't he? Maybe not. I wasn't sure. I couldn't trust my own decisions. I'd made so many bad ones in the past.

So, I sat frozen in silence, paralyzed in mind and body, a prisoner to nightmares of another time and place. Waiting for the attack. When was it going to come?

"This is it," he muttered, the mood grim.

I glanced around.

Located near "the strand," his home was just a couple of short blocks inland from where the water crashed up on the shore at Hermosa Beach. The sound was accompanied by the cool, sweet smelling breeze coming off the ocean. For a moment, the gentle feel of the elements had an arresting effect, letting me take a breath and exit the car without becoming a hyperventilating mess.

This was the first time I'd gone to another man's house where we would be alone together since I'd snuck away from Brady so long ago. It would be just the two of us.

A short path led to a small, two-story beach cottage with what looked and smelled like night-blooming jasmine growing over a wooden pergola in front of the door. It was the scent of my shampoo. Calming. I was able to take another deep breath.

"After you," Mason murmured, pushing the door open.

Expecting to find a bachelor pad, I was surprised to walk into a large, airy living area covered with gleaming dark wood floors. Wooden beams ran the length of the ceiling, and there were windows everywhere. With the open floor plan, I could see a cozy kitchen and dining nook folded into the far end of the room. Right in front of me was a cushiony sectional that invited sitting in front of a warm fire in the fireplace while watching a movie on the big screen TV just above it.

"It's beautiful," I offered, looking around with wide eyes. A home with personality. Bookshelves and artifacts, some vibrant art on the different walls. Inviting.

"Thanks." He paused to look around as though seeing it in a different way. His expression softened. "I put a lot of work into this place, and my mother made suggestions for design and decoration. My sister is the artist."

Mother. Sister. Family.

They were likely lovely and polished, full of the right kind of culture, if this place was anything to go by. They'd expect him to connect with someone like them when he was ready to settle down and have kids. Someone like Malibu Barbie. They wouldn't be expecting me.

I blocked the urge to laugh. If they ever knew...if Mason ever knew the tragic life I'd lived, existing in a desperate kind of poverty, he'd run for the hills. Who was I kidding? This thing between us wasn't going anywhere, not that I was looking for that. No way. Ever.

Absently, I rubbed my hand over my chest, feeling a sudden ache.

"There's a bathroom down that hallway just beyond the kitchen, and there's one upstairs," he said, shoving his hands in his pockets with a rough impatience.

Then there was the awkward moment with him

standing there watching me. I didn't know what he wanted from me, so I fell back on old habits. I smiled, tried to calibrate the mood so as not to make the smile too big, just enough to let him see the bright, happy face I could make, so maybe I could help him forget his frustration with me.

"Your mom has great taste."

He watched me for a quiet moment, eyes narrowing, searching my face intently, not buying what I was selling any more than Brady did, which whipped the brewing storm of my psyche up another notch on the crisis level. DEFCON 3.

"Thanks. Are you hungry?" he asked.

I was quick to shake my head. "No, I'm fine."

He frowned down at me. "Did you eat dinner?"

"Well, no, but…"

"I'll cook something," he offered, taking a few steps toward the kitchen.

"Please, don't. I don't need anything," I insisted. I'd never had any man cook for me. I was always the one who'd been required to stay on top of all things within the house. Having to cook for me would only make him madder.

He scowled, his irritation returning. "You can't go without eating."

"I'm just not hungry." I didn't want him to be angry with me. Not him. Not Mason.

"But you will be. It's no big deal." His words were clipped, like he was spitting them out. Then he was striding again toward the kitchen, and I followed quickly.

"No, really. I'm f—"

"Don't tell me you're fine." He grabbed a pot from a rack hanging over the stove, the metal clanging on the burner when he set it down too roughly. I startled, the noise jarring my already revved nervous system.

This was it. The attack was here.

The churning in my gut was growing into a twister telling me to get out. Go home. Close the door behind me and lock it.

My eyes burned with the pressure building up inside me.

"Mason, really, I am."

He was glaring when he said, "You're not. I can see it. You just aren't talking about it. Why the hell aren't you talking to me?"

"Please, just let this go," I pleaded.

"He fucking attacked you!"

"I know."

"He almost got you in the car."

"I know, but—" I could feel my voice getting smaller, the emotion balling tighter in my chest and throat until it felt like I was suffocating with it. Everything was constricted.

"There's no way you are fine. I almost lost you tonight!"

"Mason, please," I choked on my words, losing the battle on my emotions.

"Why won't you let me—"

"I don't want to be—"

"—fix this!"

"—an imposition!"

And that's when the dam broke. I couldn't hold back the tears as they welled hotly in my eyes and spilled down my cheeks.

"Fuck. I'm so sorry," his deep voice turned

gentle immediately. Soft and warm like a blanket, his tone more than his words wrapped themselves around me. His chin dropped, and he propped his hands on his hips, as though he were the one who'd done something wrong.

It only made me cry harder and turn away, rejecting this, because I couldn't trust it as much as I wanted to. Apologies were segues into why I was wrong. Why I was at fault. I wiped at my face, taking a few deep breaths. I needed to shore my strength for what was to come.

I couldn't wait for the attack a single moment more. I needed it out. Done. Gone.

I decided to save him the trouble and argue for my innocence preemptively. Swiping a hand over my eyes only to have more tears leak like I had a broken valve left me shrinking into the old me. Failing miserably. Not enough. Unable to stand up straight and tall and with my chin up. Instead, my stupid sniveling voice was pathetic when I whispered, "I didn't lead him on. I swear."

"Of course you didn't," he said in a firm tone. Turning back to him, I mostly saw the scowl on his face and backed off another step.

"I was just trying to get my bike and go home."

"He was a fucking piece of shit, Layla. I'm sorry I ever hired the bastard."

"And I know you and I had just been together in an intimate way, but I didn't tell him I wanted him. He just started being aggressive, and I didn't know what to do. I swear I don't know why he would say those things about me!"

"Layla—" The scowl gave way to outrage and confusion, his dark brows meeting at the bridge of his nose.

"And I'm so sorry you had to defend me." My words were coming more quickly, my pitch getting higher.

"Baby—"

"He just picked me up and there was nothing I could do." My sentence ended with my voice cracking, my breath coming from between my parted lips with quick sharp pants, in and out.

"I know. The memory of seeing you getting carted off, hearing your screams, is going to haunt me." Like he could no longer hold himself back, he stepped the few feet across the space and pulled me into his arms. Hard muscle scooped me gently close as he shoved his face into my neck, taking a deep breath. "I can't apologize enough. I'm so, so sorry."

Wait. What?

"Why are you apologizing? I'm the one who did this," I protested. I knew it didn't make sense, because I didn't cause it, but I was so used to shouldering blame.

"What are you talking about? You didn't do anything wrong. I should have insisted on driving you from the beginning. None of this would have happened."

"You drive me? Every day?"

"Of course! And that's what's going to happen from now on. There's no way I'm letting you ride alone when it's late."

He wasn't mad at me? He was worried?

"That's silly," I offered with a hesitation in my voice, feeling a relief so acute it was making me emotional all over again. "I've been riding my bike around here all along."

"It's always more dangerous at night when fewer people are around. When you started coming at night, I should have insisted on either driving you or following you or…I don't know…something. I don't blame you for being pissed at me. I should have seen that guy for what he was from the beginning. There were warning signs. I'm sorry, sweet girl." He pulled back to look down at me again, cup his big, warm hand against the side of my neck. His thumb caressed the skin under my ear comfortingly.

He was upset but not with me. With himself.

He blamed himself. I didn't have words for a moment like this. I didn't have strategies for emotional protection. I kept looking for emotional handholds and footholds while I felt myself falling, felt the tenderness that grew in my heart while looking into his tortured steel eyes, but there was nothing to cushion the free fall.

No one had ever apologized to me in my life and meant it.

"So, so sorry," he bent to whisper in my ear, a catch in his deep voice. "You were almost hurt because of me. I would never have forgiven myself."

"No. That's not…" I took a deep breath and cupped his head to where he'd buried his face in my neck once again because it felt right having him there. I let my fingers sift through his soft hair. "You can't be in charge of the world, and that includes me and that jerk."

"I need to trust my gut instinct. I had a feeling

about that guy."

"I thought you were angry."

His lips opened on my neck planting a soft kiss that made me shiver. "You weren't talking to me the entire way home. It was freaking me out." He planted more kisses, tender kisses, tasting kisses, nipping at the skin before his lips were back at my ear. "I wasn't kidding when I said I need you. There's something about you. I don't know, but you ground me. Just looking at you, being with you, touching you. It does it for me."

He needed me. There was something special about me. That was my crack. Right there. That and the shivery sensations that were skating over my skin, making me shiver and move closer, naturally seeking more from him. Our bodies fit so perfectly, which was surprising because he was so much bigger. Somehow, having him curled around me made me feel precious, whereas when Brady would put his arms around me, it left me feeling sick and anxious.

"And you were trying to make me eat," I sighed through a small grin, tilting my head so he could have better access to my sensitized skin, because having him there felt amazing. It was phenomenal that my body could so quickly be conditioned to recognize and respond to his touch. Swirls of heat fed off each other, amplified in a way I was becoming addicted to, spinning through the rest of my body until it was hard to think at all. "I can't eat when I'm upset."

Mason read me loud and clear. He scraped his scruff along the sensitive flesh, and I gasped with the sensation, feeling a quickening heat low in my belly. Already my arms were going around his neck, a moan easing from me with my body getting hotter. He took a nibbling bite of my lobe and admitted, "It was the only thing I could think of to take care of you. I was desperate."

"I was scared." My voice trembled, but with this addictive need, not with fear. I wanted all of him.

"Don't be scared, sweet girl. I won't let anything happen to you." He suddenly pulled back with his intense expression holding me still. "And you are sweet. Too sweet. Too nice. Too trusting. You need skills. There are ways to protect yourself from big bad guys, and I'm going to teach you. But first, I'd like to take you upstairs. If that's okay with you." The smoldering look was back, and his eyes dipped to my lips.

My body was vibrating with the need he'd created.

In answer to his question, I cupped the back of

his neck, pulled his head down, and whispered, "Yes," just before I kissed him.

The spark burned hot the moment our lips touched. Mason groaned, molding me to his warm, hard body. Tilting my head to just the right angle with a firm tug on my hair, he sucked at my lips, taking more of those naughty, nibbling bites that created relentless tingles of sensation to spiral down through my body. His rough whiskers scraped lightly over my bottom lip. I moaned with the pleasure/pain, and he drove his tongue in to seek my own, caressing me until we were both panting and kissing and desperate to taste and touch. Somehow, knowing that we were really doing this unleashed something untamed from the inside.

I shrugged out of his jacket.

He pulled his sweatshirt off.

Our lips fused again with a desperate sense of urgency. His hands cupped my breasts, thumbs circling my stiffened nipples through the fabric of my bra, and I cried out a hoarse sound into his mouth at the hot, liquid pleasure that concentrated in my pussy. I gasped and moaned against his lips. "Feels so good."

"Does it, baby?" He plucked at the hard peaks, pinching them, and I was panting and straining, arching into his hands, wanting all he could give me.

"Take this off," I pleaded, shoving his shirt up to have access to his lean flesh.

In a quick move, he yanked it over his head, letting me see the full range of his sculpted body, a body that made my mouth water. Then he pulled the straps of my bra down my arms. My breasts came free, plumped up above the material, ready and waiting for him.

"Sweet girl, these are mine. I dream about them," he murmured against my lips, his fingers already rubbing circles around the sensitized peaks. "So pretty. I want my mouth on them."

"Yes," I whispered back against his.

The moment his tongue and lips surrounded my nipple with molten heat, I cried out. It was like a live wire caused all my nerve endings to charge, and I couldn't get enough. My hands snuck around the back of his head, holding him there. He switched to my other nipple, and the pressure mounted. The feeling was so intense, I could have almost come from it alone.

"Mason! Oh my...oh my..."

"I've got you." He grinned, taking yet another

turn on the first breast.

Blood pounded with wild abandon, making the pulse between my thighs throb with its own demand for release until I was ready to climb up his body. Whimpering sounds of need escaped from my lips, and when he straightened up again, he pulled my legs around his hips with his hands supporting me by cupping and kneading my ass. He found just the right spot between my legs to titillate and torment me by grinding is rigid length there.

Then I was being tossed down onto a king-sized bed and he followed after me, parking his hips between my thighs, the weight and feel of him putting delicious pressure between my legs. Our upper bodies flesh to flesh was driving me mad.

"I need you inside me," I moaned.

"You need me here?" His hand cupped my pussy through my leggings and rubbed while delivering another hot, open-mouthed kiss. My hips rose to force more friction with his hand, and I mewled with the pleasure he was bringing me. When had this ever felt so good?

"Yes," I hissed.

"You need my cock to fill you up, sweet girl?"

"Please. I need you."

"You're so fucking wet. Right through the material. Soaked."

"You're so hard," I purred, cupping his thick cock through his denim and rubbing my hand up and down his length.

He sucked in a breath, letting me have my way, moving his hips so that he was pumping into my palm. I could feel his cock twitching and growing even bigger, but then he pulled away, saying, "I don't want this to end too soon. I still want to taste you. I've been thinking about having my mouth on you all day."

He grabbed the waistband of my leggings and pulled them, along with my underwear, down my legs, and tossed them off to the side. Then he spread my knees wide and simply stared, his eyes hungry. I was too far gone to be embarrassed or shy.

Mason reached out a hand and let his fingers sift through the moisture that had gathered, circling my opening before letting his middle finger slide in and swirl around. Then he bent over and had his mouth on me, his tongue pushing inside my core, his lips sucking on my clit. My fingers fisted the blanket beneath me, trying to hold on to something that would ground me. I felt like I was floating away. The pressure, the heat, the charge was growing stronger and stronger until I was barely making sense of my words, my legs closing around his head, my hips arching up against his face.

"Oh, god. Oh Mason. Oh, oh, oh…yes, yes, yes," I chanted, riding the edge, strung out on desire so potent I felt like I was elevating. When the orgasm hit, it rocked my body into a fetal position, curling inward. My body jerked with each wave of pleasure, and Mason kept it going. He licked at my juices and sucked on my clit until it was too much, and I had to push him away.

I'd never been so wet in my entire life.

"So fucking sweet," he said and leaned down to kiss me. I could taste myself there, and it was hot. He cupped me between my legs, letting his fingers rub through all the wetness that was nearly dripping from me while his tongue caressed mine. I was already writhing against his touch again when he pulled back to say, "I could do that all night."

"I want you inside me. I want to feel you there."

"Here?" He was kneeling between my legs, and I felt so wanton. His fingers were inside me again, and I was fucking them.

"Play with your nipples," he ordered, and it was natural for me to do just that. It was exhilarating that I had zero insecurities with Mason and that this was about both of us together. I plucked at my nipples, rubbed them and pinched at them, while meeting the thrust of his fingers, movement for movement. It wasn't enough.

"Mason, please," I cried, ready to demand more, but he was already pulling back to shed his jeans and grab a condom from the side drawer.

"I'll take care of you," he gritted, sheathing his length and taking a breath.

Then he was back between my legs, his cock jutting and heavy. He grabbed hold of my wrists with his big manacle hands. They were shackled right by the sides of my head. I couldn't move them.

Prickles of alarm cut through the sensual haze I'd been in.

I was trapped.

His big body pressed between my legs, his steel cock nudging my entrance.

I couldn't move. He was so heavy.

Alarm became fear, and I started pulling and tugging at my arms, remembering sharp, searing pain, remembering dire helplessness, seeing Brady above me, and I cried out. I slammed my eyes shut to block out the image, but it wouldn't go away.

Brady's smirk, the cruelty in his eyes, the need to see me submit to his authority.

Even if I was crying.

Even if he was hurting me.

"Layla—"

He was going to hurt me. I couldn't get the word out. I could only cry and shake my head, pulling at my arms and trying to draw my knees up to shove them into his chest, dislodge him. I scrambled out from under him until I was huddled on the edge of the bed turned away, ready to bolt. Hyperventilating.

"Layla. Baby. Did I hurt you? What happened?"

His words, so alarmed, so confused, broke through.

Made me pause. Open my eyes. Look around.

It was Mason's voice. He was concerned, not gloating.

"You didn't hurt me," I managed, barely making the words audible before smashing my face into the pillow.

That's when the wave of embarrassment washed over my entire body. My stomach churned with a sudden, sharp ache, and the tears fell with gasping whimpers escaping my throat.

Forever broken. That was me.

And here I thought I'd become so strong.

Why did I think I was anything other than where I came from?

Putting on my uppity pants, is what my mother had told me not long ago. She'd snorted with her laughter when I last spoke with her on the phone after she'd assured me that I wasn't any better than she was. *Stupid girl. You don't even realize how good you had it. Living in that nice place with a good-looking man. You need to stop all your silly dreams and look at who you are in this world. You're just like me.*

Was there no escape?

I realized I was still in Mason's room, on his bed, making a huge fool of myself yet again. What would he think of me now? I didn't want to stay and talk about it, so I muttered, "I'm sorry. I'll go."

I could call an Uber, get dressed in the bathroom, and get my tail home where I would be able to fall apart without a witness...but then I felt Mason slide his body behind mine, warm and comforting with skin-to-skin contact. My curiosity piqued, my tears quieted as I felt his movements behind me, trying to imagine what he was doing as the mattress dipped in different places. He managed to pull down the covers on his side of the bed, and before I knew it, he gently rolled me toward him, had me nestled in his arms with the warm blankets cocooning us.

After a moment of debate, feeling like the most ridiculous girl alive because my mind couldn't figure out what was right and what was wrong, if I should leave or go, I finally accepted his comfort.

Inhale. Deep and steady. I let my mind do the work I'd tried to teach it to do over the last year or more.

He wasn't Brady. *I* left *him*.

Exhale. I wanted this chance to be better. Take what I wanted. I wanted this.

My head came to rest on his chest. I swiped the last of the tears from my cheeks and sniffled.

He held me close. One hand was tangled in my hair, idly combing through the strands, his other was gently caressing a path that mapped my spine, fingertips finding and tracing each dip and hollow. His lips were pressed to my forehead, and I didn't think there was a better place to be.

I knew Mason. I could trust him. I could trust

myself. It was the strangest thing that I could go from being a weepy mess to feeling close. Cared for.

"Who hurt you, baby?"

CHAPTER 19

MASON

"I'm so, so sorry," Layla whispered, tilting her face back to gaze up at me, her dark lashes spiky with moisture.

The blue sea color of her eyes that I normally associated with a tranquil ocean on a warm sunny day was replaced by dark turbulent clouds. They were haunted with touches of hurt, fear, and shame. This emotion ran deeper than what had happened outside the gym with Greg. Someone had hurt her, and it didn't take much guesswork to realize this was her ex's doing, the same guy who was likely responsible for the creation of the rules she had me agree to when we started this thing between us.

Funny thing—I no longer wanted to abide by those rules. There was no way I could not have feelings for this girl, not that I knew what that might look like. I was still a fucking mess. Not fit for anyone, but I didn't know how to stay away from Layla.

Still, what I wouldn't give to have a piece of that bastard ex of hers. At some point, I hoped she would tell me, and in a perfect world, I would have time alone with this guy. It would be a moment of reckoning.

A few freckles dusted the bridge of her nose, but they were so light and few, they were easy to miss. I pressed a kiss there, unable to help paying homage to that spot on her face. It seemed fitting that each new discovery deserved special attention.

She closed her eyes. A kind of quiet, humming sigh sliding from between her parted lips. There was pleasure in letting my eyes memorize the lines of her face, heart-shaped with full lips that I could sink into and feast on, taking as much time as I needed to fully taste and mold and explore. But my favorite thing about her, what sucked me in and let me know all was right with the world, were her eyes. Her eyes were powerfully arresting with their pointed gaze that somehow challenged me to seek truth when I looked deeply into them.

I placed a soft kiss on each of her lids, then on the corners of her mouth, making a hint of a smile appear there. She was finding her footing again.

I held her small form cradled within the curve of my body, wondering how the fuck anyone could want to hurt her. Calming her had been like approaching a wounded animal that was cornered and needed to be finessed. She'd had her slender back turned to me, shaking, and her hair was suffocating her on the pillow.

Then I'd watched the panic fade with every calming stroke, watched as she made her decision whether to trust the situation. She'd been in full reactionary mode, fear-stricken, and now she was curled into my chest, looking up at me trustingly again.

I wanted to pummel a faceless man, but I bit back the rage, knowing she didn't need another angry male to deal with.

"There's nothing to apologize for." I brushed tendrils of hair from her face and brushed a light kiss on her soft lips. She clung to the contact, wanting to hold on, following me when I pulled back, but I didn't want to overwhelm her. I wanted her to have the time to feel right again.

Then she set her head back on the pillow, keeping her eyes locked to mine, and the connection snapped back into place.

It was her and me. The two of us.

"And yet, I keep apologizing, but I don't really want to talk about what just happened, if that's okay," she sniffed, then gave a short, deprecating chuckle, a faint eye roll accompanying the sound. "Let's just say I have issues and leave it at that. I don't want something ugly to be part of anything we do together."

"You don't want to talk about it?"

She shook her head. "But please know it's not about you. It's about me."

It was hard not to feel protective, and in feeling protective, I wanted to know who to kill for her. Again, not the best tactic when she was lying in my arms naked. "That's fine. If you don't want to talk, what do you want to do now?"

"This." She slid her delicate hand up between us until she could cup my jaw, run her thumb over my bottom lip. "I need this. Us. I need us to finish what we started here. I need this, Mason. I need to get past the freak-out and feel good."

"Are you sure? I don't want you to push yourself into something you aren't ready for." Taking a moment to search her face, all I could see was determination and a hint of shy yearning.

She whispered, "I'm still wet."

I felt my cock, which had gone semi-soft, become thick and full almost instantly. Just hearing those words, with my mind supplying vivid imagery, was making it hard to think.

"If you're sure." My tone was low and rough, as I thought about the things I wanted to do with her. That's when I pulled her thumb, which was still cupped near my lips, into my mouth. Her eyes grew round, and her breath hitched when I sucked on it, let my tongue rub against her flesh. With a hint of a smile of my own because I fucking loved how she responded to my touch, I put a growl to my voice when I asked, "Are you sure?"

"Most definitely," she breathed, her pupils dilating.

Her eyes flicked to my mouth. Her lips parted while she watched what I was doing to her digit, desire heating her gaze. I scraped my bottom teeth over the pad of her thumb. She gasped, pulling it back with a small shudder, and I grinned.

I could tell she felt my engorged cock against her stomach, because she gave me her own smile and let her free hand cup my shaft and squeeze it.

"Fuck," I hissed. "That feels so good."

"Is that so?"

"Yeah, it's so." I took another nibbling kiss from her bottom lip, used my thumb to tilt her chin down, and leisurely dipped my tongue in to play with hers, rubbing it, twining with it, deepening it with added pressure. I pulled away just out of reach as she was starting to run her fingers up into my hair. But there was something I wanted to say before I totally lost my mind to lust.

"You should also stop that."

Refocusing on my face with a dazed look of need, she asked, "Stop what?"

"Apologizing when you've done nothing to be sorry for."

"Oh," she nodded. "Okay."

Though I wasn't sure she'd fully processed my words, I couldn't hold back any longer. I dipped my head and played with her hardened nipples, rolling my tongue around one several times before sucking on it hard.

"Oh, Mason," she gasped and panted a few breaths, "do that again. Just don't...don't hold me down. Okay? I just... need to be able to move my arms."

"Whatever you want, sweet girl." I rubbed my tongue over the luscious tip, which had her chest rising and falling rapidly, her hips curling toward mine, wanting more. At the same time, I ran my fingers down through her short curls, feeling the moisture that was still waiting to be properly appreciated by my cock, and let my fingers find their way inside of her again, where they caressed the petal-soft walls of her channel.

"You make everything feel so good," Layla moaned. The sounds of her pleasure were coming faster. Breathless, she murmured, "Everything. Everything. Always so good."

I kept my fingers in her pussy and swirled them, first slow and easy, listening as her breath caught and then came out in short puffs. Then my fingers swirled harder and faster until her groans were sharp cries, her nails were digging into my shoulders, and she was begging me with desperate words.

"Oh god, oh god, oh god, please, please, please, oh Mason!" Her body bowed up on a harsh cry, her legs trapping my hand as her body jerked with the force of her orgasm.

I kept moving my fingers in and out of her slick channel, whispering in her ear, "I need to make your pussy happy, sweet girl."

"It is," she gasped out, still jerking against me, her hips continuing to move sensually with my hand, which had slowed again. "So happy."

With my lips on her ear, I murmured, "I want your pussy so happy with me that it gets wet automatically as soon as you see me. I want your pussy to know that when you see me, I'm going to take good care of her."

"Oh my god," she whisper-moaned, still coming down off her climax, her breath shaky.

I pulled my fingers out of her and used the moisture to coat the condom that was stretched over my throbbing dick, letting her watch me stroke my cock before I scooped her up and pulled her on top of me.

"What are you doing?" she asked, surprised, her legs falling to straddle my hips.

"Ride me, sweet girl. Take as much or as little as you want." When she didn't seem to follow, I added, "You be in control. Fuck me, Layla. I'm dying to be inside you. Haven't you watched a porn video where the girl was riding the guy?"

"Oh, yes," she replied, her lids going heavy. "That looked fun."

"Now it's your turn. What did the girl do in the

video?"

"Which one?" Layla grinned, but then she started moving her hips over my dick, gliding her pussy along the length of my cock, spreading her wetness all up and down the shaft. I could only grit my teeth and groan with the sensation of blood rush to my cock, loving the feel and sight of her right where she was.

With wild, dark hair tangled around her flushed face, softly rounded breasts that filled my hands perfectly, and a body that was both well-toned and soft, entirely feminine, she was a wet dream come to life. Then she was grasping me in her small grip, lining up my thick, pulsing head with her opening, and sliding down slowly, carefully, an inch at a time. She braced one hand on my chest for balance, seeming to savor the sensations.

Her lips were parted, breath suspended on a gasp. Her eyes were closed, head tilted back. Her breasts swayed with her movement, dusky-pink nipples swollen and begging for attention. She looked beautiful and sexy and like a goddess, taking me into her heat, her inner muscles squeezing me with almost painful pleasure. The moment I was fully sheathed, she tentatively moved her hips and moaned.

The fit was hot, and tight, and perfect.

Her eyes snapped open to look down at me with dazed surprise. My cock throbbed with the teasing motion, but I let her explore, doing my best to breathe through my natural instinct to thrust deep. She moved again, more definitively, lifting her hips and sliding her silken forge back down my shaft, rocking her hips forward, and we both gasped. The sharp edge of exquisite need was piercing.

"I never knew." She sounded breathed.

"Ride me, baby." My whispered words had a rough edge. "Please."

"Yes," she hissed, bracing both hands on my chest and lifting herself, slowly feeling her way through each downward thrust. My hands found her hips, helping her to maintain balance, grinding my teeth with each wave of intense pleasure rippling through my body. She was finding her rhythm, moving over me with sharp moans emphasizing each thrust, breasts taunting me with each bounce.

"Fuck, you're a sight," I growled and reached up, unable to deny myself any longer, to cup her breasts and rub her nipples with my thumbs, and she cried out with the added stimulation. She was trying to move faster.

"I want to feel you deep," she said, eyes pleading with me to make it happen.

"Like this?" I thrust up against her as she came down.

"Yes!" She cried out harshly, her face a mask of blissful desire. "Like that. Please."

"Is your pussy happy, sweet girl?" I gritted, thrusting up into her as she rode me from above. Splaying my hands over her flesh, I pressed my thumbs against her clit, making her cry out even louder.

"Yes. Oh god. Yes. You're so big. I feel full."

Her pussy was a perfect glove for my cock. I thrust deep into her sweet folds, feeling the mounting pressure, the rushing heat making my cock impossibly thicker with each thrust until my rough, guttural sounds matched Layla's desperate cries. Her face, just moments away from orgasm, was the sexiest sight I'd ever seen. We were both working for it. Reaching for it.

"Touch your clit," I growled, feeling like I wasn't going to last much longer. I worked to pound my cock into her faster and harder while she balanced herself on my chest with one hand, her other fingers working the juncture between her thighs. Her clit that was swollen with need, and Layla was crying out as her body wound tighter and tighter.

Her voice turned hoarse when she suddenly cried, "I'm coming. I'm coming. Don't stop! Don't stop!"

And when her little channel started squeezing my cock, milking it, my own orgasm hit me like a freight train. The pressure built to the breaking point, and then I was exploding with the sudden release, heart pounding furiously, incomprehensible words bursting out of my chest. I ground my cock so deep inside her that I could no longer tell where one of us ended and the other began. The sense of connection was so complete I was silently awed.

We were suspended in this other reality for several seconds, mindless, only experiencing the spasms of heat rippling from one of us to the other. My cock felt the residual contractions that still rocked her pussy, her entire body trembling with the effects of her orgasm, making my own shudder in reaction. Never had a woman felt so much a part of me. Ever.

Then she collapsed on my chest, and for several seconds we were breathing heavily, my cock continuing to pulse inside of her, her little pussy spasming around it. Both of us shuddered with echoing ripples of pleasure and panted in gulps of air. It took a few minutes to regain our breathing, but I didn't mind. The feel of her draped over my chest was right. It was only because I didn't want to lose the condom as my dick started going softer that I rolled Layla to my side. I gently dislodged my cock, tied a knot in the spent condom, and tossed it into the trash next to the nightstand. As I lay back on the pillow, the simple sight of her, a beautiful goddess lounging on my bed, arrested my movement.

She pushed damp tendrils off her face that was wet with tears, but before I had time to worry, her lips curled at the corners to show a hint of a tender smile. Then her arms draped across her forehead as she tried to better catch her breath.

Her breasts, with their pretty areolas bare, caught my attention because her movement jostled them, making them sway ever so slightly. Luscious. Damn, she was sexy. Flushed. Sleepy-eyed, not the least bit self-conscious about lying naked with me. A dream. Beautiful.

Without even trying.

My cock twitched at the sight of her, even having just come like I was having a meeting of the minds with the universe, even knowing I wasn't quite ready for round two just yet.

"You okay?" I ran my hand up her abdomen, appreciating the way my rougher, darker, sun-drenched skin contrasted with her softer, more delicate-looking pale flesh, unable to stop myself from circling one of the tips that was taunting me. It puckered instantly and an array of goosebumps popped up on the surrounding skin. She gave a delicate shiver that only served to make her breasts sway again. Maybe I could be ready even sooner.

Was it wrong to have a sense of satisfaction from her body's reaction to my touch?

I was asking her if she was okay, but I wasn't sure I was okay after what just happened.

Never had I felt so blown away by a woman. Never. When I was around her, it was like every moment was the night before Christmas. There was this sense of anticipation, and all it took was for her to smile at me, and my heart beat just that little bit harder and faster. It wasn't just good, it was so good, and that's what scared me. I'd never felt like this before. I was afraid of looking at it too closely, like she were ephemeral and could blow away on a breeze, or like it was all going to implode on me, because having anyone special in my life was not something that I'd envisioned for myself in a lot of years.

I'd been living the life of a monk with a few short-lived casual hookups to keep me going, but no one invaded my soul the way she could with a single look.

"Mmmm, I feel very good. Definitely very good. More than good. Much more." She turned toward me, stacked her hands under her cheek, her eyes tracing my face. A smile of contentment blossomed from the edges of her kiss-swollen lips, and her eyes held warmth and tenderness when they rested on me.

That look alone prompted me to pull her closer, brush another kiss on her lips, lingering over her for several seconds. Layla hummed a breathy tone of pleasure before I pulled back to feast my eyes on her face, a pillow bunched under my head.

Slowly, her smile faded, and her eyes became loaded with something heavy, something serious. There was something she wanted to tell me, so I waited for her to decide if she was going to trust me with whatever was on her mind. We stared into each other's eyes for long moments, having the kind of conversation we'd established when we first caught each other's attention.

Her eyes were asking if she should open up and let me inside. I hoped what she could see was that I was telling her yes. I was a lot of things that maybe weren't so good, but I would always keep her secrets safe.

She sighed. She closed her eyes for the briefest of moments before they flashed back to me again, soft, and vulnerable.

"I didn't know sex could be like this," she confessed in almost a whisper.

"Like what?"

She was silent a beat before offering, "Giving. Caring. Pleasurable. Playful. Safe." She gave each word its own space in time, choosing them deliberately, not rushing them. "It's never been like that for me."

"What was it like for you before?" I asked the question knowing that I needed to be careful here. Figuring I already knew the answer I was going to get, I braced myself for it. A woman didn't freak the hell out during sex unless something bad had happened to her at some point.

"He was taking. Always taking. Always expecting. Always selfish. Guilting. Shaming. Painful. Really painful. Every single time, including the first. He was my first and only." The sadness was back on her face. She hooked a hand across my chest, like she was anchoring herself to me. I let my fingers play across her soft skin, running them down her graceful shape before getting a grasp of her upper arm and just holding, locking it in place across my body, keeping her safe and secure. Only then did she add in a soft voice, "My ex was not a good man."

I figured as much. This was the shadow that hid behind her eyes and kept her on high-alert status.

"I'm not going to get too much into this right now, because I don't want him in here with us, but I want you to understand what happened earlier."

"All right."

"He controlled all parts of my life. Everything I did needed his okay or things would go badly for me. He would find ways of punishing me, and I would end up apologizing and crying. Now, looking back, I hated the memories of all the times I cried and apologized for questioning his decision or wanting to do something that he'd already vetoed. I couldn't get a job or go to school, because I had responsibilities around the house that weren't being met to his satisfaction, and that included sex. He thought my butt was too big or my muscles too soft or my hair was too short or my makeup was too much. He often liked to make belittling jokes about my white trash roots, like how I couldn't cook or drive."

"Did he hurt you physically, baby?" I asked, unable to help myself. I prayed her answer was no, or I would likely find myself serving jail time for assault. There was a slow burn churning in my gut, a need to pummel this guy who'd figured he could abuse her when he wanted.

"If you mean, did he hit me, then the answer is no, but he was cruel and manipulative. He always reminded me that I was no one and had nothing without him."

"I'm really hating this guy, Layla. Really."

"You aren't the only one." A frown creased the skin between her brows, and she looked inward a few moments before saying, "If you're asking about rape...Well, I never said no, and while I never really wanted to have sex with him, I always went along with it because I thought I had to and it was easier than dealing with how he'd react if I said no or being afraid of how he'd make me pay for that rejection somehow at a later time. He told me it was part of my job to take care of him whenever he felt like it since he was working and paying for everything in my life."

"What a dick. You know that's bullshit, right? You never have to let a guy fuck you. It's always your choice. I hope you know that."

"I do now. Except, this is where my story relates to tonight. I didn't realize I still had all this baggage hanging around in my head. The thing is, I could never get aroused by him. Never. The first time, I was a virgin, and I'd read that it might hurt, but he did almost no foreplay. I was pretty dry, and he penetrated me without any care, holding my arms down. I cried from the pain. There was blood. I was scared. He held me after, told me it would be better, and I believed him. I'd liked the kisses we'd shared. When it came time to have sex again, he had lube ready."

"Lube?"

"Yeah. It was on his nightstand, and he put some on himself before he was on me again. He climbed over me, held me down, and penetrated. No other prep. I'd tell him it was hurting, and I would cry, but he never stopped. Sometimes he would smile and thrust harder. He always told me it wouldn't hurt if I was a real woman. So many times he called me a coldhearted bitch. He told me there was something wrong with me."

"Fucker."

"The lube on the nightstand became the signal that I was expected to get into bed naked. I came to hate the smell and feel of it. The sight of it always had me shaking with fear." She took a deep breath. It was shaky, but she smiled. "Then Blessing stepped in."

"Blessing?"

"My best friend. Near the end of it all, I secretly started taking university extension classes. She was sitting at a table not too far from me in the cafeteria and heard my tearful argument over the phone with Brady. He was demanding that I come home. He'd gone through my mail and found a letter to me from the financial aide office. It was how I was paying for classes. I was pleading with him to let me stay. So, she grabbed the phone from me, and said, 'Listen, asshat. Your girl, here, is a grown woman who can do whatever the fuck she wants. Grow a pair and quit being such a whiny dickwad.' Then she hung up, looked at me and said, 'Seriously. You need to ditch that guy. The sex can't be that good.'"

"That must have been a shocker for you."

"It was."

"Did you stay and finish the class that day?"

"I did, but first, Blessing and I exchanged numbers. She became my accountability buddy. She swore she would, in her words, 'kidnap my ass' if I didn't show up."

"What happened when you got home that night?"

"The lube was on the nightstand."

She didn't need to say anything else about that. The hackles on my neck rose. As far as I was concerned, it was rape. No wonder she was so traumatized. And I'd held her hands down earlier.

"As you can imagine, Brady hated Blessing and forbid me to see her, but she wasn't going away. Over a few months, she managed to start clearing out the bad programming, and when I was ready, helped me leave. In the quiet of the morning, after Brady had gone to work, I left him a note that said goodbye. Blessing's car was already packed up because we'd been planning to move up here anyway. I have a job, a place to live, and a life because of her."

"As much as I want to kill him, I love her. So much respect for the kind of friend she was for you."

"She never gave up on me. If not for her, I know I would likely still be there with him, feeling trapped and worthless."

"Your reaction makes sense now. I'm sorry I scared you. There's no way I want you to think I'm like him."

"I know you're not," she smiled shyly. Pushing up so her lips were near my ear, she whispered, "You made my pussy very happy many times this week. You're training it to like you by giving it so much attention. Even now, just thinking about sex with you is making it get all swollen with excitement."

"Is that right?"

She took my hand and brushed it down the center of her body, over the soft dark hairs to the middle of her thighs. I took over from there, noting the growing wetness and letting my fingers move into her to bring some out to where I started circling her thickening nub of flesh.

Her breath did that hitch thing that I loved, and as my fingers worked to build tension and pleasure in her pussy, I leaned down to capture her lips in a long, lazy kiss that let me explore her lower lip with bites, sipping suction easing the sting, and playful sweeps of my tongue. Her fingers walked down my chest until she found my cock and grasped it, making my own breath hiss out on an exhale.

Already rock hard and ready for action.

It was when I moved down to her neck that she said, "Mason, I need you to hold me down while you fuck me."

CHAPTER 20

LAYLA

"Don't make me into your ex," Mason growled, his head popping up, his fingers stilling their action.

"Help me with this."

"I don't want you to see him when I'm fucking you, baby. There's no fucking way I'm going to do something that could potentially hurt you."

"I know you won't hurt me. That's the difference."

"That's like therapy."

"Exactly."

"And I don't think you're ready for something like that. Look how you reacted just half an hour ago."

"Mason," I calmed my voice and let him see how serious I was about this. "I can't let him win. I trust you. Please help me."

He was reluctant, but then he nodded and was scowling severely when he said, "If we're going to do this, you need to know that the moment you seem uncomfortable, I'm letting go."

"It's going to be uncomfortable, Mason. That's the point. How about, if I yank on my arms, you'll let go, just like you did before. Otherwise, assume that I'm trying to work through this and still come out the other side with an amazing orgasm?"

A smile tugged at one corner of his mouth. "Just one?"

"Let's call that the minimum. I suspect we can do better."

"Because your pussy is happy?"

"Yes."

His fingers were moving again, spearing my center, caressing my inner sheath while his thumb rubbed my clit. He found the most amazing spot, and I gasped out a moan, my hips curling into his hand. He continued his stroking with relentless precision, turning me into a panting, mewling mess of need.

"Is my pussy training working?" he asked against my earlobe before nipping it.

"I'm going to come. I'm going to come."

That's when he withdrew his fingers, and I cried out in protest. "Condom," he murmured.

"I'm on the pill," I breathed heavily. "And I'm clean."

He regarded me steadily for a beat, then said, "I haven't been with anyone bare for years, and I've been tested. I'm clean."

"I want to feel you in me. I don't want to feel anyone else. Just you."

"You want me to fill you up with my cum?" he asked quietly, though his eyes were growing more heated with the idea.

"Yes."

Then he was over me, sliding one of his muscular thighs between my legs in a sensual attack with hot, open-mouthed kisses and his hand skimming up my side and over my breast. His thumb rubbed circles over my nipple before he moved to cup my neck.

Against my lips, he promised, "I'm going to fuck

you until you're filled with me."

"Only you."

"Hot and dripping out of you."

"Please."

"I want you to feel me all day tomorrow."

"Do it."

His other leg slid in place, and my legs spread wide, cradling his hips. His hands wrapped around my forearms, pinning them by my head, and his cock nudged my entrance. Again, the manacled feeling started, the prickles on my skin, and I slammed my eyes closed.

"Look at me," he snarled, and it was startling enough that I opened my eyes. "I want you to keep your eyes on me. See who is fucking you. Don't you dare look away."

Then he was sliding his cock in an inch at a time, holding me in place, just the way I'd asked him to.

"Wrap your legs around me," he demanded, and when I did, he surged all the way in, touching me so deep, I gasped with the hot tingle of electricity that zapped my nerve endings.

He moved in and out of me, his every thrust

starting slow and ending with a sharp pounding like a hammer that jarred my entire body, hitting new nerve endings that were throbbing with sensitivity, that told me he was there.

Still, a part of me was tense. A part of me was too aware of his hands wrapped around my forearms, of his weight pressed into me. It had me tensing more. Some of the sensitivity began to fade, and then I was worried that this wasn't going to feel good. Then I was worried that Mason would notice I was not with him, and that's when he slowed and stopped, still deeply embedded in me. He was looking for me, searching my eyes.

"What?" I asked, a hint of fear creeping into my voice.

"That's enough for now," he grumbled. Disappointment had my heart squeezing painfully until I realized he only meant the position we were in. In the next moment, he was keeping us connected with a strong hand on my ass, but he was rolling us to our sides, so we were facing each other. He pulled my leg over his hip, tangling his own thigh between mine, but that was it. He was not moving.

"Mason…" Tears burned. Would I ever get over this? I wanted to feel normal.

"It takes time, Layla," he said in his rumbly voice. He was pillowing his head on one arm, but his other fingers were languidly tracing their way around my chest, over the curve of my breast, rubbing the tip of my nipple.

"But—"

"Be patient. It'll take time to work this out. It doesn't have to feel bad while you're doing it." He was back to kissing me. Gently at first, like he was testing the waters. And with his fingers still working me and his parting my lips to welcome the heat of his tongue, my hips started moving on their own, seeking friction. Pleasure spiked. My pussy flooded with heat and wetness once again.

"More," I insisted. "I need more."

"That's my sweet girl," he said hoarsely. He hooked an arm under my leg to open me wider, and I curled my hands around his biceps. Rolling back over me, his thrusts moved faster and harder, with my own hips pumping to meet him. The look on his face was raw pleasure, his jaw clenched, his eyes fierce as they held mine, but they didn't scare me. They got me hotter. The fire he was building inside me had raged into an inferno that was ready to blow.

Hardly able to breathe, with my own heart racing

for the finish, I moaned, "Yes, yes, yes!"

"So fucking good, baby. Hot and tight," he gritted. "I'm so fucking close."

"Yes!"

Crashing his lips to mine, he pistoned his hips even faster, pounding me into the mattress, his angle hitting the very spot inside me that his fingers had found earlier until I was moaning and crying out rhythmically, mindlessly.

I slid my own fingers toward my clit, finding the swollen flesh, slippery with my own juices, and touched myself until I was riding the sharpest edge of ecstasy.

"Are you going to come?" he growled, his breath coming in rasping gasps sounding almost animalistic.

"Yes. Don't stop, don't stop. Oh my god. Yes, yes, yes!" The molten heat of the electrical charge started in my toes, curling them involuntarily before flashing up my legs and exploding from the inside. I shouted with each convulsion of pleasure that rocked my body.

"Fuck," Mason pounded into me only twice more before he thrust and froze, his own body jerking, guttural groans echoing from his deep chest.

I felt his hot spurts of cum wash me clean from the inside out, and when he went to pull out, I tightened my leg over his ass, wanting to keep him there. He lowered my leg back to his hip and found the spot he seemed to like best, his face pressed into my neck, while catching his breath. I could still feel his cock pulsing sporadically, his heart racing.

I wanted to savor this moment when we were pressed flush, mixing our sweat, mixing our fluids, creating a scent of sex that was new and completely ours alone. It surrounded us in our own private cocoon, and I didn't want this moment to end, even as my eyes grew heavy, and my mind started to drift.

Gently, he rolled us over, pulling me on top of him where I was draped across his body with boneless fatigue. There was more that I wanted to share, but before I could tell him about what a wonderful, beautiful, and amazing experience this was, that maybe I was wrong about keeping us casual, that maybe we could try to start a relationship because I wanted to be with him, I fell asleep.

My bladder woke me up to the bright sunlight that seemed to be pouring into the room, along with a variety of minor aches that reminded me of what we'd done the night before. I smiled until I noted that the other side of the bed was empty, and weirdly, perfectly made up. Blankets were smoothed, the pillow looking fluffed without any indication that Mason had used it.

Hospital corners. I cringed. I got caught up in the tight sheet because it was tucked in so sharply. A glance at the clock on the nightstand showed it was almost ten in the morning.

Wondering if he was already in the bathroom, I got out of bed and couldn't find any of our clothes on the floor to grab. There was a slight chill to the air, and besides that, I was a little self-conscious. Even at home, I didn't walk around naked. I'd learned to stay covered up, not wanting to give Brady any encouragement.

I was sure we'd dropped the clothes on the floor during our bout of sexual gymnastics, but I didn't see them. Unable to ignore my bladder any longer, I opened one of the two other doors in the room and found myself in a walk-in closet. Backing out, I opened the other door and found the bathroom. Thankfully, it was empty.

But where was Mason? And why was the bed made up on his side?

It didn't take long to conclude my business, but

while washing my hands, I noted that all his towels were perfectly folded and centered on the towel racks. I reluctantly dried my hands on one, then made sure to straighten it again. I didn't want him to get mad at me for leaving his bathroom a mess.

My skin prickled with the thought. I was starting to feel insecure and needed to find Mason, but I didn't want to do so naked.

I went back into his closet and turned on the overhead light. Perfectly hung clothes grouped by occasion. One side of the small space had his dress clothing with a few suits and dress shirts taking up space along with some items hanging in a plastic zipped bag as though they were being protected. The plastic was cloudy clear, and it seemed like I could see a dark jacket with gold buttons, dark blue pants sticking out the bottom. They looked all too familiar.

My heart kick-started a few beats, and I got a strange feeling in my gut. With a slow pan of the rest of the closet, I saw the other side had more casual clothing, perfectly hung, perfectly aligned, his shoes and a pair of black combat boots perfectly perpendicular to the wall with the same amount of space separating each pair of shoes.

"No," I whispered under my breath, gazing at everything with a hint of panic making my eyes grow wide.

There were dresser drawers on one wall, and I figured he had to have a T-shirt in there somewhere. This new alternate reality only got worse when I saw his socks and boxer briefs carefully placed with precise folds in the top drawer, and in the next drawer, his shirts were the same. Quickly, I grabbed the topmost T-shirt and pulled it over my head, but just as I was about to leave, I saw the dog tags and felt the blood drain from my face.

He was military. Just like Brady.

I had to know. I had to know now. I had to find him and ask him point blank, because I wanted nothing to do with the military. I wanted nothing to do with precision and commands and orders and control.

I walked quietly into the hallway outside the bedroom and saw that there was another door on the far side of the landing. It was open, and from where I was standing, I could see it served as an office, a desk set up in front of the window. I was about to head downstairs when I heard a noise and froze.

It was a whimper coming from that room.

"Mason?" I called tentatively.

Moving closer to the office, I saw that a futon

was pushed off into a corner of the room and that Mason was there. He was drenched in sweat, his hair sticking to his forehead in clumps. He moved restlessly within his sheets, and a hoarse cry erupted from him, startling me. It was only partially muffled by the pillow and followed by incomprehensible words. His face suddenly contorted with a tortured look, and he moaned with agony, reaching toward something that only he could see in his mind.

He whimpered again, cried out, "No!"

He was having a nightmare.

Suddenly, he sat up, his steel eyes frantic, and roared, "Get down! Get down!"

"Mason?" I called to him. Was he awake or asleep?

He suddenly jerked away, scrambled back so he was flush against the wall, muscles tense, his bare chest heaving breaths, and blinked several times, looking around. His eyes zeroed in on me, and I could see his memory returning incrementally, percolating through the layers of consciousness to a sense of awareness.

On a shaky breath, he sat back, the sheet still tangled around his body, and leaned his head against the wall, turning away from me. It was a look of such despair, I was struck silent for several moments, torn between the knowledge that he was military and wanting to hug him close and smooth the pain from his face.

"Are you all right?" It felt like a stupid question. Of course he wasn't all right. He looked like he'd just fought off the devil himself.

"I'm fine." Brief. Clipped. When he looked at me, there was just a flat affect, none of the warmth I was used to associating with him. "Give me a minute."

It was a cold, hard dismissal. My stomach bottomed out with dread. I didn't recognize this Mason. I hadn't seen him before. Heart pounding out a fierce warning, this moment only reinforced my own fears that I could get emotionally entangled while he could remain emotionally cold and unavailable just like Brady.

Just like Brady. Oh my God. My breathing turned shallow as my heart sped up. It became a struggle to take a deep breath. I needed space. Air. I backed out of the room and practically ran back to the bedroom I'd slept in. Panic set in. I was only wearing a T-shirt, but I didn't know where my clothes were.

Just like Brady, my brain screamed, flashing the

memories at me like a warning beacon.

His beautifully cruel smile. Me constantly crying. Apologizing for living. Learning to hate myself. Burning pain with each thrust, his face above me, holding me down. Praying for it all to be over fast.

There was a glass door opposite the bed that I hadn't noticed the night before. With some relief, I slid it open, taking a deep gulp of the cool breeze coming off the ocean. It sent goosebumps over my body, making me shiver, but I welcomed the distracting sensations. The crashing waves and salty scent of the moist air was immediate and calming. From the balcony, I could see a small patch of dark blue water rolling toward shore between two homes that were a block closer to the beach.

Just like Brady, my brain said, but this time in a whisper. I continued working to pull deep breaths into my lungs.

A flash of color caught my attention. The balcony overlooked the backyard and stacked against the wall were a couple of surfboards. There was a small patch of grass and a short path that led to a gazebo that had vines with purple flowers growing vibrantly. It looked like there was a hot tub.

Mason put a lot into this place. He worked hard. Never took shortcuts. Never expected anything. Not like Brady.

I heard his approaching footsteps. Still, my body tensed. Ready for a fight.

Instead, his words softly remorseful, he said, "I have some sweats you could borrow."

"It's all right." My voice was all croaky. I didn't turn around, just kept my gaze fixed on the patch of ocean and took a breath. My muscles wouldn't relax. Even my fingers had a white-knuckle grasp of the bannister. Nervously, I offered, "Sorry I had to grab a shirt from your closet, but I couldn't find my clothes."

He bent to lean his forearms against the wood railing and said, "They're folded in the laundry room."

"You did laundry last night? After…after…" It took a couple of tries. It was funny how in the light of day, even after all the ways we'd been intimate with each other, I was suddenly shy. "After sex?"

He took a moment to answer, his head tilting downward to sightlessly view his yard, contemplating his next words. "I have a condition. It looks a lot like OCD, you know, obsessive compulsive disorder. Things have to be in their place. Organized. Neat. I need…"

He seemed at a loss for words, so I gave him a side glance, the disappointment saturating my tone. "Hospital corners when you leave the bed, even if it's still in use? No dirty clothes on the floor, even if they got there because we were stripping for each other? No dirty clothing at all?" He grimaced, a flush staining his sun-kissed cheeks, and shook his head with a look of embarrassment, like he had something to be ashamed of, and I felt like a jerk suddenly. A condition like that didn't make someone bad. "I'm sorry."

He just shrugged my words off. "Something like that. It's complicated. That's part of it at least. Something to do with controlling my environment. It…I don't know. The shrink said something about how it makes me feel like I'm keeping bad things from happening."

Part of me wondered why he'd had to go to a counselor and if he was all right, but more than that, I refused to get sidetracked. The new Layla was not going to let her emotions become a weapon to be used against her. Not again. I had to close off my heart to protect myself, because he could be just like Brady. I had to remember that.

"I told you I wasn't interested in anyone from the

military, but you deliberately kept that from me."
The hurt was there, the feeling of being betrayed
because I'd communicated my needs to him, and
he'd pretended to care. All I could see was once
again, a man was getting what he wanted without
caring about me. Anger turned my gaze accusing
when I stared up at him. Mason, who'd at first
looked surprised, now had a frown building across
his dark brows.

"What are you talking about? I've never hidden
who I was," he growled his surprise. "You're the
one who told me it had taken a year to get
comfortable with me, know me, approve of me,
trust me. You were the one who approached me.
What did I have to hide? Why would I think you
didn't know?"

"I didn't know! I…" My cheeks grew hot as I let
his words sink in. He was right. I hadn't asked
enough of the right questions. My foolishness gave
way to a self-directed anger. I turned away from
him to gaze desperately at the sliver of rolling blue
waves, feeling like I was somehow drowning. Such
a freaking idiot. My heart had slowed some from its
mad pace, but it was still beating a little too fast.
Just couldn't get my breathing to regulate.

"I work with disabled vets, Layla. How is this a
surprise?" He gentled his deep, rough voice like he

cared. I felt edgy and overwhelmed, so it wasn't surprising that tears pricked my eyes. I ached with the desire to be cared about, wanted to just throw my arms around his big strong body, but this had to be all wrong. It had to. He could be just like Brady. Cold. Unavailable. My rules kept me safe. Obstinately, I tried to shut off the effect his voice had on me.

"That doesn't have to mean you were in the military. I told you at the coffee shop I didn't want a man in the military." Even if my original assumptions had been wrong about him, I knew I'd been up front with him, making him aware of my exceptions. "And I opened up to you. Last night. I shared things with you that I've never shared with anyone else. I let you in. I trusted you!" And he'd been so sweet and attentive. But that wouldn't last. It hadn't the last time I'd trusted someone.

"That's not how it happened. Back at the coffee shop? I told you about the guys I worked with, and you said no to dating one of them. That's all you said. You said no or never or something like that, which I didn't understand, but you wouldn't talk about it. Remember?"

"I meant 'no' to anyone in uniform."

"So it's my fault that you were unclear? You refused to talk about it, but it's my fault that I misunderstood your vague statements? I'm now a bad guy?"

"No..." Again, his words filtered through my brain, and I had no emotional leg to stand on. Past and present emotions were becoming entangled, fighting for space in my head. I was emotionally strung out, fear the most intense feeling overriding my racing thoughts. Fear of what, I didn't even know. Shadows? Memories? Or the ghost of relationship future where I make the same mistakes over and over again.

I sniffed back the coming moisture, bit my lip to stop it from quivering. My nose was starting to run, my eyes going watery. This was all messed up, and it was my fault. None of this was his fault. How stupid of me! This was becoming a shame spiral once again.

Mason watched me a moment, care and worry radiating from him, causing him to reach out. I shook my head, backing away, rejecting his comfort. He dropped the hand, exhaling sharply on a rush of frustration.

"What the hell is wrong with guys in the military? Please help me understand." He suddenly scrubbed his hand through his dark hair. "I don't even know why this is a point of contention. The guys I've known have been fucking heroic. I'm doing my best not to take this personally." But he was taking it personally. I could hear the tinge of hurt in his tone.

This was going to be the confrontation. This was it. My heart restarted its race, pounding too hard and too fast. Immediately, I was tripping over myself to explain. "Of course what you all do is heroic. It's not about that. It doesn't even make sense. I shouldn't even be talking about this. I'm sorry."

"What did I say about apologizing? You haven't done anything to be sorry for. Tell me, Layla. Please. Let me understand." There was a stark plea in his beautiful eyes. He wanted to know. Face value. I'd always been able to take Mason at face value. He'd never actually done anything to hurt me.

Taking a deep breath to calm my heart, I faced the ocean and began talking. "My ex, Brady, is in the Navy out of San Diego. Life with him was a nightmare. He needed hospital corners. He needed things cleaned and organized in a very specific way. If they weren't done to his standard, he would berate me for being low class and hopeless before making me do it over again. It didn't start out that way. He was sweet to me at first, trying to get to know me. We met when I came out from Arizona to visit my sister who'd managed to find a position at a bar near the base. By the end of our relationship, he'd tell me I was lucky he took me out of the trailer park, even if the trailer park stink never completely left me."

Mason had turned his gaze back to the ocean, and while he didn't say anything, I could feel his anger on my behalf. It had a strange calming effect. I really wanted him to understand and accept why this couldn't happen between us. He deserved that from me. The full truth.

"There was always an implied threat that he would take me back there because he knew how much I hated it. I would agree to anything to never see that place again. My mother should never have been a mother. She never took care of my sister and me, so we took care of ourselves. When things were rough, and they always got rough, I went to the library to escape. When the lights were shut off, I went to the library. When she had some shady man hanging around the house, I went to the library. I couldn't run away for real, so I ran away into as many books as I could get my hands on."

Mason looked at me again, and this time I couldn't keep my own eyes from swinging to his. They grabbed hold of me the moment our eyes met. Comforting, but I still pushed back a step as I talked, not wanting to feel reliant on his warmth and strength. More than anyone else, I knew these feelings weren't real.

"One time, Brady threw me into the deep end of the pool while we were at his friend's party. Other guests, friends of his, their girlfriends, were spontaneously jumping in, playing around. I almost drowned. I just kept swallowing water when I yelled for help and...and was sinking."

"I want to kill this guy," Mason's tone, for being quiet, came out in a vicious hiss, which took me by surprise.

"To be fair, he didn't know." The memory of the afternoon flooded my mind. "I'd been embarrassed to let him know, because it would have been further ammunition that he could use against me. I thought I could take care of the problem by just wearing shorts, you know? I mean, I don't even own a bathing suit. Anyway, he'd had a few beers with his friends. They all started to horseplay with their own significant others, so he grabbed me up, only he didn't listen when I told him to stop. I was clinging to him, practically crying, but he didn't listen. Just tossed me in the deep end."

"Fucking bastard."

"I thought I was going to die. I really did. I

swallowed so much water."

The memory brought back the feelings of panic. Horror. Desperation. I closed my eyes, feeling the shudder of fear raise goosebumps on my arms. I held them tightly across my chest and opened my eyes again, falling into Mason's steady gaze. I held on to him, took a deep breath and exhaled the memory away.

"People make mistakes, I mean, I know, but the worst part was how he handled it. He was embarrassed that he had to fish me out. Started making fun of me. Said I was…flailing around like a beached whale. Everyone laughed, including Brady. I'd been terrified, and he thought it was funny. He never apologized. The feelings that I had for him died a slow death because he found ways to manipulate them, twist them and take advantage of them to suit his own selfish needs. In the two years I spent with him, he even denied me the library. We didn't live anywhere near it, I had no friends to take me, and he wouldn't take me. So I didn't even have that. There was no escape. I got to a point where I was trapped. My time was spent trying to keep him happy, anticipate his wants and needs for the sake of my own survival."

"You were completely dependent on him."

"He told me I was fat, that I had a jiggly ass, so

you know what I did?" I smirked inwardly. "Started going to the gym. At least now I'm going because I like feeling healthy. Blessing helped me realize that I needed to stop trying to get along and instead to get gone. Her words. Anyway, I found your dog tags. You're military."

"I was," he narrowed his eyes.

"I'm telling you this because I promised myself I would stay away from anyone associated with military, someone used to giving orders and expecting them to be obeyed."

"Are you comparing me to him?" Mason suddenly stood to his full height, his frown now a look of anger. "You think I would treat you like that?"

"No. Of course not. You aren't like him at all." I pressed fingers to my eyes, starting to feel confused. The dots weren't lining up the way I expected them to. "Look. We were going to keep this casual, but last night didn't feel casual. It felt like the beginning of something, and I'm not ready for that. I'm not ready to have a man watching over me, having a say in my life and what I do."

"When have I given you the impression that I'm going to tell you what to do?"

"It would be so easy to fall into that again and start caring more about your wants and needs and ignoring my own. I've been there and done that."

"I would never want you to do that."

"I'm falling for you." Just saying that out loud had me reeling with fear at my own words, had him searching my face with a kind of urgency, but I had to make sure he understood why this was dangerous for me, so I repeated, "I'm falling for you, and it's scaring me. I saw the precise way you keep your closet, the way your clothes are organized and your shoes line up perfectly. Do you know that in my own place, while I'm not a slob, I deliberately leave my shoes laying around? I like knowing they're there when I get up in the morning. I walked around the room this morning trying to find my clothes, and they weren't where I left them, where I wanted to leave them. I lived like a prisoner for years, and now I'm free. I can't live afraid anymore. Did you know that I was worried that you would be mad because I dried my hands on your perfect towel?"

A curtain suddenly collapsed over his face, muting the angry expression, and dampening his frown, wiping away the expression there. He went from being part of the conversation to retreating to some remote location where I could no longer feel him. Through this talk, I'd felt him right next to me but hadn't realized it until he'd pulled back, and that pinched my heart, hard. It was startling.

He looked down at his bare feet, avoiding my gaze. He shook his head and said, "I don't want you to be afraid of me. And you're right. We were going to keep this casual." He sounded like he was saying goodbye, and then he looked back up at me. His expression confirmed it.

The look of pain on his face, the instant reversal, had me backtracking. He was giving up. Right here. Right now. He wasn't going to fight this. It was what I wanted, right? That was what this talk was about. Right? And yet, a sliver of panic pierced my heart, had it jumping. He was going to walk away. Wasn't this what I wanted?

Feeling like I was stumbling emotionally, my words rushed out quickly when I insisted, "I'm not saying you're like him. I'm not afraid of you."

He shook his head. "I don't want to hurt you. It's the last thing I want. I'll get your clothes and take you home." Then he walked off.

What had I just done?

I stood alone with a sense of loss. The silence was sudden and heavier than I knew what to do with. It condemned me. The moment he went inside, it was like the cold water was suddenly turned on, splashing me awake. The cold awareness trickled down my body. He'd left me alone. Given me what I wanted without further question. I'd treated him like he was going to behave like Brady, but Brady would never have done anything I asked. He would have put me down. Had me crying. Insisted that who I was wasn't enough without him. Mason would never do that.

What just happened? It was so sudden. What did I do? I pushed him away.

Did I just make a huge mistake? No. He was military in nature, even if he was no longer in the service. He needed his life orderly and regimented to survive. I needed random chaos. There was no way.

I swiped at the tears that fell onto my cheeks. Hot. Splashing. It was what I'd said I wanted. He was giving it to me.

The drive to my apartment was done in silence. Our connection was gone. It felt like we were two strangers inhabiting the same four-foot-wide space, but with an emotionless mile between us. Casting a quick glance his way, I saw there was an air of loneliness surrounding him. Sadness. He was keeping himself closed off from me, and it hurt in a deeper more poignant way than it ever had with

Brady. What did that mean?

We pulled up to my place and sat for a few moments in silence. It was excruciating, especially since memories of the night before had begun sliding through my mind.

He'd been so careful. So thoughtful. So generous. But the near panic attack from this morning was still fresh in my mind, throwing my thoughts into a jumbled mess.

"You coming to the gym next week?" He broke the silence.

"Yes."

"You should go back to morning times, so you're safer. Maybe take the bus until you can fix your bike."

I nodded, my eyes burning. He worried about me. What was I doing? Why was my mind such a mess? Knowing that tears were close, I leaned over and pressed a kiss to his cheek before hopping out. I didn't look back as I disappeared into my apartment complex and opened the door. The tears were welling, about to fall, clouding my vision, which was why I didn't see my sister right away.

She was lounging on the couch watching TV, a smirk twisting her lips. There was a smell of old grease and something else hanging in the air. I saw that her stuff, while contained to one corner of the room, was still a disaster area. "Blessing called the landline. Seems she couldn't get you on your phone and you didn't show up for work."

"Oh," I started, already digging for my phone in my bag.

"Girl's a bitch if you ask me, getting all uppity and snippy like she's better than me."

Uppity. That was my mother's word. It was meant to invalidate, and I was surprised to hear my sister say it. We'd both hated hearing it when we were kids. Our mother used it nearly every conversation on the rare occasion I called her, like her birthday or Christmas. In any case, I ignored Nadine's random comments and focused on the missed calls and texts that Blessing had sent me.

"Asked about my job," Nadine continued, giggled like she'd just heard a joke. "She thought I had a job. Like I could have a job. I told her not to be such a goddamn stiff."

I was in the middle of my text when I heard her comment. First, it occurred to me that her words sounded slurred, and then I processed her actual words and looked up. Text forgotten. I really looked.

Unkempt hair that needed washing. Tank spotted with grease and showcased hickeys on her neck and chest. Eyes bright and shiny. She had a big glass of something the color of weak cranberry juice in her hand and a half-empty bottle of vodka on the floor at her feet. At the far end of the couch, in the bottom half of a flimsy cardboard container from a nearby burger joint, was what looked like cold, congealing chili cheese fries, the grease darkening the cardboard as it bled through to the cushion below.

My stomach dropped and familiar dread choked my throat. She was wasted, having sex on my couch, eating… "Nadine! You're drunk! Oh my God."

"Nooooo," she snorted, then laughed and held up her thumb and index finger so they were barely separated. "Maybe just a touch. Weasel brought it over, and you know what happens when Weasel lets out his weasel." She laughed. "Then I got hungry."

There were so many things wrong, I didn't even know where to begin. The disappointment, the sense of being deliberately misled yet again—it was a slap to the face. "You don't have a job? Why did you tell me you had a job?"

"I needed a place to stay," she pouted, but she wasn't completed gone. I could see the calculating look in her eyes. She'd been drinking, but she was fully aware of what she was doing. "I went to Weasel's first, but then his parents kicked me out."

"So you came here."

"I came here."

"You came here and started doing whatever the hell you wanted to do."

"It's not that big a deal."

"To you! I told you not to eat on my nice sofa. There's a perfectly good table like five feet away."

"The couch is more comfortable. Besides, I'm being careful. See? Still in the box." She leaned over, nearly sloshing the cranberry drink in her hand, and grabbed the box. A few patches of oil were left behind. She set the box right back down on the same spot with an exaggerated gasp. "Oh. Oops. That was an accident. I didn't think it would hurt anything."

She didn't give a shit about my feelings. She was not the Nadine from my loving memories and never would be again. This was ridiculous. I was tired of thinking I had to keep her happy. I didn't. I wasn't in charge of her life. If something happened to her, it would be because she was making that choice. I'd been living long enough without someone else treating me like shit to accept being treated like that by her.

My anger became a battering ram and slammed through the door, exploding with the force of so many repressed emotions.

"You never do. Never. You only ever think of yourself and what you can get out of a situation at any given moment. You became our mother, a huge wrecking ball that smashes precious things to bits when you touch them, including relationships with people who actually care about you. By the way, I paid five hundred dollars for this couch, and I didn't want anyone eating on it, including me." I stormed over to grab the damned food, tossed it in the trash under the sink, and slammed the cabinet door closed before whirling around and glaring at her again. "I pay all my bills now. I work my butt off to have the right to decide what happens in my apartment—"

"Okay, okay! Way to kill the buzz." Initially, my sister had been wide-eyed and surprised by my reaction, but then she fell into a scowl, letting her arrogant attitude catch up to her again. "Since when did you become such a bitch?"

"Since I grew up and started taking care of myself."

"I don't know what you have to be so proud of.

This place is a shithole," she sneered, a sweep of her arm encompassing the space. It was the arm holding the drink, and some of the claret liquid nearly spilled onto the couch.

The hurt was sharp. I was proud of being able to stand on my own two feet and was proud of the things I'd been able to buy for my own place. She hadn't been able to do that for herself yet. More interesting and thought provoking was the question that I came to next: Why did I keep looking for her approval? She wasn't ever going to see the value of what I was doing, not as long as she was an addict.

I took a breath, knowing my next words were going to shove her out the door. Weighing them in my mind, they felt right. I never thought I'd be saying this to my sister, someone who meant so much to me, but it was either this or continue to accept her wrecking-ball treatment.

I took a deep, centering breath. "No one's making you stay. In fact, you weren't invited to begin with."

Just that quick. Decision made. Power taken back. One breath to the next. Maybe she'd leave, and maybe this would be the end of a fucked-up familial relationship, but I'd just have to live with that.

Nadine was now glaring at me. "Fucking cold. Brady was right."

The words were slow to process. She knew how personal my sharing that was. How could she throw those words back at me? "What did you say?"

She clammed up. After running off at the mouth with all her opinions, she zipped her lips and refused to make eye contact.

"What did you mean by that?" I approached slowly, wanting to see and hear every nuance of her answer.

Like caution flags had waved in her mind and had her mouth shutting momentarily, her lips pressed together. She shrugged and said in a small voice, "I'm just saying…"

"What exactly are you saying?" I snagged her drink out of her hand and held it away from her.

"I'm just saying you could have had it easy if…"

"If what?" The anger was seething, waiting for the rights words, the right nuclear code to attack. "Don't be shy now. You started this."

She gave a big sigh. "You could have pretended. You could have sucked it up and pretended. Brady wouldn't have known the difference."

"What are you talking about?"

"Sex! You could have pretended to like it, and you wouldn't be in this place getting on my case about food. You'd have a good TV and more than a shoebox for an apartment. He wouldn't have kicked you out!"

"Kicked me out?" The laughter that bubbled up from my throat was the crazy-sounding, cackling kind that was the exact opposite of genuine amusement. It was the kind that stems from horror. "*I* left *him*, Nadine."

"That's not what he said."

That was the missing piece that struck me momentarily stupid. I gaped at her. "You talked to him?"

"Yeah." She grabbed her drink back from me and wobbled from lack of balance and coordination. "When I called looking for you."

"You called him to find me?" I needed to get this straight.

"Then I called mom for your number and address when he said you guys weren't together anymore."

"When did you talk to him?"

"What's the big deal? Recently."

"When?"

"Maybe three weeks ago? He said he was willing to take you back."

"Take me back?"

"Yeah. He wanted to know where you were. He's been worried about you all this time, so I had Weasel drive by on our way up from Mission Beach. I saw him on my way to see you. We could move in tomorrow. He's got this amazing, huge condo up on a hillside with views—"

"We?" I suddenly realized what she was doing, the horror of it. "You and me?"

"He said I could live with you guys until I got back on my feet."

"I can't believe you." A nightmare unraveling, threatening all that I'd worked for.

"What?" She was still scowling.

"How quickly you threw me under the bus to make life easier for yourself. You don't care about me at all."

"That's not true."

"It's completely true. You come and go as you please. You never call me unless it's because you need something. You haven't tried to get help, or get a job, or look into going to school, or even clean up after yourself when you do come over. Everyone's supposed to take care of you like you're the queen of England. You come into my house and do whatever the hell you want, which is how you treat anyone who's nice enough to try and offer help. How many bridges have you burned between Los Angeles and San Diego since you left Arizona ten years ago?"

She suddenly gritted her teeth and snarled, "You owe me!"

"I owe you?" I scoffed. "That's rich coming from you. What does that even mean?"

"I protected you!"

"When?"

"You don't even know. No one knows." She took a gulp from her glass and hugged it to her chest. She was starting to shake, tremors attacking her body as she sat back down on her blanket. "I never told. I promised."

The distress on her face was real. Instant. My anger deflated as my alarm rose.

"What are you talking about, Nadine? What happened?"

She took another gulp of the drink, then sniffed and stared into it. When she looked up at me, there were tears filling her eyes, the moisture quivering before it overflowed down her cheeks. "I never let him come near you. He promised he would never touch you if I went along with him."

"Who?" I asked quietly, but I was afraid I already knew the answer. There were only a couple of men who my mother had been able to keep around long term, back when she was still pretty and used it to manipulate men. Of those men, there was only one who'd ever given me the creeps. The meaning behind her words was making itself clear.

She nodded, seeing the light dawn in my eyes, and sniffed. "Glen."

Glen. Our mother's live-in boyfriend when we were little girls. My adult eyes looked back through the mist of time to interpret what my little girl eyes had seen. Shadows drifting through the bedroom door. A quiet whimper.

She's all right, Layla. She's having a nightmare. I'm taking care of her. The man's voice was Glen's. *I'm just holding her until she goes back to sleep.*

All right. I remember answering with the complete trust that a child gives to an adult automatically.

I remembered Nadine changing over time. Becoming quieter. Quicker to fight with me. I remembered trying harder to make her smile. Do things for her. Share candy with her, even when she'd had her own. By the time Glen finally moved on, Nadine had been in middle school, and I'd been in elementary. Five years had gone by. That's when the drugs and alcohol started.

"Nadine." It was the soft sympathy in my voice that triggered her reaction. Her eyes frosted over.

"Good old Glen liked 'em young. He liked touching me, having me touch him, and toward the end, he started fucking me all the way. I was twelve, Layla. Twelve. It fucking hurt. I hated him. So much. He would catch me alone. Remember all those times you ran off to the library? I was expected to wait for him, or he would start fresh, training you. That's what he said, and I wasn't going to let him fucking do that."

"Oh, Nadine," I moved to sit beside her.

"No!" She put up a hand to stop me. "I don't need your sympathy. I need a place to crash."

"All you're doing is crashing. You deserve better than that. You need to talk to someone. You need to go to the police."

She barked a laugh. "You think I haven't tried that? I got sober three years ago and decided to start kicking ass. You know what happened when I went into the police station? Nothing. No one gave a shit. It was old news, and when they looked at me, they saw a junkie with a record. They didn't even believe me."

"I believe you. I remember him coming into our room. You have a witness now."

"Whatever. I don't even care."

"Nadine, please let me help you." I went to give her a hug, but she shoved me off, and in doing so, sloshed the remains of her drink onto my couch. We both stood up and looked down at the mess of the one piece of furniture I'd put sweat equity into. Covered with cranberry vodka and patches of grease.

All because of her. But even as the anger rose, I let it fall again. How many times had she probably looked for help and not found it? Felt unprotected? Unsafe? Violated? Like her life wasn't worth as much as everyone else's? I now understood. The real question wasn't why did she turn to alcohol and drugs but why wouldn't she?

"Oh my god. I'm so sorry," she cried, setting the glass down on the coffee table and rushing to get napkins to soak up the mess. It wasn't helping. Tears were now flooding her face. Genuine. Remorseful. "You're right. I'm this big fucking mess, a fucking wrecking ball."

Somehow I wasn't surprised that the couch was ruined. I crossed my arms loosely under my breasts, surveying the damage, and shrugged.

"It's a couch." She and I were both damaged, and after the abuse I went through with Brady, I wanted to hold her tight. I wanted to cry with her, but she was backing away from me, so I figured she needed some space.

She'd been a child going through all of those same abuses. And she was right. She'd saved me at the expense of herself. But letting her implode for the rest of her life could not be the answer. I needed to find a way to help her. She didn't need to crash anymore. I gentled my voice, calmed it, hoped she could hear my love for her in it.

"It's a silly piece of furniture. You are more important than that. Don't worry about it. Look. You should rest for now, and when you're up for it, we can talk more later. I need to get a shower and grab some food."

"There isn't any here." She hung her head. "You're going to need to go out and get something."

Again, I bit back my irritation. I'd already had an emotional morning before this talk with Nadine had started. Fatigue was setting in. I needed space to think about everything. On a sigh, I said, "All right. You need help. Let's work together to figure this out, okay?"

She kept her eyes on her feet, not wanting to make eye contact. "I'm sorry about going to Brady."

"It's all right. The truth is I left him, Nadine. He was a controlling jerk, and I ended up sneaking out, like, two years ago, to get away from him. He doesn't even know where I live."

She took a deep breath, shaking her head with wide eyes. "That's not true."

"What's not true?"

"He knows where you live."

My eyes narrowed with sudden apprehension. "How?"

"Because I told him."

CHAPTER 21

MASON

"She coming?" Zeke asked, leaning against the machinery in the room I used for rehabilitation, Jay sitting in his wheelchair near the free weights.

"I don't know," I growled, sitting on the weight bench. It was Monday, and somehow, I made it through the weekend, which went by at a crawl. I could still smell her on my sheets and was able to fight the compulsion to wash them just to keep her scent close.

That had been a breakthrough.

"She'll be here," Jay nodded. "She's in love with you, man. I've seen the way she looks at you, and the way you look at her."

I shook my head, not wanting to hear it. My

insides had felt like miles of road rash since dropping her off on Saturday. "I'm not the guy for her. She doesn't need some guy with more baggage than sense. I've got…issues. Things I haven't told you much about."

"You clean everything or some shit," Zeke gruffed in his craggy voice. "I went by the office the other day. I don't know what the hell you did to that place, but I couldn't find a damn thing."

"And she doesn't want a guy with the smell of armed forces coming off him. Her ex…It was bad. This isn't going to happen. She doesn't need to deal with all my problems."

"So you let her go," Zeke snorted, somehow managing to look disappointed at the same time that he smirked. "And here I thought you were some big shot with all the answers. You told me not to make decisions for my daughter and granddaughter, but you're doing that with your woman. She deserves to know who you are, so she can see that we aren't all the same."

Jay rolled up closer in his wheelchair, a frown creasing the lines around his dark eyes when he said, "You sent Zeke's ugly mug to my place to set me straight, but you're going to act like you don't deserve someone who gets you?"

"It's not the same. She can do better than me." I scrubbed my hand over my face. *G-man. Gone forever. How can I deserve a life more than he did?* But my reasoning was starting to sound hollow to my own ears, especially after having the gift of her sweetness and inner light. That's what I saw most when I looked at her. Just thinking of her was making me feel choked up.

"Now why the fuck do you say that?" Jay demanded, his lips twisting in a frown.

"I…" No one had ever heard the full scope of how it was all my fault. I looked Jay then Zeke in the eye and hung my head again. It felt so heavy on my shoulders. Would it feel lighter if I shared with them? They would get it. All they knew was that I'd survived an accident. They didn't know I'd caused it. "I got my best friend killed. Missed an IUD when I was walking point. He died in my arms with pieces blown off."

They weren't saying anything, and I lifted my head to gauge their reactions. They both looked grim, but neither seemed shocked nor looked at me with judgement.

Jay leaned back, still keeping a bead on me. "I thought I saw something in the rocks when we were rolling by in the Hummers. Figured it was hot and my mind was going wacky because we were in the middle of nowhere, expecting nothing. Just transporting shit from point A to point B. Simple." Jay looked away then. Grinned, but there was no humor. "I didn't say anything. Then our shit suddenly blew the fuck up. Three guys dead in our truck. I lost my legs. It was a guy with a fucking rocket launcher and a scope. Score. Am I to blame?"

"Fuck no," I scowled.

"But it wasn't me, by the way. It was a guy in the truck behind us who saw something in the rocks. I said it was me to prove the point because our truck was hit, not his. I still don't blame him."

"You didn't set it in the ground, Mason. You aren't in charge of when someone gets their timecard clocked out. If you keep thinking that somehow you could have done something different, you're going to end up going nuts like so many of us, and we'll be burying you six feet under. War is bullshit. Fucked-up things happen. We do the best we can. The end," Zeke scowled.

"If I'm being forced to talk to someone about this shit, and Zeke is forcing himself to finish his chemo, then you better get your ass in to talk with someone. Do the fucking work, brother. Live your life well. That's how you honor your best friend."

"Dammit. I tried that…" My sentence fell off midpoint as I saw Layla enter the gym. Fuck she was beautiful. Her striking eyes, rounded and looking like a clear summer sky, scanned the floor, bypassed the cardio section, weight machines, free weights, and stopped when they landed on me in this separate room. The connection snapped into place in an instant. I could read her eyes. They were telling me that she was still with me, and I was telling her that I was grateful.

My eyes burned just seeing her. I was having trouble breathing. G-man would have loved her. He would have fallen to his knees in front of her with whatever offering he could find, either on his person or on the ground, even if it was a rock, and propose to her with it in some goofy way. For a moment, it felt like he was next to me, rolling his eyes and asking what the hell I was waiting for. If he were here, he'd pull up his ukulele and come up with a song that cracked us all up at the same time that it made fun of me for being dumb and not fighting for her.

My heart clenched with his smiling image in mind. Honor him by living well? Was I dishonoring his memory by reliving his death over and over again? Trying to think of some way that day could have had a different outcome if only…?

Our eyes were still connected. She was always able with just a look to hold me captive. A willing prisoner that wanted to live in their blue depths, feel the sweetness of her soul, breathe in her essence.

"Did you really try? What, once or twice? Then it got too hard and you said 'fuck it.' Am I right?" Jay asked. His voice had receded to the background, like he was narrating the moment. "Doesn't she deserve to have the man she wants? It appears to be you for whatever fucked-up reason, considering I'm a prime example of man flesh here. Can't you be strong enough to come to her the best version of you that you can be?"

"Go to counseling. Take the meds," Zeke demanded in his sandpaper voice.

"Don't be a hypocrite, Mason." Jay added, not pulling any punches. "Have some fucking balls, confront this shit that's been eating you alive from the inside, and fight for your woman. I waited too long and mine stopped trying. That's on me. Don't make my mistake. Who knows? Maybe Amanda isn't so far gone that she wouldn't hear an apology from me. Maybe she'll wait for me just a little longer. I've listened to you all this time, brother. You helped me when I didn't think I could do this. You sent me Zeke when I had my doubts again. It's time for you to start listening now."

Layla hitched her bag farther up on her shoulder and hesitantly came toward the room we were in. She ran a nervous hand over her dark hair, making sure all the tendrils were tucked into the ponytail, then pushed the glass door open. She was wearing her usual spandex that showed off her curves. Part of me was proud of how hard she worked to sculpt the body she wanted, and the other part of me wanted to cover her up so only I could see. I knew what was inside her clothes. I'd had my hands, mouth, and tongue all over her.

She was mine, but was I hers? Did she want to claim me?

I stood as she came toward us.

"Layla," Zeke greeted her in what was his warm voice. It was actually a gentler rumbling sound like a car engine with a deep purr. He'd somehow damaged his vocal chords while he was at war, which had given his throat a perpetual rasp.

"Zeke." She gave him a warm hug and kissed his cheek. "It's nice to see you again."

"I'm Jay." Jay rolled forward with a big smile creasing his face.

"Nice to meet you." She shook his hand with a small smile. "I've seen you working in here for the past year."

"Mason's keeping me alive."

"Good to hear it." She nodded and turned to me. Moving closer, she held my gaze, looking up at me from a foot away.

"We've got to get to the clinic," Jay said as he picked up his gym bag from the floor and set it on his lap. "Zeke, wheel my ass out of here, would you? My arms are noodled."

She only looked at me. After a moment, she reached up to cup my cheeks in a caress. I was surprised to realize she was wiping tears from my cheeks. Tenderly, she pulled my face down and whispered, "Don't be sad," before brushing her lips across mine.

My arms snaked around her, my face found her neck, and it was like coming home. Taking a deep breath of her scent with her small frame tight in my arms and her fingers threaded through my hair, my heart eased.

"I know I'm not who you wanted," I murmured into her neck.

"I don't know my own mind anymore," she whispered by my ear.

"Just, please don't walk away. I don't know what this is between us, but I know I want us to talk."

"I can't seem to walk away. You're all I've thought about for so long now."

I pulled back to search her face. "Can we hang out later?"

"Yes," she replied, and her own eyes misted.

"What is it?"

"My sister left. I found her drunk when you dropped me off on Friday. We had it out. Some things came to light that explain why she changed. It's a long story." She shook her head. "We were supposed to talk more, but she managed to pack up her stuff and sneak off while I was out getting food."

"You don't know where she went?"

"She doesn't have a phone that works consistently."

"When will you see her again?"

"It could be a few weeks, a few months, or even a few years. It could be never."

I thought about that possibility and hugged her closer, hoping she didn't ever have to bury her sister. "I'm sorry, baby."

"I think she knows I'll help her when she's ready, but until then, I know she's going to be on self-destructive mode, which was what we were fighting about. She takes everyone down with her. The thing is"—she pulled away— "she told Brady where I live, and now I'm wondering if he was the man in the black car."

"Thursday night?"

She nodded.

"Shit. Layla, you've been in danger the last three nights alone?"

She shook her head, and said, "I'm safe at my place. It's got a security gate."

"Those are fucking easy to get around. Why don't you just come stay with me?"

"Because I'm not sure that it was him in the black car."

I relived the moments of seeing her getting hauled off and felt my stomach twist. "I need to protect you, Layla. The idea of a man taking you is literally making me sick. That's one of the two things that've been bothering me."

"What's that?"

"I want you to be able to protect yourself. There are ways to take down grown men bigger than you. I want to teach you some moves and have you practice them."

"Really?" she asked with surprise.

"Absolutely. Work with me for the next half hour. Let's make this part of your workout."

She was already nodding, which told me she was a little freaked out herself. "Show me."

"All right. Now, the thing is, it doesn't matter how much of a badass a guy is, how big he is, if someone grabs his balls and does a squeezing twist, he's going down every time."

"A ball grab?" she asked horrified.

"Or a dick punch. No guy would see that coming."

CHAPTER 22

LAYLA

"This is quite the shitstorm, Wonder Woman."

Blessing was wearing a *Game of Thrones*-inspired, artfully ripped, brown halter top with worn, leather-looking, fitted utility pants and biker boots. Her blond hair tumbled in waves down her back, and she took a moment to shove her glasses back up her nose.

"It might not be him," I frowned, wiping my fingers on a napkin, and tossing it into my brown paper lunch sack.

"Don't be a freaking ostrich and live with your head in the sand."

"You know they don't actually do that."

"Do what?"

"Bury their heads in the sand. It's all a myth." I tilted my head back to enjoy the sun that decided to break through the clouds at midday. We were lunching on the roof. I'd already given Blessing the lowdown over the weekend. She'd even come over to help me decompress when my sister showed up missing yet again.

Luckily, nothing of mine was gone.

Unfortunately, the material on my couch was toast.

It would be a while before I could replace the fabric. Maybe next time, I would get something in a dark pattern. In any case, if I could do it once, I could do it again.

Blessing glared at me. "Don't miss the point. You were fine for all this time until your sister came to town. Then all of a sudden, some guy tries to grab you off the street. I'm telling you, even if you don't want to stay with Mason, you need to stay here. At least until we find out what rock Brady's been hiding under. Have you shared this info with the police?"

"What if I'm wrong? It's purely a guess."

"Until you're missing, and no one can find you."

"Well, you aren't the only one who's freaking out. Mason might have flipped out this morning. Then he had me practice self-defense moves with him for almost an hour. I know I'm going to be sore."

She leveled me with a narrow-eyed stare, and I knew she was about to ask me the tougher question. "Tell me again why you ran off from this man who saved you from a kidnapping, insisted on teaching you self-defense, and turned you multiorgasmic?"

I shook my head. "It's complicated. I mean, he's got PTSD stuff that's making him all neat freak crazy. His need to be organized had me right back in San Diego with the cleansers and the toothbrush and the hospital corners."

"He wanted you to clean?" she asked.

"No, but I panicked and realized that I don't want to be stuck ever again."

"Are you the same girl you were four years ago when you decided to live with Brady?"

"Well, no. Of course not."

"You kick ass, that's why." She held up her hand tapping each finger as she listed my accomplishments. "You've been working overtime to finish the last of your classes online for the associates degree you started, while you work your tail off with this complicated, demanding job, and while you're thinking about going back to finish the rest of your bachelor's degree, even though you're now earning sufficient money with great potential for making more as we go on. You won't ever be who you used to be. I can guarantee it. You are not a girl who makes the same mistake twice, and you have a badass friend who won't let it happen besides. Seriously, you are a fucking rock star, Layla. Cut the man some slack."

"But that's what I found out when I stayed with him. I'm not as strong as I thought. I freaked out. I had multiple panic attacks. I saw Brady lurking in every shadow, reminding me that it would be so easy to fall into that trap again. I thought I was strong, but when I care, I stop thinking about what's good for me. I can't ever live that way again."

"Exactly. No one gets things right the first time or the second time, but once you learn what's right, you don't make that mistake again. You are fucking strong, girl. You survived until you could find a way to live the life that you wanted. And you won't ever accept less than that. Trust yourself again. You learned this lesson. Now take it with you and thrive. Take things slowly with Mason. Get to know each other. But I'll tell you this, and you're going to get mad at me, but he's still controlling you."

"Brady?" My voice turned shrill with the very idea. "Not even close."

"He's every single reason that just came out of your mouth for you not taking a risk and seeing where this thing can go with Mason. Brady's the one lurking in the shadows because you keep letting him exist there. And look, I'm not saying to be stupid and dive into this thing with Mason headfirst. I'm saying Mason seems to be a good guy who truly cares about you. It's all right to let this flow organically. See what happens. People meet and they couple up happily all over the world. My parents have been together for like forty-five years because they can't stand to be away from each other. I'm the 'oops' baby that happened when my mother was forty, which is why my sister is like fifteen years older than me."

I knew this was all true.

"Big girl panties, Layla. You have to keep growing in this life, or you start dying on the inside. And you know, from what you told me about what happened, it sounds like Mason needs you too. I think you guys could be good for each other."

"Right, well, that's a lot to think about."

The sound of a high-pitched drill filled the air, and Blessing whipped her head around toward the noise, the set of her jaw showing her aggravation. In a voice loud enough for me to hear above the noise, she said, "This shit started at seven-thirty in the goddamned morning. Woke my ass from a dead sleep."

"The new owner?" I asked.

"Yeah. His crew said this would be happening for the next two fucking weeks. I need my sleep. You know that I do my best creative work late at night, and now I'm going to lose out on sleep for the next two weeks? Fucker."

"Did you try talking to him?"

"He's out of state right now. Not to be disturbed." There was disgust in her tone. "Anyway, we've got Thanksgiving with my parents in a couple of weeks. They want to take us all skiing in Colorado. You up for that?"

I'd been spending all my holidays with Blessing's family the last few years. It had been eye-opening to see how kind and loving a family could be. And she was right. Her parents were crazy about each other. Finishing each other's thoughts. Whispering naughty things in each other's ears that caused blushes of embarrassment and Blessing to pretend outrage when she was secretly proud of their happiness together.

"Yeah, sure. If they don't mind me tagging along," I said absently.

"You know they love you. They want to adopt you."

I laughed. "Let's do it."

"I'm only half joking. So, you going to stay here tonight?"

"Well, I told Mason we could hang out tonight. He's picking me up at five."

Blessing's smile lit up her face. "Good girl. Blow him well, my young Jedi. Blow him well. Feel the force…of his dick that is."

I arched a brow at the same time that heat climbed into my cheeks.

"What's the word again?"

Knowing she wasn't going to let me go without saying it a few thousand times, I grabbed my lunch bag and said, "Pussy, pussy, pussy, pussy…" I was still chanting it as I stood and made my way toward the sliding glass doors. I didn't even flinch.

I thought I heard her say, "And…my work here is done."

The rest of the workday went by in a flash, and

when it was five, Blessing walked me out to the sidewalk where Mason was already waiting for me. He was leaning up against the Jeep, looking like a delicious feast for my eyes. An unbuttoned pale blue flannel stretched across his broad chest, thrown over a simple gray T-shirt with yet another surf logo on it. Jeans and leather flip-flops completed his casual look, but it was the feeling I got when looking in his eyes that I craved most.

A feeling of completing a circuit, if that made any sense. Searching the sensitive depths of his beautiful eyes, making sure there were no new shadows, gave me an added surge of strength, like he was solid. Steady. He showed me in the way he looked at me that he had nothing to hide.

I realized that I'd always felt this from him. He was nothing like Brady. Nothing at all.

"Blessing, this is Mason."

"Mason the Hunk." She grinned, eyeing him boldly. He blushed the lightest tinge of pink but pushed away from the car door and stuck out his hand, which she took readily.

"Nice meeting you," he smiled, but his tone was serious. "From everything she's told me, you have been an amazing friend."

It was her turn to flush. She shrugged and said, "It went both ways. I'm not exactly normal, as you can see. She accepted me with the packaging I arrived in."

"Okay, guys. Too many feels here," I said, but with a big smile on my face.

"No more of that." Mason dropped a kiss on my head, slid his arm around my back. It was warm and strong and supportive. Comforting.

"I don't want her sleeping alone with her crazy ex possibly lurking about. If she decides against boning you tonight, bring her back here, all right?"

This time, Mason chuckled. "For sure."

"Text me when you know. I don't want to worry like I did on Friday."

I hugged Blessing and said, "For sure," mimicking Mason's response. "Mason told me to call in sick on Friday, but then he distracted me."

He chuckled. "I did."

"Keep up the good work," Blessing saluted.

With a toodle-oo wave of my fingers, I got in the Jeep, and he pulled us into traffic. With all the thoughts and feelings that were radiating from my heart, there was still one theme my mind kept coming back to: being with him filled me with such warmth and tenderness that I couldn't wait to talk to him any longer about what I was thinking. I turned toward him, and he sliced a quick glance my way.

He looked worried.

"What's up?"

"I owe you an apology, too. I wanted to apologize for the way I skipped out on you Friday morning, especially after everything you did for me."

He shook his head. "You don't need to apologize."

"I do because I've had some time to think. I also have a nosy friend who has my best interest at heart, and she made me realize some things."

"What's that?" he asked, dividing his time between the road and my face.

"You are nothing like Brady, and all my freaking out was about letting him continue to have a piece of me. I was so afraid of being caught up that I started seeing problems to give myself an excuse not to try."

"I can understand that." He nodded, his eyes

turning sad, turning inward.

"Here's my takeaway of this situation." My heart picked up a few beats. I could feel my blood rushing, the vein in my neck pulsing. My words sounded a little shaky when I said, "I've never felt like this about anyone before. I think about you so much of the time. It's like you said earlier: I don't know what this is, but maybe, if we go slowly, we can see where this goes."

"Really?" He suddenly grinned at me. It was contagious.

"Really."

He abruptly turned down a street and pulled into a parking lot. When the car was off, he reached for me, pulled me across his lap, and planted a hard kiss on my lips that had my arms drifting up around his neck, my nails sliding into his hair. Just when I was getting good and hot, my bottom wiggling against his growing erection, he set me on my seat again.

"What…" I knew I looked confused.

"We're here," he announced, a twinkle in his eyes.

"Here…where?" I looked around, realizing we were in front of a store.

"Remember this morning I told you there were two things that I needed to address with you?"

"Uh, I think so."

"One of them was self-defense, which I plan to keep training you in. Maybe I'll even see about getting a guy to do a once-a-week night class for free for all females. Seeing you get carted away took years off my life."

"Okay. That's a great idea, but what's the second thing?"

"Swimming. There is no way you can live in this part of the world and not know how to swim. We're here to get you a suit."

"A suit?" I looked around. He'd parked in the Becker Surfboards' lot. Mild alarm creased my brows. "Why do I need a suit? You don't have a pool or anything. I'm telling you now. I'm not getting in the ocean. I'm just not. Maybe around my ankles and knees. I mean…" I'd started babbling my nerves just thinking about it.

"Hear me out," he ran gentle knuckles down my arm in a light caress. "My parents have a pool, and Saturday we're celebrating my dad's birthday."

"So…" He couldn't be suggesting I meet his parents. Not now. Wasn't it too soon? Here was something else to worry about.

"So, come with me on Saturday, and let me give you your first swimming lesson."

"To your parents' house? On a special occasion?" I shook my head. "I mean, it's so last minute. Isn't that rude?"

"It's fine."

"You want me to meet your parents? I'm not...I mean...Isn't it...Aren't we..." A full sentence refused to form, mostly because I wasn't sure what to object to.

"They will love you. Everyone is laid back, and you'll be making my mom happy. She's been trying to get me to bring someone every time there's a get together. She'll be excited to hear that you're coming."

"Swimming?" Parents and swimming. It was all so much, but I could see this was important to him. I let my fear dissipate. If his family wasn't going to like me, I guess now was as good a time as any to find out.

"You need a couple of suits. They've got a whole section here for women's beachwear."

"A couple?"

"Yeah." A sly grin slipped over his lips, and I found that I liked that playful expression. I found myself mirroring it. He added, "Maybe one of them you wear for me, and one you wear for the rest of the world?" He looked hopeful and happy all at once, and I found myself nodding immediately. I liked the idea of taking on the seductress role.

Beckers was fairly empty when we entered, particularly as it wasn't prime beach season, but there were still a number of suits displayed on the racks. After grabbing a few that looked cool, if not small, I went into the dressing room and worked my way into the first. It was shockingly brief, but even I could whistle and admit that working out did a body good.

"Let me see," Mason called when he figured I'd been in the room too long.

"I don't know," I hesitated, suddenly shy. The top was strings and triangles that pulled my breasts together, and the bottom was basically just shy of being a thong. There was a whole expanse of smooth, soft skin, shaped from the work I'd put into it, but not overly so. Fit. Feminine.

Wow. I'd never worn a bathing suit in my life, and from the way I'd seen other women wear these, I was rocking it.

I opened the door.

Mason's jaw dropped. The sense of feminine power that flooded my body was intoxicating, especially when the man I was having an effect on was this big, tough-looking, ex-military guy who could throw grown men around. With a casual step forward, I spun to give him the rear view, pausing just long enough to strike a quick pose, cocking my hip, before turning back to face him.

"Do you like this one?"

He shifted from one foot to the other, gave a quick glance around, and moved me back into the dressing area, closing the door behind him. Pushing up against me, he showed me with the feel of his rapidly hardening cock against my stomach how much he liked it. He bent to growl in my ear, "You are so fucking hot."

"So you like it?" My words came out sounding breathless, and I realized this was flirting. I was teasing him, making him sensual promises. I rubbed my tummy against his erection, as his breathing deepened.

"It's perfect on you." One of his fingers ran under the cup of my top, gently feathering over my nipple, pulling the material out of the way so his lips could close around the stiff, distended point, his tongue curling hot and wet around the aching tip. Now he was making promises.

"Mason," I whispered, biting my lip to keep from panting, "we can't do this here."

"Just letting you know I like this one," he whispered against the aching tip, and my pussy contracted with sudden heat and moisture.

"I have more to try on," I protested, but my hand was still cupping the back of his head, fingers threaded through his short dark hair as his tongue rubbed sensuously and his lips sucked hard and fast.

I moaned and panted, arching into him, unable to get enough.

He flicked it with his tongue one last time before stepping back. "Let's finish up so I can take you home."

CHAPTER 23

MASON

We were barely through the door when I had her pushed up against it, my dick finding its pleasure in grinding against her soft body, my lips buried in her neck where I could be immersed in her scent.

"Oh my god. Hurry," Layla gasped, trying to unbutton her shirt.

She'd only managed to get it halfway undone when I lifted her up to nuzzle her breasts through the silky, transparent satin of her bra, her legs automatically hooking around my waist. Her nipples were particularly sensitive. She shivered and moaned, sounding more desperate by the second, which was why I was driving us both insane taking turns with each ripe tip, scraping my teeth over the fabric. They were tight buds pushing out against the material

"I need you inside me. Please," she demanded despite the plea. "My jeans need to come off."

The couch was an easy decision to make. Setting her down on her feet, I grabbed her hand and pulled her toward the arm of it before spinning her around so her back was to me. Sliding my hands down her stomach, I took it upon myself to unclasp her jeans and shove both them and her floral scraps of underwear down her hips to her ankles, where she kicked them off.

Before I could stop her, she was on her knees working on my own pants, making short work of the belt and buttons. She looked up at me hesitating, her expression suddenly uncertain, and while I wanted to be inside her, I also wanted her to know she had skin privileges. She was allowed to touch me however she wanted whenever she wanted. To that end, I held her gaze and nodded. She went back to my pants that were now hanging on my hips. Pulling them down until my cock sprang free, thick with need for her, precum on the tip. And with eyes looking like they wanted to feast, she wrapped her mouth, hot and silky, around my cock, making me shiver with the intense pleasure.

"Fuck," I breathed out, fighting the urge to straight out fuck her mouth because if felt so good. I didn't want to scare her, but the sight of her on my dick was almost enough to send me over the edge. Then she started moving.

With our eyes locked, she worked her hand and mouth in tandem, wringing groans and guttural sounds from my throat that I was sure I'd never made before. I was powerless under her innocent blue eyes, her eager lips and tongue. The heat grew like a wildfire through my body. I felt the tingle in my spine, my balls tightening, the warning that I was going to blow if she kept this up, and carefully pulled her off my cock.

She protested until I told her, "I want to fuck you until we're both coming so hard the neighbors are fucking jealous."

Her answer was simple. "Do it."

I turned her toward the couch and bent her over the arm, gently caressing her gorgeous, round ass cheeks, kneading them before letting my fingers slide between her legs. Her wet arousal coated her swollen lips and pink clit, with more to be found inside her channel. I slid two fingers inside of her, and she started panting and moving back toward me, trying to get them deeper. She was soaking me with her need, and I knew she was close, shaking with it.

"This okay, sweet girl?" I asked, not wanting to do anything that would take her out of this moment. We still had a lot to learn about each other.

She looked over her shoulder, a soulful appreciation darkening her eyes before she said, "Yes. I want your cock there, Mason."

That was all I needed to hear. My pants were on the floor by my feet, and I slid into her hot, tight pussy. I only paused when I was balls deep, both of us moaning with the intense feel of it. "This isn't going to last long, baby. You feel too good."

"Hard, Mason. Fast and hard."

With my hands grabbing her delicate hip bones in a firm grasp, I tunneled into her, her entire body jerking with every thrust of my hips. The slap of our flesh was accompanied by her cries of need that were growing louder and louder. They matched my own growls of building, tightening desire.

Moving one hand to the base of her spine, I held her firmly to the arm of the couch while my other hand worked around to where her swollen clit throbbed under my fingertips. Finding a new rhythm, a new angle, I worked the dripping wetness from her pussy over the hot button of nerves with my fingers, and her cries became shouts, her hands hooking around the arm of the couch she was bent over to push back, meeting me thrust for thrust until she shouted, "Oh my god, oh my god, oh my god, I'm coming! Don't stop, don't stop, yes!"

Then she went stiff, and her body shook with the explosive impact of her climax, her channel squeezing my cock, taking my orgasm from me with a roar ripping from my lungs until I was coming like a fucking locomotive. By the time my own body stopped pulsing in her pussy, she was laid out like a rag doll. Gently pulling out of her, I picked her up in my arms and settled us on the couch. I pulled the blanket draped off the back cushion until it was settled over us, making a cocoon of intimacy.

She was tucked into my body, her ass pressed to my groin, drowsing, and I was struck with a feeling of gratitude that she was here with me at all. It made my stomach turn to think that a simple twist of fate could have kept her from me, like if she hadn't had the courage to defy her ex and register for school, or if she hadn't met Blessing.

With my hand absently tracing a line over her hip and back to her stomach, I realized I still questioned my worthiness and that the guys were right. If I wanted to have a life worth living, I was going to need some help, but she deserved to know what she was getting herself into.

"You know I have this weird condition, right?" I murmured next to her ear.

"Condition? That's right. An OCD kind of thing?" she asked, then lifted a hand backward to cup my neck and run her fingernails up my scalp. It did two things instantly. It sent shivers down my spine and arched her breasts out, making it impossible to ignore them, so I didn't.

"Sort of," I murmured, letting my hand change course so it skimmed up her abdomen and cupped her breast, lazily thumbing the nipple that was already straining toward me.

She sighed, shivered, and asked in a voice that was breathy, "Do you need something to happen right now? Some sort of clean up?"

"No, nothing," I said, which was amazingly true in this moment. "It's just that I didn't tell you how I got this way, and I think you should understand who I am if you're thinking of signing on with me at all."

She paused her movements, and then she was turning around to face me, giving me her full attention. "I want to know everything about you."

I dropped a soft kiss to her lips, reacting to the sincerity in her eyes, falling into their peaceful ocean blue depths. They were my soft landing. I never wanted to be without her, which meant it was time to confront the shit and stop hiding from it. I leaned back to look up at the ceiling and took a deep breath, finally ready to talk about him. For the first time, my chest wasn't getting tight. Instead, there was a sadness, but with it, a warmth. I hadn't allowed myself to think about him at all, and it had hurt to deny myself the memories.

"George was one of my best friends from about middle school on. Always getting us into trouble that he usually planned. Not that I wasn't a willing participant, but he always tried to shoulder all the blame, too. I never let him. Still, he was that kind of guy. He'd walk through fire for you."

She remained silent, simply resting her hand on my chest. Let me think through my memories of him for a moment, knowing there was more to come.

"My family had some money, so it was expected that I would go to school once we graduated, but George's family wasn't as well off. He came from a home with a single, working mom, and he didn't have the best grades. His mother was not going to let him miss out on college, so the solution was going into the military and capitalizing on benefits afterward. I could never let him do that alone, so I went with him."

George and his stupid ukulele that never left his side. The image popped into my head, and it actually made me smile.

"Just the funniest guy, you know. Clever. Always had a perfect comeback. Could make up a song, whether it be corny or dirty, that would always capture a moment to perfection."

Layla grinned up at me. "Blessing is like that."

I mirrored her smile. "I can see that about her. She doesn't hold back."

"Not even a little."

The smile faded as I went into the part of my memory that was raw, that stung, that I was afraid of peering into. "Needless to say, we were sent to Afghanistan. Hot as fuck, and with all the gear. Relentless. So many missions that had us walking for hours under the sun. But there was George, always bantering with the rest of the guys, trying to keep the morale up on those fucking death marches. So, this one day, I was walking point guard for IED detection with my dog, laughing at the bullshit the guys were harassing each other with, and…"

I saw it clearly in my mind. Had my eyes doing their scan, watching for my dog, Sadie, to alert.

Amazing little girl. So smart. Loving. Always by my side. One floppy ear on her shepherd's face that could make the hardest Marine smile.

My eyes burned thinking of her. Loyal.

I remembered fighting the fatigue of being weighted down. Felt the scorching heat of the sun. Remembered the thoughts I was having, imagining being in the cool waters of the Pacific Ocean and bobbing out on the swells, waiting for a good set to come rolling in. Was remembering how George and I would ditch school back in the day to hang out at the beach if there was a good swell.

My breath hitched and came out with deliberately controlled exhalation to try and calm the sudden rapid beating of my heart. Could I really do this? Despite the effort, my breathing got heavier. Sharper.

"It was like the end of the world. There was this exploding roar that left me momentarily deaf and…and mindless. Uncomprehending. Smoke. Bodies. There's no way to describe it except mad chaos in fastforward. Someone grabbed my arm and yelled something in my face. Maybe the words were 'take cover,' but I couldn't hear anything. Then we were running. I was looking for him. George. He'd been somewhere behind me in the field. Couldn't find him right away and started freaking the fuck out." I needed to pause. Emotion swelled in my throat. I needed a moment to swallow it back down.

Soft, delicate fingers crept up my neck to my cheek, cupped it gently, her care bleeding through my skin to warm my heart. She didn't say anything. She didn't need to. Just that one touch made the memory less lonely. I rubbed my face in her palm, closed my eyes for a moment, managed to take a deep breath again, even though my heart still hammered away. This was the part that hurt the most. My guilt.

"I knew what I was doing. I mean, it wasn't like I was a fucking rookie. I'd done it countless times. I knew what I was looking for and how to find it. Being able to view the environment as a whole and look for what seems strange or unnatural in the landscape. I'd trained. Practiced. I had experience." I shook my head, thinking about how the world changed from one moment to the next. "I keep thinking that maybe I was distracted, listening to the guys and just missed the signs. But I can't go back and investigate. I can't remember. I can't find the missing link, what I could have done to prevent it."

"Was it unusual for George to joke around when you guys were out?"

Thinking about it, I admitted, "No. Not really."

"Did you find other buried IEDs?"

"In all the time I spent out there, I managed to locate eleven."

"So you saved your guys on at least eleven other occasions. Were the IEDs easy to find?"

"No. It's like finding a needle in a haystack."

"Or a bomb in the desert?" She sounded dismayed, and her arm tensed, hand sliding down to cup my neck, holding me tighter, like she wanted to protect me from the memory. "Holy crap. You lived a nightmare."

"I had a metal detector, and between it, my dog, and my own observation, I caught most everything. A hundred and twenty patrols, and we found eleven IEDs. I felt successful until the day when everything went wrong."

"What happened after the explosion?" Her hushed voice reflected my own.

"Bullets were flying everywhere, popping the dirt at our feet, then one whizzes past my temple, and I feel the air puff kissing the hair by my ear. We all scramble. Everyone's screaming, running for cover, and I realize G-man is just gone. I don't know where he is. I can't see him in the smoke, and I sure as hell can't hear him calling. I stumble onto

him some distance away while I'm
checking…bodies."

I closed my eyes, back in the battle, seeing
George laid out, and felt the thick emotion rise up
again in my throat, distort my voice.

"When I finally understood what had happened, I
don't know, maybe a few seconds later, I saw him
lying there a couple feet away. I knew he couldn't
survive. On some level, I knew he couldn't possibly
make it, but my brain just couldn't think that way. I
needed to save him. Didn't even realize I had
shrapnel piercing my body or that I was a fucking
bloody mess. All I could think of was crawling over
to him. He was all fucked-up. He'd been closest. I'll
never forget how he looked. Panicked." I knew he
was going to die. I couldn't stop it.

A harsh cry broke from my chest out of nowhere.
I felt bleeding from deep in my soul, and my hand
went up to cover my eyes like I could somehow
stop the vision, but I couldn't. It was vibrant. Clear.
His blue eyes were so round and confused looking
up at me. They were permanently etched in my
mind, along with the feeling of horrifying
inevitability. I could still feel the burning heat,
smell the smoke, taste the fear, and know that my
best friend was going to die right before my eyes.
Another harsh cry, and I tried to sit up. Move away,

so I could hide the pain, but she wouldn't let me.

"Mason. Sweetheart," Layla rolled onto me, moved up to press her cheek to mine, cradle my face to her. She was wiping the moisture from my cheek with her thumb, holding me tightly, her soft lips whispering, "It's all right, baby. I've got you."

And she did have me. I buried my face in her neck and snaked my arms around her slender form, holding her tightly to me as the wave of sorrow racked my body. G-man. So young. Both of us. So naïve. Our dreams cut down in a single moment.

It was several minutes later that the wave of emotion subsided, the quiet settled between us. I was able to take a breath again. There was more. It all needed to be said. I needed to get it all out. I loosened my grip, and she continued to sprawl over me, but now with her head on my chest. Her hand was still cupping my face, and I was glad to have it there. A new calm washed over me.

Taking a deep breath, I continued, "He was straining against the pain. Shouting at me in sobbing bursts of words I couldn't hear because of the ambient noise and the ringing in my ears. It haunts me."

"Oh, Mason," Layla sniffed. I'd been so caught up in my own memories I hadn't realized how affected Layla was. Surprised, I saw tears were streaming down her face when I turned my head to look at her. She offered, "I'm so sorry. He died, didn't he?"

I wiped the tears from her face and nodded, holding her gaze for strength. "His leg was gone. His arm was mangled, sort of hanging off him. The blood was so much. More than I would ever have thought. And so red against the dirt. I didn't know where to start. I didn't know what to do."

"There was nothing you could have done." She planted soft kisses along my jaw, reaching the corner of my mouth. "Nothing."

"I could have found the fucking IED. They were still waiting to ambush us, but maybe we could have taken evasive measures and had fewer casualties. Maybe George would still be alive. I don't know." The words felt empty when I said them out loud this time, and that had me stumbling in my own thoughts.

"You aren't Superman, and that war was not your fault. There is nothing you could have done to change what happened. You are not some all-knowing deity. You are not that powerful. No one is. There is nothing you should have been able to do that you didn't already do." Her fingers traced a caressing line down my neck, around my pecs, and around the different muscles in my abdomen. Her lips gave nipping kisses along my neck. A shiver worked down my spine as she loved on me, pausing to add gently, "I still work on that part myself, wishing I could have known or understood who Brady was sooner. I had to give up that kind of thinking, or I wouldn't have been able to be here with you. In the now. Trying to live my best life. Maybe it's better because I know how awful things can be. George sounds like he was a good man and a great friend."

"The best." Remembered love and warmth trickled out through the pain.

"He loved you. Probably like a brother."

I nodded, swallowing past the lump in my throat as the warmth spread through my body.

"Maybe he would want you to live the life he couldn't have?"

George never would have wanted me to stop living for his sake. I let her take me away with soft hands and gentle attention, each touch like a gift of warmth to my soul. The knot in my throat subsided, and I turned to catch her lips for a feathery touch, partially turning to settle a leg between her thighs, appreciate the feeling of being skin-to-skin.

"Is that why you were sleeping in the other room when I woke up on Friday?" she asked, while rubbing her lips to mine.

"I still have nightmares. They're violent and leave me thrashing around."

"You relive those moments? Still see them in your mind when you least expect it? When you're defenseless?" She leaned up and kissed each eyelid with a reverence. My heart swelled with the warmth of her care.

"When he's in my arms, dying, and I'm shouting at him to hold on, that I'm going to get him out of there."

"Oh, Mason," she kissed me again, only this time longer and deeper, taking her time. Her hands were sliding down my chest, her caresses lingering, lovingly sculpting the shape of my muscles before wrapping around my already hardening cock. There was a qualitative difference in the way she was touching me.

She was making love to me.

It was the why that I'd been looking for. I'd never felt closer to a single other person in my entire life.

I pulled back to see her eyes, find that

connection that always recharged me, and felt her legs shift. Open. Rolling toward her, my hips settled in the cradle of heat between her thighs, and it was like coming home. I was right at her entrance, and together we arched our hips on a sigh. Tender kisses and murmured words of encouragement hung on the air between our lips. Legs wrapped around me, hands curled over my ass, pulling me deep in slow, steady thrusts.

"Tell me if it's ever not okay," I said with a look that demanded she listen.

"I promise," she responded, and it was there on her face.

Our eyes held and we watched the electricity charge up with each thrusting glide that we choreographed, each moan that we shared. Then we were both gasping and holding each other through the waves of pleasure that rocked us.

I was falling in love with her.

On that thought, I started drifting off, ignoring the sound of my phone buzzing from somewhere in the room.

CHAPTER 24

LAYLA

"There's no freaking way I'm going to meet your parents for the first time in my bikini, and especially not that skimpy, hootchie-mama bikini, and you're just going to have to deal with that."

Meeting a guy's parents was not something I ever did, not even with Brady, and my stress button was already getting pushed over and over again, as evidenced by the state of my bedroom. My closet had been turned inside out in an attempt to find the perfect outfit that simply did not exist. I'd settled on my nicest jeans that were slim fit, ballet flats, and a feminine button-down blouse with a blue floral design that outlined my shape and left an attractive V open neckline.

He'd said casual.

Mason showed up in cargo shorts and a T-shirt. That got me worried that I was overdressed, and he spent the next ten minutes talking me out of changing my clothes yet again.

"You look gorgeous, sweet girl," he growled in my ear, curling his big body around me from behind when I went back to survey my closet. Of course, any time he called me that, my heart got a little mushy and warm. It was the first time I'd ever had a pet name, and my heart clung to it. I let him coax me out of the apartment with his promise that everything was going to be okay.

I believed him. Trusted him. It felt scary, but it was also exhilarating. Like letting go of the rollercoaster handlebar, trusting that it would hold me in when I lifted my hands overhead to simply enjoy the ride.

It also turned out my stress was all for nothing.

We arrived at his childhood home, a lovely place on the beach in Manhattan Beach. Mason walked us through the glass house that was designed with casual beach elegance in shades of blues and creams with dark hardwood flooring. It was beautiful, bigger than any house I'd ever been in before, but comfortable and lived in. It wasn't like a scary museum of wealth where you couldn't touch things.

As we neared the far end of the entrance hall, comfortable chitchat punctuated by light laughter drifted like happy musical notes through the air accompanied by smells of something delicious. It was a house with love and warmth vibrating through it. How amazing for kids to grow up in this kind of place. Food to eat. Space to play. Sweet-smelling air instead of the filth that always seemed to cling to Naddy and me.

I think I'd hated that the most. The filth. Sometimes, I still felt dirty, and it was hard to remember that I didn't live that way anymore and never would again.

"Hey guys," Mason called out. At the end of the entrance hall, we cut through the living room and formal dining area with its picturesque view of the gorgeous ocean that was right outside the sliding glass door. It was breathtaking, but we kept moving. The next archway led into the kitchen, and that was where everyone was gathered around a bar that overlooked a stove.

"Mason!"

"You're here."

"Hey, brother."

It was a chorus of greetings with lots of heartfelt

hugs and pats on the back. Watching them for these brief moments let me see what a beautiful family he'd come from. His father was an older, Nordic blond version of both the guy standing by the stove, who I assume was Mason's brother, and Mason. His sons inherited his distinguished, chiseled features, even though they had their mother's golden-brown skin coloring. His sister was petite like their mother but had her father's Nordic coloring. A bright, genuine smile lit up her face.

His mother found me first. She was surprised, if the widening of her eyes was anything to go by, which made me wonder if he'd let them know I was coming. But then, her smile grew wider, instantly warm, and welcoming.

"Well, introduce us to your friend, Mason. Don't keep us waiting." His mother gave me a friendly wink. Then everyone's eyes found me behind him. My cheeks heated under all the curious looks. I was totally out of my element with this whole meeting the family kind of thing. As always, my fears that I would give away my upbringing had my heart racing at the same time that I yearned to be accepted.

Mason snagged my hand and tugged me forward, sliding his arm around my waist and giving me a comforting squeeze. "This is Layla, my girlfriend.

We've known each other for a while. We met at the gym, and for some reason, even though I'm a giant pain in the ass, she's agreed to go out with me."

There was a moment of silence before they all grew big smiles on their faces. I exhaled my relief at the same time that I realized I was being foolish. They were lovely, not judgy.

"At least you aren't deluding yourself." His brother interjected. "You are a huge pain in the ass."

"I learned from my big brother," Mason returned, reaching out to fist bump the guy. It was fun and lighthearted, this joking. They were close, the way Naddy and I used to be, which warmed my heart. Then he was saying, "This is my mom, dad, my little sister, Savannah, and my brother with the big mouth, Travis."

The enthusiastic greetings were sudden and overwhelming, starting with his mother, who gave me a warm, tight hug. "Layla, we are all absolutely ecstatic to finally meet you. I can't tell you how very, very glad I am that you're here. You should call me Nancy, and this is Sam." She pointed to her husband.

"Layla," Sam greeted warmly, his dark blue eyes reflecting something like hope when he shook my hand, and it was the same with Travis. Even Savannah spontaneously gave me a quick, brief hug, her long blond hair swooshing around me. I'd never been hugged by so many people at one time and wondered if this was how normal families behaved. My cheeks burned with the amount of attention.

"So nice to meet all of you," I said, now unsure of what to do with my hands. I clasped them together at my waist and tried to keep from twisting them. "Thanks so much for having me here. Your home is beautiful."

"Thank you, and you're welcome," Nancy answered. "Can I get you a drink?"

"I'm fine for now, thanks."

A quick glance at Mason showed that he was happy to lounge against the counter behind me, a contented smile resting on his face. He looked relaxed. I'd never seen him with that look before. It suited him.

"Oh!" With a mildly panicked look, Nancy hurried around to the stove and turned the fire down on something, gave it a quick stir and looked up at Mason. "Creamed corn."

"I love your creamed corn," Mason groaned.

"I know," she answered, her eyes taking him in with the look only a loving mother could have.

"It's my birthday, but she's cooking all their favorite foods," Sam grumped, but he wasn't serious.

"You get all your favorites all the time," Nancy smirked.

"Damn right I do." Sam kissed the top of her head and she blushed. It was adorable, the obvious love they had for each other, just like Blessing's family. I still wasn't used to seeing this whole family dynamic thing, and it made me realize exactly how much I'd missed out on as a kid. No wonder I'd fallen for Brady's charm. No one had ever taught me, just by example or role modeling, to insist on being treated well. I'd had to learn that through trial and error.

"How did you guys meet?" Savannah asked, situating herself on the barstool again. She patted the one next to her own, inviting me to have a seat. "Get comfortable."

It was like she was inviting me into her space, like she wanted to get to know me for real. My confidence grew more, and I felt a genuine smile spread across my face. "Thanks."

After I took a seat, Mason shifted so he was behind me and rested his hands on my waist. He nuzzled the top of my head. "She joined up a little more than a year ago, and I couldn't take my eyes off of her. She was beautiful and confident and wasn't afraid to work hard for what she wanted."

"That's so sweet," Savannah singsonged.

My cheeks grew hot as I thought of the night at Zeke's when I first propositioned him, but I admitted, "It was mutual. I was impressed with the work he was doing, rehabbing the vets in the morning, and he was easy on the eyes."

"He is pretty," Travis added.

Mason arched a brow. "Keep talking, brother. I can take you now."

"You wish. Muscles don't make up for skill."

"Good thing I have both."

"We'll have to see about that."

"Why don't you guys take it outside, and while you're at it, get the grill started," Nancy ordered, but there was happiness in her voice. She was clearly enjoying having all her kids at home. "Go do your manly grunting and scratching outside and leave us to gossip about you."

"You're okay in here without me?" Mason asked quietly by my ear.

There again was an example of how thoughtful he was. First, every time he touched me, he made sure it was okay with me. He made sure I consented, which was sexy unto itself. And now, here he was making sure that I would feel safe and secure if he walked away. I had no doubt that he would stay with me if I gave any indication that I needed him near me. This was what it looked like when someone treated you like you were important. I was important to him.

The thought had me blinking back the sudden burn, but when he started to frown with worry, I smiled wide to reassure him.

"I'm fine," I said with a smart wink. After searching my eyes for a moment, giving me a chance to center myself within the steady strength reflected in his eyes, he rubbed a soft kiss on my lips that left me flushed, that had everyone grinning around us, and followed his brother out through the French doors into what I could only assume was the side yard, an area large enough to have a little plot of grass, an outdoor grill, and a small lap pool.

"I'll supervise," Sam smirked. "Holler if you need me."

Nancy patted his cheek. "I know where to find you."

Sam looked back at her with what could only be described as a lecherous expression. "Anytime, sweetheart."

She flushed, fought back a smile, but kept her look semi-stern. "Sam."

"I know, I know. Not in front of the kids." He headed for the back door mumbling, "Like they don't know we've done it."

"You mean we didn't hatch out of an egg?" I heard Travis' voice in mock horror drift in through the open door.

I looked at Nancy and Savannah, then we all giggled, and Nancy rolled her eyes. "Men."

"How can I help?" I asked, wanting to feel useful.

"Do you know how to chop lettuce and vegetables?"

"I'm sure I can manage."

"Then you and Savannah can help me make the salad."

And that's when we all relaxed and started

chatting.

Savannah was about my age, and even though she continued working on her own artistic painting projects that she laughingly warned were forced on all family members when they were completed, she was formally following in her father's footsteps with architecture, specializing in using sustainable building materials.

If her artwork at Mason's house was anything to go by, her architecture was likely out of this world. I shared about my own love of design and using technology to help make companies more accessible, the user experience easier and less intimidating.

It wasn't long before Savannah was asking me to look at the website for her father's company, Garrett Architects, because it was outdated and could use a new look. I promised to do it as long as they let me do it for free, which got a protest out of both Nancy and Savannah.

Our conversation flowed easily, and soon enough, the food was ready, and Savannah left the kitchen to set the table. Nancy stopped me when I went to help.

"You know"—Nancy dried her hands on a towel and faced me— "I can't tell you how happy I am that Mason found you. He hasn't been the same since he came back from war, and it breaks my heart to see the way he's isolated himself from everyone. But today, for the first time, I see the old Mason coming back, and I can only assume that it's because of you. He's contented. My heart is so filled. I can't thank you enough. There isn't anything I wouldn't do for him, and it was driving me crazy that there was nothing I could do." Her eyes watered with the pain she'd experienced as a mother.

I swallowed a lump in my throat, remembering the story he'd told when we were lying in each other's arms. Had he told anyone else? I had a feeling he'd kept it all inside, unable to let himself forget. Using it to punish himself for something beyond his control.

"You know, I don't know if I'm an influence or if he's just ready to heal, but I do know he's an amazing man, and I feel lucky that I found him," I admitted. "I love the way he's so selfless, giving his time to others who need him. It shows how kind and gentle he is. Honorable. He makes me want to be my best self."

There was pride shining from his mother's eyes, but then she whispered, "He's got a thing he does. You know. Moving things around."

"I know." I gave a self-deprecating smile, thinking of the way my apartment seemed to make him edgy. Left alone, he'd likely work his way through each room, organizing it. "He's going to get help with his PTSD. I'm afraid my own need to have things disorganized will be a special kind of hell otherwise."

"Professional help?" she asked with surprise.

I nodded, and she had me in a big hug instantly, this time, the tears in her eyes shimmering.

"I'm so relieved. So happy. Some mixture of PTSD and survivor's guilt have had a stranglehold on his life for so long now. On all our lives. We've all been so worried about him. You're the first girlfriend he's had in years, the first he's brought home to us in a long time, and we're all just so pleased to see that he's trying to get back to living life again. He had a terrible time with…well, it's not important." His mother broke off suddenly, a quick frown at whatever thought was in her mind.

I wondered what he'd had a terrible time with. I was dying to ask because I wanted to know everything about him, but I didn't. I felt like it would be too forward when what I really wanted was for her to approve of me. "He wants this for himself now, and I think that's what will help him be successful. He doesn't strike me as someone who gives up on what he wants."

"He isn't." She sighed, looking out the window toward the ocean view, where the sun was getting lower in the sky. "No matter how old your kids are, they're always your babies, you know?"

I didn't know, but I could see from the way they treated each other. Maybe there would be a day that I could share more about myself with her. I realized that for the first time, I wasn't afraid of thinking about a future where I might be connected to Mason.

It was when we were all moving into the dining room, Nancy directing everyone where to sit at the beautifully arranged table that was covered with dishes of mouthwatering foods, that the doorbell rang.

"Are you expecting anyone else?" Sam arched a brow at his wife.

"No one," she replied.

"I'll get it."

Savannah went to answer it, and within a few seconds, high heels clicked along the wooden entryway and rounded the arch to reveal beautiful, Malibu Barbie. Bethany appeared, a huge smile on her face as she surveyed the room. My stomach dropped.

Had Mason invited her?

The thought made my stomach burn with a sense of betrayal. The growing warmth and feelings of belonging that had been flittering around my insides seemed to vanish. Bethany looked as perfect as she had the last time I'd seen her, her long blond hair windblown and silky. With her linen pants and cute, strappy cami, she was like a model stepping out from the pages of an ad titled *Town and Country*. It was a harsh reminder that there had never been anything elegant or sophisticated about me.

"Mom! Dad! How are you guys?"

My brain recoiled further, processing her greeting.

Mom and Dad?

CHAPTER 25

LAYLA

Smiles dropped, laughter stopped, and several glances were cast toward Mason and then me.

The sound of the other woman's voice caused an immediate, discordant lull in the boisterous conversation, and everyone seemed to wince or visibly cringe. Mason shoved out of his seat, scowling, and along with the rest of his family, I slowly stood from my seat and moved around the table with the group to face the new guest.

Now I was confused.

"Bethany. This is a surprise." Nancy gave her a neutral greeting, but there was also a *why are you here* embedded in her tone. "I'm sorry to hear about your mother's illness. I haven't been able to keep up with her since she sold the house and moved away."

"I know," Bethany moved with confidence, bustling over to give Nancy a hug. "It's so good to see you all. I've missed you and missed being here. I think I might have spent more time here than in my own house over the years, and then Mason and I were together for so long. What was it?"

"I don't know," Nancy said, subdued as she pulled away from Bethany's hold.

"Seven years? Who knows what would have happened if not for that war, right?" She caught sight of me, and I could swear I saw the flash of both surprise and anger in her gaze before she pasted her smile back on. "Oh, it's you. The little groupie from the club. The girl who was playing around with Mason in his office." It was said breezily, but it was meant to sting, and she hit the bull's-eye. My face burned, and I felt myself caving from the inside for a moment before trying to distance myself emotionally.

They'd been together? For years? Would still be together under different circumstances?

Surprise and shock bottomed out my stomach.

He hadn't told me.

My gaze slid down to my shoes, my cheap knock offs that were from a discount store. There was no way to compete with her.

Mason probably still loved her. I mean, how could he not? Logically, it made sense. It sounded like she'd been a part of his life forever, and she was still coming around. That explained why he'd been reluctant to start something with me. There was a chance that they were going to get back together. Had I even asked?

My heart stuttered a few steps. No wonder she was like part of the family. He'd been truthful that they weren't a couple anymore, but he'd omitted the part about their long history together.

Blindsided. My eyes stung, and when I looked at Mason, he was watching me intently, telling me with a look that we needed to talk. Damn right we did. I hoped that's what my silent message back to him was. There was no way I was going to be in a situation ever again where I was treated as unimportant. And there was no way I was going to be a substitute for someone else. I was not going to be second best.

"Anyway, Mason and I are working together on a project," she added with a bright smile before going to Sam and giving him a hug. He gave her an awkward one-armed pat on the shoulder, but his gaze sought Mason's. There was concern there.

Mason scowled, his eyes snapping to Bethany. "No, we're not."

"Of course, we are." Bethany stepped back from Sam to give everyone the benefit of her perfect smile. "Mason invited me to come so we could talk about my new business."

"We are not working on a project together, and I never invited you here, Bet. I specifically left you a message telling you I'd give you a call because I was going to be busy here." A muscle ticked in Mason's jaw, and his voice took on a distinctly cold, unfriendly sound.

Unfazed, she waved a dismissive hand. "I must have missed it. I've been out of town. Anyway, I didn't want to pass up a chance to see you all again. It's been too long, and besides, I haven't eaten."

"Unbelievable. Bet—" Mason was gearing up to unload, but his mother cut him off.

"We have enough. Let's set a space. Maybe we can do a little bit of catch-up before you have to go." Nancy gave Savannah a look, and in turn, Savannah rolled her eyes and moved to grab a setting from inside the buffet.

At least it consoled me to know that the family seemed uncomfortable with her. Maybe she wasn't as much a part of them as she was trying to make it seem.

Savannah quickly set the extra place, and everyone moved within the awkward silence to sit.

That's when Bethany planted herself by Mason, leaving me the odd man out at the extra seat by the corner, on the opposite side of the table from Mason. And seeing them side by side, my insecurities scowled at me inside my head even more harshly, and I couldn't help but recognize that they were the perfect-looking couple. She was this beautifully elegant creature with a china doll complexion and sweet brown eyes who clearly knew how to dress and act in all types of company, and he was this big, strapping, handsome man who matched her.

Her eyes widened with that well-practiced, mean-girl move, a pretending-to-care expression creasing her face, and she raised a well-manicured hand to her perfectly lipstick-lined lips. "Oh! I'm sorry. The last time I was in this house, we were a couple, and this was my place at the table." She started to get up.

I shook my head at the new slap of information.

She'd had her own place at the table.

I didn't belong. Hadn't I always known that? The trailer park stink was always hanging in the air around me. It was the cloud over my head that cast a perpetual shadow, one I couldn't seem to get out from under.

"I'm fine here." I pasted on my own calm smile, the one I'd learned to use while living with Brady.

"I'm not." Mason stood.

"No." I shook my head, feeling the heat rise in my cheeks. This was becoming the most embarrassing social situation I'd been in since my time with Brady. "Please. Let's just eat."

The sooner the better. This had gone from wonderful to nightmarish in nothing flat. *What am I doing here*? How ridiculous to think that I could actually fit in here, with this family. Me. The ultimate hillbilly who preferred bare feet and soft grass to heels and makeup.

Brady's voice filtered through my mind, reminding me of what it was like to be the last one across the finish line in life.

"Are you really going to wear that?"

"Can't you try a little? Maybe wear some makeup or something?"

"Christ, can't you do anything right?"

"She burns toast and has no idea what quantum physics is. What else is she good for?"

The voice swirled around in my head, and I fought it back. Took a breath. Picked up the napkin from the table and set it in my lap.

Mason's eyes found mine, anger and concern flaring from their flinty depths, but I had an automatic smile painted across my face. It was the smile I'd learned to wear when I was trying to keep others from seeing too much, too deep.

Mason wasn't buying it. He refused to sit next to Bethany and instead stated, "Bethany, we need to talk."

"After dinner is fine."

"No. Now."

"What's the problem, Mason? You sound angry. Aren't we old friends? We grew up together." She had a coquettish smile on her face, but even I could see that it was calculated, meant to gain his sympathy.

"I don't know what we are, but we're not friends," he growled.

Her giggle was a light tinkling sound. "We're business partners. Haven't you told your family?"

"We're nothing and haven't been for years and years. I don't appreciate you trying to give any other kind of impression. You came here uninvited and pushed my mother to invite you to stay because she's a nice person. But you like taking advantage of nice people."

Something else was going on here.

I suddenly realized I'd been making this about me instead of seeing the situation for what it was. Should Mason have told me about her? Maybe, but maybe not. We were new. In time, she would have come up, but they hadn't been together for years. More important, no one wanted her here. She'd barged in on a special occasion and was being completely fake about it. She didn't give a shit about anyone in this room, including Mason.

Had I really been about to back off and let her sink her claws into him again? She'd only hurt him, likely had already in countless ways. I was here to love him.

I bit back a gasp realizing that I loved him. There was some panic in thinking the words, but then I looked at him, at his handsome face that I felt I knew so well. We still had a lot to learn about each other, but I knew his heart. It was beautiful.

Did we have things we needed to talk about? Sure. Later. For now, the voices of insecurity fell silent. I clasped my hands together in my lap and watched the scene play out, knowing this was where I belonged.

He needed me. It's what he'd told me, and I believed him.

I thought of what Blessing would say. She'd be proud. She'd probably tell me to cut a bitch who put her hands on my man. I bit back the grin but agreed with the sentiment. Mason's gaze flicked to me for a moment.

Whatever he saw in my expression had him looking confused, so I winked. His head cocked ever so slightly, like he couldn't make out what was going through my mind. The side of his lips were thinking about quirking. Hopefully, my eyes were telling him that I was staking my claim.

There was no way I was going to leave him vulnerable.

Women could be freaking evil creatures.

The other amazing takeaway for me? The battle with my inner Brady voice was becoming easier to win. I could see a time in the future when it might be eradicated.

"We're trying to have a nice family birthday, Bethany," Nancy said in a firm tone. She came around the table to stand by me, put her hands on my shoulders. I was on their team. Supported. She added, "What is this all about?"

Bethany looked up at Mason with an exaggerated look of surprise. "Didn't you get my email? I sent you the material you asked for. It's all there. I'm ready for us to sign a contract."

"No."

"Why not?" A hard note entered her voice.

"You really want to do this here?"

"Where else?"

"I checked into the material you sent. It's all fraudulent. It was all faked. None of what you sent me checks out."

"That's not true!"

"This is never going to happen. Never. Get that straight right now. I won't do business with you, because what you're trying to sell me is an unknown substance." His voice grew steely, his eyes narrowing to make his point. "Listen to this part carefully. That makes the product dangerous. And selling unknown drugs to the public with false assurances makes you dangerous. You're dangerous when you give people substances to ingest when you don't know what's in them."

"Dangerous? Me?" It was like his words ripped the pleasant mask off her face, her nose and lip curling in conjunction with each other. She was suddenly so very ugly, and she snarled, "I'm not the one who's dangerous. I'm not the one who has a police report for domestic abuse against his partner!"

"Bitch!" Savannah gasped with anger. "My God, you don't know when to stop."

"You owe this to me. I gave you years!" Bethany's words were nearly a shout.

"Bethany, you need to go home," Nancy spoke firmly. "Come back when Mason has properly invited you."

"You're kicking me out?" She shook her head confused. "I've practically been a daughter to you!"

"You're nuts, Bethany," Savannah said through a mask of fury, clearly reacting protectively.

"I'm nuts? I'm not the one that killed my best friend in Afghanistan when I didn't do my job right.

I'm not the one who sleeps with a gun under my pillow night after night. I'm not the one who goes berserk with nightmares and beats on anyone who's near." She suddenly swung her gaze to mine, her expression looking feral when she said, "Get out before you end up with a broken nose, stitches, and a black eye like I did!"

Her cruelty had no bounds. There was a hint of glee in her eyes. She was enjoying hurting him. A glance at Mason showed me that his jaw was clenched, his hands were in fists at his sides, and his breath was beginning to heave. Was he having a panic attack?

Look at me! I begged him silently, and when he didn't, I glared at her.

"You don't believe me? I've got pictures. I can text them to you. The hospital took them, and I look at them every day and thank my lucky stars I left him before he killed me."

"Then get out, Bethany," Travis interjected, vibrating with his rage. "Make us all happy and leave. You aren't welcome here anymore."

Again, I looked at Mason. He wasn't denying any of it. He hung his head, avoided eye contact with me. In fact, he looked ashamed, and I wanted to jump the bitch and claw her eyes out. A wave of protectiveness rose.

Had he actually done what she'd accused him of? I couldn't imagine it. He wasn't an abusive guy. There had to be more to this story.

"I'm leaving. Screw all of you people." Bethany's final words sailed back through the house, followed by the slamming of the front door.

Her absence created a vacuum.

Silence fell.

"Travis, will you give Layla a ride home?" Mason didn't hesitate more than a few moments— met my eyes for a fraction of a second but long enough for me to see the hurt there—then he was out the door.

"I never liked her!" Savannah suddenly growled. "Even when they were together. She was selfish then and she's selfish now. God, I hate her!"

"You should have slammed the door in her face," Travis muttered, shaking his head. "Where do you think he went?"

"I don't want to lose him again," Nancy said, her voice trembling. "He was so happy earlier."

"He's strong." Sam's tone was low, but his

nostrils flared with his ire. "Trust that."

"But what he went through…" Nancy shook her head. "Others have lost that battle."

"He won't," Sam assured her, dropping his hands on her shoulders. She turned her face into his chest.

Savannah looked at me. "Do you have any ideas where he might have gone?"

It was strange that they were all looking at me with hopeful eyes. I didn't want to let them down, but I didn't know where he would go to soothe his soul. "I wish I knew, but I don't think you have to worry. He's got a support group. Friends who've gone through what he's gone through. Honestly, I think he needs some time to process what just happened. I'm hopeful he'll talk with me about this later. When he's ready."

I wondered if he would seek out Zeke or Jay or the beach, but figured he needed time to get his head wrapped around what just happened.

There was a moment when three sets of eyes studied me, thinking about what I said.

"You're right," Sam nodded. There was a collective acceptance that there wasn't anything they could do except be supportive of him in spirit.

Nancy seemed lost for a moment, not sure what to say. She cast a quick glance at Sam, who was glaring at the doorway that Bethany had stormed through. She looked back at me. "Are you able to eat some food?"

The idea of prolonging the painful awkwardness now that Mason had left caused a prickling sensation in my gut. I couldn't pretend everything was okay. "I-I think it's best if I get home, but I hope we can try this again. I had such a lovely time with all of you."

"Absolutely. Make him bring you back for Thanksgiving. It's only a couple weeks out, right?" Nancy came around to take my hands, holding them warmly.

Savannah nodded. "A little less than two weeks. You don't want to miss her mashed potatoes and stuffing. They're to die for."

"I'll make sure he does."

"Let me make you a plate to take home. I'll give you enough for two. That way, if Mason shows up, you can eat together."

"That would be lovely."

Sam ended up being the one to take me home, a drive that was no more than twenty minutes. We were about halfway when he said, "You know, when he first came home, he was having these nightmares. More like night terrors, really. And you couldn't wake him up from them."

I thought back to the morning I woke up and saw him in the spare bedroom moving around restlessly. I nodded. "He still does. I found him thrashing around on the futon in his spare bedroom. He was in the middle of one, shouting for me to get down."

Oops. I might have just overshared, but he didn't say anything.

"It used to be worse. He would be back in combat, and his eyes would be open. He'd actually get out of bed and shove anyone off who tried to wake him up, mistaking them for the enemy attacking him in his dreams."

I gasped, realizing how Bethany could have gotten hit, and looked at Sam. He met my gaze, confirming what I thought.

"Did she try to wake him up?"

"If you've ever seen night terrors, it looks like the person's awake, but they're living an alternate reality that's in their minds. He was thrashing around in the middle of the nightmare. She tried to wake him up, but she couldn't. He was shouting, jumping out of bed to take cover, and she got elbowed in the nose, which of course, caused her black eye and lots of blood."

"It was an accident," I murmured.

"Exactly. But Bet wanted to make it out like he was an abuser. I just wanted you to know the truth before any of her words sunk in too deep. Mason would never knowingly hurt any woman."

"I know." I struggled for a moment, wondering if I should over share again, and decided it would put his mind to rest. "I was at his house the other night, and he opted to sleep in the other room. I think it was because he knew he had these dreams. I know he doesn't want to hurt me."

Sam nodded and relaxed. "You're good for him. I'm so glad he found someone who can be patient. He can get better, but it's going to take time. He needs to be surrounded by people who care, and he needs to talk to the right professionals. Somehow, I think you had a part in motivating him to rejoin this path, so I want to thank you for that."

I could accept that. "This is my place," I volunteered as we got close to my building. The sun had gone down and streetlights flickered on. "Thanks for the talk and the ride, Mr. Garrett."

"Sam. Please. I hope we see you again soon."

"I have a feeling you will."

With a short wave to Mason's father, I pulled my bag firmly over my shoulder while digging for my keys and phone. I found the phone first and sighed when I saw that there wasn't a text or a missed call. Switching my phone to the other hand, I dug around for my keys and was glad to feel them almost immediately, because I could see that Mason's father was waiting on the curb to make sure I got through the gate all right.

I quickly brandished the keys to show him and sent another wave before I unlocked the gate and pushed through. With my unit on the other side of the complex, I paused to quickly text Mason to let him know I was home and dropped my phone back into my bag as I walked on. So deep was I into my own thoughts that I didn't hear anyone behind me until I heard the voice.

It was a voice I knew well.

I'd lived with it for two years.

It still had the power to make my heart pound, my skin break out into a cold sweat, even as the temperature was falling.

"You into old guys now?"

Brady. He was standing right there. In the shadows of a tree in the common courtyard not five feet away. The menace in his casual stance stole my breath instantly. Larger than life. Not just a memory. Not just the monstrous voice in my head.

My heart jumped into my throat, pounding like it had the fear of God put into it, and it had. By this man. Panic held me frozen. My muscles refused to move. My brain refused to think.

The trembling began instantly.

He looked the same.

His familiar blond good looks were marred by the cruel twist of his lips that could never give a truly tender smile or a loving kiss. Selfish. Abusive. Angry. Vengeful.

I saw the lube on the nightstand in my mind's eye and was about to start hyperventilating. The memory of him holding me down. Pain. Despair. The smell of his cologne that clung to my own skin after he touched me, the clammy feel of his body that always made me recoil, even as I was forced to submit, like it wasn't my choice.

I bit back a horrified whimper at the vivid memory.

"Brady," I murmured just loud enough to carry.

It came out a touch shaky.

He liked that. A lot. With his eyes crawling over my body, a sense of ownership reflecting back at me, his smile grew wider. I knew I needed to think; I needed to keep calm but facing down my living nightmare had my thoughts turning chaotic.

I took a breath.

It helped.

Judging from his expression, he figured that he still had power over me. Did he? Was it that easy? Had I learned nothing? Taking another, deeper, calming breath, I tried to get my brain back online.

An image of Mason with his fiercely protective demeanor pulled up in my thoughts. Just thinking of him was helping me to overcome the fear coursing through my veins. I focused on his steel eyes that were always connected to mine, the way his embrace was strong and firm but gentle and caring as well.

Would he arrive here soon? Did I need him to handle this, or could I?

"You look good, Layla. Started working out?" A hint of the sneer I'd become so used to seeing curled his lips. He'd often criticized me for being soft. "You should have done it sooner."

Bastard. Another breath.

"What do you want?" My voice came out stronger. Hearing it gave me confidence. I stood up straighter.

"I thought maybe we could talk." He approached, his body as big and muscular as he'd ever been, as big and muscular as Mason was, but while Mason got my body humming, I had to will myself not to back away from Brady. My stomach churned as he came closer, but I didn't want to show anymore fear.

"Stop right there!" I held a hand up.

His brow raised with surprise at my outburst, but he didn't stop. In fact, he kept walking toward me in his slow, rolling gate, now smiling his sick smile. He was ignoring my command, deliberately, to show how my words meant nothing to him. I was hyper aware of his every move, the threat of violence nauseating. I didn't know what to do.

Then I remembered my voice was a weapon.

"I'm going to scream if you come any closer to me!" I yelled, my voice getting loud enough to echo off the buildings. He paused, and relief trickled through me.

"Now why would you do that?" he taunted, but

464

his smirk morphed into a glare. He was still several feet away, casting a quick glance around before settling his eyes on me again. "I'm here to see you. I'm worried about you."

Were any of my neighbors home? Maybe I needed to be louder.

"There's nothing left to say. My walking out was the last thing I wanted to communicate with you. Period. Now leave. I don't want you here."

But he wasn't leaving. He was still standing there, studying me, trying to calculate his next move. The fear took hold again. What if he tried to grab me? I had to be on my toes. Ready for anything.

Instead, he softened his expression.

"I don't think you mean that. You need me. Your sister called not too long ago and told me you were living a shithole existence. I wanted you to know you don't have to do this anymore, baby. I'll take care of you. I'm here for you," he crooned, switching to a gentle tone, and I could now hear the fake care. I'd fallen for this same voice time and again when I first came out here needing love, needing someone to pay attention to me. Shit, I'd been so gullible!

Disdain had my nose wrinkling when I spit out, "Don't call me that."

"What?"

"Baby. I'm not your baby."

He gave me his signature charming grin. "Sure you are. I love you, Layla. You know that. And you love me."

"Not even a little bit." Surging anger burned through my glare, and my fear started to fade. "I don't need you. I don't love you. I can take care of myself."

His eyes hardened, even as his mouth kept a sweet smile.

"What about Nadine? I can help your sister get into a rehab clinic, Layla. Can you? Where do you think she is right now? Blowing some guy for money to buy drugs? Hanging out with junkies, exposing herself to diseases? I can help you find her."

He evoked horrifying images of my sister that could highly likely be true, but she needed to figure out what she wanted in life. I couldn't do that for her. It was time to get back some of what he took from me.

"I don't need anything from you. I don't want anything from you. She called all on her own without any prompting from me. She's living her own life. I had nothing to do with that." Controlling, abusive asshole. It was all so clear. I could see he was a sad imposter of a man. "I want nothing from you. Do you hear me? You need to leave before I call the police. I'm about to scream this place down like it's my own personal horror movie! I'm fucking done with you!" It felt empowering to face him down, but that didn't mean he wasn't still dangerous.

If I could just get inside my apartment, I could lock it behind me.

Brady scowled away his smile, his menacing voice low when he threatened, "You need to watch your language, Layla. Such bad habits you've developed since you left. I'll need to start training you again. We can't have you embarrassing me in front of my friends." Then he lurched forward and snagged my arm.

"No!" I cried, the fear returning in a rush. He'd dropped the caring act.

He snarled into my ear, "Enough of this bullshit. It's time for you to come home. I'll help you grab your shit." He yanked me harshly toward my apartment, making my keys go flying. With sick dread, I could see he already knew which apartment was mine.

"No!" I shouted and dug my heels in, trying to jerk away. Trying to blindly grab for my phone in my stupid cavernous bag, but his hand only tightened, crushing, hurting my arm to the point that I thought he might break the bone.

Where was my god damn phone?

He frog-marched me toward my own place. It was only feet away.

"Fucking cold-hearted bitch," he hissed in my ear. "We're not done until I say we're done."

I tried jerking my arm from his hand again, but his grip was too tight, and I couldn't stop the cry of pain from my lips. My bag fell off my other shoulder, spilling its contents over the ground, just like it had the other night when I was attacked. I flashed back to the gym parking lot when Greg was grabbing me while the car pulled up. And then it all clicked into place.

It really had been Brady. He'd tried to kidnap me a week ago.

"That was you in the black car," I gasped, trying to jerk around to face him.

"I have no idea what you're talking about." His smile was evil.

The way he was simply assuming he could do whatever he wanted, take me against my will, take away my choices, force me to accept his abuse again suddenly triggered something deep inside me. Blessing was right. I was not that girl anymore. Never again. This was my life. Mine. He had no right to it.

My rage knew no bounds. It grew suddenly large and feral. It erupted from the depths of my soul in a powerful flurry of shoving and kicking and fighting to get free.

"Let me go, asshole," I shouted for the mountains to hear me miles away. Filled with a wild fury that came from deep in my gut, I screamed loudly before shouting, "Help! Please help me!" He covered my mouth, panicked, trying to cut off the sound, but I bit down hard enough that he snatched his hand away and grabbed my other arm as well, squeezing, cutting off circulation so my hands throbbed.

"Shut up! Where the fuck are your keys?" He shook me with his frustration, angry at this new creature I'd become. "Give them to me. You aren't coming back here."

"You're going to jail. The police have video footage of your car." I wrenched my arms again, but he yanked me closer.

"There's lube on your nightstand, love," he snarled in my ear. "Right next to your pretty blanket with all the delicate flowers sewn on."

"You were in my apartment?"

"I packed your clothes and your computer. Nothing else is worth taking."

Couldn't anyone hear me scream? Where was Mason?

Mason! What were his words earlier this week? Hurt the gonads. Do a dick punch, a ball grab with a twist, or a knee to the fruits and berries. It would bring down a man any size. I'd practiced this all week.

I was in the perfect position.

With all my might, I shoved my knee right into his crotch.

Bull's-eye.

Direct hit.

He cried out. Shoved me away. Fell to his knees, grabbing his junk with a groan of pain.

"I'm never coming back! Never!" I backed off, ragged breaths heaving, and spotted where my phone had fallen out of my bag. Scooping it up, I called emergency. The moment the operator picked up, I managed to say, "I need help. There's a man trying to kidnap me. I'm at 223 Havenhurst Avenue. Please hurry."

"This isn't over," Brady snarled, surging to his feet. Instantly, I kicked for the goal. Jammed my pointy-toed ballet flat straight into his balls, and for a second time he shouted out a raw cry of pain. I could keep this up all night. He'd underestimated me for the last time because now I had something to lose. I had a life.

The game was up. I was finally free.

"Layla!" Mason came bursting through the courtyard in time to see Brady crumple in a heap on the ground. He snarled, "Motherfucker! You just made the worst mistake of your life."

"The police are on their way," I interjected, pushing in front of Mason, so he'd be forced to stop. There'd been so many emotional bombs dropped in the last hour, I didn't want him to do something foolish that would land him in jail.

"You called them?" he asked, only taking his eyes off Brady to look me over and pull me close.

"Fuck. I heard you screaming. I had to jump the gate."

"I'm all right. I called. They're coming." Relief had me shaking now. I couldn't stop trembling.

"Fuck you, fucking coldhearted bitch," Brady moaned, holding his crotch protectively while curled up on the ground. "You can fucking have her. Fucking crazy bitch."

"Better stay down, or I'll beat your ass, motherfucker," Mason growled, stepping around me to put his big, muscular body in front of mine. He was being my shield. With a sneering grin, he assured Brady, "It would be my fucking pleasure. Believe me."

"Yeah? Fuck you, too." The words were harsh, angry, but Brady remained down with Mason standing guard over him, muscles flexed and ready. I was nervous at first that he was going to add his own punishment, but Mason had complete control of himself, and Brady was smart enough to know when he couldn't win.

It was only a few minutes more when, for the second time in a week, sirens filled the air. Some of my neighbors came out to see what was happening, showed their concern for me. I hadn't even realized what kind neighbors I had.

The police took Brady into custody, and by the end of the evening, it came out that after learning where I lived, he'd followed me to the gym. He'd been doing that for several days, trying to figure out my daily schedule so he could do his worst. I remembered that I'd begun to feel like eyes were on me when I was biking home.

The gym is where he'd happened on Greg standing outside smoking a cigarette, ready and willing to make some quick money, get him to call and report when I was there.

I made sure to watch as they took Brady away in handcuffs, and when he made brief eye contact with me through the window of the police car, I managed a grim smile.

This really was the end of a long, terrifying nightmare, but this time, I killed the monster.

CHAPTER 26

MASON

"Christ, Layla," I sighed, "you've got to stop doing this to me."

It was several hours later, and my hands were still shaking. Layla was lounging against me on the sofa, a fire was going in the fireplace, and some mindless TV show was on. I wasn't sure either one of us was really paying attention to it.

We'd only just arrived with a bag of her clothes because the idea that her ex had been prowling around her apartment was creeping her out. I was glad to have her where I could take care of her, but we really needed to talk.

It was time.

"I can't believe Brady's actually in jail," she

said, her fingers tensing where they were previously relaxed on my abdomen. I picked them up, appreciating how soft her skin was and how small and delicate they seemed enveloped in my hand. Twining them with my own, I lifted them to my lips for a kiss.

She looked up at me, an adorable flush tinging her cheeks. I wondered if she was feeling confused about dealing with her ex again. Sometimes feelings could be tricky things.

"You kick ass, sweet girl. He's right where he should have been all along. Dishonorably discharged because he was pressuring other women using his authority. He didn't have anything to lose in coming after you. You're not the only one he did this to, and you've done your part to make sure he doesn't do this to someone else." His car was identified on the video footage from the gym, and he was now facing breaking and entering, kidnapping, battery, and a load of other charges that were going to keep him locked up for some time.

She turned to face me, drawing her knees under her, a thoughtful expression creasing her forehead. "I'm glad he's there, but I think I feel safer, too, because I realized how small he is, you know? Clearly, I don't mean physically, but that he plays small and always has."

"He's a fucking dick is what he is." Kill. Rip him to fucking shreds with my bare hands, had been the singular thoughts in my mind, even after she dismantled his nuts using the moves I'd shown her. "And you took him out. I'm so fucking proud of you."

She blushed, but there was still more on her mind.

"Yeah, but what I'm saying is even bigger than that. I used to be so impressed with him. I used to think he had it all together, and I was always willing to give him everything, let him take over my life, because I didn't think I could do anything right. I felt so small and ineffective in the world. In a sense, I gave him this power over me, but tonight was different."

"How so?"

"I saw him for who he was for the first time. He's weak. Tries to force his will on others because he can't compete on any other level. I see the coward under the mask. Aside from being a criminal, I realized I'd grown too big to accept any more abuse from him. I guess I'm saying that I'm proud of myself. I am strong."

"Hell yes, you are," I grinned, rubbing her arm. "You're a 'go big' kind of girl. If I didn't know it before, I knew it after you came on to me at the club."

She laughed, covering her face that went tomato red, then peeked at me through her fingers. "What can I say? I wanted you. If I'd waited for you to ask me out, we'd still be suffering in silent, horny agony."

"Porngasms forever," I joked, but quickly lost the smile to cup her face with a gentle touch. "You're so strong. I'm in awe of you."

She held my gaze and insisted, "Part of the reason I could see his weakness was because you showed me day by day what it meant to live with integrity."

My throat tightened, and I worked to swallow as I thought of the night Bethany was hurt by me. "I didn't mean to hurt her. Bet."

"I know." She turned her face to kiss my palm. "I managed to get it worked out in my mind pretty fast. I saw your nightmare, what you go through. And I get why you were sleeping in the other room."

"It used to be so much worse. Bet was our neighbor, lived in the house next door, and we always knew each other. She's maybe a few years older than you, a few years younger than me."

"How old are you? I don't think I've ever asked."

"Thirty-one."

"I'm twenty-five."

"That's around what I figured. Anyway, we started going out in high school and then through college. It was never really a perfect fit. She needed to be taken care of, which was fine until I came back from the war with my own injuries. She couldn't handle the problems I was dealing with psychologically."

"Can you tell me about what you're dealing with?"

"PTSD. The psychologist I went to yesterday explained that during a horribly tragic, traumatic moment, like when your friend blows up in front of you, your brain reacts in a different way, sort of remembering all the minute details of a given situation when it wouldn't normally do so, but without a context for it. So, I can get triggered by anything that reminds me of that time, making my brain react with red flags that tell me to panic. It can be emotion, like when I was afraid for you, or when things are chaotic in some way. The OCD and nightmares are a symptom of the trauma."

"So how do you get help?"

"By talking about it, writing about it, noticing what causes an episode that needs to be talked about, and giving it a proper context. There are different therapies that can be tried. I think something called EMDR was mentioned, but we didn't get too much into the details. Basically, it's going to take time, and anyone who's part of my life will have to have patience. This will take years." I wanted her to see the seriousness of my gaze. This was also a message to her.

"No wonder things didn't work out with Bethany. She didn't strike me as particularly understanding or patient." She snuck her hand in mine, squeezed it. Her eyes were telling me she was in.

"You noticed, huh?"

"The thought of that she-beast having access to you is unacceptable."

"Jealous?" I asked with a teasing smirk.

"More than that, I didn't want her to have the chance to hurt you again."

Her comment, so telling, gave my heart a shot of

warmth. It took a moment for me to ask, "So what was your smile about? When you were sitting at my mother's table."

"That?" she chuckled. "I was just recognizing that I was going to protect my territory."

I grinned, feeling a flush of pleasure touch my cheeks. "Am I your territory?"

"Absolutely." She grew serious. "I wanted to protect you from her hateful words. I wanted to make sure no one ever treated you so coldly again, but how could I do that if I wasn't right by your side, taking care of you? All it took was a deep breath and a decision to take a leap of faith. Once I made that step, it was even easier to realize that...I love you."

My heart swelled, making it hard to breathe, and my eyes stung. I pulled her to me and sealed my lips to hers, just a tender, intimate touch of our lips, our breaths mingling. "I love you, too, sweet girl."

"I'm so glad I'm not the only one," she smiled against my mouth, her eyes opening to look at me. I found myself grinning back and pulled away just a few inches. The connection snapped right into place as it was always meant to.

"So, if I'm your territory, then you're my

territory, too?"

"Fair is fair."

EPILOGUE

MASON

Eight months later

"What did he do to her in the video you watched?"

Dawn was breaking over the water, and I'd managed to drag Layla to the beach to play in the ocean and watch me surf. She'd finally let me teach her how to swim, despite her fear. Her courage, and her trust in me, knowing I'd keep her safe, humbled me every time she stepped into the water. It took time to get past the memory of nearly drowning in the pool that one time with he who would never again be named, but she faced it down in baby steps. Before long, she was floating, learning how to hold her breath, doing simple strokes.

It took about three months to get her to move in with me. We started cooking together, watching crappy reality TV together, arguing over who was going to control the remote, and fucking like bunnies all over the house. Therapy was one of those things that was ongoing, teaching us valuable lessons on communication. I started sleeping with Layla under the strict promise that if I was having a nightmare, she needed to clear away from me. She agreed. Funny thing—I hadn't had a nightmare in several months.

I still had moments of needing to breathe through spells of OCD, particularly when Layla first moved in. She tried to make sure common areas were organized, but when it came to the bedroom, she was less so. Not that she was messy, just that she wasn't dedicated to making sure everything was always in its place.

Sometimes, she could distract me from an oncoming panic attack with a sexy blow job, sucking my cock deep into her throat and cupping my balls. It was our own personal therapy. Now, there were times when the sight of her clothes draped over a chair or her shoes kicked off wherever she'd left them got me hard. Maybe she was doing the whole Pavlovian dog training on me. It was working.

I was getting hard now just thinking about it.

"Video? Whatever do you mean?" she asked,

recognizing the heat in my eyes with a wicked smile of her own. She knew what video I was talking about. It was the one I'd caught her watching just before bed the night before. Remembering what followed got me even harder. Everything about this woman drew me in.

Her dark, wavy hair had dried, and the breeze was blowing it gently around her face. I moved to brush it away from her neck, but my eyes got pulled south to the soft swell of her breasts, her hips, the barely-there scraps of her bikini bottom.

She knew what her bikini did to me. It was the one that had only the ties on the sides of her hips keeping it up. I'd been fixated on those ties while she jumped over waves or swam under them in the shallows. After getting out of the water, she'd wrapped a towel around her shoulders and sat on the blanket we'd laid out close to the water below a sand dune, away from prying eyes. I'd brought along a basket of food that was holding down a corner of the blanket.

I hadn't lasted long in the waves. Those ties.

I leaned in and nipped her bottom lip, tasting the salty ocean on her skin before licking it to soothe the sting. She gasped and shivered with the cold drops of water that were still dotting my skin, her blue eyes darkening, going slumberous as they locked on mine.

"The porn with the guy coming up to the girl on the beach. Did he lay her back in the sand?" I leaned over her, sliding an arm around her legs and physically manipulating her body, pulling her down so she was flat on her back. It was so fucking hot that she wanted to reenact moments of porn that had turned her on.

I loomed over her.

Excitement shined in her eyes.

"Something like that," she murmured, reaching to pull me down, but I caught her hand, pulled it over her head to pin it on the blanket and casually rested on my side, my elbow propping me up. I made sure to leave her other hand free. It was what we'd worked up to. She still needed to feel like she had some physical freedom, and there was no timeline on healing. We both knew that.

"Tell me what he did," I insisted, making my voice deeper and rougher sounding, the way she liked it.

The flush spread from her chest up to her neck and cheeks, and she bit her lip, a mischievous smile curling her lips. Fuck she was hot. Then she whispered, "He gave her an orgasm."

"How?"

"He put his fingers inside of her, and she couldn't help but come."

"Did he play with her tits first?" I asked, lightly pulling the material away from her breast.

The nipple was tight and beaded, anxiously waiting my attention. I bent my head and licked at it, rubbing it with my tongue while she moaned under me, doing her little pants that made me so hard.

"Did he?" I asked, pulling away from her breast just to stretch this out.

"Yes," she hissed, so I sucked her nipple into my mouth and raked my teeth over it, making her cry out. The wind carried the sound away to the seagulls flying overhead.

"Then his fingers likely found their way into her suit bottom like this." I pulled the tie, peeled the wet cloth aside, and just like that, I had my fingers sliding over her swollen clit into her soaked channel. I slid my finger in, curling it into the exact spot that drove her nuts, and swirled it back and forth, in and out, my thumb riding the button of her clit.

"Mason!" Now she was panting, her eyes closed,

and I slowed my movements.

"Eyes on me. I want to watch you come."

Her beautiful eyes were on me again, and in them I saw desire, confidence, trust, need, vulnerability, and a future that was mine to share. She whispered, "Please. Make me come. I'm so close."

"I'll always take care of you." My voice was husky with emotion, and I added another finger. Her hips were meeting my thrusts, her moans growing louder with my thumb rubbing her clit in tight circles. She was taking what she needed, her fingers sliding over her breasts to pinch her own nipples. The sight and sound of her desire held me captive, had me drowning in my own lust.

Fuck, I needed to slide my cock inside of her. She was so fucking beautiful.

"Oh my god, oh my god, oh my god," she whispered in her chant that told me she was close. "Mason, I'm going to come, I'm going to—"

I covered her shout with a kiss, felt the explosion in her body, the way it jerked under me, and I couldn't wait anymore. With a quick glance around, relieved that no one else was out just yet, I nosed the triangle of cloth off her other breast and sucked her nipple into my mouth, nipping at it, sucking at it, tonguing it at the same time that I kept moving my fingers in and out of her.

In minutes she was panting and moaning again.

"I need to be inside you," I growled, sliding a leg between hers, giving her a chance to say it was all right.

"Fuck me," she said breathlessly, reaching between us to undo my trunks.

I shoved them down just enough to give her access, and then she was wrapping her hands around my length, pumping it, positioning me at her entrance. We both groaned feeling the tight, hot fit of my cock as it slid into her little pussy, filling her up. She was a glove, squeezing me.

"You feel so good inside me. So perfect," she breathed. "Always."

"You're mine, baby." I moved a slow steady pump of my hips.

She panted her moan, meeting the thrust. "And you're mine."

"This is going to be fast and hard. There's no way I want anyone to actually see you. Hold on tight," I muttered against her lips.

She wrapped her arms around my neck, and her legs around my hips, opening herself to me completely. With my fingers sliding down, pinching at her sensitized, engorged clit, I pistoned my my dick into her hot, wet sheath. Every slide of friction was winding us both up, feeding the pleasure and the need and the heat until we were hanging on by a thread, desperate to reach the climax, chasing it down as the electrical charge surged through every nerve ending.

"Shit! Mason! Oh my god. It's too much!" Each phrase was punctuated on a desperate, panting cry.

"Come for me, baby," I gritted.

And she did. She cried out, her back arching off the ground, her pussy spasming all over my cock, squeezing it with each of her convulsions, until my own orgasm had my balls drawing up tight. The pressure grew, the tingling almost painful in its intensity, and then I was growling with each thrust, uncaring if anyone heard me until I was exploding, only wanting to fill her with me the way she always managed to fill me with her.

Despite the fact that we were still gasping each breath, we were quick to pull our clothing back into place. There was no way we wanted to risk actually getting caught. With a blanket wrapped around our bodies, cocooning us within our own small space on the sand, we watched the horizon until the gray light of dawn became the vibrant rays of sunlight.

By that time, there were more people moving about. Joggers. Other surfers bobbing on the swells. Die-hard beach-going families were setting up their little beach camps for the day, breaking out the sunblock for impatient little ones who were ready to start building their sandcastles. Lighthearted chatter mixed with the squawk of seagulls carried to us on the wind. Life.

This was what I wanted. This life with the partner who was perfect for me.

Layla had even reached out to Bethany, which had been one of the most selfless acts of kindness I'd ever seen, considering who Bet was. Of course, all the drama and excitement had had to do with trouble she'd gotten into with a married partner at the law firm, which had ended up getting her fired. Layla had talked her into going back to school and living at home with her mother to save money instead of looking for another guy to support her. Bet actually seemed more content than I'd seen her in a long time.

"I'm hungry." Layla leaned into me and nipped my neck. "If you don't feed me soon, I'll have to eat you."

"Don't tempt me." I grinned. Nerves made my heart kick up a notch, beat a little faster before I said casually, "Unpack the food. Let's eat."

"What did you bring?" she asked, more to herself than to me. The moment she turned away to check the basket, I kneeled behind her, waiting for her to turn back around. "Hmmm. This all looks good. Bagels and cream cheese? Ooooh, chocolate covered strawberries. What's…this…" She broke off, turning back to me slowly.

There was a small black velvet box in her hand that she was holding out to me. It was shaking. Her eyes were fierce with emotion: excitement, hope, and fear. I took the box from her, flipped it open, and showed her. It was a beautiful pearl in an intricately designed white gold setting surrounded by diamonds.

"This belonged to my grandmother," I started, and already her eyes were filling with tears. "Hard times in life shaped her to be the strong woman she became, which is why she loved her pearl ring so much. You know, a pearl can only become its most beautiful self through adapting to perpetual friction. It reminds me of you. The struggles you've faced in life shaped you to be more caring, more loving, and more compassionate. I've never met a more beautiful person in my entire life. I thank my lucky stars every day that I have you."

The shimmering tears spilled down her cheeks. Her lower lip quivered, but she held still, listening, love shining in her eyes. I couldn't just see it, I could feel it coming from her, filling me up, making me stronger by being near.

"Every day, I see how you strive to be your best self—working hard, facing down fears, taking care of the people around you, most of all, me. You accepted me as I am, with all my damage and broken parts. I'm not perfect. There are so many jagged edges, but you saw who I was. Being with you inspires me to live my best life. How could I not want to spend my life with you?"

"I feel the same way," she half sobbed. "I didn't know what it meant to love until I experienced it with you. All I'd ever known was mistrust, pain, and a desperate desire to live another life without knowing what it could look like. You helped me push myself to demand more and be brave enough to reach out for love again, even when I was scared."

"We did that for each other. You are the most precious part of my life."

"And you are mine. Heart and soul."

"Heart and soul. I love you, sweet girl." I pulled the ring out of the box. "I want everything with you. Will you marry me?"

"Every day for the rest of our lives. Yes."

I pulled her in for a kiss, barely hearing the cheers and claps of those who'd happened upon this most special moment.

I didn't care.

She was my forever.

EPILOGUE 2

BLESSING

Meanwhile… 8 months ago

He could definitely be Batman to my Catwoman.

Mr. Eye Candy was standing just inside the sliding glass doors on his side of the patio, like a creeper, just watching me. I was fine with that because what the real estate agent told me was right on. He was a panty-wetting hottie. Dark hair that was ruffled, like he'd run fingers through it, and muscles that were a gorgeous view to behold since he wasn't wearing a shirt. I couldn't see eye color, but the way he was looking at me was intense, his brows furrowed with concentration, like he was studying me, hard.

All I could say was, yum.

I was sure he could do a body good, just like milk.

My girl parts thought so. They were perking up a bit. My blood pumped a little faster the longer we stared at each other. It felt good. I'd been working on my project so long; I'd forgotten what it was like to get all hot and bothered by a dark stare that, if it were translated to language, would state clearly: I want to fuck you.

That was all right, too. I didn't have any hang-ups about sex, which also didn't mean I jumped any warm body, but he was definitely inspiring thoughts. Not that I would ever fuck a guy who lived next door to me. I mean, really. What happens when the music stops? We'd still be sitting in the same musical chair, right? Nuh-uh.

It would be fun to tease him, though.

I was wearing my sexy, Laura Croft, jungle adventure kakis that were nicely fitted to all my best features. I know I've got good tits and ass, and there was definitely cleavage visible since my shirt had multiple buttons undone down the front. I even had a nice whip hanging from my very cool utility belt, a whip I actually knew how to use.

This was one of my best outfits.

Giving him my superlative, with lots of exclamation points around it, pin-up girl pose, hand on hip and bending just a bit to give a good showing of my lush, perky girls, I blew a kiss his way. It made me realize I didn't have a Betty Page look ready to go. That would be my next trick to drive him insane.

With a rose queen wave, I strutted my stuff back inside. Playtime was over.

I was about to set the gaming world on its ass, cause minds to be instantaneously blown, because the baby I'd been creating for the last decade was about to become a reality. I wasn't bragging. This was a fact. I knew exactly what I had. It was eerie, this knowing that sat over me.

My game was going to create the biggest sensation, and I couldn't wait.

* * *

Thank you so much for reading ONE BREATH TO THE NEXT!

I hope you love Mason and Layla as much as I do. The next book in the Hermosa Beach Memoirs series follows Blessing and her exciting jump into the passion project she's dreamed of realizing. She suddenly finds herself with a new mystery neighbor,

Ian, the man who may be her partner in crime or her ultimate downfall. You can preorder FIERY BLESSING now!

And don't miss the NEW RELEASE, that celebrates Christmas in July with a steamy winter weekend at a cabin in the woods. Ever skinny-dipped in a hot tub with snowbanks surrounding you? Sparks fly when Beck finds Cat in this quick, sizzling read. He won't let her hide out a moment longer in WINTER HEAT, available now!

And, to find out about new books, sign up for my newsletter: http://danubeadele.com

Turn the page for an excerpt of FIERY BLESSING.

FIERY BLESSING

Chapter 1

Ian

"Get. The. Fuck. Off. Of. Me!"

Sharp. Female. Angry.

I scowled into my fridge while the overly bright inner light pierced my eyeballs. Early morning brain fog had me blurry-eyed and confused, but after hearing the words spoken loudly and clearly, I paused, shot a glance around the kitchen. Who was that? Where was the voice coming from? For a moment, I forgot that I was in the middle of foraging for breakfast.

"You think you're so damn cute, but you're not!" Irate female. Was that my new sexpot neighbor? It had to be. It sounded like a lovers'

spat.

The thought was souring, not that she was an option. Never do your fun where you do your work. Not that she knew she was work. Not yet at least. But it didn't hurt to look. Appreciate. Enjoy.

Watching her prance her cute little ass around in all her cosplay had been pure pleasure. Yesterday, she'd been a female version of Indiana Jones, everything feminine and fitted, showing off all of my favorite parts on a woman. The day before, she'd been a psychedelic go-go dancer with a short skirt that showed plenty of long leg on top of platform boots.

"Leave me alone!"

I winced against her shouting voice.

Nice pair of lungs, that one. Nice pair of tits, too.

She'd caught me checking her out. Standing just inside my sliding glass door, I'd been about to come out on the roof patio that we shared. Seeing me there, she'd struck a poster-girl pose that made my dick jerk with surprise. She'd blown me a kiss through her full lips and completed a pageant girl wave goodbye before disappearing inside her own set of glass doors on her side of the patio. I thought there was even a whip hanging off her hip. For fuck's sake. The images that brought on…

The memory spread a sleepy smirk across my face. The moment begged the question, what kind of panties did a female archeologist wear, if any? Unfortunately, it seemed I wouldn't be finding out anytime soon. I was here to work a deal. Negotiate. It was what I was good at. I was setting myself up to be the new CEO of Gamecon. This was going to be the deal of a century.

So why did her voice sound like she was in the same room? Her words had come across clearly.

The orange juice was sitting on the shelf, one of the few items I'd grabbed at the corner mom and pop market the previous night. The cold air from the fridge reminded me that I had disgusting cotton mouth and a dull ache behind my eyes. I grabbed the carton, needing to soothe the dryness in my throat. It had been a late night spent working. There were so many cogs to put into place before I put forth an offer on what was sure to be an epic deal.

"Let go of my pants! Let go!"

Swigging from the carton and swiping my chin, almost in the same move, I replaced the carton, closed the fridge, and cocked my head toward the sound of her voice. Scratching at my chest absently, I wondered if there was a vent between our apartments? I knew we shared a wall, and this was an old building, but had figured on thicker walls. Could she hear me as clearly? Because that would be...

"Let go of my pants, you bastard! Get off of me! Now!"

And that's when I realized she was being attacked.

Adrenaline shot through my system. Shoving past the furniture in my living room to get to the door, I launched out of my apartment. Images of my petite neighbor being forced in any way had my blood pumping furiously.

I'd beat down a motherfucker for forcing anything with her.

Deaf to everything but blood roaring through my ears, I pounded down the hall, and kicked open her front door. Wood splintered from around the door frame, pieces of it exploding inward. The door slammed open and bounced back toward me. Shoving it back out of my way, I stepped into the room and looked for danger, my breath coming in panting huffs, muscles tensed.

"What..." she yipped, head snapping my direction.

There was no danger.

Everything was summed up in a fraction of a second. There was an exceptionally large, black and tan dog playing tug-o-war with a pair of pants. The owner of the pants, my little blonde bombshell neighbor, was, unfortunately, partially wearing the pants. Hands on the waist, both legs only halfway encased in the tight legs of material, she was bouncing on one leg while the dog yanked on the empty cuff of the other.

My entrance had startled her. She looked up at me, her big blue eyes, so light they were almost gray, rounded in surprise. Her moment of distraction gave the large pooch enough of an advantage that he won the tug-o-war instantly. With a victorious yank, the dog knocked her off balance, took her feet out from under her, which set her back on her ass, and stood there triumphantly with her pants in his mouth.

That left her pantless. She jumped up to her feet, squinting and glaring at me and the dog, nice, rounded tits heaving in her tank top. Her long blonde hair, nearly platinum in color, was tied back in a sleek ponytail.

"What the hell were you thinking?" she blasted.

"Are you talking to me or the dog?" I asked,

because seriously, I wasn't sure where she was directing her anger.

"Both of you!" she snarled, hands on her hips. She spun on the dog. "Some scary dog you are. Aren't you supposed to be a Rottweiler or something? Give me my fucking pants you worthless beast!"

"Me, or the dog?"

"The dog!" She threw her hands up with frustration.

"You know he can't understand, right?"

She rolled her eyes and moved toward the dog who danced away grinning his doggy grin, begging for her to chase him.

"Dammit!" she charged after him, giving him exactly what he wanted, and giving me a sight to behold. A gorgeous, heart shaped ass, encased in some flowery thong, flashed me as she dove after the squirrely beast. I silently cheered him on. This was a better stimulant than coffee any day of the week.

A half-naked sexpot was trying to chase down a dog. Based on the situation happening in my boxerbriefs, which I realized was the only clothing I happened to be wearing, all systems were functioning. Funny thing. We'd never officially met, but it was like we were having an underwear party.

Leaning against the door frame, I watched for a few seconds, enjoying the view.

"Where are your glasses? Can you see him?" I asked casually, realizing why she was squinting so hard. I'd usually seen her wearing a pair. It was adorable, not that I was about to say this out loud. She'd probably kick me in the balls for admitting that to her.

"Help me. Don't just stand there," she tossed me her cute "angry" look. "Mad kitten" face. Was that a thing? If not, it was now.

Noting she was creeping up on the dog from one direction, I went the other, and he was cornered, trapped between a coffee table and the couch. He crouched down, gave a growling, muffled bark, and I knew he was moments away from jumping over or even onto the coffee table.

Using my deepest, most ferocious, no-nonsense CEO tone, I growled, "Drop it. Now!"

The dog looked up at me with surprise. Paused for a moment to stare into my eyes. And dropped the pants. Sweet sexpot girl stared down at the dog for a moment, dumbfounded. Then she threw a scowl my direction before turning it back on the dog.

"Really?" Exasperation underscored every jerking motion of her arm as she snagged up her pants, turned away from me and yanked her pants up her legs, hiding the sweet curve of her ass before zipping up and turning back around. She squinted down at the pooch. "You're a bad dog."

"He's a puppy," I laughed, not trying very hard to hide the satisfaction of having the dog listen to me when he wouldn't listen to her.

"How can he be a puppy. He's like, over a hundred pounds."

"You don't know for sure?"

Her eyes searched the area a beat before she huffed yet another breath. "Where the hell are my glasses? I can't see to find them. They got dislodged when I was fighting off the Kraken, here."

"Hold on." I saw they were flung open on the arm of an overstuffed chair opposite the couch. I handed them over. She started cleaning them with the bottom of her tank, flashing smooth, pale skin.

"Thanks. Anyway, my nephews brought him in when they showed up last night, and now they're in class, and I don't want to text them because it might get them in trouble. I was too busy to ask questions. I now realize I should have. They didn't bring his food, a leash, or anything." She finally put her glasses on and huffed a breath, studying the dog. "I'm about to go buy him some food. So, you think he's a puppy? Should I get puppy chow or something?"

"He looks like he's maybe somewhere around two. He's still romping. Doesn't look completely filled out yet." The dog was calming down. He had a short stub of a tail that was wagging madly as his eyes flicked between the two of us, waiting for some clue as to what would happen next.

"And you are in your boxers?" She was now looking down at my dick that was still at half-mast. Partly, I was gratified to see her eyes widen with what looked like appreciation at the same time I felt a dull flush hit my neck.

"I thought someone was attacking you. I heard you yelling next door."

"Well," she arched her brows consideringly, her eyes lingering on my cock a beat longer before looking up at me. "Thank you? If someone were attacking me, you would have saved me, Mr. Eye Candy."

"Eye Candy?" I grinned. "I like that. Especially since I've been secretly calling you Sexpot."

"Sexpot?" she laughed, and her face lit up. "I like it. Sexpot it is. And while we seem to be the most informal of strangers, you know, running around in our underwear together during our first meeting, it might be good to know what else you are called. In case the delivery man shows up with a package for you."

"Right. They won't be looking for Mr. Eye Candy."

"Nor Ms. Sexpot, either."

"Ian."

She shook my outstretched hand. It was small and soft. Engulfed by my grasp. Knowing that the rest of her was probably just as soft didn't help the situation in my boxers one bit. My dick liked the idea of exploring all of her soft places. She'd fascinated me from my first glimpse of her. It was time for me to head back before my cock pointed due north.

But I wasn't the only one affected.

Her own cheeks pinkened, and she pulled her hand away quickly, saying, "Ian. You're the guy making all the noise next door when I'm trying to work." It didn't escape my notice that she was crossing her arms to shield her breasts from my gaze, but it was too late. Of course, I noticed her nipples had gone hard. I'm a guy. And she was attracted to me. I might be able to work that in my favor.

"It's Mr. Eye Candy to you," I cocked my head, playfully.

"Yeah, well, I'm trying to meet a deadline, and you're fucking up my schedule with your noisage, Mr. Eye Candy." She forced a scowl.

"What are you working on?"

"Just, some tech stuff." She looked down at the dog with a sigh. "I still need to buy him some stuff. He probably needs a walk or something, right? Shit. I don't have time for this. I don't know why my sister didn't mention the dog before doing a drop-off and run. But hey, are you about done over there?"

"About. A few odds and ends left. I can arrange the time to better suit you."

"That would be great. I work late and get up late. Except for this week. My nephews are staying with me." She sighed a groan. "How can boys be so messy in less than a twelve-hour period?"

"Talent?"

"Maybe." She shuffled toward the door, and I followed behind gladly. I knew exactly what was hiding under that denim. "I amend that. Boys can be messy in minutes of showing up. Is that my door, shredded off the hinge?"

"It is. I'll send someone over to fix it today if that's all right."

"I'd appreciate that. By the way, my name's Blessing."

"Nice to meet you."

"Now we won't be strangers."

"No, we won't."

But I already knew her name.

In fact, she was the reason I moved in to begin with.

PREORDER FIERY BLESSING TODAY!

MORE BOOKS BY DANUBE ADELE

Kiss and Tell

Book 1: WINTER HEAT

Book 2: TRUTH OR DARE

Hermosa Beach Memoirs Series

Book 1: One Breath to the Next

Book 2: Fiery Blessing – preorder

ABOUT THE AUTHOR

Danube Adele believes that a good nap can solve most problems, diving into new adventure kickstarts creativity, and quiet walks along the beach soothe the soul. Add a mango margarita paired with chips and salsa to the mix, and you get a happy life. Author of the paranormal, sci-fi romance series Dreamwalkers, she can often be found either eagerly typing away at an HEA on her laptop, or lounging on the sofa with a hot, sexy romance novel in hand. She's lived in southern California her entire life, and much of that time with her greatest fans, her loving husband and two brilliant sons.

Sign up for Danube's newsletter:

www.danubeadele.com

Like Danube Adele on Facebook:

www.facebook.com/Writer.D.Adele

Goodreads

https://www.goodreads.com/author/show/7340150
.Danube_Adele

Twitter

www.twitter.com/DanubeAdele

Made in the USA
Monee, IL
11 September 2022

13761570R00285